THE SCHOLARS
OF NIGHT

ALSO BY JOHN M. FORD

NOVELS

Web of Angels
The Princes of the Air
The Dragon Waiting
The Final Reflection
How Much for Just the Planet?
Growing Up Weightless
The Last Hot Time

SHORT STORY COLLECTIONS

Casting Fortune
From the End of the Twentieth Century
Heat of Fusion and Other Stories

POETRY

Timesteps: A Selection of Poems

THE
SCHOLARS
OF
NIGHT

JOHN M. FORD

TOR

A TOM DOHERTY ASSOCIATES BOOK
NEW YORK

THE SCHOLARS OF NIGHT

Copyright © 1988 by The Estate of John M. Ford.

Introduction copyright © 2021 by Charles Stross.

A Tor Book
Published by Tom Doherty Associates
120 Broadway
New York, NY 10271

www.tor-forge.com

Tor® is a registered trademark of Macmillan Publishing Group, LLC.

The Library of Congress Cataloging-in-Publication Data is available upon request.

ISBN 978-1-250-26917-1 (trade paperback)
ISBN 978-1-250-26916-4 (ebook)

Our books may be purchased in bulk for promotional, educational, or business use. Please contact your local bookseller or the Macmillan Corporate and Premium Sales Department at 1-800-221-7945, extension 5442, or by email at MacmillanSpecialMarkets@macmillan.com.

First Edition: February 1988
First Trade Paperback Edition: September 2021

Printed in the United States of America

0 9 8 7 6 5 4 3 2 1

INTRODUCTION

BY CHARLES STROSS

In his forty-nine years, John M. ("Mike" to his friends and colleagues) Ford proved himself to be bewilderingly versatile. He wrote poetry; he wrote extensively for the Traveller and GURPS tabletop role-playing games; he published children's fiction; he emitted novels. And what novels! *How Much for Just the Planet?* stands out as being both a Gilbert and Sullivan comic operetta *and* a Star Trek novel. *Web of Angels,* published when he was twenty-three, invented most of the tropes that later became recognized as cyberpunk a few years ahead of schedule—a prodigious, precocious feat. As for *The Dragon Waiting,* words fail me: just read it. (It won the World Fantasy Award in 1984.) And then we come to *The Scholars of Night.*

The Scholars of Night is a classic British Cold War spy novel— ironic, for Mike was American through and through—written in the mold of a forgotten master of the field, Anthony Price. (John le Carré is best remembered today, and indeed gets a tip of the hat in the narrative, but Price was at the top of his game in the 1980s and stands up to comparison with le Carré and Len Deighton.) Price was all about the intricate and lethal games historians and academics play, the scholars of night who plot treason and sell their souls to the agencies of state power. Mike follows his scholars, Allan Berenson and his protégé Nicholas Hansard, back to the roots of their profession—to the Elizabethan playwright and libertine Christopher Marlowe, reputedly one of Sir Francis Walsingham's spies during the cold war between Protestant Tudor England and the Catholic French and Spanish empires. Not only is the entire novel a meditation on Marlowe's precious but murderously truncated career, Ford's plot hinges on a long-lost and lately rediscovered play of Marlowe's: its discovery precipitates a terrible and potentially world-ending act of revenge, a tragic game of sixteenth-century assassins that plays out anew in the fever-and-chills atmosphere of the mid-1980s.

The Scholars of Night was first published in 1988, which means, knowing how publishing schedules work, that it was probably written in 1986. If you're under fifty years old you don't remember that period clearly. (If you're under thirty, it ended before you were born.)

On the assumption that you're under fifty years old, I'd like to give you an ideological Rosetta Stone for the world in which *The Scholars of Night* is set—a world that now reads as being as science-fictional as anything else Mike wrote.

Let's set the controls of our time machine back to 1986, when Mike Ford was writing about The White Group and their deadly game of analysts. This book is a time capsule from a half-forgotten, bafflingly alien world: a world before laptops, internet, and smartphones, bizarrely overflowing with nuclear weapons and coin-operated phones bolted to the walls. It was a nail-biting period to live through if you paid any attention whatsoever to the news. I suspect that most of us who were adults when the wall came down were traumatized by the experience of growing up knowing that we could be flash-fried or poisoned with radioactive fallout at fifteen minutes' notice, all because of a faulty sensor or a diplomatic game of chicken gone wrong. I had nightmares at the time, and almost every contemporary I've checked with had the same experience of creeping terror combined with fatalism. (The psychology of the school active-shooter drill and the creeping dread of climate change renew the trauma for the younger generations.)

Nor is it only the technology and the nuclear nightmares that have changed. *The Scholars of Night* unblinkingly reflects the unremarked homophobia and sexism of the 1980s. It was a decade when antibiotics still mostly worked, but AIDS was a death sentence and being openly gay was perilous—if you were in government service you would be prosecuted or fired as a security risk if you were outed.

In 1986 Ronald Reagan was midway through his second term as president of the United States. Margaret Thatcher was prime minister of the UK, and a very new and perplexingly different general secretary of the Communist Party of the Soviet Union, Mikhail Gorbachev, had just come to power. The word "perestroika" had just begun to be heard in the USSR; superpower relations were still in the deep freeze they'd descended into after the death of Leonid Brezhnev. By accident, during the Able Archer 83 exercise of November

1983, NATO forces in Western Europe nearly precipitated an all-out nuclear war with the Soviet Union. Subsequently both superpowers backed away from the brink—nobody actually *wanted* the world to end—but like two cats sizing one another up, they were both primed and expecting an attack. In 1986 the USSR was seen by many in the West as an existential threat, and the existence of roughly 60 thousand thermonuclear weapons underlined how seriously the threat was taken by both sides.

Perhaps the weirdest, most alienating difference a time traveler from the world of 2021 to that of 1986 would notice is not the bipolar macho politics of nuclear superpower confrontation, but that *nobody saw the victory of capitalism as inevitable.* History had not yet turned a very important corner. In 1986 there existed a globe-straddling colossus, a revolutionary superpower that—with its satellite states and fellow travelers like China—represented a third of the planetary population and held two-thirds of its weapons. The Soviet Union was a utopian project gone to seed, but nevertheless it saw itself as blazing the way for the true future of humanity. Despite all the terror and purges, despite the famines and concentration camps along the way, the communist states were founded to pursue the goal of building a better future for everyone, and even in 1986 not *all* the gold leaf had worn off the skeletal saint's relic beneath the bejeweled rhetoric.

Utopian ideals are both desperately dangerous and terribly attractive to a certain mindset. There was a reason why many in the West were willing to work to bring about the workers' paradise. (And the echoes of that idealism can still be seen today. We all measure our politics using a yardstick that is part of the ideological payload of the French Revolution—the dialectic of left versus right—even though the revolution appeared to be dead only three decades after the storming of the Bastille. Who today can confidently assert that Lenin's children won't ever find their way to a new October, and get it right the second time round?)

History has a way of brutally and rapidly rearranging your understanding of the parameters of life. Since the end of the Cold War in 1989 and the collapse of the USSR in 1991, a Whiggish triumphalism about capitalism's victory over socialism has come to be the norm in the United States. But this state of unquestioned supremacy seemed anything but inevitable at the time in question. The attitudes of 1986 seem as bafflingly alien as the world before COVID-19, or before 9/11.

Which brings me full circle to a reappraisal of *The Scholars of Night*. This is a multilayered book: on the surface, a gripping spy thriller and a tragedy of revenge from beyond the grave. But on another level, it's a commentary on the deadly games academics play—games which spill over into real life (and death) when the players undertake work for their peers in the intelligence services. It's an old, old game— one Christopher Marlowe reportedly played himself—as the dissident freethinkers and heretic intelligentsia lock the doors and freely play what-ifs with human lives as counters, and the timeless nature of the game is reflected down the hall of mirrors from the 1580s to the 1980s.

Read it as a historical artifact of a bygone age, or read it as one of Mike's most enigmatic science-fictional tragedies. It works well either way.

THE
DEATH
OF
SOCRATES

PART ONE

FAUSTUS MUST BE DAMNED

The stars move still, time runs, the clock will strike,
The devil will come, and Faustus must be damned.

—Doctor Faustus, *V, II*

Nicholas Hansard knew that he was trapped. He looked into the face of the last heir of the House of York, and knew that Richard Duke of Gloucester meant to be King of all England; he saw the naked dagger in Richard's hand, and knew the duke meant to stop at nothing. There was no way to fight his way clear; Richard had twenty picked men behind him. But maybe there was a way out.

"You don't want to kill me, Your Grace," Hansard said calmly.

"I don't? Tell me why I don't."

Hansard kept himself from smiling. Richard was given to striking in haste; making him pause was half the battle, if not much of the war. "Because of what I can give you, Your Grace. I have some wealth, I have houses that can shelter and feed you—"

"All of which will belong to me anyway."

"The gold, the stones, yes, but the people within? And the people without—in one of those houses is the contract for a hundred Burgundian crossbowmen and fifty lances of horse."

"They'll fight for me as well as you, if I pay them."

"Indeed, indeed—or anyone else, if he pays them. And I regret to say that on my death that contract will most swiftly be delivered to—well—another, who also has the means to pay them."

"You're trying to blackmail me for your own life."

"A man might have worse reasons for it."

"True enough," Richard said. "But do you know, I'd rather take the chance of having a bunch of fickle Burgundians against me than your fickle self with me. I'm going to kill you."

"Christ, Rich."

"Praying won't help, Professor Hansard. You're dead."

"Well, you're in character, Rich," Hansard said, reaching out to the table and picking a piece from the gameboard. "Okay, I die, I sink." Hansard scooped a stack of cards from the table on his side of the board, and handed them to Richard Sears. The twenty-year-old Duke of Gloucester was wearing black twill jeans and a VALENTINE COLLEGE: *You Gotta Have Heart* T-shirt. "All my transferable properties and estates." Hansard picked up another card, held it out to another player. "But Lady Anna gets the Burgundians."

Anna Romano, the senior surviving Lancastrian heir, was a graduate student, a small, slim woman with short dark hair. She took the card representing the mercenary troops and added it to the stack of her faction's forces. "Thank you, Professor. We shall offer prayers for your departed soul."

"Watch the 'we' until you're crowned," Richard said, and sat back in his chair. "I thought he was bluffing about the Burgundians."

Hansard turned to Paul Ogden, the fourth player. Paul was seventeen, just out of high school and visiting the Valentine campus before starting classes in the fall. "Well, Paul, we now have the classical three-way endgame of a strong faction from each royal house and a third party—you—in control of Parliament. What are you thinking?"

"I'm thinking I could use a beer," Paul said.

The other students laughed; Hansard said quite seriously, "Bad enough that you'd concede the game for it?"

"What?" Paul said, then, "Oh, I get it. As Chancellor of England, I could call a Parliamentary vote on the kingship, and I control enough votes in both houses to force the outcome . . . but I can only make Rich or Anna win, I can't do it myself."

"Go on," Hansard said. He scratched at his blond hair and rubbed his sharp chin.

"To win for myself, first I'd have to get a senior heir away from one of them . . . and that could take years. I mean, hours."

"'Years' is okay," Hansard said. "You should be thinking in game time, months and years instead of so many turns."

Richard said, "It's why we play out those little scenes, instead of just saying, 'I kill your character and take his cards.' If you don't think about what a real person in your situation might have been thinking, then the game's just *Kingmaker* with some house rules."

Paul said, "In other words, do I want to give up winning because I'm tired and it's late . . . or historically, let some other noble faction control England because the war's gone on so long already."

"He achieves synthesis," Anna said.

"Of course," Paul went on, "I'm also thinking, 'Why not quit? After all, it's just a game.'"

Anna said, "Two syntheses in three minutes. Bravo, Paul."

Hansard said, "That's exactly right. It *is* just a game, not historical fact. If *Kingmaker* or *Diplomacy* ever repeated the events of the real York-Lancaster war or World War One, I might start believing in the Tooth Fairy again. But there are lots of facts around—and lots of things pretending to be facts. I'm trying to teach process, the things that go through people's minds at 'historical' points. Your desire to quit the game because you wanted a cold beer isn't the same as wanting a long dynastic war to be over—but there *is* an analogy there, and I believe it's a useful one. If you can think like a person of the fifteenth century, or whatever period you're researching, the real facts will stand out from the fake ones, just as a man in doublet and hose would stand out in midtown Darien."

"In certain parts of midtown Darien, at least," Anna said. "Are we still on the subject of a cold beer?"

Hansard said, "It's up to Paul and Parliament."

Paul said, "You're kidding."

Richard said, "He isn't, Paul. Professor Hansard is Socratic to the limit. You want a brew, you're going to have to call Parliament."

Paul looked at Hansard. Hansard grinned. Paul said to Anna, "Do you want a beer badly enough to marry me for it?"

"Marry—why, you precocious bastard," she said, and looked at the board. She shoved the piece representing Margaret of Anjou into the Canterbury Cathedral space. "All right. Margaret marries the Chancellor of England, who had better not be a near relative, we're in enough trouble with Rome as it is. Now call Parliament and let's get that beer."

"You didn't even send me a wedding invitation," Richard said, and hunched his shoulders. "Oh, well, now is the winter of our discontent made glorious summer by this sun of . . . uh, Lancaster."

"I told you not to kill me, Rich," Hansard said. "The beer's in the refrigerator."

Back in Hansard's den after the refrigerator raid, Richard and Paul and Anna sat on the leather couch with a beer each and a shared reefer. Hansard sat in a wood and fabric armchair, drinking coffee from a mug labeled HEMLOCK. ("I told you," Rich told Paul, "Socratic to the max.")

"What happens if they catch us with this stuff?" Paul asked, between cautious tokes.

Richard said, "This is Connecticut. They put you in the stocks."

"See what happens when you take up with evil companions?" Anna said. "Rich's a junior, he can plead on his age, but me, I'm a grad student, I've got no excuse." She giggled and glared at Hansard. "And don't you *dare* say 'insanity defense,' Nicholas."

Paul said, "I mean, what happens to you, Professor Hansard? Isn't this like, well . . ."

"Illegal? Last time I looked. But don't worry about it, Paul. Valentine College is too liberal to push an issue like grass and too small to have a reputation to worry about. Anyway, I'm not a full professor here, I don't have a regular course schedule. I run seminars, which are very often games—like this one, but more elaborate, with more players—and I'm away some of the year, on research."

"You can make money doing historical research?" Paul said, a little hazily. Richard laughed.

Hansard said, "It can be done." He looked at his coffee mug, at the poison label. "Are you interested in being a career historian?"

"I didn't know . . . I mean, I wasn't sure there was such a thing."

"It happens. It happened to me." Hansard tapped the mug. "Sometime I'll tell you about the fellow who gave this to me."

"*Homo fuge;* flee, man," Richard said in a deep voice, "flee, lest you become . . . a *protégé!*"

Paul's eyes were suddenly quite clear. "Would you be my faculty adviser, sir?"

"It's a little early for that," Hansard said. "Fall term doesn't start for four weeks yet, and you won't properly be a student till then. Give it a while."

The beer and the conversation ran out a little before midnight. Richard and Paul were headed for the summer-residence dorm, Anna for her apartment just off campus. As Hansard closed the door behind them, he heard Paul say, "So is it always like this around here?"

"This is just summer," Rich said. "Wait until fall term starts. We get thirty players in a game, and it's unbefuckinglievable. . . . Say, you ever been in a Civil War battle?"

Hansard poured himself another cup of coffee and sat down by the *Kingmaker* board. During the game he'd had an idea for a new rule, for assassination attempts against nobles, and now he wanted to take notes before the thought passed.

The doorbell rang. Anna, he thought at once.

And then he thought of Louise, because he never thought of a woman without thinking of Louise, despite that Louise was dead. Or perhaps because of it; for twenty months of Nicholas Hansard's life his principal occupation had been watching Louise Hansard die, in and out of hospitals, never out of pain.

Before Louise, he had never seriously considered marriage; for a time after Louise, he could not seriously consider sex. But the one thing had changed, and the other did as well.

Anna.

Hansard opened the door, and it was not Anna. It was a man in motorcycle leathers and helmet, a pouch slung over his shoulder. His bike, a big Harley with huge cargo panniers, was at the curb, lights still on.

"Would you sign for this, sir?" the courier said. There would be no names spoken: The courier would not prompt him with what name to sign, nor say who had sent him.

Hansard knew both already. He wrote *Christopher Fry* on the courier's pad, then waited as the man matched the signature against his sample. Hansard felt slightly silly, signing the playwright's name, as if he were faking an autograph; he made a mental note to choose someone more obscure for next month's code name.

"Just a moment, sir," the courier said, went back to his cycle, did something concealed by his body. Hansard had been told the bike carried elaborate alarms, and sometimes explosive destruct charges. The courier came back up the walk with a flat parcel. Hansard took it. "Thanks."

"Not at all, sir. Good night."

The courier rode off, quietly. Hansard looked up at the sky; it was a cool night for August, very clear. He went inside, sat down with his coffee, and opened the envelope.

Inside was a set of black-and-white photographs. They had been taken underwater; a frogman was visible in some of the pictures. The main subject of the first two photos was a boxy object Hansard finally realized was a jeep, half buried in bottom silt, a white Army star half-visible on its flank. The next pictures showed a leather briefcase. There were markings on it, barely readable; a long word seemed to be INTELLIGENCE. A chain ran from the case's handle to—

That was the subject of the next photographs. They were disturbingly clear. Clipped to the last one was a typed sheet reading:

```
TENTATIVE IDENTIFICATION OF REMAINS AS T. C.
MONTROSE, MAJOR US ARMY INTELLIGENCE, MISSING IN
ACTION GERMANY 20 MARCH 1945. REMAINS DISCOVERED
NIEDERKESSEL GERMANY 10 DAYS PRIOR THIS DATE.
RECOVERY IN PROGRESS. RSVP.—RAPHAEL
```

"Can you make money doing historical research, Professor?" Hansard said softly to himself. "Sure, if you know the right people."

He picked up the telephone and began to dial.

■ ■ ■

The German sky was blue, the grass was green, the crane was olive drab, and the water of the river was dark as private sin. Chains and cables ran down into the brown murk, and on the banks were soldiers, leaving bootprints all over the travel-poster grass. The soldiers were mostly American engineers; some were Bundeswehr. They all had guns, nothing unusual about that.

Two frogmen popped up from the water, and signaled to the crane operator. The big machine rumbled, and the chains went taut. The dark water stirred.

A little distance up the riverbank, a man in a gray leather jacket was sitting on the ground with his knees drawn up. He had bushy black eyebrows and steel-rimmed glasses and a smooth, plain face with a calm expression. A notebook-sized portable computer was propped against his knees, and he was typing on it, a little at a time. Every few minutes he would look up at the crane and the soldiers, and look back down, and write a little more.

A few meters behind him was a black Mercedes sedan, at least ten years old. A hard-faced woman in a green down-filled vest leaned against the driver's door. The vest was open in front, and the butt of a pistol was just visible within.

A brand-new black Mercedes pulled up next to the old one, and a man in an expensive dark suit got out. He bowed slightly to the woman, who pointed at the sitting man without speaking.

The man in the suit went down to the bank—walking carefully, minding his trouser legs—and looked down. "Mr. Rulin?"

"*Ja,*" said the sitting man.

"My name is Kreuzberg. My office—"

"*Ich hab' Deutsch,*" Rulin said flatly.

Kreuzberg stopped, then continued in German. "My office, I believe, told you I would be coming."

"They did," Rulin said. He looked up at the crane again; he still had not looked at Kreuzberg. "However, they did not tell me what you were coming for."

"The documents—"

"They're American documents."

"But found on German soil. —In German water, I should say." Kreuzberg laughed politely. "And besides, they are so old—"

"If you start back to Bonn now, Herr Kreuzberg, you should be home in time for dinner."

Kreuzberg stared. "I don't understand," he said, and Rulin knew it was the truth. Rulin said, without any audible rudeness, "I will explain. Those men are going to raise the jeep. The man in it, or rather what remains of the man, will be put in that aluminum coffin you see over there. The box will be sealed and flown to a laboratory in the United States; you can see the helicopter, and the plane should already have its engines warm."

"But the documents—"

"The photographs show the briefcase is chained to the man's wrist. There it will stay. I've seen limbs fall off bodies in that state: If that should happen, we'll carefully put it on top of the rest of him."

"This is not what I had expected."

Damn straight, Rulin thought, and said nothing. He hadn't let Kreuzberg present any credentials, or speak English, or otherwise get one up on him. He didn't owe Kreuzberg anything.

Kreuzberg said, "I am empowered to—"

"You're empowered to do absolutely nothing here, Herr Kreuzberg, and you know it. You are *cleared* to observe, which you are doing. You're not going to look into that briefcase, I'm not going to look into it, nobody is until it's in that laboratory. *Das ist fast alles.*"

Kreuzberg muttered something, neither German nor English.

Rulin said, "I grew up in a place called Hamtramck, Herr Kreuzberg, and I can cuss pretty well in Polish myself. But in fact I'm not a CIA bastard. My credentials are through CIA, but I'm here as an outside adviser. Sort of a civilian tech rep."

"You are not—Intelligence?"

"Let's not be any more insulting than we must, Herr Kreuzberg. I have a degree in archeology. I'm an expert in opening tombs, digging up graves, that sort of thing. I was the most appropriate person to send."

"And who did send you?"

"A man called Raphael."

Kreuzberg thought for a moment. "I do not know this Raphael."

"Your office does. Why don't you drive back and ask them?"

"And if I do not?"

Rulin said, "You're cleared to observe. I should warn you, though, that Ms. Donner over there is cleared to kill you if you try to do anything more than observe."

Kreuzberg turned. The woman in the green down vest grinned at him. She dug in her pocket, unwrapped a piece of bubble gum, popped it into her mouth and began to chew.

Kreuzberg stared at her, his mouth slightly open.

Rulin said, "She calls her gun Blitzen. You've probably heard stories about Americans who give their guns names. In her case, I'm afraid they're all true."

Donner worked her jaw, and cracked the gum so loudly that two of the soldiers turned at the noise.

Kreuzberg said softly, *"Donner und Blitzen . . . ? Toll. All ganz' toll."* Then he turned back to Rulin and said, "I will make a full report of this, of course."

"Of course," Rulin said.

Kreuzberg stamped back to his car. He paused to take a last look at Donner, who cracked her gum and waved. Then Kreuzberg got into the car and drove away.

When he had gone, Donner spat the gum into the grass. "Do you think he'll put that stuff about 'Donner and Blitzen' in his report?"

"He's very precise, according to his file."

"He's an all-day sucker."

"But a reliable-rated all-day sucker, in the K Directorate's book."

Donner frowned. "So I have to start calling my pistol by some stupid name, because you wanted to piss somebody off?"

"Convince him, Carrie, convince him. Whatever else Kreuzberg is thinking right now, he believes we're very, very serious about whatever's in that briefcase." Rulin stood up, tucking the computer under his arm, brushing at his trousers. He looked down the road where Kreuzberg had gone. "And that's just what he's going to tell his employers."

"Which employers?"

"Oh, both of them," Rulin said, "but Moscow first. Kreuzberg's priorities are very important to him." They began walking along the riverbank, toward the crane and the soldiers.

The water below the crane had begun to bubble and roil. The chains ground link against link and the machine whined with the load. The jeep's headlights broke the surface, mud running from their slitted wartime covers, looking like the eyes of an enormous frog.

"Ever seen *Psycho?*" Donner said.

Water and gravel were pouring from every part of the jeep as it cleared the river. Forty years of river water had buried it halfway in the riverbed; the divers had dug it clear enough to raise, but it was still coated and crusted almost to the fender tops. On the driver's door, the painted white star showed surprisingly bright where the diver who had found the wreck had scraped the silt away.

And then there was the driver, still more or less upright in the seat, one arm hanging over the door. From this distance, he had a sort of cartoon expression. His mouth was open wide, very wide. Some of the soldiers looked nervous. Rulin supposed a few would be sick; at least one always was at a time like this. Rivers or tombs or pyramids, it didn't matter; for years now, new discoveries had been linked in his mind with the smell of vomit.

"All right, hold it there," Rulin said to the crane operator. "Let it drain a bit before you bring it in."

The morning sun caught the dripping water and river silt, and they sparkled like diamond rain from the clear blue sky.

■ ■ ■

The sky over Edinburgh was dull but not plain; rain clouds in a dozen shades of gray and indigo and steel ran together, a literal watercolor.

Allan Berenson pulled his topcoat close, pushed his trilby onto his head, and walked across the road that divided the huge chain hotel from the tiny stone inn where he was staying, where he was expected. The big hotel's electric sign was haloed in the mist, and its glass front shimmered like a package wrapped in plastic film. Ahead, the bed and breakfast was dark and Gothic in the rain, quiet, faintly brooding, but infinitely warmer.

"Hello, Doctor," said the plump old woman behind the desk as Berenson picked up his key. "A bit damp out today."

"A bit."

"May I send you up some tea?"

"That would be lovely, Mrs. Cromie. Two, please, milk for me and lemon for the lady."

Mrs. Cromie nodded and smiled conspiratorially. "I'll have it up quick, Doctor."

Berenson smiled back and climbed the stairs. He knocked lightly at the door, then opened it. There was a single room, ten feet by twelve, with well-worn and sort-of-matched furniture: a Morris chair, a dresser with mirror, a tea table, a double bed. A woman in a blue jersey dress sat on the bed, slipping off her stockings.

"Not so soon after the stairs," Berenson said very softly, "my heart won't take it."

"I shouldn't let you do the buttons, then."

"You'd very well better," he said, went to her, and ran his hand down the line of buttons on the back of the dress; he kissed her neck. "But Mrs. Cromie's bringing us tea. Let it wait that long."

"How long—" There was a knock. Berenson went to the door and accepted the tea tray. When he turned, kicking the door shut, the woman was sitting straight up, her hands demurely folded, her bare ankles crossed, a bright schoolgirl grin on her face. Berenson laughed, nearly spilling the tea service.

"Do you think I pleased the old voyeur?" the woman said.

"She's an old darling," Berenson said, "and more discreet than a whole firm of Swiss bankers." He put down the tray. "Now, tea first, or buttons?"

"The tea will get cold," she said. "I'm—"

"Hush." He poured the tea. The woman's dress slipped to the floor. She put it on a hanger on the door, went into the tiny bathroom, reaching for her bra clasp.

Berenson turned to face the window, draining his teacup, looking through the small diamond-shaped panes. The rain was coming down hard now. Between the tracks of the drops, he could see Arthur's Seat, the crouching lion of mountain above the city, the black shape of Edinburgh Castle—and of course the chain hotel.

"Goddamn imperialism," Berenson said.

The woman said, "We had the Empire." She came out of the bathroom wearing a gray silk kimono. She sat down on the bed.

"Not like this. We export our lousy fast food and our lousy fast food hotels everywhere in the goddamn world. At least you had some respect for the local cooking. And the architecture. We want to put the goddamn Golden Arches over the Forbidden City." He turned away from the window. "And you know what's really funny? That chunk of transplanted Ohio over there is where the KGB boys are staying." He looked back for a moment, at the glow of the sign. "My cut-out to Palatine is in room 614 right now, pretending to be a Louisiana oil man, charging like mad on his American Express Gold Card."

"Where do the CIA stay?"

"Here."

"That isn't funny, Allan."

"It isn't a joke, my dear. I learned about this particular bed and breakfast from a friend who also happened to be a Company case officer. In

London, he stayed at a tiny place in Covent Garden, a dozen rooms, no restaurant. He swore Graham Greene was a regular—which may have influenced his choice."

"There's no chance he'll turn up—"

"He's retired now. He lives in Oregon, and fishes." Berenson went to the small bed, sat down on the chintz spread next to the woman. "The Russians like the most American hotels. The Americans like local color . . . and of course, they like to feel like international spies, too." He slipped his hand inside the collar of her robe, stroked the back of her neck. "Where the hell does the KGB get American Express Gold Cards? Does Moscow Narodny Bank count as a 'major financial institution' on the application?"

"And what do the English like in hotel rooms?" she said. "Besides being scratched just . . . there."

"The English like things understated."

"That must be what I see in you." She put her hand inside his unbuttoned shirt, against his chest. "You're so elegantly understated."

"I'm too old for you, you know."

Her hand moved down, across wiry gray hair and stiff scars. "That's what attracted me to you, don't you know? I thought, look at that doddering old relic, he must be desperation itself in bed."

"That wasn't a joke either," Berenson said softly. He ran his fingers into her hair. "'What door is there will let the traitor in, except that gate the traitors call their own . . . It opens for the infamous, and when it closes, it is with the axe's sound. . . .'"

"That's from the Skene Manuscript?"

"It is."

"And you're memorizing already. Do you think it's really by Christopher Marlowe, then?"

Berenson's hands paused. "It could be," he said thoughtfully. "If it's a forgery, it's a damn good one. Not to mention the problem of motive: Why forge a Christopher Marlowe play, instead of Hitler's diary or Howard Hughes's will?"

"Whose will? Oh, the mad billionaire, with the ice cream."

"They have excellent ice cream in Moscow."

"That's not from Christopher Marlowe."

"I was in Moscow last a couple of years ago. I wondered, if I had to live there for the rest of my life, just what I would do to keep from going insane."

"And you thought about ice cream. What about me?"

"I didn't know you then."

"I could keep you sane." She giggled. "You could have ice cream, too."

"And when I'm gone?"

"Then *I'll* have ice cream."

"I'm serious."

She was quiet for a moment. "Yes, I see that you are. Very well then. You don't intend to flee to our Eastern comrades and neither do I. If we did, they'd only play loyalty games with us for the rest of our lives—me more than you. No. We'll find someplace quiet and neutral, one of those little speck islands in the Caribbean, and live all alone, like Ian Fleming characters."

"Harlequin Romance, more likely. Excuse me, I mean Mills and Boon . . . and if there isn't anywhere neutral? Because I really don't believe that there is—the Ross Ice Shelf has gotten awfully political of late."

She cradled his round face in her hands, massaged his temples with her fingertips. Her hands were very strong, her nails short and perfectly trimmed. "Then we shall prostrate ourselves upon the threshold of CIA, or whatever MI6 is calling itself this week, and beg to be taken in; and they will kill the fatted calf and put rings upon our fingers, because better a prodigal come home than another bloody defector in Moscow."

"I met Philby . . ."

"I know you met Philby. I don't want to talk about Philby. I don't want to talk at all, and neither do you."

"You're braver than I am," he said. "You've got a whole life to lose if this goes wrong."

"And you don't?"

"I have you. Just you."

"*Allan.*"

"I'm sorry. Palatine sent word that NIGHTMOVE has approval from both the T and S Directorates."

"'Sent word'?"

"Palatine doesn't leave London anymore. They know he's near retirement, so as long as he stays in a small orbit, they don't pay too much attention to him." He paused. "You won't be missed—"

"I won't be missed, Allan. What's the matter?"

"Things are going into motion so very soon now . . . first-night jitters, that's what it is."

"You never had first-night jitters. Not even on the first night." She laughed, then stopped suddenly. "Something *has* frightened you, Allan. Tell me what it is."

"Promise me," Berenson said, "that if anything happens to me before the day, you'll go to ground."

"What about the other agents?"

"They only know their specific roles. Only you and I know the overall scheme of things."

"You and I and KGB."

"*Almost KGB.* That's the point. KGB has the plan, and the network roster—but they can't execute. The roster's encoded."

"What?" She had an astonished, and delighted, smile.

"The names are encoded, but not very elaborately. I'm certain they can break that—and so are they; that's why they accepted the list as it is. But each of the agents has a keyword . . . and the words on the list are fakes. I've instructed all of them that if they receive the keyword on the open list, they're to run for cover. The real words are—well. I don't think Moscow will guess them."

"You haven't told me any of this before. What's my secret word?"

"There hadn't seemed . . ." He shook his head. "And you don't have a keyword. I . . . don't think it's necessary, for you."

"You bloody brilliant man. So what frightens you?"

"Nothing," he said, "nothing," and hugged her to him, losing himself in the scent of her hair. Her fingers slipped inside his waistband, and he gasped.

"Hmm," she said, tugging at his trouser fly, "full French tab. Only one thing for that . . ." She began to bend down, but he caught her head in both his hands.

"Not yet," he said. "I want . . . to look at you a little longer."

She frowned. "Tell me what's wrong . . . please, Allan."

"A footstep on my grave, that's all."

"No regrets, now."

"Only for you," Berenson said. "I should have loved you in the open. There are people you should have known . . . there are times I think . . ."

She said, "Are there times you don't think? Let's find out . . . no, now I can't either. Think what?"

"That we might have done as much in some other way. Some way we could have shown everyone. That all this scuttling in the dark has been unnecessary."

Very gently, she said, "You must be Doctor Faustus, mustn't you."

"And must be—"

She stopped his mouth with hers. After a minute, or more, she loosened her grip without releasing it, said, "You're going to change the world, Allan. Don't be afraid."

"Change the world," he said, in a small voice.

"Yes."

"It has to change the world, doesn't it . . or it's just common treason."

He held her tight again, and he sighed, and he trembled.

■ ■ ■

Major Montrose was scared, and not of the Germans. The Krauts knew the war was over; there wasn't any front here, no organization, hardly any troops but the *Volkssturm*, old men and kids given a rusty rifle or a rocket-propelled grenade and told to defend the Fatherland. Montrose stomped on the gas and the jeep rolled on through the cold damp night.

Mortar rounds lit up the cratered road. Montrose could see some soldiers, Wehrmacht from God knew where, running from one burning farmhouse to another. He thought about driving after them. The worst thing they could do to him would be to kill him. That might not be a bad thing at all.

Cecily would get a telegram: REGRET TO INFORM YOU THAT YOUR HUSBAND WAS KILLED WHILE ON A SECRET MISSION OF THE UTMOST IMPORTANCE TO THE WAR EFFORT. There'd be a medal in a box. Major Montrose had sent some of those telegrams himself. Secret mission. War effort. Killed. Cecily, oh, Christ.

A salvo landed on the road behind the jeep. Fragments whistled past. Montrose held the wheel white-knuckled. The cuff to the dispatch case cut into his wrist. He looked for the Kraut soldiers. It wasn't really such a bad idea. Even if the bag made its way to whatever passed for a headquarters around here, the Germans wouldn't do anything with the papers; it was too late in the day for the SS Security Service, much too late for the Abwehr. And then there was the Gehlen Service . . . Christ, Montrose thought, he could have worked for General Gehlen. Should have. Gehlen would get out of this mess with every hair on his ass intact.

Montrose realized suddenly that he was lost, literally as well as figuratively. He didn't have a map, he was behind enemy lines and wasn't supposed to have a map; suppose he was captured, couldn't have the Krauts learning important secrets, like where their own goddamn towns and roads were. More artillery exploded, whistle-crump, whine-wham. There was the occasional pop of a rifle, but no sustained small-arms fire. So there wasn't any fighting nearby. The artillery could be coming in from anywhere.

The road ahead ended in a T, and beyond it was a river, flat black. Montrose slowed down, and thought. If this was the river he thought it was, if he hadn't gotten totally turned around, then it ran east and west.

The Americans were west, the Russians were east. And never the twain shall meet, Montrose thought, and turned right, turned west.

The road was clear. The black ribbon of river streamed past on his left. If there was a bridge ahead he could be in trouble, the Air Force had it in for German bridges; but this was just a little country road, it shouldn't have a major bridge along it.

He might actually make it.

A cluster of rounds went off all around the jeep. A tire exploded. Montrose leaned over the wheel, hugging it, trying to keep control; then something hit his left wrist like a thirty-pound sledge. The wheel spun. Montrose's leg spasmed with the pain and slammed the gas pedal to the floorboard. The jeep left the road, half leaped the bank, hit the dark water.

Major Montrose was under water before he quite realized what had happened. First he tried to open the door of the jeep and get out, but the door wouldn't open. Or maybe it was his hand that wasn't moving to open it. He couldn't see anything, but he could feel the water, and smell it and taste it. He kicked down. Nothing happened. He should be floating, bodies floated, he'd seen enough of them. He tried to raise his arms, to stroke downward, but they wouldn't come up. Okay, the left one had gotten hit, but the right—

The right one was chained to the dispatch case, *and the case was stuck—*

■ ■ ■

"He can't have had more than about thirty seconds of air," Nicholas Hansard said, and pointed to the folder with Major Montrose's postmortem X rays, stacked on the table with the photos and transcripts and marked maps Hansard had used to reconstruct the Major's last drive. "His left wrist had been broken by the shell fragment, his right leg by the impact. Even if the briefcase hadn't gotten hung up, he probably wouldn't have made it. It's not a big river, but it's surprisingly deep there."

Hansard stood up. The conference room was paneled in light maple, lit by shadowless fluorescents. There was padded brown carpet and a white acoustic ceiling; it was very, very quiet. The only furnishings were Hansard's document-covered table and two leather swivel chairs. Hansard scratched his head absently, twisted his head to loosen the neck muscles, and finally, almost unwillingly, looked at the other chair; at Raphael, who had been sitting silently, listening to Hansard's lecture, for almost two hours now.

Raphael wore a white suit, crisp blue satin-stripe shirt, dark blue silk foulard tie with a fine gray pattern. There were no creases in his clothing or his flesh. A smooth curve of fine gold hair swept across his high forehead; the face below was all planes, sharp bones under taut translucent skin. His eyes were large and very blue, with a terrible clarity. There was something unsettling about Raphael's face, something not entirely human, as if he were some kind of alien being that had chosen to appear as a man, but could not make the illusion perfect—or could not be bothered to.

Raphael was the Director of The White Group; what that meant was never exactly defined, just as The White Group itself was "a research and advisory agency on matters of intelligence policy and international affairs," whatever that meant. Even its headquarters was a vague brownstone in Georgetown, like a hundred other buildings fronting a hundred other things.

"Ever you amaze me, Dr. Hansard," Raphael said. "Would you detail some of your deductions to me? How do you know Major Montrose was lost?"

It was not lost on Hansard that Raphael always asked, "How do you know . . . ?" and not "Why do you think . . . ?"

"Time," Hansard said, looking back at the map, pointing at it, avoiding Raphael's blue eyes. "We know that the Major made his contact on time—given the nature of the meeting, if he hadn't been on time he never would have met the contact—and we know the distance he had to cover. There's no place he could reasonably have stopped, even to take—even for a few minutes. He must have been driving from the end of the meeting until he went into the river; and to have spent that amount of time driving he must have taken almost every wrong road in the area."

"Suppose he paused. Hid in a farmhouse, say, to wait for the friendly advance."

Hansard shook his head. "The fuel tank of the jeep was nearly dry. We have the motor pool record of its last filling. That corroborates the driving time."

"And the time of the crash?"

"The Major's watch caught the mortar fragment. Stopped it precisely at 2323 hours."

"How very fortunate for our analysis," Raphael said. "And Major Montrose's agitated mental state? He had been on missions behind enemy lines before this one, I believe."

Hansard nodded. "But not like this one." He picked up another folder, opened it. Inside were computer-enhanced photostats of the waterlogged documents from the Major's briefcase. He paused. "You've read these . . ."

"Yes. What do you think of them?"

"If they're authentic . . ."

"Dr. Hansard."

"Sorry. Yes, I think they're authentic. The fidelity to period is perfect, and the physical correlates—length of immersion, paper analysis, and so forth—all fit for 1945. Tell Stringer he did a hell of a job, as usual."

"That will please Stringer." Stringer was The White Group's head of research.

"But, I mean, if it's *true*—"

"Yes?"

"The documents can be authentic but not true," Hansard said. "They could be German black propaganda, intended to discredit the people they incriminate."

"Do you believe that to be the case?" Raphael's voice was cool, distant, a radio message from a faraway star.

"Unfortunately, no." Hansard dropped the folder on the table, took off his glasses and polished them. "The file claims that seven highly placed officers in Western Allied Intelligence were actually working as free-lance spies, accepting payment to deny information to the Western Allies. They did this both for the Germans *and* the Soviet apparatus. For instance, one of the seven was aware that certain members of the German High Command were actually part of the Red Orchestra, the Russian spy organization inside Germany, but did not reveal this to his own Intelligence service. . . . If Stringer's notes are correct, at least three of the Orchestra members wound up in the postwar West German Intelligence, and one helped the Soviets install one of their people in the top West German counterintelligence job. You remember the scandal when he defected—"

"I remember."

"There's going to be a lot more of that kind of thing, if the rest of these seven men had the same sort of influence. Well, six of them, anyway."

"Major Montrose was the seventh, of course."

"Yes. Which explains why he was so worried."

"Indeed. . . . I'm curious, Dr. Hansard—on what do you base your reconstructions concerning the Major's wife?"

"There were letters in his pocket." Hansard paused. "She didn't— that is, there's no reason to believe she knew he was anything but a completely loyal Intelligence officer. Naturally there's nothing in the

letters, Montrose would have expected them to be censored, but . . .
I did some outside research. Cecily Montrose was certainly never involved with espionage."

"Mrs. Montrose is not still living, I believe, Dr. Hansard."

"She died in 1969."

"Yes." Hansard could not decide if that was an agreement, an approval, or . . .

Raphael said, "Thank you for your analysis, Dr. Hansard. The
usual payment plus bonus is in order, I think."

"Raphael . . ."

"Yes, Dr. Hansard?"

"Is Allan Berenson a member of The White Group?"

"Dr. Berenson of Columbia?"

"You know who I mean."

"I was making certain. Is Dr. Berenson implicated by these documents?"

"I . . . don't know."

"The only appropriate answer under the circumstances, Dr. Hansard. There is a great deal of data analysis left in this matter. But to
answer your question, no. Dr. Allan Berenson has never been associ-
ated with The White Group."

Hansard forced himself to look at Raphael. He might as well not
have bothered; there was no expression there to read. "Thank you,
Raphael."

"Of course, Dr. Hansard. The White Group exists to provide accurate advice. And Dr. Berenson was at one time considered as National
Security Adviser, I believe."

"He said that he—yes."

"Any other questions, Dr. Hansard?"

"No, Raphael."

"Then I will say good day to you."

"Good day, Raphael."

Hansard watched Raphael stand up and walk out of the room, in
what seemed all one fluid motion. The door closed behind Raphael.
Hansard shivered. He looked at the papers on the table, and with a
sudden stab of pain across his face realized that his jaw was clenched
tight. He gathered up his own papers and went through the cool,

quiet corridors, out into the haze and soggy heat of Washington in August, and tried to think of what to think about first.

■ ■ ■

Raphael's office was paneled with white travertine marble; the ceiling was a metal grille enameled in deep blue, the floor carpeted in the same blue. Broad blue-green ferns in white ceramic pots hung suspended on white cords. The ferns waved gently in a silent flow of air from the overhead grille. Around the walls were maps, a world-time clock, and a dozen video monitors. The nearest monitor showed a street scene, just outside The White Group's door; Raphael watched as Hansard left the building. He stood on the sidewalk for a moment, apparently looking for a taxi, then walked off in the direction of the nearest Metro station.

Raphael touched a button on one of the control boards built into his glass and steel desk. "Stringer."

"Yes, Raphael?"

"Dr. Hansard usually visits the Smithsonian after this office, correct?"

"That's right."

"Tap the Metro cameras, check it, please. Then come here, with the file on the Montrose recovery."

"Yes, Raphael."

Raphael switched off all the monitors, sat back in his chair with his fingertips tented together. He did not move until Stringer came in.

Stringer was dumpy and jowly, with short black hair and a narrow mustache. He wore cheap white shirts and narrow ties in dull colors, dark trousers with suspenders. In the offices he also wore reading glasses with angular black half-frames: Stringer was acutely farsighted and the glasses were necessary, but they looked ridiculous on his fat face. Some people thought Stringer resembled Oliver Hardy, and by the kind of subconscious voodoo reasoning that often passes for logic in Washington they assumed the glasses were a joke. This was incorrect. Stringer had no sense of humor.

Raphael put a delicate hand to his sharp chin and said, "The discovery is convenient. Is it too much so? Why were the divers in the river?"

Stringer said, "They were looking for a local girl. She'd threatened to jump off a bridge if her parents didn't let her marry a local boy, a garage mechanic. The parents said no, she disappeared, the boy said he hadn't seen her, and they dragged the river."

"This is authentic?"

Stringer raised the file folder he was carrying, snapped it open. "Donner and Rulin checked with the local cops. The girl'd gone to her boyfriend to elope, told him she was pregnant, the usual. He killed her with a wrench, buried her under—"

"Verifications?" Raphael said.

"All clear to standard depth. The parents and the boyfriend are all lifetime locals. Donner says there's no reasonable probability this was a virgin sacrifice." If convincing the other side to accept fake information required a death, it was often more efficient and less expensive to use someone outside the apparatus. Some organizations considered it better espionage as well, in the same way that hunters after deer try to shoot one another only by accident.

"I concur, considering that the death only located the documents. But tell Donner to note any claim that the parents knew of the jeep going into the river."

"Next action?" Stringer said.

"Deliver the file to CIA as per agreement. Thank them for offering us the analysis project and providing Rulin with credentials, and invoice them at the usual rate plus fifty percent for short notice on the project, and one hundred percent for speed of analysis." Raphael tapped his fingertips together. "And prepare a memo to Mossad indicating a low probability of General Gehlen's involvement." Gehlen had, in one of the everyday ironies of the Intelligence business, been a party to the creation of the Israeli secret service.

Stringer made notes on the folder in tiny, precise handwriting. "Any other action?"

"Not at present. CIA will doubtless think of something to do." Raphael exhaled slowly; it might have been a sigh. "As will KGB. As will the rest of them."

■ ■ ■

In the shopping arcade underneath the RCA Building in Rockefeller Center, a woman in a gray tailored suit was speaking into one of a long bank of pay telephones. "Yes, that's fine, I'll get back to you," she said, to a person she did not know and would never speak to again in her life. She hung up, leaving several other women in suits talking on phones, and joining a steady flow of women in suits through the arcade. This particular woman had never read a book about dressing for success, but she had passed a particularly difficult course in dressing for not being noticed.

At the subway entrance underneath Sixth Avenue, which New Yorkers would rather die than call "Avenue of the Americas," the woman was met by a man in a brown suit coming from the McGraw-Hill building. They greeted each other in the manner of acquaintances who aren't sure they want to become friends, and together went through the subway turnstiles to the uptown platform, where after a short wait they boarded the first car of the B express. Two stops uptown, at 59th Street, they got off the train and waited for the K local, which another man joined them in boarding.

The three people were being called Boris, Neil, and Susan, which were neither their real names nor the names on their passports but work-tags picked by computer as part of initiating the action phase of this operation. Neil was the man in the brown suit; he and Susan carried briefcases. Boris wore a sweatshirt, jeans, and sneakers, not new but clean, and carried a backpack. Boris also had a bicycle clip on his trouser leg, though he did not have a bicycle. In Manhattan no one is surprised if your bicycle is no longer where you said it was ten minutes ago.

The K was held briefly at the station for unannounced reasons, then proceeded uptown, under Central Park West. This was the phase of the operation that gave the planners the most headaches. In New York City, an average of two operations per month had to be aborted, and a further four reorganized in progress, because of subway delays. The planners had tried taxicabs, but they were frequently unavailable when needed, and the drivers could not be counted on to forget the passengers, especially since the advent of the computer-printing taxi meter. Private cars got gridlocked and could rarely be parked in a convenient location; once a vehicle was left untended for three minutes in central Queens, and vanished forever, along with an embarrassing quantity of weapons and explosives.

For the most critical operations, the organization had actually secured a legitimate medallion taxicab of its own. The vehicle, with modifications, had cost $35,000. The medallion cost another $280,000. The planners were terrified to send it out on the streets.

The three operators left the K train and parted company, each walking several blocks by a different route to the target building, a Victorian brownstone on an exceptionally well-kept block. Neil and Susan waited on the sidewalk while Boris climbed the stone steps and pretended to press one of the doorbells. He then picked the lock, which took thirty seconds—it was a good lock—and opened the door. Neil and Susan followed him inside. Susan and Boris got into the elevator and rode to the fifth floor, while Neil climbed the stairs.

The building was very convenient for the operation: It had no doorman, and only two apartments to a floor. 5B was occupied by a cellist who taught three days a week at the Brooklyn Academy of Music; the controller Susan had telephoned from Rockefeller Center had confirmed the musician was still at BAM. Even if she was called home instantly, she could not possibly return before the operation was completed.

Boris and Susan went to the door of 5A. Neil stood near the stairwell. He opened his briefcase and took out what appeared to be a water pistol: a gun made of glossy plastic, colored bright green, with a tiny nozzle instead of a rifled hole in the end of the barrel and fake safeties and other details molded onto its surface. It would not have alarmed anyone for more than an instant, especially in shiny grass-green.

Susan rang the doorbell of 5A. The man who answered the door was wearing a bathrobe over pajamas, slippers, black-rimmed eyeglasses. The glasses were a problem, but a small one. The man appeared to be the operational target, but protocol required one more point of confirmation before final execution.

"Dr. Allan Berenson?" Susan said.

"Yes?" the man said, and then his eyes narrowed slightly and he said, "Did you ring from downstairs?" but by then he had ceased to brace the door and it made no difference.

Neil began walking briskly toward the door as Susan flat-kicked it wide open, the edge whistling out of the startled target's grip. Susan turned smoothly, making room for Boris to hit Dr. Berenson below the sternum with the extended fingers of his right hand, while his left neatly picked the glasses from Berenson's face. The target's breath puffed out and he staggered back a step, raising a hand toward his face. Neil held out the bright green toylike gun. He had a broad, bright smile. He pointed the green gun directly into Dr. Berenson's face and pulled the trigger. There was a click, sharp but less loud than a toy cap pistol, and a whitish cloud of mist sprayed from the gun exactly as Dr. Berenson gasped to fill his empty lungs.

Dr. Berenson fell, and was dead when his body struck the Persian carpet or within two seconds thereafter. His skin had a blue cast. The medical term is *cyanosis,* from the same root word as cyanide.

Neil watched Berenson fall, and looked at his body for a moment longer. Neil was still smiling. Then he said, *"Na'zdrovye,"* to Boris and Susan, and went down the stairs, tucking the gas gun back into his briefcase.

Boris and Susan went into 5A and shut the door. Boris gave the glasses to Susan, then crouched by Berenson's body, got his hands beneath it and lifted. One of Berenson's slippers fell off; Susan picked it up, in the same gloved hand that held the dead man's eyeglasses.

Boris carried the body into the kitchen. There was a half-eaten sandwich on the table, a half-full coffee mug that said HEMLOCK on the side, and an open book, Berenson's place held with the handle of a teaspoon.

"Nice setup," Boris said, not breathing hard under Berenson's weight. "Americans are such cooperative people. Table?"

"Refrigerator," Susan said. She opened the refrigerator door. Boris lowered Berenson's feet to the floor, holding the body upright in front of the open refrigerator. Susan slipped Berenson's glasses back onto his face. His eyelids were half-open, showing slivers of white eyeball. Susan said, "All right," and stepped back.

Boris rocked the body back and forth for a moment, like a man lining up a billiard shot or a golf putt. Then he gave Berenson a small push and let him fall forward. The body hit the refrigerator shelves with a rattling clang. A chop wrapped in plastic film fell to the floor, and a plastic milk jug tipped over and began to drip rapidly.

Susan looked at the angle of Berenson's bare left foot, and tossed the slipper along the same general line. Precision was neither necessary nor desirable; few things are less predictable than a dying man's twitch.

Boris said, "Did you see the—"

"Wait." Susan reached into the refrigerator and took a large, ripe tomato from a low shelf. She dropped it. It exploded on the floor, spattering Berenson's face with seeds and fluid.

"What's *that* for?" Boris said.

"The juice raises hell with lab tests," Susan said. "Don't you read the service briefings?" She went toward the door. "The box is on his desk. Mind the stuff on the floor."

"I don't need the briefings to know that," Boris said stiffly, and followed Susan out of the kitchen, avoiding the splattered tomato and the milk that was beginning to puddle against the body.

Berenson's desk was an antique rolltop, with a green-shaded brass lamp, envelopes in the pigeonholes, a pocketful of small change in a heavy bronze ashtray with the University of Chicago crest, and an elaborate electronic telephone fitted with a wood case to make it look a little less out of place here. On the center of the desk blotter was a box of black metal, with black web straps. The box was open, and inside it was a stack of pages, somewhat tattered at the edges, covered with a spidery brown script.

"That's it," Boris said. He reached into his backpack and produced a Polaroid camera. Taking a step back, he pressed the button; the flash fired and the motor ejected a developing photograph.

"We need the typescript, too." She looked around the study. "Try the living room."

Boris returned in a moment with the stapled, typed pages. Susan took them, placed them carefully on top of the antique manuscript in the box, then closed the box and began fastening the straps.

Boris opened Susan's canvas briefcase and took out a black box identical to the one on the desk. "Ready?"

"Yes," she said, and lifted the manuscript case from the desktop. Boris set the one he carried in its place. He undid the web straps, lifted the lid. Within was a typescript on top of a large manuscript, brown-written pages looking just like those in the original box.

"Nice work they do," Boris said, as he adjusted the box to match the Polaroid photo.

"What they get paid for, just like us," Susan said.

Boris pointed to the new typescript. "It won't have his prints on it."

"Kitchen floor," Susan said.

Boris nodded, picked up the stapled papers and opened the kitchen door. He leaned inside. There was a rivulet of milk running right past the table where Berenson had been reading. Boris gave the typescript a gentle toss into the milk. He looked for a moment at the HEM-LOCK coffee cup, then chuckled to himself and closed the door.

Susan was closing her briefcase, with the manuscript case inside. "Time?"

"Twenty-two minutes." Boris took a last look at the photograph, then tucked it and the camera into his backpack.

"Nice working with you, Boris."

"Someday we must have that drink together, Susan," he said, and they both laughed. It was a trade joke, funny and sick at once: funny because they would probably never meet again, sick because if one of them should be invited for a drink and find the other waiting, it would mean that someone like Neil would also be quite near, smiling, for the only thing that Neil's sort ever smiled for.

■ ■ ■

Nicholas Hansard sat with the HEMLOCK mug in his lap, the coffee in it gone quite cold, thinking about the man who had given him the cup and bade him drink.

It was six months after Louise had died, died finally, and Hansard was at loose ends in New York, with a degree and a teaching certificate nobody wanted and a medical debt beyond human comprehension. He was spending his dinner money in the Compleat Strategist game shop on 33rd Street, and noticed a listing on the store bulletin board for *Diplomacy* players. In the corner of the card, below the phone number, was the note *Ph.D. Required.*

Hansard called the number. "Ph.D History," he said. "I prefer playing Austria-Hungary." The voice on the other end laughed and invited Hansard to Berenson's apartment on the Upper West Side.

Diplomacy was a board game of war and power politics, set in a fictional turn-of-the-century Europe. The rules were simpler than chess, but chess was a duel, no quarter asked nor given; *Diplomacy* had seven players making alliances and breaking them, offering deals and waiting for the correct moment to renege. Dr. Berenson's group was composed of professors and politicians and genuine diplomats; there were about fifteen New Yorkers, and another twenty who stopped in for a game when passing through the city. A doctorate was not actually required for membership, Berenson admitted: "To be honest, I'm waiting for someone to call and say, 'to hell with degrees, let me in.'"

They would gather in apartment 5A, dressed in Savile Row suits or safari jackets or T-shirts and jeans, once in a while full embassy white tie, and play the game on an oversize board, walnut-mounted and glass-topped, with custom-made wooden pieces representing armies and navies. Above the board was a plaque reading:

YOU MUST BE PROUD, BOLD, PLEASANT, RESOLUTE,
AND NOW AND THEN STAB, AS OCCASION SERVES.

"Christopher Marlowe," Hansard said when he saw the sign, "from *Doctor Faustus*."

"Correct," Berenson said, sounding pleased as only a professor could with a right answer. "One of the most relevant dramas of our time, I think."

Which led them into a discussion of drama and relevance, and then politics and relevance, and politics and history. Inevitably a brain trust such as surrounded Berenson could not confine itself to playing a board game, not with all of reality to play with. . . .

At two o'clock one Sunday morning, after Hansard had led the Turkish Empire to a narrow victory, he and Berenson sat watching the House of Representatives debate aid to Nicaragua on all-night cable television.

"Goddamn imperialism," Berenson said.

"You want the Sandinistas to win?" Hansard asked.

"I want to stop handing them an excuse for not winning. Ortega's gang is using the *contra* war to cover up every failing of their administration. They murder the Miskitos, ration everything in sight, suppress the newspapers, and rail at the Church, all because somwhere there's a man with an American-made gun."

"Moscow will continue to back the regime."

"So what if they do? It's their hard-earned money. Look, let me tell you the dirty little secret of modern war: Nobody can afford to fight one. And I don't mean big bombs blowing up, though those are certainly in the numbers. The cost of mobilizing the big powers has become impossible."

Berenson stood up and went to the *Diplomacy* board, looked down at the colorful map. "Only theater nuclear war is affordable, because it relies entirely on existing equipment, expended after use. You don't have to buy spares for a missile once it's launched, or provide it with hot food and medical care and a dry spot to sleep. It doesn't draw a paycheck and it doesn't get shipped home, in a boat or a box. It even buries itself, so to speak." He swept a hand across the gameboard.

"The trouble with good old Theater Thermo is that, as far as the military issue goes, it accomplishes jack shit. As we've both told a million students, war is an extension of politics. Asking won't get you what you want, so you beat on the guy until he gives.

"Now, if you think you're going to survive—and I mean *survive,* not win, nobody's fucking *won* a war since 1870, and nobody's *ever* fucking won a theater-level war—you can say 'give me what I want or I'll kill you.' And even if you don't think you'll survive, you can say 'give or I'll fuck us both over so bad you'll be sorry.'" Berenson stood up from the couch and went to the *Diplomacy* table, his face reflected in its glass surface.

"But nobody ever actually says that, because the threat isn't credible; believing in the end of the world doesn't come easily. Part of the wonder of diplomacy is how little we actually believe in, compared with how much we claim to believe in when the other side is listening."

That was Allan Berenson: irreverent, theatrical, wringing out the language for the words he wanted. It was not long after that that the letter from Valentine College had shown up in the mail. Hansard had never heard of Valentine, let alone applied there, and when the job came through he was certain that Berenson had been involved.

Even after the first call from Raphael, the first projects, it had always been in the back of Hansard's mind that Berenson was connected to The White Group, that somewhere, somehow—

"Never fall in love with a theory," Hansard said out loud.

Allan Berenson again, on another late night: "*Foreign Affairs* magazine would be a lot truer, not to mention a lot better reading, if someone called someone a lying bastard now and then. But that's the problem with us: We're all play-acting. The world *is* all a stage, you know. Theater of cruelty, theater of war, theater of the absurd. We play *Diplomacy*, but the real thing is a game too, of lying about what you truly care for, so you can bargain your junk for the other fellow's heart's desire."

"Allan," Hansard said, a slight blur of Foster's Lager on his tongue, "were you *really* almost an adviser to the President?"

Berenson laughed. "Was I really? Yes. I was almost really. National Security Honcho Himself. Let me tell you about that. . . ."

Which he did: It was a tangled Washington tale of illustrious names and powerful committees, which ended when a certain Senator's wife heard a certain word used at a certain dinner party on the White House lawn.

Berenson said, "So the Senator said, 'Professor, I hope you can explain yourself in plain terms.' And I told him, 'I don't know how much plainer I can be, Senator: A Marxist propagandist would say that the means of production ought to be in the hands of the people, but I'm just telling you to go fuck yourself.'"

That was the part of the story that Hansard remembered. Not the committees or the illustrious names.

Until he read two of those names on Major T. C. Montrose's list, the men who had begun by selling intelligence but graduated to selling their authority and reputations, helping to plant spies in the highest ranks of the Western services.

Philby had been on the short list to become head of British Intelligence. An Israeli agent, Eli Cohen, had been so well and truly infiltrated into Syria that he had become a prime candidate for Syrian Defense Minister. A Soviet sleeper as the American President's Security Adviser wasn't such a bizarre notion. Nor that the plan to plant the agent should fall apart because someone wholly irrelevant was offended by a wholly irrelevant word.

Hansard stood up, walked around his own game room. There were framed historical prints on the walls: a page from Domesday Book, the plan of St. Gall monastery, a Confederate recruiting poster. Wooden shelves held artifacts: a bullet from Lexington, a stone from the magic circle at Avebury. There was a bit of cord and clay in a glass cube, a fragment of an Egyptian tomb seal that The White Group's

Vince Rulin had given him last Christmas. And of course there were books, for research or passing interests or simply because their bindings had pleased him, many books because love knows many reasons.

The room was, Hansard thought, very much like one in Allan Berenson's apartment. There was no deliberate imitation, and historians were packrats by nature, living nested in glittery bits of the past. Berenson had never been to visit, though the invitation had always been open; it was such a busy world . . . Hansard suddenly wanted very much for Allan to see the room; not necessarily to admire it, or even to comment, but just to know that it existed.

Hansard looked at the telephone. Berenson's number jumped into his mind. He picked up the receiver and began to dial. Allan would tell him if it was not true. Allan would surely tell him if it was.

He put the phone down again, poured a double shot of Irish whiskey into his cold coffee and drank it straight down. He went to bed and was asleep instantly.

Hansard woke early and unrested. At eight A.M. the radio announced that Berenson was dead.

■ ■ ■

"Cheese," said the cabdriver, as he drove Hansard across Amsterdam Avenue. There were more than a dozen black stretch limousines parked on Amsterdam and Cathedral Parkway. "Who you suppose died?"

Hansard said, "This'll do," and the cab pulled sharply over to the first clear spot on 110th Street. Hansard tipped the driver a third of the meter and started walking east, back toward the Cathedral of St. John the Divine. Gargoyles smiled down at him.

There were police cars among the limos, and black sedans with curious antennae on their trunk lids, and men who carried radios in one hand and raincoats in the other. It was cloudy in New York on the twenty-ninth of August, warm and humid and threatening thunder. The raincoats had nothing to do with that.

One of the men with the radios said, "Excuse me, sir," to Hansard. "Private function today."

"I'm a guest," Hansard said, and got out his driver's license. The man called in Hansard's name and Social Security number. He asked to look through Hansard's briefcase. "Sorry, sir," the man—Secret Service, FBI, who?—said, "precautions. Our job."

"Yeah." Hansard closed the briefcase and walked on.

The limo drivers were clustered around one of the long black cars, smoking and drinking Diet Pepsi from cans. They all wore the same black suits, white shirts, narrow black ties. Black peaked caps were piled up on the car's hood. Hansard noticed their eyes: They all wore identical metal-rimmed aviator sunglasses. Some of them were tall, broad-shouldered, athletic; beach boys under the crisp livery. Others had creases across their shirts from steering wheel against paunch. But under the blacked-out eyes there was the same look on all of them. They could drive the big cars too fast, and no one would stop them; park the cars where they pleased, and light cigarettes with the tickets. The privileges might belong technically to the men they drove around, but these were the ones who could run red lights.

Hansard thought that Allan would have called it "trickle-down in action," and they would have laughed at that.

Another limousine pulled up, and a muscular driver got out to open the door. The passenger was wearing a dark blue suit with a deep red ascot at the throat, an extravagant ring on his thick hand. His face was wrinkled, still rather delicate, his hair gone mostly white.

Hansard said, "Hello, Ray."

Arnold Rayven said, "Well, hello, Nicholas. Well met, ill occasion."

One of the guards asked for Rayven's credentials. The man looked at the card he was given, said, "Sir, do you have something with a photograph?"

Rayven pulled out a laminated plastic card, held it next to the guard's walkie-talkie. "Arnold Rayven, Vectarray Technologies." He tapped the nameplate on the radio. "We charge the taxpayers a lot of money to build these things. Why don't you use yours?"

The man just said, "Yes, sir," as politely as he had said anything else, and cleared Rayven through; Rayven and Hansard went into the Cathedral. It was cooler within, and quiet, and dark, the stained-glass windows all dull with the day.

"Do you like this place?" Rayven said, gesturing at the gray stone arches.

Hansard looked up: It was more than a hundred feet to the ceiling. Ahead, the nave stretched on through arch after arch, like a trick with mirrors. "I haven't been here that often. It's . . . impressive."

"It's *big*, Nicholas. But then I'm prejudiced. Johnny Rockefeller put a half million into building the thing. Seems to me that the Devil offered Christ a palace once before, and He said no."

Hansard felt himself smiling, just a little. "Where would you have held this?"

"No question in my mind: the Agora in Athens. But that's out of the question, of course. Not Athens. Not this year. Our friends outside with the Uzis under their coats would swelter at the thought. I wonder what they thought of our Saturday night poker parties at Allan's apartment?" They turned a corner, walked through the Cathedral gift shop, past note cards and miniature gargoyles, out into the air again.

They were in the stoneyard, where the carvings for the still-unfinished Cathedral were stored; around a small grassy plot were stacks of facing and cornice blocks, slabs and cubes of marble piled like toys. Out on the grass a tent had been set up over some chairs and a table with a punchbowl; people in dark suits and black dresses were walking about on the grass, conversing in little groups. There were perhaps thirty people altogether.

"Quite a technical problem, actually," Rayven said. "Where do you let all these miscellaneous diplomats and millionaires gather for a little quiet and reverence, without some branch of the guns-and-grenades brigade crashing the party?"

"Where are the ashes?"

"Rob Cullen took them. He's on his way to the Antarctic, going to scatter them on the Ross Ice Shelf."

Hansard chuckled. "The last nonpoliticized spot on earth. Yeah, that's lovely. Rob's idea?"

"Allan's. Apparently he suggested it to Cullen about a year back."

Hansard's jaw clamped shut. If Allan had known—if he had been ill, if the Montrose file and Berenson's death were really only a coincidence—"He didn't know," Hansard said vaguely.

"We all *know*, Nicholas," Rayven said, surprised. "Did you ever know Allan to be a fatalist?"

"No."

"Damn right. Maybe it was just a whim, or a joke . . . it just happened to be an Arctic explorer he was talking to. With another of us it

might have been 'bury me with the *Titanic* wreck,' or on the Moon."
Rayven scratched his head. "I wish I'd thought of it; Arianespace
owes me a favor. We could have put him in orbit." He shrugged, gestured. "Ah, there's the Lady Herself. Shall we?"

Several people were clustered around a thin, elegant, gray-haired
woman who sat in a wheelchair, chainsmoking custom Nat Sherman
cigarettes. She looked up, and smiled. "Nicholas."

"Tina." Hansard took one of her age-spotted hands in both of his.

"You're a young flirt, to call me that. But you may."

Augustina Polonyi had been shot in the spine while fleeing Hungary in the collapse of the '56 revolution. Since then her name had
come up a few times in consideration for the Nobel in economics, but
she had always been too much something or not enough something
else for the committee. She did some sort of advisory work.

Hansard suspected that she and Allan had at one or more times
been lovers; but he had never given it a great deal of thought, and this
was not the day to do so.

Rayven said, "If he's flirting, what am I to do?"

"Hello, Ray. Western Vacuum Enterprises, Hiland to Furthest."

A man standing behind Polonyi said, "Oberstrasse Kosmei, any
cargo to Brackenbury." The speaker was a retired astronaut.

"Just a minute, just a minute," Rayven said, and took a wallet out
of his coat. Inside the leather was a checkbook-sized computer with
dozens of keys and a liquid-crystal screen. Rayven punched buttons.
"You realize that I'm going to have to call the others and get their
moves now. In the interest of fairness."

"All's fair—" the astronaut started to say, and then he stopped, and
nodded, and said, "No, you're right. Today, you're right."

Hansard said, "What's this one?"

"*Space Trader III*," Rayven said. "Tramp freighters on the last
frontier. We've got a ninety-planet database, two hundred forty trade
goods, a terrific set of research rules . . ."

"You didn't ask me," Hansard said.

Rayven frowned, tapped his hand computer. "Uh, the money's
real, Nicholas. Buy-in was twenty thousand."

"Oh. By me, then." He paused, sensing Rayven's embarrassment.
What would Allan have said? "Besides, I'm more into history than

science fiction. Anybody for a round of *Annales de Medici* with real poison?"

The others laughed, and Hansard began to laugh too.

A man's voice said, "You people are playing *games?* At a *funeral?*" There was an abrupt silence, and they all turned.

"Who," Polonyi said, her voice as precise as a scalpel, "are you?"

Hansard saw one of the guests make a quick hand signal. He felt a sudden tautness in his stomach.

A guest he recognized, a professor named Sandridge from McGill University, came up behind the man who had spoken. "He's with me," she said.

"Couldn't you get a sitter?" someone muttered.

"Larry didn't know Allan," Sandridge said.

There was another uncomfortable silence.

Hansard said, "This isn't a funeral. It's a—memorial, for want of anything better to call it . . . if you'd known Dr. Berenson, you'd understand that there isn't any better way we could remember him. Most of us knew him through games. I met him over a gameboard, and half of what I learned from him, I learned there. We keep on playing because it keeps him alive."

"I, uh, I'm sorry," Larry said. Sandridge touched his arm, said, "Come here, there are a couple of things I ought to tell you," and led him away.

After a moment, Polonyi said, "Thank you, Nicholas."

Hansard took a breath. There didn't seem to be any more laughter. "I thought it was pretty glib, myself."

Rayven said, "Man's completely surrounded by politicians, diplomats, and general blowhards, and he kicks himself for talking glib."

Another guest, an ex-ambassador, said, "Glib? Do you remember the night we had Hank Kissinger playing Austria-Hungary, and . . ."

Hansard looked at Augustina Polonyi, who looked back at him, and everything else was shut out. He wanted to tell her about playing the game to keep Berenson alive, because Hansard had played his little game with the Montrose documents and helped to kill him. But it was all secret, the papers, the reasons, the acts. Nations had privileges and imperatives, but they all trickled down to people who killed and people who died.

"You're in the will, you know," Rayven was saying.

Hansard said, "The will?"

"There isn't much—the money goes to a couple of endowments, and since the apartment's in New York City there'll have to be some wrangling over it." Rayven sighed noisily. "I think making me executor was his last joke."

Hansard thought, No, I'm the last joke. It just isn't very funny.

Rayven said, "The furnishings and small property are to be divided among several of us, including you, Augustina, and me. I'm having an inventory done, but there's been some fooling around about government papers Allan might have had, so it'll take a few days."

"I'm not going anywhere," Hansard said.

Rayven nodded. "There's Kay Parks, she's on the list too. See you later." He walked away.

Hansard noticed that he and Polonyi were suddenly by themselves. Polonyi lit another cigarette and said, "Have you observed anything in particular about this group? I shall be disappointed if you haven't."

"Don't say that," Hansard said, then softened it with "please."

"But you have already seen it," she said. "When you set Dr. Sandridge's companion straight about our purpose here."

"When I . . ." He was suddenly distracted. She wanted him to think and not brood. Very well, he would think. "When I said it wasn't a funeral . . . nobody's mourning. Not a wet eye in the house."

"Yes," Polonyi said slowly. "Funerals are to say goodbye. But we're not at that point yet. It happened too suddenly, too far out of sight, to be absorbed. . . . But these people are used to gathering around Allan—and you know how much he was the centerpoint of any group."

"Here we are with no center," Hansard said. "Makes it very obvious that he really is gone. . . . People are leaving already."

"Allan had no use for fools," Polonyi said. She looked up quickly. "And if you say, in any tone whatever, that he found a use for you, I shall never forgive you for it, Nicholas. *I mean that.*" She stopped; her expression cooled. She took a puff, turned away from him and blew smoke. "No eulogies today; you're right, they would only have been glib. Are you going now, Nicholas?"

"I think so," he said. "It's an awkward trip back." He pointed at the handles of her wheelchair. "May I—"

"Always flirting," she said, and he could hear the tiny strains enter her voice. "I'll be fine, thank you. Good-bye, Nicholas."

"Good-bye, Tina."

The sky was quite dark with clouds now, and there was a faint ripple of distant thunder. Hansard turned at the Cathedral door, saw Polonyi sitting alone, smoking, looking at nothing.

He caught up with Rayven in the long walk through the nave; they walked side by side, but neither spoke. When they reached the street, Rayven's chauffeur straightened his cap and glasses and pulled the car door open. Rayven said, "Can I give you a lift someplace?"

"No . . . thanks."

"Yeah, I've got nothing to say either. I'll send you the inventory. We ought to get together . . . when we do that."

"Uh-huh. I'd . . . like the *Diplomacy* set. Unless someone else—"

"I'd figured that was yours all along."

Thunder popped in the dead air.

Rayven said, "Excuse me, Nicholas, but it's time I went home and cried my goddamn eyes out."

He got into the car, and it glided away. Hansard loosened the suddenly choking knot in his tie, and went to find a cab before the rain began.

■ ■ ■

On the twenty-ninth of August in London, it had been raining since before dawn. In a flat in Bloomsbury, not far from the British Museum, a woman in a blue jersey dress was sitting all alone on a hard chair beside her narrow bed. On the bed was a copy of *Time* with a short obituary for Dr. Allan Berenson, under the heading of "Milestones." There were also some documents from the Ministry of Defence Games Centre, all marked SECRET, and a double-edged knife cast in one piece of clear resin, difficult to see against the patterned bedspread. Berenson had called the dagger a "CIA Letter Opener." It held an edge better than stainless steel, and was invisible to metal detectors.

"Such gifts you give people," she had said when he had presented her with it.

The woman flipped the magazine shut so that she could not see Allan's name any longer. An American Senator was pictured on the cover: According to the caption, he was "Issuing a Challenge to Washington." He had the fatuous simper American politicians wore for all public occasions. Berenson had once told her a story about that Senator, and a party, and the means of production.

Inside the magazine, the obit. had said that Dr. Berenson had no living relatives.

The woman picked up the telephone and dialed a number. The man who had given it to her had carefully instructed her never to write it down. She had not, of course, but the man had no need to know why.

Neither had Berenson known that she had the number. He would have made her promise never to use it, as she had promised to abandon NIGHTMOVE. It was bad enough to break one promise to a dead man.

There were two rings at the other end, then a voice spoke a single name. The name was just a word, a step in the dance of concealments and recognitions.

"This concerns a set of heirloom silver," the woman said. "I was told that you might have the pieces I need to complete the collection. The pattern is a Sheffield, 1821. . . . Yes, I'll wait."

After a pause, the voice said a few more words. The woman said, "Yes, I would like to pick up the pieces at your earliest convenience. . . . Splendid. And the address? . . . No, I'll remember it."

She hung up the phone, and compared the false keyword address the voice had given her with the list of meeting places in her memory. Heathrow. The Holiday Inn. *The Russians like the most American hotels,* Berenson had said, that day in Edinburgh. Right as usual.

She snatched up the magazine and threw it to the floor, then slipped from her chair, knelt against the bed, and cried.

PART TWO

SUCH AS LOVE ME

To some perhaps my name is odious;
But such as love me, guard me from their tongues . . .
—The Jew of Malta, *Prologue*

It was August in Washington, the steamy apex of the unlivable District summer. Nicholas Hansard had his linen jacket off, folded over his briefcase, and his tie loosened. That helped a little, as did the trees shading the Georgetown street. But through the branches the sky was still white as sour milk, the sun seeming to fill it all.

The street was lined with high, narrow townhouses, some granite, some brick, with black ironwork railing their steps and grilling their windows. Most of the doors had engraved brass plates naming doctors or lawyers or consultancies. There were some flags on eagle-topped poles; the banners hung limp in the heat. On rooftops, air conditioners bailed heat and moisture from the buildings back into the air.

The roadway was too narrow for parking, though there was a black Mercedes stopped and empty anyway, a couple of yards from a NO PARKING ANYTIME sign. The car had diplomatic plates. Hansard felt a sudden wild urge to kick the damn thing, caught himself starting to do it. He looked around, embarrassed, but no one else was visible. He smiled at the windows of the house where the car was parked, just in case anybody's Intelligence service was taking his picture. "Must be the heat," he said, in case they were taping, and walked on.

It wasn't the heat, and he knew it. It was Allan Stovall Berenson, deceased.

Hansard walked up five granite steps to an oiled oak door. The plate, polished brass like gold, said:

THE WHITE GROUP, LTD.
Contract Research

There was no mention of "appointments only." That went with the neighborhood. Hansard pressed the doorbell, smiled again for the cameras. After a moment, the door clicked, and Hansard pushed it open. The air inside was blessedly cool. There was a short corridor; at the other end was a grille door, as on a bank vault. The grille stood open. Hansard stood still for a moment, letting the air dry him out, and went through into a small room, furnished in tweedy Edwardian style. There was a door on each wall.

A young man, younger than Hansard, sat behind a large and cluttered oak desk. He looked up through black-framed glasses and said, "May I help you?"

Hansard said, "I want to see Raphael."

"Are you a member, sir?"

"You know damn well who I am, and I'm not going to play today." Hansard took out his ID card, a thick rectangle of white plastic, and tossed it onto the desk. The receptionist moved a leather-bound book to expose a dark glass plate mounted in the desktop. Hansard put his right hand on the plate, and the young man slid the ID into something out of sight beneath the desk. White light warmed Hansard's palm.

"Good afternoon, Dr. Hansard," the young man said. "Raphael is in a meeting just now, but if you'll wait in the lounge I'll make sure he knows you're here."

"Is he really in a meeting?" Hansard said.

"Yes, Dr. Hansard. He really is."

"Sorry," Hansard said awkwardly.

"Not at all, Dr. Hansard. It's a very hot day." The receptionist gestured, and one of the doors swung open magically. Hansard took his card and went through.

The lounge was comfortable enough, with leather armchairs, books and recent magazines—*Foreign Affairs, Punch, Smithsonian*—a bar stocked with expensive liquors and brandy in a wooden cask. Hansard poured a cup of coffee; it was fresh, as if they'd been expecting someone. He sat down. There was a Turner on one wall; on another, floor-length velvet drapes pretending to hide a window. The street face of the building had windows, and at night lights showed from some of them, but he had never seen an interior room with a window or skylight. They were too vulnerable, to bombs, to burglars, to lasers that could pick sound off a vibrating pane. He glanced around; no camera was visible, but there certainly would be one watching him.

Suddenly a bit self-conscious, he went into the small tiled washroom and washed the Foggy Bottom sweat from his face and hands, combed his hair, cinched his tie. He sat down again, sipped his coffee, looked at a copy of *The Economist*.

There was a trilling sound from the table at Hansard's elbow. He nearly dropped his cup. It was the ring of an electronic telephone. He picked up the angular black handset.

"Dr. Hansard," Raphael's voice said. "Please come up. Bring your coffee." A door opened on a small elevator. Hansard got in, and rode down.

Raphael was in his cool, white office, sitting behind the desk in a tan silk suit, khaki shirt, dark brown tie. Around the room, the hanging green ferns rustled faintly, and the monitor screens were all dark.

"You should have called, Dr. Hansard," Raphael said. "I would have told you a meeting was scheduled; you needn't have waited."

"It's all right," Hansard said, hearing himself sound hoarse. "I just wanted to give you this." He reached inside his briefcase, took out a long white envelope, put it on the desk.

Raphael didn't touch it. "And this is?"

"My resignation. From The White Group. Effective today."

"I'm sorry to hear that. Your work has been very valuable to us."

There was a pause. Raphael didn't seem to move at all, not even to blink. The envelope just sat on the desk, a little white island in a sea of black. Finally Raphael said, "Is there anything else, Dr. Hansard?"

"You don't want to know why?"

"I had assumed that these papers"—he touched the envelope—"would explain that."

"Yes. Well . . . I suppose they do." Hansard took a breath. "Is this going to affect my position with the College?"

"You are not, I presume, resigning your professorship."

"Not voluntarily."

"Dr. Hansard. You seem to be expecting me to threaten you. I confess I can't imagine why. Have you had any reason to believe that your work here was in any way coerced?"

"No."

"Or that your professorship was somehow contingent on your performance here?"

"No."

"I should hope not. This is an information agency, you know, Dr. Hansard—I like that word better than 'intelligence,' it presumes less—and blackmail is a generally unsatisfactory method of gathering information. Do you think I would have anyone in the Group who did not wish to be? If you were discontented, you would in time begin to betray us."

"I'm not—"

Raphael raised a hand. "I'm not talking about defection or treason, Dr. Hansard. I don't mean anything deliberate, in fact. Just small shadings of interpretation. You're a teacher; can you not tell a student who hates the subject from one who loves it by the papers they write? . . . If you were to begin lying directly, of course, you would be found out soon enough." Raphael fixed Hansard with his colorless eyes and smiled innocently. "As you would. As we would."

There was another long pause. Hansard said, "Well. I guess that's all, then."

"Not quite, Dr. Hansard. There is a courier en route to you, with a new document we wished your opinion on."

"What is it?" Hansard caught himself. "Oh. I'm sorry."

Raphael's lips bent; it looked like a smile. "There's no difficulty in telling you. It has no security importance. Have you heard of the Skene Manuscript?"

"Of course," Hansard said, startled. "The new Christopher Marlowe play."

"That's not verified, as I understand. A copy of the manuscript came into our possession, for possible verification."

"Why you?"

"A matter of interagency relations. There are a large number of academics in the British services, as you surely know. . . . You see now why I'm so sorry to lose your services just now. But." He put his fingertips together. "When the courier arrives, simply refuse delivery, you know the procedure. And please turn in your ID plate at the desk as you leave. Thank you, Dr. Hansard. It's been a very great pleasure working with you."

"All right, I'll do it," Hansard said.

"Pardon me?"

"Is this your idea of not blackmailing me?"

Raphael said, "Dr. Hansard, you asked me what the document was."

"And it isn't Intelligence-related?"

"If you mean, is this the secret work you've decided you no longer wish to do—" Hansard felt a chill. Sometimes it seemed that Raphael knew everything. "—you know my attitudes concerning secret material."

"Yes. Of course."

"But it was unkind of me to tantalize you. Do you genuinely wish to resign from the organization, Dr. Hansard? The issue of the manuscript entirely aside."

"I meant it," Hansard said.

"Very well. As you recall, your arrangement with us includes severance pay only on the dissolution of the Group. But if you were to perform this analysis, we could pay the usual fee and bonuses. Would that be acceptable?"

It was three times his annual college salary. "You want me to authenticate the Skene Manuscript . . ."

"Dr. Hansard, I want you to be satisfied. I've already explained that."

"I'll . . ." Hansard swallowed. *Proud, bold, pleasant, resolute,* he thought, *and now and then stab.* "Tell me honestly, Raphael—is this connected with Allan Berenson's death?"

"I regret that you suspect me of dishonesty, Dr. Hansard. Do you have reason to believe it might be connected? That would be of interest, of course."

"He was—very fond of Marlowe. It was Allan who first told me about the Skene papers. If there was a copy in the United States, I'm certain he would have known it . . . now he's dead, and you have a copy."

Raphael nodded. "You're a very gifted analyst, Dr. Hansard. But it isn't quite so coincidental as that. We have actually been in possession of the manuscript since before Dr. Berenson's death."

"You didn't tell me then."

"I intended to. But the Montrose analysis came up suddenly, and frankly it was of much more importance."

"Yes. I can see that. . . . So there's no connection." Hansard supposed that he was trying to detach himself from Allan's death; he supposed that Raphael knew it.

"If there is a connection, I am not aware of it."

Hansard nodded. He supposed that Raphael might tell the truth, or he might lie if it suited him (though Hansard had never caught him in a lie), but for him to falsely deny that he had a piece of information—to say "I don't know" and not mean it—that was unthinkable.

Hansard said, "I'll need some resources. Almost certainly need to go to England."

"Your expense account will be kept active." Raphael picked up the resignation envelope in his perfectly manicured fingers. "I'll file this, unopened, until you've completed your work. That way there's no question about expenses. Keep your ID as well; it could open doors."

"All right. I'd better go home and meet your courier."

"No hurry. He isn't due until tonight. Good day, Dr. Hansard."

"Good-bye, Raphael."

Hansard went out of the office. As the door closed behind him, Raphael's hands moved over the switches on his desk, lighting monitors. He watched Hansard make his way out of the building, back onto the sweltering street and off in the direction of the Metro. He picked up the envelope, put it in a drawer. Then he stood up and went into the next room.

Stringer was there, and four other people, seated around a conference table. In a corner, a large-screen monitor showed Raphael's office from a view over his shoulder. Stringer pushed a button to blank the screen.

Raphael sat down at the head of the table. "Opinions?"

"He didn't take much convincing," said Josiah Blaine Carteret, Ph.D. Political Science. He was a tall and athletic man, blond and sharp-faced, with a Carolina accent. "Then, he's always seemed a ratha' malleable young fella."

"I should hope he'd rise, given the bait." Robert Booker Applewood, Ph.D.s Linguistics and History, was black and barrel-chested, with a curly, graying beard. "A lot of people would do a lot of things to get hold of a Skene copy. Are you quite certain he didn't know that Berenson had the manuscript?"

From the far end of the table, Stringer said, "Berenson acquired the copy on his last visit to the UK, ninth August. His last contact with Hansard was thirtieth June."

Linda Gould said, "Last known contact." Gould's doctorate was in mathematics. She was short, dark, muscular. "The surveillance on Berenson was lousy."

"This isn't Bulgaria," Applewood said.

"If it hadn't been lousy, Berenson wouldn't be dead," Gould said.

"Possible but no longer relevant," Raphael said. "And certainly never our responsibility."

Carteret said, "Suppose Hansard looks up the man Allan got the manuscript from?"

Applewood said, "You're paranoid today, Joe."

"Yes, Brother Bob, that I am. Ever since the Montrose list showed up, I am right enough crazy."

Stringer said, droning a bit, "Berenson received his copy of the Skene Manuscript from Sir Edward Moreton Chetwynd OBE, Cambridge University . . . and MI6 Research Intelligence Section paren Central close paren. Berenson and Chetwynd were longtime acquaintances, but Chetwynd is vetted completely clean. He has no links to the Montrose group."

"Thanks for small favors," Gould said. "The British are taking it hard enough from that damn soggy satchel, without having a head of section named."

Applewood said, "They're sensitive to the issue, Linda."

"More than we are," said the last person at the table, "and Allan could have been much worse than the Philby ring."

Raphael said, "Dr. Hansard was your recruit, Dr. Polonyi. Do you have any comments now?"

Augustina Polonyi sat slightly back in her wheelchair, tilted her head. "About what, Raphael? He feels tremendously guilty over Allan's death; we nearly lost him for it. If he knew the extent of the disorder the Montrose list has created, I suspect he would recoil, freeze completely. We'd lose him for a long time, if not forever. Joe calls him 'malleable,' and that's right enough. It is exactly that receptivity to ideas, to other modes of thought, that makes him brilliant." She lit a fresh cigarette from the stub of the last. "You should have seen him across the *Diplomacy* board, playing a head of state with more concern than most of the real things can marshal; ah, he drove Allan nearly to tears of joy." She ground out the slightly smoked cigarette. "Nicholas is a responsible, open-minded, serious young man, who *is* still working for us, correct, Raphael?"

Raphael pressed his hands together. "Correct, Dr. Polonyi." He looked up. "Stringer, give us the chronology, please."

Stringer opened a plastic folder, peered at it through his half-frames. "Tenth August, Allan Berenson returns from the UK, where we are standard-depth certain he made contact with KGB control. He also returns with a copy of the Skene Manuscript, acquired from Edward Chetwynd.

"Twelfth August, Berenson has Skene photographed. The film is mailed to an address in the UK that proves to be a cold drop. Servicing of the drop is not observed."

Carteret went *hmm, hmm, hmm.*

Stringer continued, "Fourteenth August, a White Group contractor enters Berenson's apartment and photographs the manuscript.

"Twentieth August, the Montrose documents are recovered; twenty-second August, they are authenticated by Dr. Hansard and the findings passed to CIA.

"Twenty-fourth August, Dr. Berenson is terminated in semi-clean fashion, body discovered by housekeeper on the twenty-fifth, reports transmitted to The White Group as per request on the twenty-sixth."

Raphael said, "Very well. Dr. Applewood, your analysis of the manuscripts."

Robert Applewood said, "Slides, please, Stringer," and Stringer pushed a plastic cube of slides into a socket on the table, adjusted a control. The wall screen showed a sheet of worn paper, covered with spidery handwriting.

Applewood said, "The Skene Manuscript was discovered six months ago during a renovation of Skene House in Lincolnshire. Workmen broke through a wall into what was apparently a sealed priest's refuge. There were several Catholic books and documents within, and, in a wooden case, the manuscript of a verse play, in the Elizabethan style, entitled *The Assassin's Tragedy,* and signed by Christopher Marlowe. The script compares closely to that in documents believed to be in Marlowe's hand. Next, please.

"This is page twenty-one of the Skene Manuscript, as photographed by our contractor on the fourteenth of August. Next, parallel, please."

Another slide appeared alongside the first. It also showed a page of manuscript, apparently the same one. Several places in the text were circled in red.

"Page twenty-one of the manuscript found in Dr. Berenson's apartment after his death," Applewood said. "The text is similar, as is the hand and even the cracking of the paper. But there are differences in all respects. Next."

The screen showed magnified parts of the manuscripts side by side. Gould said, "Yes, I see. The descenders are much sharper on the right."

Applewood said, "Next."

The slide showed two columns of typescript, listing words and phrases side by side from the two manuscripts. "There are two hundred and twenty-three changes to the text. Most of these are trivial, and do no more than create an alternative version of the play. There are, of course, alternative versions of plays known to be by Marlowe, including *Doctor Faustus.* But several of the changes are anachronisms and incorrect usages, some subtle, some not. The extremest case is in the last act, in the description of the banquet at the court masque during which the King is to be assassinated. Slide, please, Stringer . . . Now, this *could* be a world-class coincidence, but I see no way to read it other than as a description, in rather fine Elizabethan blank verse, of a Big Mac, fries, and a chocolate shake."

Linda Gould said, "All right, what's the point?"

"The point," Applewood said, "is that the Skene Manuscript found in Berenson's apartment after his death is not the same one he had two weeks earlier. Stealing Skene and leaving a forgery, even a bad forgery, in its place would be understandable. But this is a very good forgery; in fact, the forger must have had close access to the original. The changes were deliberate. The question is, who and why?"

"And when," Gould said.

"No, I think that's clear," said Dr. Polonyi. "It must have been done after his murder. The box was open; he had been studying it very recently. He would have noticed the change."

Carteret said, "Suppose he knew about the switch? Had a hand in it?"

"Then he would not have been studying it."

Gould said, "Has this copy been compared to any others?"

"There aren't any others," Applewood said. "Not in this country. The researchers involved are all extremely concerned that this doesn't become a media circus, like the one around Hitler's diary—especially if Skene turns out to be as much a forgery as those."

Carteret said, "But Berenson had a copy. . . . He wasn't even a historian."

Polonyi said, "You know as well as I, Joe, that favors were done for Allan, sometimes extraordinary ones."

Gould said, "Then you think this play means something useful to us."

Applewood shrugged and looked at Raphael. Raphael said, "We are virtually certain that Dr. Berenson was operating a network of agents. The Intelligence services have, unfortunately, almost no leads to those agents. We have been retained on the usual basis to"—he seemed to smile, but perhaps it was only a trick of the light—"explore those possibilities available to us."

Gould said, "Hansard's looking up a four-hundred-year-old *play,* for God's sake."

Polonyi said, "Which, for some reason, Allan chose to send to one of his agents through secret channels."

"All right," Gould said, "it clicks. It's all we have. And I trust the fee is enormous?"

Carteret laughed out loud. Stringer looked up, with a pained expression. Raphael just said, "Does anyone have anything to add on the conduct of this operation?"

"Just wake me when it's over," Carteret said, and stood up. "You'll all excuse me; I've got a lecture—"

"Of course, Dr. Carteret," Raphael said. "Next formal meeting in two weeks."

Carteret went out of the room. Applewood and Gould said goodbye and went out together, picking up a conversation about cipher mathematics they had left in the middle. Stringer stood, nodded to

Dr. Polonyi, and waddled out. The door slid shut behind him with a faint hiss.

Dr. Polonyi lit another cigarette, using a steel Zippo with the Foreign Legion Paratroop crest. Raphael sat entirely still as she took a slow puff and exhaled it.

Polonyi said, "When did you decide to use Nicholas for this . . . exercise? Before he announced his intent to resign, or after?"

"You agree that he is the correct choice."

"He's the perfect choice, as you know very well. Now answer my question."

"Haven't you just answered it?"

After a moment, Polonyi said, "You don't think you'll lose him, do you? You expect to keep using him until he . . ."

"It was entirely Dr. Hansard's choice to present his resignation, as it was his choice to take the Skene assignment."

"He feels guilty; he feels responsible," Dr. Polonyi said. "He's a genius at finding historical cause and effect; did you expect him not to see one here?"

Raphael nodded. "Go on."

"We could have told him the truth. That Allan had been under surveillance and suspicion for more than two years. We might even tell him about Sevenage. I'm sure he would find it fascinating."

"Would that lessen his guilt?" Raphael said. "I'm not asking rhetorically, Dr. Polonyi. I have no objection to revealing that to Dr. Hansard—if it will improve his mental state. I am not convinced that it will. . . . And of course you know that we do not have the authority to expose Dr. Hansard to Sevenage."

"Since when have you ever observed the niceties of clearance?" Dr. Polonyi toyed with her cigarette. "Perhaps you're right. It might only . . . further complicate matters. I withdraw the suggestion."

"It was a reasonable suggestion."

"'So are we all, all reasonable men.'"

"Dr. Berenson was your friend," Raphael said. "Dr. Hansard is your recruit. Albeit an unknowing recruit."

"I shall miss Allan terribly," Dr. Polonyi said, with no particular emotion in her voice, certainly not grief. "I shall especially miss the *Diplomacy* games . . . have you ever played *Diplomacy*, Raphael?"

"I am familiar with the game," Raphael said, "but I do not play."

"No, I understand," Dr. Polonyi said, and smiled. "Why would you feel the need? Good-bye, Raphael."

"Good day, Dr. Polonyi."

She crushed out her cigarette in the overfull ashtray, turned her wheelchair and rolled it to the door, which whirred open to let her pass and closed again behind her.

Raphael stood up, went through the connecting hall into his office. As he left the conference room, a sensor saw that it was empty and turned the lights out.

Raphael sat behind his desk, palms together, watching his screens. After a few minutes, Stringer came in, carrying a black folder. He put it on the desktop. "Latest report on the Berenson termination."

Raphael opened the folder, flipped through it, snapped it shut. "Yes. . . . I can remember when every agency had its own style of execution. They were proud of it; it was part of the operation. 'Thus die all who oppose us.' Then all the passion went out of the killing, it became one more expediency, and it had to be done in an expedient fashion. Efficient, tightly built, without much to distinguish one from the next. Like Japanese automobiles."

"Does it matter who killed him?"

"Not much. Keep the file open. Where is Dr. Hansard now?"

"The Folger Shakespeare Library. He went there directly after leaving this building."

"Ah." Raphael smiled slightly, as much as he ever did. "The Skene papers haven't even arrived, and already he's in research mode."

Stringer looked vaguely puzzled; Stringer was never out of research mode. "Do you want a trace on him there?"

"No purpose in that," Raphael said. "As Dr. Polonyi has just been reminding me, if we could find out what Dr. Hansard does in the historical sources, he would not be as precious as he is. . . . He will be going to England very soon. Arrange surveillance."

■ ■ ■

The woman in the London hotel lobby was dazzlingly ash-blonde, and wore wraparound sunglasses and silver and bronze earrings as big as the palm of a hand. She was dressed in a Karl Lagerfeld oversize white trenchcoat over a black ribbed top and leather skirt. The accents—

scarf, gloves, belt, perilously high pumps—were all fresh-blood red as her lipstick.

Everyone in the lobby found something particular to watch, heels, hips, enigmatic lips; everyone watched. Reading stopped, writing postcards stopped, collecting keys and counting out change stopped in midair. When the elevator doors finally closed behind her, something like a shudder of relief shook the room.

She left the elevator on the nineteenth floor. The hall was dim, and cool, with burnt-orange carpeting and wall covering like lacquered burlap. From an alcove came the grinding thrum of an automatic ice maker.

She knocked on a door. "Come in," said a man's voice from within. She entered.

The room was spacious, furnished with imitation French furniture. Allan had called the style "Louis-irrational-number." She found it amusing that the London KGB *rezident* should have such a quintessentially imperialist desk.

Palatine stood by the windows, his back to her. He wore a conventional black City suit, pinch-waisted and crisp. "Good morning," he said, and turned around. His eyes widened, just slightly, and he smiled, just showing teeth. "That's a quite . . . striking outfit," he said. His voice was authentically British, she thought; not the pure Oxbridge that only foreigners spoke, but a little west of BBC. "You were not observed?"

"I was observed like mad," she said, "but I wasn't followed. And this isn't how I usually dress." The outfit was in fact borrowed from a friend, supposedly for a romantic lunch.

Palatine examined her face, the sunglasses. "Yes, I see. Protective coloration. Very good."

"I'm glad you approve," she said, not too dryly. "Do you have the operational file?"

Palatine spread his hands. "Surely we have other things to discuss first. Changing the principal of an operation can be quite complicated—and as I'm sure you're aware, the group I represent is not known for its loose organizational structure."

The woman said, "We have nothing to discuss. The original terms were five hundred thousand pounds in gold for the delivery of the

COPE LIGHT unit, and another million contingent on the success of NIGHTMOVE. Those are also my terms."

"You learned this from the former principal?"

"I don't know where else I'd have heard it."

Palatine nodded. "The S Directorate has requested me to tell you that, if you consider the full NIGHTMOVE operation to be beyond your resources, they will pay seven hundred thousand pounds for the delivery of COPE LIGHT alone."

"Tell the S Directorate thank you, but I'm quite up to the full operation. In fact, I'm not interested in anything less. Now, I'd like to see the operational file."

Palatine said, "We are also willing to provide you with a field operations specialist. This will not diminish your payment for services—"

"No. The file."

"As you wish." Palatine went to the desk. He produced a piece of blank gray metal the size of a charge card, slipped it into the crack above one of the drawers. There was a buzz and Palatine pulled the drawer open. He took out a file folder labeled LINE ZN.

"The list is encrypted, of course," he said, handing over the file. He was smiling like a man with a wonderful secret.

"Naturally," the woman said, and smiled back. She opened the file, scanned the list of agents' names. "WAGNER," she said, giving it the German pronunciation: *Vog*-ner. "Of course." She began to laugh softly.

"WAGNER is one of the agents on the list," Palatine said. "You are acquainted with him?"

"I *am* him," she said, and immediately regretted it; better to have lied, to have kept Palatine and KGB completely at her mercy.

Palatine said, "May I?" and reached for the file. She let him take it. He examined it. "WAGNER. . . ." he said. "I presume you're fond of his music? An amateur musician, perhaps?"

She said, "He did it, didn't he. He told me you couldn't decode the list, and you can't. You'd have been all over the shop if I hadn't decided to walk in."

Palatine said, irritated, "We are not without resources."

"Good for bloody nothing."

Palatine looked thoughtful for a moment. "I'm sorry, miss—"

"WAGNER will do," she said lightly.

Palatine smiled and nodded. "Of course your assistance is greatly appreciated, and will be rewarded. NIGHTMOVE is an extraordinary plan, a brilliant conception."

"Don't try to flatter me by flattering Allan," she said. "This isn't going to stand as a monument to his memory. It's espionage, and treason, and it's going to be murder, and he knew all of that."

Palatine shrugged, no longer upset or nervous in the least. "Then do nothing. Expose the plan; expose me. You might be able to rehabilitate Dr. Berenson's name."

"Give me the list."

Palatine did so. "Is there anything else I can do?"

"Yes. I'll need some money, at least ten thousand pounds cash; I'm going to have to travel, and I can't leave a trail of cheques behind."

"Quite sensible. We'll make it twenty; don't want you running short in the field." His voice had turned school-masterly pleasant; she wanted to punch him in the mouth. "Well, then—"

"And a gun," WAGNER said.

"Excuse me?"

"Something quiet. Bullets or gas or darts, I don't care." She grinned at him. She'd practiced the effect, with the sunglasses and makeup, before a mirror: It was definitely spooky. "Don't worry, I'm a big girl, I won't leave any messes."

"Yes, very well," Palatine said, his neck just slightly flushed.

"Then I'll say good day, Mr. Palatine." She took the papers out of the folder and slipped them into her coat.

"Good day," Palatine said.

Palatine watched as the door closed behind the woman. He sat down at his desk, took out a duplicate of the Line ZN roster, the operational plan notes, and the support files. He made a note that WAGNER had now been identified, penciled *Cipher key: Musical preference?* below it, then added *Unconfirmed.*

He did paperwork for a few more minutes, organizing the delivery of the money and weapon through cold drops, setting up a surveillance of WAGNER. As he finished with the documents, he stacked and squared them neatly. They would be ash and dust in twenty-four hours, an incriminating liability once their plans were in motion, but

Palatine saw in that no reason to be disorderly. He was proudly neat, even fussy.

KGB did not really trust fussy men, he knew very well. Despite the mountainous bureaucracy, they still fancied the image of sword and shield; knights in armor did not square up forms. The CIA cowboys were exactly the same.

It was why Palatine loved the British station: This country appreciated a neat desk and a pressed suit. Oh, that was a stereotype, to be sure; most of the real stuffed popinjays were dead or retired, but still there was an *image* there, and it would take generations to shake it, just as the Soviets were still shadowed by Beria, the Americans by Wild Bill Donovan.

Palatine himself was one of the last, perhaps *the* last, of the perfect illegals. His parents had been given impeccable documentation as British nationals—an easier thing before the Hitler war, before computers and lasers and retinal prints. All Palatine had done was to be legitimately born to them, and His Majesty's Government had provided the rest of the documents. He had grown up English, attended the public schools and Oxford. He had debated in Eden's favor on Suez. The Communists—the wrong Communists—had attempted to recruit him, and he had dutifully reported them to the Head.

He had come by his place in the City and the old-boy network as honestly as anyone ever did, establishing the reality of his British self even as the details of his Soviet self piled up. He had medals he had never seen, a uniform he had never worn, a whole ghost personality in an office on Dzerzhinsky Street.

Palatine noted that the surveillance operators were to report immediately when WAGNER located the agent with access to the COPE LIGHT device. At that point they would intervene, seize COPE LIGHT, conclude the operation.

Palatine had not lied to the woman: NIGHTMOVE was in fact a brilliant plan. But it was also wildly audacious, and insanely risky. Typically American.

S Directorate, the KGB scientific-intelligence section, estimated that the COPE devices had cost in excess of forty million dollars to develop. The Rhombic-series satellites were each worth half a billion, the National Security Agency's pride and joy. Doomed, all of them, because of a college professor and a handful of disgruntled people in positions of trust. Allan Berenson had called them his "sunshine traitors." A whole network, Palatine thought, with no direct ties to the KGB, with an almost ridiculously low potential for backfire, with a genuinely ridiculous price—NIGHTMOVE would be a bargain even if they paid the million and a half pounds. Which they would not.

There was still a good deal of room for concern. There wasn't enough surveillance in depth, Palatine well knew, but there couldn't be, not and preserve that wonderful deniability. Further, they did not dare call attention to the security loopholes that made the operation possible until those gaps had been fully exploited.

Palatine sat back in his chair, and folded his hands, feeling rather amused at himself. Was he beginning to think like an American—a buccaneer of the secret ways? *You must be proud, bold, pleasant, resolute,* Allan had quoted to him, *and now and then stab, as occasion serves.*

Palatine had become terribly fond of Berenson. They had started with a mutual contempt for each other's goals and politics, but in time learned that they were more alike than different: two intelligent and educated men who had discovered that the world was mad.

Palatine had been faced by the truth in 1961, only a few years after he had been activated as an agent in the UK. The game was much wilder then, only partly real—Ian Fleming and John Kennedy had done that, between the two of them, blurred the lines between reality and fantasy. For a moment, the whole business became mythical: people read tales of spies as they had once read tales of Hector and Achilles. (Palatine's classics professor had pointed out that the *Iliad* contained a cracking good spy story.) And, inevitably, the spies themselves began to believe the fables of greatness and invincibility.

In September of 1961, Palatine had been given a directive for transmission to his superior. It called for the murder of a prostitute named Christine Keeler, in such fashion as to incriminate MI5. Palatine made certain that the order never reached operational level—a bold thing to do, though he did not do it boldly. It bought the first in a series of favors and honorable debts that had finally put him in this room, in this chair, thinking about stupid murders.

He wondered who had ordered the death of Dr. Allan Berenson. Perhaps it was as well he did not know; if he did, he might issue a directive of his own, and the shame of the times was that there were no longer any young men to lose the orders that needed losing.

He thought for a moment more about revenge, and pride, boldness, resolution. He opened the NIGHTMOVE agent roster, and made a note above WAGNER's name: *Terminate immediately upon obtaining target.*

■ ■ ■

"So what's it about?" Anna Romano said, and handed Nicholas Hansard a folded shirt.

Hansard put the shirt in his suitcase, said, "Some damn papers."

"Fall term starts in a week and a half."

"Yes, it's that important."

"Rich got a letter from Paul Ogden. It was mostly about you."

Hansard looked up. He almost asked who in hell Paul Ogden was, then remembered the *Kingmaker* game, and nearly bit his tongue. "Look . . . I'm not moving away. I shouldn't be more than a couple of weeks. Paul can wait that long to decide what to do with his life." He stuffed socks into a corner of his bag.

"At least that long," Anna said, then more loudly, "When's your plane?"

"Eleven o'clock out of Kennedy. I'm on the commuter at nine."

"Shit."

Hansard stopped, his hands full of underwear. He looked at Anna, into Anna's eyes, so gloriously large and dark. "What time is it?" he said, hearing an adolescent squeak in his voice.

"Seven-forty-five."

It was a good half hour to the local airport, and he wasn't nearly done packing. "Shit," Hansard said, and Anna laughed and gave him a long, wet kiss. "Oh," Hansard said, "that's a big help."

"I'll drive you to the airport," she said. "Nothing like prolonging the agony."

Prolonging wasn't quite the word. Anna drove a gun-metal-gray SVO Mustang, cranked up to stock-car speeds on the twisting country roads. "Warp eight, Mr. Scott," she shouted as they shot the railroad underpass at seventy-five, and Hansard replied, "Och, Cap'n, the engines'll never take it," but for most of the ride they were silent.

He could have told her the reason for the trip. Anna was no gossip—he knew that well enough by now. But he was being cautious. . . .

No. He was being scared, irrationally, superstitiously. He couldn't shake Allan's ghost.

In the depths of his wife's illness, there had been moments away from it. He would walk out of the hospital, and sit down on the grass; watch the world going by, alive with joyful indifference, and know that life went on.

Now everything seemed underlaid by an invisible network of death, and life went on only until one of the threads was pulled, and snapped a neck decades and continents away.

He wanted to make Anna understand what was happening, but without drawing her into the web: wanted to say *what you don't know can't hurt you,* and was disgusted with himself for even thinking such a thing.

The regional airport was one runway and a cinderblock terminal building. The terminal had chipped fiberglass chairs, a candy machine that had seen heavy action before the Korean War, and a television set (COURTESY OF BUD'S TV-RADIO SERVICE) perpetually turned to a local old-movie channel. Tonight it was showing something Italian, with spaceships. There was an attendant, watching the movie, and two other passengers waiting: a fat man in a three-piece suit, reading *Forbes* and looking bored, and a college-age kid with a sweater draped over his shoulders, reading *Fanny Hill* and looking bored. Hansard and Anna went out onto the apron; the attendant started to tell them that they couldn't go out yet, then shrugged and turned back to the TV.

The plane, a twin-prop Beechcraft, was sitting there, door and nose cowling open. The pilot was walking around it, finishing preflight.

Anna said, "Mind telling me where you're going from Kennedy? Or do we just wait to read about it in *Foreign Affairs?*"

"Oh . . . God, I'm sorry. England. I'll be . . . running around, I expect. If you want to write, send it to the American Express office in London." There was a *clang;* Hansard turned sharply, but it was just the flight engineer closing the plane's cowling. He turned back to Anna. "Look, about Paul . . . have him send me a letter. And I promise I'll talk to him as soon as I'm back."

"Okay."

"I mean it, Anna."

"I know you mean it, Nicholas," she said gently, then pointed at the Beechcraft. "Now get on that plane, or you'll regret it . . . maybe not today, but—"

He kissed her. The attendant was leading the other passengers past; Hansard ignored them and held Anna.

"I said, get on that plane," she said finally, and then smiled and said, "Us . . . well, we'll always have the fifteenth century."

Hansard got on the plane. There were only eight passenger seats; he squeezed forward into the one just behind the pilot, alongside the port propeller. The door was shut, and the prop spun up.

Anna was waving, silhouetted against the little terminal's greasy windows. Hansard waved back as the plane began taxiing. He wondered how old the ritual of "seeing someone off" was, supposed it must be ancient. Ships sank, trains derailed, planes fell, all roads ate their travelers. How terrible to imagine that one had turned away a moment too soon.

So many ways to dusty death, and no proper way to say good-bye. They turned onto the runway. The little plane roared and rolled and bumped and lifted, banked hard right, and was swallowed by darkness like outer space, between night sky and Long Island Sound.

Two hours later, Hansard was looking out of another airplane window at the dark. There had been no one to say farewell this time. There *was* a security guard who was convinced that the battery-powered reading lamp in Hansard's briefcase was some sort of infernal device and demanded its partial dismantling, and a gate attendant who spent some time making certain Hansard had a valid passport before the airline invested fuel, a seat, and a foil-wrapped meal in ferrying him to Europe.

Just as well Anna had not been there. The small goodbye gestures, sweetly romantic at the tiny regional field, would have been utterly lost in the comic inferno of an international airport. As it was, he thought about her, waving, and all between faded out, like a commercial that had interrupted *Casablanca* on the all-night channel.

Hansard was sitting in the front row of business class, no seatback obstructing the space in front of him, and the adjoining seat was luckily empty. The attendant had brought him a double bourbon and Coke; he had his pocket tape player running, headphones masking the thunder of the 747 with Creedence Clearwater Revival. Hansard reached into his briefcase, took out photo-reduced copies of the Skene Manuscript and several documents from the Folger Library, and the controversial reading light. He clipped the lamp to a plastic padholder; it threw a cool circle of light onto the papers.

The airplane had headphones and a reading lamp, of course. But the built-in lights were always dim and badly aimed; the onboard music was never to his taste. Working environment was important, and Hansard carried his own with him. On trains he brought his own whiskey, but there was a law (ass, idiot law) against that on airplanes.

The attendants unfolded the movie screen, and the cabin lights went down. Hansard barely noticed. Tucked up in his sphere of light and sound, he began to study the pages, reading not for content but for inference, looking for the mind behind the lines.

He sipped his drink, and time began to dissolve.

■　■　■

The taproom stank of old cheese and stale beer and fresh vomit. Students do not drink to be sociable, nor because it makes their hearts light: They drink to get drunk, and all else is sophistry. Somewhere outside the room, it was full day in Cambridge, and breezes rippled the river and the grass upon its banks; but within the tavern it was perpetual late twilight, a land of splinters washed in bad wine.

It was April, 1587. Christopher Marlowe was twenty-three years old, a student at Corpus Christi College, with a divinity scholarship. His Latin classes were meeting at this very moment; he was not meeting them. Marlowe sat, and drank, and tried to shut out the world. But the world crowded in.

There was a loud young man across the room, more or less entertaining a circle of more-or-less friends. The speaker, who read law, had been at Fotheringay two months earlier, to watch the execution of Mary Queen of Scots, and the tale was still good for a drink, or two, when embellished.

". . . and there was an alchemist there, a proper old wizard, who

told me he was trying to get a phial of Mary's blood, for his spells."
The wizard was a new twist on the story.

"Papist after a relic, more like," someone said.

"No, no," the law student said, "blood for a charm, he said; said he
could call up the Devil with a Papist queen's blood."

"'Twere no maid's, that's sure enough," said another of the listen-
ers, and there was a round of guffaws.

"Why did the wizard tell *you* this?" one of the younger students
said, thoughtfully, missing the point. "He must have known what he
was risking."

The law student jumped on the opportunity. "Aye, well enough,
and I told him so; but he says to me, 'As well be hanged for the Devil
as the Pope.'"

The storyteller collected his laugh, and another beer. By the next
telling, the wizard would be Doctor Dee himself. Or perhaps the
Devil would make an appearance. *The bad queen dies,* Marlowe
thought. *Hell is discovered.*

It was an interesting idea for a scene: the execution of Mary presented as a parable of damnation. He wanted paper and a pen. Suddenly he wanted some air as well.

Marlowe stood up, started to move quietly toward the door. But
the room was too small. The law student shouted, "So, you don't like
our conversation?"

Marlowe ignored him.

Someone slid a chair back, blocking Marlowe's way. Marlowe felt
his chest tighten. His chin was round and receding, his eyes brown
and mild, his beard light. He looked an easy mark. And he was alone,
which sealed it. The law student—Marlowe had entirely forgotten his
name—said, "I asked you if you liked our conversation."

"As well be deafened by an ass's bray as a church bell," Marlowe
said, and shoved the chair in his path, spilling the man in it to the
floor. The others stood up. Off to one side, the barmaid crossed her
arms. She knew who to name to the constables if they did too much
damage, and it had been a slow day.

Marlowe heard mutterings and grumblings. Not everyone wanted
to fight. No one would flee, of course, it would become too infamous,

but in a group, in a crowded little ale-hole, it was easy enough to appear to take part without ever getting one's knife wet.

And they all did have knives. Any man did, in such a day and age. There was a sound like cloth ripping—

—as the cabin attendant pushed back the curtain to first class. The main cabin lights came on. Hansard looked up; dawn was leaking through the airplane windows. Hansard stretched a bit, looked out and down at the Atlantic through broken pink clouds.

He put the papers away, took out a tiny battery-powered shaver and stumbled back to the lavatory. As he shaved and tried to tidy himself—not entirely easy in a stainless-steel phonebooth—he thought about the Marlowe he was creating. Too broody, he supposed; too much a reflection of himself. (Hansard peered into the lavatory mirror.) He was on firm ground with the tavern brawls; there were plenty of records of that. Marlowe had died in a taproom knife fight, supposedly over the bill. That explanation was too convenient for a number of modern people, the sort who got their history from obese novels and flatulent miniseries. Every male figure in the whole past was now perceived as Richard Chamberlain in a tight velvet suit, doffed only to bed Jane Seymour in a candle-lit room.

Corpus Christi College had what was supposed to be a portrait of Marlowe: a soft, roundish face, with a little beard and mustache, large brown eyes . . . a bit of a knowing smirk on the lips. The face of a supporting character, maybe, but not the hero of a Major Motion Picture or Unprecedented Television Event.

They did have documents of the secret mission to Rheims. Sir Francis Walsingham had sent seven young men to infiltrate nests of Catholic scheming. That much was known. Marlowe himself seemed never to have written of it. At least, not in open terms. But there were the plays, with their assassins, their turncoats, their masterminds. (Hansard stretched the skin of his cheek and scrubbed at it with the whining razor.)

Who would play Walsingham on the little screen? Orson Welles was gone, Richardson was gone. There was Edward Woodward, who'd done *Breaker Morant* and then the television show about the retired spy. There was a face that had seen things.

Hansard looked into the mirror, and wondered if he looked worldly, or just like death on the night flight.

■ ■ ■

Marlowe looked intently at the small-paned window, though it was quite dark outside; he watched the lamplight slide like golden oil over the facets of glass. He thought of Tamburlaine, burning cities as the pyre of his dead wife Zenocrate. The scene would be lost if the fire was only described: Marlowe wanted fire on the stage.

"The Masters of the College have proposed your expulsion," Walsingham said levelly. "They say that you are absent from classes."

Marlowe turned to face Sir Francis, who sat behind a small writing table. "I am. Of course, I was abroad for a time. As you may recall."

Without reacting, Walsingham said, "You are a brawler."

"Do you mean by that that I am a failure as a murderer?"

"And it is said . . ." The old man paused, frowned slightly. ". . . that you are impious."

"*Well,*" Marlowe said with a sudden bitterness, "as well be hanged for a blasphemer as an assassin."

"What am I supposed to do with you, man?"

Marlowe shot back, "What did you do with me in Rheims?"

"Used you," Walsingham said, just as quickly. "I used you as the workman uses a good tool."

"And a fine piece of work it was, too." Marlowe pressed his palms together, turned his head. "All that death in a little room." He turned back to Walsingham. "Where did you find that creature?"

"Poley?"

"Even the devils have names."

"He was in prison, on a charge of violence."

"Oh. He was no amateur, then. No unschooled genius."

"You were not like this upon your return. What's bred this in you?"

"Time," Marlowe said, "and the thought of blasphemy. Our Lord instructed us to do no murder, yet we did murder there in France."

"Spare me a scholar's fine logical arguments—"

"*Bene dissere est finis logices,*" Marlowe said: *To argue well is the chief end of logic.*

"—those people were traitors to the country of their birth, murderers themselves, would-be regicides."

"And so they deserved to die, for their lives were damnable."

Walsingham said, "Just so," in a very ordinary tone.

There was silence for what seemed a long time. Marlowe said finally, "I am leaving the College."

"Leaving it for what?"

"My play is nearly finished. I mean to go to London, and see it performed."

"This is the *Queen of Carthage*?"

"I'm not happy with that. I've put it away. I've written a life of Tamburlaine."

Sir Francis nodded. "An epic, I hope."

"At least, my lord, I'll say it's large in scope."

Walsingham chuckled at the extempore verse. "Obtaining the notice of a company, and a production, will be easier with connections. Connections will come more easily to a graduate of the College. It isn't so long until the end of term."

"You yourself said the Masters mean to expel me."

Walsingham smiled, the smile of a man who knows where he is strong. "They are gracious men. They will make allowances for the Queen's loyal servants. I will make clear to them that your absence on the Continent was in government employ."

"But not the nature of that employment."

"Naturally not."

"And if I do not choose to accept your assistance?"

Walsingham shrugged. "Your life is your own."

"Yes," Marlowe said, "yes, I suppose that it is." He went out of the office, into the dark corridor, thinking of Rheims; of the Catholic conspirators who had accepted Marlowe as one of them, and then been led carefully to their destruction.

If they had wanted *things,* lands or gold or offices, why then they would have been plain folk, greedy and comprehensible. But though the cell spoke of being laureled as heroes, they knew there was nothing like that in store for them. Marlowe had seen the plan that they had made and refined: It had been wonderfully direct, and simple, and after one breath's space for the mob to catch its wits the killers would have been torn to pieces. Men had killed kings for infinite reasons; yet among the members of the Rheims cell there had been a strange, invisible alchemy that made the immoral act moral, and therefore imperative . . . that made this murder holy.

He could muster no such madness for himself.

■ ■ ■

Hansard and the rest of the passengers spilled down the chute into the glass corridors of Heathrow Terminal 3. He hitched his garment bag high on his shoulder and began slaloming past the tourists as they tried first to absorb the fact that they were *actually not in America anymore* and second to decipher the airport signage, a form of minimalist art easily lost amid the posters inviting visitors who might be short a machine-tool plant to build it in Milton Keynes. Flat morning sunlight came through the corridor walls; the sky was promising blue. It was 5:30 A.M., an unholy hour anywhere on earth but with one distinct advantage at Heathrow. . . .

Hallelujah for the dawn patrol, Hansard thought as he reached the Customs area: The maze of roped corridors leading to passport control was nearly empty. He had more than once stood in the ghastly little labyrinth for two hours and up; but today there were only a few people ahead of him.

And one couple behind him. . . .

"Whaddaya think they did with the bags?" she said.

"I dunno," he replied.

Hansard looked straight ahead. Less than twenty yards directly in front of him, just past the passport-control desks, was a massive set of electronic signs displaying baggage-carousel locations.

"Look at this line," she said. "You'd think they didn't want us t'come at all."

"Yeah," he said. "Made a big stink about we's gonna ruin 'em."

"We want in!" the woman said shrilly. A pair of policemen turned at the sound. Like all the airport teams, they carried automatic rifles.

"Look at those guns," she stage-whispered. "You think there're terrorists here? Suppose there was somethin' in with the bags?"

"Oughta all have guns," the man said. "Give me a gun, nobody gonna hijack *that* plane for sure—"

The line cleared by divine mercy, and Hansard picked up his bag and walked on.

"Business or pleasure, sir?" the Customs woman said.

"Pleasure," Hansard said. She stamped his passport and handed it back. Hansard walked on. He had said "pleasure" with a hint of a British accent. It was a habit of his, an unconscious reflex, not at all deliberate. He hoped not, anyway.

Overhead, the baggage board was reporting handling delays for all flights. Hansard shouldered his luggage and walked on toward the Underground station. His step was light.

PROCESS
OF
ELIMINATION

PART THREE

THE TENT OF WAR

From jiggling veins of rhyming mother-wits,
And such conceits as clownage keeps in pay,
We'll lead you to the stately tent of war . . .

—**Tamburlaine, Part I,** *Prologue*

In the Combat Information Center of the cruiser USS *Wright,* four men and three women sat at desks, each with a computer screen framed in gray metal and two banks of lighted switches. Above the consoles were rear-projection status screens, able to show electronic maps, weather charts, status reports, whatever was required, even television pictures of the sea if that should be considered important. Higher still hung special-purpose displays for aircraft and satellite control, nuclear weapons management. The ceiling glowed dull red with background illumination, a genial halo of hell.

The seven people, four of them in United States Navy uniform, two Royal Navy, one West German Kriegsmarine, saw the world through the screens, heard through earphones, replied through headset microphones and fingers on switches. Their purpose was to tie together the sensors and weapons (or, as the manufacturers would insist, the sensor and weapon *systems*) of *Wright* and the eight other ships making up NATO Task Force CT-59, current mission to patrol the North Atlantic one hundred kilometers west-northwest of Scapa Flow.

"Sonar contact," one of the operators said, and pressed a key; an area chart drew itself on one of the large screens, marking the friendly ships in green and another in white. "Looks like an attack sub . . . dunking the phones now. Yup. Diesel for certain." Numbers annotated the hostile boat's symbol on the screen.

"It's turning," said an ensign. "Why aren't we—"

"We're not on the bridge," said the Command Duty Officer, Lieutenant Commander Susan Bell, Royal Navy.

An engine-room repeater displayed a rapid change in engine RPMs. The Soviet sub edged close to the symbol for *Wright,* then slipped in front of it.

The communications operator snapped a switch. "CIC *Wright* to *Glamorgan,* hostile boat on intercept course, acknowledge." The woman covered her microphone, said, "Bastard's going to ram."

"It does seem so," Bell said offhandedly.

The sub did. The green and white symbols intersected on the screen. An annunciator screen lit red.

"CIC *Wright* to task force, *Glamorgan* has been collided with. Stand by." The comm operator turned. "She's taking water. Expects to lose power anytime."

"She's out of the net," the detection operator said. "Hole in radar coverage, 280 to 295, and neatly done too."

"Can you stretch to cover?" Bell said. The crew was getting a bit too excited, a little too eager to congratulate the enemy.

"Increasing the sweep rates." All right, Bell thought, that was good. Click, click. "*Damn.* Three bogies, airborne, fast. Where'd those come from?"

"Pop-up missiles."

"*Wickwire* is firing Phalanx," the weapons operator said. Phalanx was an electric Gatling gun that fired clouds of bullets at incoming missiles; it worked pretty well, which was fortunate, because so did the missiles. "Got one, got two."

Congratulatory attitude again. "What about three?"

"Impact on *Wickwire.*"

"That takes the radar down to starboard. NTDS has a pair of missile boats on the horizon. We're firing."

A voice crackled in Bell's headset. "CDO *Wright* . . . On my way," she said, and slipped the phones off. *Just when the war was getting interesting,* she thought, and said, "I'm being relieved. Keep to your stations."

"Aye, sir."

LCdr Bell went around a bank of equipment and through a door. The light in the hallway beyond was painful after the dim CIC; Bell shut her eyes and put a hand against the wall for guidance.

The floor was linoleum tile, the walls paneled in wood veneer, the lighting fluorescent through diffuser panels. It looked like any office corridor. Which it was. There were doors up and down the hall, leading to more gaming rooms: At the end of the hall was the bridge of the "ship" Bell had just left. USS *Frank Lloyd Wright* was a fully commissioned naval vessel consisting of three rooms in the London War Games Centre.

Bell turned a corner and went into the duty lounge. It was carpeted, with low tables and plastic-covered chairs, a tea cart in the corner. Two lieutenants, one American, the other Canadian Navy, were sitting with their ties loosened and foam coffee cups in their hands. Both wore dark aviator-style glasses, to save their dark vision for the game rooms.

"How's the crew doing?" the American said.

"They're having a bit too much fun yet," Bell said, "but they're all right. Pretty soon they'll be getting sick over the side." She looked at the analog wall clock, tied, like all the clocks in the Centre, to a master time computer belowstairs. "Time, gentlemen."

"'Down to the sea in ships,'" the US lieutenant said, and the two men went out of the lounge, cups in hand. The American was replacing Bell on the *Wright;* the Canadian was headed for Room 41, which was the primary flight deck of the carrier *Vicksburg.*

Bell made two cups of strong tea. Just as she was adding the milk, the lounge door opened and Gareth Rhys-Gordon came in. Bell handed him one of the teas. "Good morning, Gareth."

"Morning, Suze," Rhys-Gordon said. He looked at his watch. "Time to drink it, too. Super."

Gareth Rhys-Gordon was a short, very slight man with huge spidery hands. His face was skeletal, and grooved by an old scar from the corner of his eye to the corner of his mouth; it gave him a perpetually sardonic look. He was not quite ugly, but one tended to look past him without meaning to. His straw-colored hair fell straight down all around his head as if plastered there by a sudden rain. He was wearing a tan tweed jacket, twill trousers, battered brown shoes; Rhys-Gordon usually had on indifferent clothes of indifferent color and fit.

Bell said, "Long night?"

"Special procedures for today," Rhys-Gordon said. His voice was soft, with a faintly musical Welsh accent. "Five minutes to think 'em up, three straight nights of paper-chasing to make 'em work. We're on for a big 'un today."

"New baby has to do trials for Uncle," Bell said. "Pruett's offering five quid it doesn't work."

"Is that a fair bet?"

"That's classified information. You're not going to entrap this working girl, Mister MI5 Sir."

"Fie, and I haven't bagged my limit for the season." He smiled with his crooked lips, looked over at the tea cart. "Bit of a biscuit left?"

"Some shortbread, I think."

He dipped a wafer in his tea. "Have you actually seen this wizard's cabinet?"

"COPE LIGHT?" Bell shook her head. "Diagrams in the manuals, that's all. Apparently there's only two of the things, and it . . . Is that where you were last night? Bringing it up from Edinburgh?"

Rhys-Gordon said, "I've been down and back the last three nights running. You're just going to have to guess which cup the little pea was under." He held out his teacup. "A pox on all traitors and Inter-City Rail." He swallowed the last of the tea, said, "Now it's your turn. Shall we?"

They went out of the lounge, got into the lift. Rhys-Gordon rubbed the back of one big hand with the callused fingers of the other. There was a lively speculation among female Centre staff about Rhys-Gordon, and a complicated joke about a box of Durex condoms with the Official Secrets Act printed on the side.

The lift took them down to the third sub-basement, where the generator rooms and secure storage areas were. The Vaults Duty Officer, a Royal Marine sergeant-major, examined their badges as another Marine stood by with a machine pistol. Rhys-Gordon reached into his jacket and carefully brought out a Walther pistol, which the Duty Officer stowed away in a locker. The VDO finished his checks by telephone and video screen, said, "Just a moment, please."

The outer door opened; there were two more Marines standing in the steel corridor beyond. They and the Duty Officer accompanied Bell and Rhys-Gordon to one of the vault alcoves, a reinforced metal door with a wax and wire seal hanging from its lock.

LCdr Bell took an envelope from the pocket of her uniform blouse, tore it open, and shook out a piece of card. She compared the illustration on the card to the markings on the seal. "All correct," she said, showing the match to one of the guards for confirmation, and stepped back. Rhys-Gordon passed her, taking out an envelope of his own. There was a key inside. Rhys-Gordon broke the seal and put the key in the lock, then waved to the Duty Officer, who was standing several paces behind. The VDO nodded and brought out a large key, a T-shaped handle on a multipin electronic plug, that was chained to his belt. He inserted it in a socket on the wall.

Rhys-Gordon said, "Now," and turned his key simultaneously with the Duty Officer's. There was a loud buzz as the bolts retracted, and Rhys-Gordon pulled the vault door open.

Behind it was a plain metal closet, containing an aluminum suitcase a bit larger than an attaché case. Rhys-Gordon held the vault door—it was balanced to close and relock automatically if left unattended—as Bell removed the case.

Bell, Rhys-Gordon, and the VDO each signed a paper form and entered secret approval codes into the record computer. When Bell and Rhys-Gordon were finally allowed to leave the vault, another pair of armed guards, Special Air Service this time, were waiting for them. Rhys-Gordon took his pistol back, checked the magazine, and vanished it clean away into his coat.

They rode up to the first basement level, passed through another checkpoint, leaving the guards behind, and entered Computer Room One. It was nearly thirty yards on a side, with one skewed glass wall that looked out on the Situation Room amphitheater. Most of the floor space was taken up with the machines, long gray cabinets, amber CRT displays, diode status lights hard as winter stars. The floor itself was made up of pale blue tiles two feet square, actually a false floor concealing power and data conduits. Overhead, the fluorescent light was bluish behind thick glass, ground-wired lest stray currents from the bulbs interfere with the computers. There was a perpetual thrum, through the surfaces and in the air, and a perpetual stale chill as well, from the eternally pumping fluorocarbon refrigerant that kept the most powerful of the supercomputers from melting themselves down by sheer force of thought.

In one corner, blocked by cabinetry from the Situation Room windows, there was a table covered with loose papers, empty sandwich and sweet wrappers, used and half-used coffee cups, a copy of *Which Car?* halfway inside a *New Scientist*. There was a man in a white jacket, wiping pastry crumbs from his fingers, and a British Army signals officer.

The technician in the white coat said, "Hi, Miss Bell."

"Hello, Pruett. Five quid still on?"

Pruett looked at Rhys-Gordon, blinked and coughed.

The Army man, Captain Michael Doheny, said, "So that's what all the fuss is about?"

"You don't know the half of it, Mick," Bell said, and stopped herself before saying anything more. She and Doheny had a comfortable, stable, and gloriously erotic relationship of fifteen months' standing; Rhys-Gordon didn't necessarily know about it (though Security-In-General surely did), but either way discretion was no fault, especially not this morning. And Pruett wasn't entitled to know *any*bloodything.

"Where's the engineer?" Rhys-Gordon said.

"Late," Pruett said. "The front door called a minute ago; they're checking him in now."

Rhys-Gordon picked up a telephone. Captain Doheny offered him some coffee, which he accepted, drank, grimaced over. "Security Desk, please . . . Tom? This is Gareth. What's the tale on Mister Yates? Ah. Well. Can't hold that against him, can we." He put the phone down. "Poor fellow had to come up from Edinburgh yesterday, and he's barely recovered from the journey. Overslept himself on account of it." Rhys-Gordon's expression was either philosophical or just sour.

Five minutes later the door opened to admit a tall, thin man in a white lab smock over a black suit, security badge pinned on crookedly. He pushed back coarse dark hair and said, "Morning. Sorry I'm late." He held out his hand. "Lewis Paul Yates, Vectarray UK." Hands were shaken, introductions made.

Finally the aluminum equipment case was set on a folding table next to one of the computer cabinets. Pruett unfolded a kit of electronics tools. In the high corners of the room, television cameras swiveled to follow and record the operation.

Captain Doheny and Yates the tech rep took keys out of sealed envelopes and unlocked the equipment case. Inside, cushioned on black antistatic foam plastic, were three circuit boards, black epoxy and silver solder on gold on green, and a thick ringbinder. Bell removed the book and opened it.

Yates pointed to the boards in turn. "This is the emulator module. You notice we've used thirty-nanosecond EEPROMs, with an equally improved erase-and-reprogram time. This is the modem board—fairly conventional design, but with top-hole error checking. And this is the decryptor module—"

"You've sold me, mate, just have to convince the wife," Doheny said, just too softly for the audio monitors to catch, and Yates shut up.

Pruett had opened the front panel of the gray cabinet. He reached inside carefully and pulled a metal frame; it came out easily on rollers. There were a dozen boards in the rack already, and another half dozen empty slots.

Bell handed the manual to Yates. "All right, stand back, I'm a doctor," she said, "scalpel, please, nurse," and Pruett handed her a screwdriver. She began unbolting a retaining clip on one of the motherboard sockets.

Installing the COPE LIGHT boards was nothing if not anticlimactic. They fit perfectly; they passed the initial continuity and function tests without a spark or a wisp of smoke. In thirty minutes the cabinet was closed and they were out of the computer room.

"Lunch?" Doheny asked Bell, when they were back in one of the main corridors.

"Lunching with the Red Queen," she said. "Boring girlish fancies."

Doheny snorted. "You can't fool me, Lieutenant Commander Bell. You're going to talk about war."

"Never on a game day," Bell said. "Besides, Friday night you're taking me to dinner, and the theatre, and we'll have the whole night after that to talk about war."

"Hmm."

"All's fair, Mick." Bell looked up and saw her lunch companion coming up the hall. "So there you are! I've got something to rake over with you."

"Yes?" the other woman said.

"This morning *someone* threw a bloody kamikaze submarine right at one of my cruisers. That wouldn't by chance have been you, would it?"

"I'm terribly sorry, but I cannot discuss official naval doctrine with unauthorized Westerners," said the woman whose secret name was WAGNER, and she and LCdr Bell laughed as Captain Doheny shook his head.

■ ■ ■

"So did the black box go in all right?" WAGNER said, cutting a piece of her kidney and bacon.

"Ssh," Bell said. "Gareth's got spies everywhere." She speared a bit of hard-cooked egg from her salad plate, chewed it thoughtfully. "Well, the eggs are fresh at least. The cheese has seen better days, though."

They were eating in a pub half a block from the Games Centre. Its sign was the Bear and Staff, which led to a number of Cold War-flavored jokes. On days when the Centre ran at full staff, like today, most of the lunch crowd was in uniform.

"I'm beginning to think Pruett's right, though," Bell said.

"What on earth would make you agree with Pruett?"

"This box isn't going to work. You know what it's programmed in?"

"Ada, I suppose."

"Nope. Sadie. Specialized Ada Implementation. American Defense spends God knows how many millions developing their ultimate computer language, and God knows how many more selling it to us, and already they're inventing supersets and variations. . . . How've you been coming with Ada?"

"All right, I think. I thought you liked the language."

"I like it all right. It's a pretty good language, as such things go, but like everything else it'll be obsolete in five years and dead in ten. By which time we *might* have enough programmers trained so that you people don't have to do your own coding." She leaned over the table. "See, that's the problem with the whole Centre: It's a mess of half-developed ideas and equipment. Nobody knows if you can run a sea battle from those damn' CICs, but does that stop them? And they're building them for the Army as well. They all seem to think they're going to sit in the front parlor and run World War Three by telephone. . . . All except Mick, and he wants to lead his men through shot and shell."

WAGNER said, "You sound more like a pacifist every day, Commander Bell."

"I'm just a workin' girl sees things as they are," Bell said, in her best Eliza Doolittle voice.

It was true, WAGNER thought. Bell had never spoken a secret: but she saw things the way they were, and said what she thought of them, and that was much more important. She had done nothing at all improper in teaching WAGNER the Ada programming language; far from being a secret, its developers were trying desperately to get it accepted and adopted. But without the training—and Bell's explanations of how to make the computers do what they were actually supposed to—WAGNER's part of NIGHTMOVE would have been impossible.

Her original part, at any rate. Things had become much more complicated since then.

"Have to run," Bell said, shoving her salad plate aside half-finished. "It's showtime. I trust you have something absolutely delightful waiting for them?"

WAGNER said in a stage-Russian accent, "I? How is a peace-loving Socialist People's Republic having dirty little surprise waiting for imperialist reactionary Ramboite West?"

As they walked back up the street, Bell said, "So when's your holiday start?"

"Friday," WAGNER said. "Two weeks of nothing much important."

"You'll be back to play the bad guys for BLUE CRYSTAL, won't you?"

"I'm looking forward to missing it. Besides, I've already put my hand in. Peace-loving Socialist People's gameplayer has programmed all her dirty little surprises."

"Wouldn't like to give a girl a hint."

"Leak military secrets?" WAGNER said, and they both laughed as they turned into the building. On the pink brickwork by the door, someone had spray-painted GREENHAM WIMMIN ARE EVERYWHERE in brilliant green.

■ ■ ■

LCdr Bell checked back into the Centre, went up to one of the women's lounges to tidy her uniform and adjust her makeup. She hated this, but there was no way around it for these productions. The last time she'd had to chaperone a crowd of visiting brass, she had gone in barefaced, as if it were sea duty; two days later Rhys-Gordon tipped her that she was "suspected" of being a lesbian. Mick Doheny had been in an absolute rage, and watching his anger had defused her own; eventually they ended up laughing over it, in bed, always a good place to laugh.

The Red Queen was wrong, Bell thought: She wasn't turning pacifist. With a war on there wouldn't be time for the hypocritical crap that went on in peacetime.

She went back out into the Centre, almost too deep in thought to return salutes. At the end of a plain blue corridor, a guard in a booth opened the outer door to the Situation Room. It closed behind her, and the inner door opened.

The Situation Room was four stories high, with nine tiers of computer consoles, like desks in a school lecture room, facing the Main Display boards. The central screen was a color computer screen projected twenty-five feet long by fifteen high, currently showing a square map of the North Atlantic from Scapa Flow to Iceland, ship positions marked in green and white, flanked by status reports on ships and aircraft. Above the board were smaller screens, much like the ancillary displays in the simulated Combat Information Centers, and a set of digital clocks for Universal Time, Washington, and Moscow. UT, one hour earlier than Greenwich Daylight Time, was 9:40 A.M. The date was 31 August.

She crossed the floor, looking up at the console tiers. Operators were settling in at the desks, checking headphones, testing circuits. It wouldn't do to have a burnt-out bulb or a telephone fault interfere with the day's entertainment. To Bell's right, at the side of the Main Display, were stacks of plastic symbols, and a pair of extensible poles with grippers: If the Display shut down for some reason, it could still be used as a manual plotboard, just like the good old days.

The wall of the room to the left of the display was angled to face it, and fronted with glass, giving a sort of cross-section view of the Centre. Bell boarded a small metal lift, mounted to a track on the wall, and rode up.

The lowest level housed the computer room, even duller and grayer from without than within. Above it was the Operations Room, where the Centre's functions were coordinated: data kept running to the right rooms, machinery from computers to air conditioners monitored. She waved to Mick, who had his tunic off and headset on, and was standing over a table cluttered with printout. The tech rep, Yates, was in the Ops Room as well.

The top two levels were viewing galleries, with carpeting and comfortable chairs. She passed the lower room, where a crowd of shavetail junior officers sat ramrod-straight while a lecturer gestured in front of them, and got off the lift to enter the topmost level. Lambert, the Centre's civilian director, was there, along with a dozen miscellaneous observers: generals and admirals, a man from the American State Department and one from the Ministry of Defence, another that Rhys-Gordon had identified as being with CIA. Coffee was being dispensed from a silver service.

Lambert turned. "Ah. Gentlemen, lady—" (by God, Bell thought, there was a woman admiral in the group) "—this is Lieutenant Commander Susan Bell, one of the development officers here at the New Centre. She'll be answering any questions you have on today's exercise."

The visitors settled into their chairs. Bell saw that their makeup—the hair dyes, the contact lenses, the corsets and the sunlamp tans—were all in order. These were the very models of a modern, and so on. One never knew when the conduct of a war might be interrupted by a television interview. Colonel Blimp had exploded over New Jersey.

Bell put on a lightweight headset, plugged into a wireless belt pack. She had access to UNICOM 1 and 2, general talk channels, and SPECCOM, which overrode the others in case of priority bulletins or emergencies. Data-repeater screens lit up on the viewing-room walls. Some of the visitors turned to watch them, but most gave up after a moment or two and turned back to Bell and the Situation Room window. There were telephones and computer hookups available, but it was a polite secret that part of the room's function was to control just what information reached the observers.

Mick Doheny's voice came through on U-1. "Final stations, exercise on line in one minute."

Outside, the Main Display map zoomed out to include most of

the UK and the Norwegian coast. Ship data were wiped and re-drawn. A red arc swept across the top of the map, and satellite sym-bols appeared.

There was no way to get through this, Bell thought, except to play the game. She took a deep breath.

"You'll all have been briefed on today's exercise," she said, neces-sary prelude to telling them what was in their unread briefing folders, "but just to recap, we'll be simulating a part of the BLUE CRYSTAL naval exercise that's to begin ten days from now. This is a fully com-puterized run; there are no live ships involved, although some of the simulated ships are being operated by trainee crews in the Centre's game rooms while others are fully computer-controlled."

"What about the hostile fleet?" one of the admirals asked.

"Hostile forces are all simulated, under the direction of members of our Red Pool. The New Games Centre has a considerably larger and more diverse pool of hostile-force players than the old centre. We think that this, along with more sophisticated computer models, will provide a much more challenging maneuver enemy."

"You mean more accurate?" someone said.

"We're hoping for an accurate reflection of hostile-force doctrines, yes," Bell said, wondering again at the lengths they were expected to go to avoid naming the "hostile forces."

"What about the COPE system?" the Ministry man said.

Bell said, "We've just finished the installation of the Command Persistence system. The working prototypes are interfaced to the sit-uation computers through signal-generator and receiver links, so that they send and receive exactly as they would in a field situation. . . . Now, if you'll look toward the Main Display, you can see that the exercise is under way. . . ."

They watched the screen, the ballet of the moving ships as they existed only in cabinets of silicon and wire; but Bell could see that it didn't matter. They were playing the game too. She listened to Doheny's voice, calm on the general channel, and began to relax.

"What's *that*?"

Bell looked up, saw the moving trace on the screen. A blue square drew itself over the spot, and a corner of the Main board showed the indicated area in closeup. "That's a missile," she said, "identified hostile." More shorthand symbols appeared on the small screen. "It's a medium-range missile, probably an SS-N-4."

"Is it nuclear?" someone asked, in a startlingly tense voice.

The missile symbol flashed into a red blossom. People at consoles looked up. As the burst faded, it left an empty sea. "Yes," Bell said, "it was nuclear."

"Shee-it."

Bell got the data from the screens and UNICOM 2. "High air-burst reported . . . what you're seeing represents loss of data links, not necessarily ship casualties."

"An EMP blinder?" someone asked.

"That's right," Bell said, "an ionizing-radiation burst to knock out our data systems." Without thinking, she added, "The Red Queen right on cue."

"What?"

"One of the Red players," Lambert said. "She's the ranking woman in the Red Pool . . . thus the name." Lambert smiled, too damn sheepishly for Bell's taste, but she knew better than to compound the issue.

"You said 'on cue,'" an American Marine colonel said (to Lambert, who hadn't said it at all). "Was this arranged?"

Lambert looked at Bell. She said, "The EMP strategy is considered standard. It's one of the reasons for the creation of the COPE system. I was just referring to the excellent tactical timing of the maneuver."

"Do the Russians have any women strategists?" the State Department man said. Bell thought that if anyone, especially Lambert, mentioned Rosa Klebb from *From Russia With Love* she might do something regrettable. But the CIA liaison just said, "Yes, they do," in a somewhat depressed tone.

Bell said, "If you'll look now, you can see the Command Persistence system being activated. There are three components. COPE CHANTER, which is part of all maneuver units, stores tactical data during an interruption, ready to transmit it in bursts when the channels reopen. The COPE PHAGE unit automatically hunts for free channels, using any and all links available. Do you see the green line to the satellite-location arc above the map? That indicates that COPE PHAGE has switched from microwave to laserlink."

"It's punched through directly to the satellite?"

"That's correct. Now COPE LIGHT comes on-line. The COPE LIGHT module can transmit and receive data through the PHAGE links. It contains a programmable emulator"—no, she thought, easy on the jargon—"essentially it pretends to be a weapons control or data acquisition system. We can receive tactical information from any device that we can link to, and with the CHANTER and PHAGE modules we can link to almost anything."

"You said weapons control as well. It can fire weapons?"

"No, it was designed to fail-safe. It can, however, *deactivate* a weapon system that it's emulating."

The CIA man said quietly to the man from State, "You remember the memos on battlefield nuclear-cancel, sir? This gives us the capability to arm units, and then disarm in the field."

Ships began to flicker back into existence as communications links were restored. Bell pointed out the casualty calculation screens; she called down to the Machine Room and had them recalculated into color graphic displays, bar charts of broken ships and dead sailors.

After that point, she became superfluous. The audience was caught up in the video game now, and all they wanted to do was play. Which, following tea break, they did: that was what the Centre was for, after all.

■　■　■

WAGNER opened her shoulder bag at the Games Centre main entrance, produced two Ada programming manuals for the guard's inspection. He ran a bar-code wand down the books' spines, satisfied himself that they were unclassified material properly signed out.

"Hey," Susan Bell said. "Want to celebrate the survival of the West? No thanks to you."

"I do my best," WAGNER said. "But not tonight, Suze, thanks."

"You have a date."

"I have a holiday coming, and work to finish."

"*Oh.* I promise, I won't tell anyone."

Bell was cleared out. Gareth Rhys-Gordon came through, passing his gun around the metal detector. "I assume the magic device worked," he said to Bell.

"Perfectly. Obviously you didn't drop it . . . like to have a pint to celebrate, Gareth?"

"Yes, I could do with that, Suze," Rhys-Gordon said, in a curiously flat voice. WAGNER turned, just slightly, to look at him: There was a grin on his creased face, a look of almost embarrassed good humor. Then it was gone, replaced by his usual weary half smile.

WAGNER said good night to both of them and went out. It was nearly eight o'clock, a last bit of summer twilight on the horizon. She caught her usual bus on the corner, but rode most of a mile past her usual stop, getting off in the City near St. Paul's.

The address she had been given was a narrow glass building-front, a misplaced bit of modernization between two old stone business blocks. There was a bank of bell buttons: She pressed one for an office on the eighth floor. The door lock buzzed. She went inside, got into the small lift and pressed for fourteen.

The fourteenth-floor corridor was empty. There were glass doors with the names of small brokerages, record companies, a private investigator. All of them were dark within. And just around the corner was a red metal panel covering a fire hose and extinguisher.

She opened the door. On the narrow shelf below the hose was a purple plastic bag, from Liberty's department store. She picked it up, shut the door, and paused.

The Liberty bag was a bit too convenient, she thought. Commonplace, certainly, easy to carry out, but also easy for someone on the street to spot her carrying out. She reached into the bag and took out a brown paper parcel, the ends neatly folded and taped. Her coat had large practical pockets, one of which swallowed the packet. The shopping bag went into the ashtray by the lifts.

She took the tube home, with one unnecessary change just to keep in the habit. She went into her flat, sat down on the bed, and cleared off the bedside table.

She put the brown parcel on the table and opened it. Inside were twenty thousand pounds in respectably used notes, a silver cigarette case, and two metal boxes the size of chewing-gum packets wrapped in a folded paper. Handling them very carefully, she folded out the sheet of instructions.

The flat silver case fired small-caliber bullets with a cyanide filling, five shots. The boxes were spare magazines. There was a friendly warning in the sheet not to count on the bullets alone to kill a man, "but the poison is reliable in one minute or less."

She folded up a newspaper, propped it against a pillow, and pointed the lighter at it from a few feet away. The gun made a small bang, like a book falling to the floor; the bullet—which she was cautious not to touch—went through a hundred and fifty pages.

It wasn't ideal. The range was short, and the bullets were pretty damned obvious. But it would do.

She put the money and the gun away, took out the NIGHTMOVE file and began studying it. Now all she had to do was find the rest of Allan's network.

Besides her own, there were four names, four short dossiers—or things pretending to be dossiers. She didn't think they were real. Which left the question of whether they were code, or just camouflage.

The code names were KING BYRON, who had the COPE LIGHT unit; ROCK STAR, an electronics technician; FRIAR BACON, who had access to the weapons they needed; and CROWN PRINCE, who had a boat to deliver the weapons. But Allan had told her that they wouldn't answer to those names, only to second code words.

She put the folder down, made a cup of tea. He hadn't explained that just to make pillow conversation, she knew now; certainly not just because she'd been prying. Allan was much too discreet for that, and much, much too good a planner. She was the backup system for NIGHTMOVE. Which meant that the puzzle had to be one she could solve.

What might Allan have used, that he would have expected her to know? History? Marlowe's plays? He'd sent her the copy of *The Assassin's Tragedy,* but she was fairly certain she knew the reason for that, and—

If not Marlowe, then perhaps Doctor Dee. Dee, the Elizabethan court sorcerer, had left notebooks filled with doubletalk that actually concealed his cosmological theories, in terms designed to keep him from the burning court.

WAGNER read the dossier for KING BYRON. It was a bland description of a middle-aged, blonde lady; but one sentence popped out: *Not a plain woman. Always seemed quite tenable, here running fourth.*

It made no real sense. But it had to be there for a reason. *Not a plain woman.* How did that encode a contact?

COPE LIGHT was built in Edinburgh, she thought. Edinburgh sat on the Firth of Forth.

And its telephone code was 031. *Not.* Three letters. *A.* One letter. *Not a plain woman. Always seemed quite tenable, here* . . . 031–556–6574. A perfectly reasonable telephone number.

"I see it now, Allan," she said, "halfway home now." She ran her hand over the bedspread, missing him more than the loss of sight or hearing, put the teacup down and went back to the folder.

■ ■ ■

Nicholas Hansard picked up his teacup and looked around the foyer of the National Theatre; it was half an hour before curtain time, and there was a fair crowd over tea and sandwiches in the foyer buffet, milling around the bar, examining the paintings on the concrete walls and the merchandise in the glassed-in bookshop.

The foyer fronted two theatres, the large Olivier and the somewhat smaller Lyttleton, on half-a-dozen levels with bars on each. The building was a bit industrial, with its raw concrete walls, angular balconies, long airspaces floor to floor, but not unpleasant. A pianist and guitarist were playing just across the floor, the lighting was comfortable, Hansard's quiche wasn't too awful.

The ushers were opening the doors to the Lyttleton. Hansard finished his tea, bought a program, and took his seat.

The play was Jonson's *The Alchemist,* done in modern dress. Subtle the phony alchemist was a white-coated scientist, the house he and his associates "borrow" to con their customers was a Bauhaus extravaganza in black and white and gold, further fitted out by Subtle with computers, elaborate glassware, and laser beams (Laser Effects by The Short Wave, the program said). Hansard was generally wary of "updated" period plays, dressed up for the sake of "relevance" as if relevance originated in the costume shop. Replacing the plague, which in the original accounted for the house owner's absence, with something about a condo in the Bahamas, seemed a bit forced, and rather a strain on the word "vacation." But he laughed, and the relevance—Jonson's, that is, not the prop department's—came through. He rode the tube back to his hotel in a pleasant mood, drank a cup of tea, and fell asleep thinking of black lacquer and green laser light.

■ ■ ■

WAGNER opened her eyes. She had been lying back on the bed, concentrating on KING BYRON's dossier, and she had fallen asleep.

She shook her head, massaged her eyes, stretched uncomfortably. She began to undress, trying to pick up the thread again.

Who was King Byron? A character in a play? Not a Marlowe play, certainly, not even *The Assassin's Tragedy*. There wasn't a historical King Byron she could think of. There was good old mad-bad-and-dangerous George Gordon, but he hadn't been king of anything. What if—

She froze, hands sliding her dress down her hips. What if, indeed. Byron hadn't been a king—but he might have been; there was an excellent chance that he might have become King of Greece. As detailed in a collection of historical essays called *What If?* One of Allan's favorite books.

King of Greece. She laughed out loud, tossed the dress in the air and caught it.

Then she paused again. It was too simple, too well known an almost-fact. There had to be something else. She went to the dresser, took the copy of *The Assassin's Tragedy* from the bottom drawer. She looked at it, and thought a moment, running through the catalog of characters in her memory. No, there wasn't a King of Greece. There was a "Fabianus, King of the Germanies," the assassin Didrick's intended victim, but the mere alliteration wasn't nearly a good enough connection.

There was a copy of Marlowe's plays (the verified ones, she thought) on the shelf, a battered Penguin paperback. She began riffling through the *Dramatis Personae* pages.

She found it in *Tamburlaine, Part Two*. One of the crew of Christian kings who gave Tamburlaine something to conquer: Gazellus, Viceroy of Byron.

She looked at her watch—nearly eleven, she thought, Macbeth doth murder sleep—picked up the phone and dialed. There were several rings, then a click, and a hiss. She knew at once it was an answering machine: British Telecom about to tell her she'd guessed wrong. Then a man's voice said:

"Hello. This is Lewis Yates. I can't answer the phone myself now, but if you'll leave a message—"

She hung up at once.

Lewis Yates was the Vectarray UK tech rep. He'd been at the Centre that morning. Now, where had they put him? The Strand Palace, right. She riffled through the directory and dialed.

"Mr. Lewis Yates's room, please." There was a pause, then a ring, and a click.

"Yates here."

"I'm trying to reach Gazellus," she said, trying to keep inflection out of her voice.

There was a pause. "Good God," Yates said. "I'd thought—"

"Never mind that. Can you make delivery?"

"Yes."

"St. James's Park, east end, eleven tomorrow. Bring nothing, this is to arrange the purchase only."

"How will I—"

"I'll know you." She hung up.

■ ■ ■

Lewis Paul Yates looked up at the sky over St. James's Park. It was cloudy, and prematurely chill, but no rain was in the newspaper forecast. Certainly the weather wasn't dissuading the tourists, who were accumulating like drops into puddles to watch the Changing of the Guards just across the street.

Yates sat down on a bench facing the pond and watched the ducks glide by, a child tossing them cheese-dusted corn puffs in defiance of the signs. He folded his copy of the *Telegraph* to the crossword puzzle and took out his pen, but he couldn't really concentrate on it; he was thinking about the achievement of COPE LIGHT, wondering who the woman was who had called him. The American, Berenson, was dead now, Yates knew; but then, that was the whole reason for the system of code names. Berenson had been a marvelous planner. They had met at a wargamers' convention in Bristol, over a Civil War miniatures battle.

Their meeting was no accident, of course. During lunch break from the battle, Berenson bought Yates a whisky, and as they sat outside in the sun drinking, asked him about Vectarray and Command Persistence.

The American had presented it to Yates as an intellectual puzzle, like the mathematical poser in *New Scientist* but for rather higher stakes: twenty thousand pounds if he could work out a way of removing one functional COPE LIGHT device. He had even given Yates a thousand on account, just for thinking about it.

The thousand had kept Yates's bookmakers happy for an entire week. Twenty, well, twenty would be very nice. But of course gentlemen never talked about money in naked mathematical terms. Twenty thousand implied rather vaster sums.

And Yates had never for a moment believed that the money might be for the *plan* to steal COPE LIGHT. Sooner or later, the hardware would be demanded. And in fact, as he worked out the method, bit by bit (a little computer humor there, Yates thought), he realized that he might as well be doing it. So he did. In for a penny, in for twenty thousand pounds.

There were only two working COPE LIGHT prototypes, VUC-2-LTX-1 and -2, and they were in a vault checked six times daily at random intervals. James Bond couldn't have removed them without someone noticing.

But real laboratories never much resemble the ones in James Bond movies; they're rarely so efficient and never so tidy. It isn't possible to build exactly one piece of equipment, or exactly two, or exactly any number. The road to a working prototype is littered with burnt-out power supplies, mis-etched or clumsily soldered circuit boards, worn cables, and mangled edge connectors.

The junk from a Secret project is supposed to be destroyed. In practice, the still-usable parts are salvaged—chips removed, parts desoldered, cables clipped—and the remaining hulk goes to be smashed and compacted. This is called Cost Control and Materials Efficiency, and everyone agrees that it is a good idea. It is not even a compromise with security, provided that everything is tallied up at the end of the day. Which, at Vectarray UK's lab in Silicon Glen, it was. There was a ledger with a precise chip count: number returned to the bins, number destroyed, signed by the engineer and security officer on duty. Yates had considered switching good chips in central stores for faulty ones, assembling a unit piecemeal, but on further thought he decided it was an invitation to disaster: If random chance drew too many duds at once, there would be an investigation.

Yates had purchased a batch of ICs from electronics stores, one in London, one in Liverpool. Two, so the purchase wouldn't be too large in one place; only two, so the number of storekeepers who might remember him was minimal. Most of what he bought were random gates and flip-flops out of the bargain bins; he had to pick up a few fancier ones to match the specialty ICs. All that really mattered was the number of pins.

It wasn't any trouble at all to bring them into the Vectar-ray lab; sorted by pin counts, they went into little polythene bags and then a toffee tin; then the tin went into his briefcase with the usual clutter of small tools and reference books, crossword puzzles and candy bars. Then he just carried the case in to work. The security man, a decent enough but utterly unclever chap named Borden, checked it in with a casual look—they might worry about someone bringing in a bomb or a camera, but this sort of junk?—and a wisecrack about them all being packrats. "Like Doctor Who," Borden said. That was what passed for science with Borden.

Yates took the tin into the supply-room annex, where defective parts went to be logged and destroyed, and hid it. The annex was a cramped concrete room with steel shelves full of dead electronics, cabinet parts, stray tools, and an electric furnace. Yates wasn't in the least afraid that security would find his box, only that someone might come across it while looking for his or her own hidden contraband.

He was set up for the circuits. Now he needed a board to mount them on. The COPE LIGHT main board began as a slab of copper-coated green plastic fourteen inches by eighteen. The raw board material was coated with an acid-resistant chemical in the pattern of the desired circuits; then it was dipped into zinc chloride etching solution, the unwanted metal eaten away.

The next step was for an engineer with a continuity checker—really just a box with two wires, a battery, and a light bulb—to test the main circuit paths. The VUC-2 circuit design was quite complicated, and one board in three had faults in the etching, almost impossible to see but making the board worthless.

The boards were made three in a batch. Yates got the job of testing a set, VUC-2-MB-52 through 54, and, true to form, board number 53 was faulty. Yates opened the etching-room ledger and entered *Board 54. Failed continuity test.*

Board 54 of undeserved ill repute went straight to the disposal annex. There wasn't close control over naked boards; they weren't salvageable, and of little value to spies, industrial or otherwise.

Reconstructing COPE LIGHT from the pattern of lines on the circuit board would have been like assembling a Formula 1 racer from an oily tireprint. So Yates wrote down that it was destroyed, and that was accepted—even though it was actually duct-taped to the wall behind a tagboard reference chart on transistor equivalencies. Now he had a board. And very soon the chips would be joining it.

He would have been happier assembling the unit on faulty 53 himself, but supposed it was better, cleaner, for another part of the team to do it. Which they obligingly did. The chip sockets and the discrete components (thankfully few of those, and all commonplace stuff) were installed, the board hooked up to the testbed, and—nothing. D.O.A.

The board was carried into the annex for autopsy and disposal. Yates sat at the bench, the board in front of him, the toffee tin in his lap, unsocketing chips, switching them for lookalikes, then marking the dummies with a red paint pen and dropping them onto a board for disposal. The toffee tin filled up with genuine circuits.

Borden came in right on schedule. He examined the chip sheet, going by pictures—what else did he have to go on? To him they were all just little black blocks with gold legs. The paint marker took care of a few telltale control numbers. Yates fired up the electric oven, bringing it to a temperature that would burn epoxy.

Borden helped Yates toss the chips into the furnace, and sang about roasting chestnuts on an open fire.

"Where's the board?" Borden said.

"Right here," Yates said, and displayed the green and gold panel. "You want to use the hammer, or shall I?"

Borden was delighted to take up the steel sledge and slam it through the circuit board. Then its splinters too went into the fire.

When all of the parts were burned, Borden and Yates signed the ledger. Yates thought that Borden was a right fellow, for a company cop, and told him so. Borden laughed, and when they got off work they had a pint together.

"Again sometime," Borden said as they left the local.

"Sure, mate," Yates said. It wouldn't do, of course.

He began taking the chips out a few at a time, hooked to the hem of his underwear like gold-legged lice. Getting the board out was another matter entirely. It would fit into his briefcase, barely, but it was always inspected on exit. He considered building a false bottom into the case, but Borden, despite his technical ignorance, seemed competent enough at his job. Yates could not rid himself of the notion that Borden would somehow naturally perceive the alteration in depth of the briefcase.

There was a recreation room just off the building cafeteria, with two Apple computers and a stack of illegally copied game disks. (It also had two pinball machines; some of the programming staff were purists.)

Over an intense *Elite* tournament, Yates complained that the rec room looked dull. Two days later, he brought in a large envelope containing some computer graphic posters. After a stop in the stockroom to pick up a roll of tape (and something else), the posters decorated the bare walls. Behind one of them was the COPE LIGHT board.

A day after that, Yates went into the rec room and locked the door. He popped the lid of one of the Apple IIs, to reveal the metal-cased power supply and several circuit cards mounted vertically to sockets in the chip-covered motherboard. He unbolted the mother, lifted it out, then laid the COPE LIGHT board against the bottom of the case. Yates covered it with a sheet of plastic to protect the etched circuit paths, then replaced the Apple works on top of it, tightening the mounting bolts with the greatest care. Then he removed the multiple-pin connector from the disk-drive controller board, painted the pins with typewriter correction fluid, and plugged it in again. Finally he replaced the lid, which fit with a hair to spare.

Yates opened the door. One of the programmers was just reaching for the handle, a cup of coffee and a biscuit balanced in his other hand. Perfect, Yates thought.

The programmer said, "Hello, Lew."

"Hi, Jack. Has anybody noticed anything funny about Apple Beta?"

"Not that I know of."

"Well, she just died on me. Right in the middle of a German fighter offensive, too."

"Shit! You've tried, you know, jiggering it?"

Yates snorted. "Come take a look." He put a disk in the drive and switched the machine on; it sputtered and coughed and finally came up with an UNABLE TO LOAD message.

"Well, *shit*," Jack said. "Do you think you can fix it?"

"That's why I'm an engineer and you're a programmer," Yates said, with a smile and no sarcasm. "But you know there'll be hell to pay if I'm caught using the company shop. I'll take her home and see what I can do."

And he did.

"Gazellus," said a voice from behind Yates. He looked up. The ducks were swimming around the floating cheese snacks. The voice said, "Please don't turn around."

"Wouldn't think of it," he said, then looked at his crossword. "'Stout start for mortal,' five letters. Any idea?"

The woman said, "You have the unit for sale?"

"If you have twenty thousand to pay for it."

"Very well. Do you know where the Bear Gardens Museum is, in Southwark?"

"I'll find it."

"Eleven tonight, then."

Yates said amiably, "You don't suppose we're attracting attention by *not* looking at the cavalry, do you?"

There was no answer. He turned. There was no one behind him, not counting a couple of thousand tourists watching the Changing. Pity, he thought. She'd had an attractive voice, and if she had the mind for this sort of thing . . . no, that would be a fatal attraction.

Aha. *Stout start*—FAT—*for mortal*. FATAL. He filled it into the crossword, then tucked the paper under his arm and walked away. As he stepped off the curb at Birdcage Walk, a leather-clad messenger on a motorbike roared past him with nothing to spare. Good old London, Yates thought, watching the cyclist turn hard left without signaling. Dangerous place.

He walked on toward Westminster, beginning to calculate how he would kill the woman tonight.

■ ■ ■

There were four motorcycles parked by the embankment curb, just next to the red iron Hungerford Bridge. The drivers, all in full black riding leathers, leaned against a bridge pillar, smoking, talking. A ragged man came up to beg a cigarette; given one, he went back around to shelter beneath the bridge, inside a cardboard box.

The cyclists watched him go, silent just a moment, then went back to talking about cars and women, making no special distinction between the two.

". . . low-slung bird h'out'a Manchester, see, h'an'she says, 'hoo leather . . .'"

". . . four-liter Bentleys. Do they only sell 'em to rich young City twits, or what?"

"'. . . up the spout,' she says. 'How many times since Monday,' I says . . ."

They were couriers between calls. With their black jackets and leather jeans they wore high-buckled boots, and plenty of chrome trim. One had a little spanner fastened to a zipper pull, *Mad Max* style, but it was a joke: This was a weekday job, and you couldn't go tramping into a high-ticket office in Death-or-Glory kit.

All four had radiotelephones on their hips, the microphones clipped at the shoulder for calls on the fly. They were young, none over twenty-eight, faces prematurely weathered with the road and the squint they affected in imitation of racing drivers' photos. Two were typically English blonds, one dark with gypsy curls, one tall and red-haired, with scars on his cheekbones.

Their bikes were all high-powered Japanese machines, with big panniers in the rear, helmets on the pillion, worn copies of *A-Z London* guides somewhere about.

The red-haired courier's phone chirped. He punched the microphone. "Cherry, yeah." The radio gave an address. "Yeah, got it." He started for his bike. "Later."

"Later, Cherry," one said, and the others waved.

Cherry rode into the East End. He parked the bike in front of a squat gray building with barred windows. There was a red Jaguar, a good one, an XKE, parked just in front of him, and a big black Rolls across the street. Cherry blew a kiss at the Jag and went inside. He came out again a minute later with a large envelope. He tucked it in a pannier and roared off. Business as usual.

A couple of blocks farther on, he turned into an alley, took out the envelope and opened it. There was a photograph inside, a slip of paper with an address and a few special instructions, and five thousand pounds in cash. Cherry stuffed the money inside his jacket. He found the address in his street guide, stared for a couple of minutes, then rolled both papers tight and stuffed them into an already overfull trash bin.

The address was another alley, a fairly clean one not too far from the office where he'd picked the papers up. He walked to the end, just past a small steel door, leaned against the damp stone wall. He unzipped a pocket in his jacket and put his gloved hand inside, closing the fingers around wood. He waited. He shouldn't have to wait long.

He didn't. A man in a Burberry with a cashmere collar came out. He was a big fellow, but stooped, with only a little gray hair left. He leaned forward to lock the door. Cherry stepped behind him.

"This is from Cody and the lads," Cherry said, as per instructions. The target went very stiff for a moment. Long enough. Cherry shoved the icepick into the back of his neck, and he fell down twitching like a wrung chicken.

There was a second thud as he fell, a metallic one. Cherry looked down. There was a gun on the ground, dropped from the target's fingers. Now, that wasn't nice at all, he thought.

He examined the pistol without touching it. A Browning. Good weapon. But he had a couple of guns.

He left it where it lay and went down the alley. He got on his bike, kicked the starter, and pulled out into traffic, and in an eyeblink was lost among hundreds of cars and trucks, dozens of messengers exactly like himself.

■ ■ ■

It was twenty minutes before eleven. A few vehicles rolled over the Southwark Bridge as Yates crossed it on foot, the artist's portfolio containing the COPE LIGHT board in his hand. His step was jaunty and his mind was racing. He had worked it all out, in detail.

He wore a cheap plastic raincoat, purchased at Marks & Spencer that afternoon. Its pockets were weighed down with metal, the results of purchases elsewhere. There was a cheap Italian stiletto in his right-hand pocket. When the woman asked him to hand over the case, it would be in his grip, against the case handle. When her wrist was near, he would trigger the spring-loaded blade with his thumb—he had spent an hour before the mirror in his hotel room, practicing the maneuver—and cut her. It would almost certainly not be a serious wound, but it would startle her, and surely spill blood. Then the steel whip in his left-hand pocket would crack her skull, and another stroke from the stiletto would finish the job. He had no plans to hide the body; Southwark was a notoriously bad neighborhood, and a scouting trip earlier today had established that the spot in question was not well traveled. In fact, he might have picked it himself.

It was a long way from any tube station, and Yates would certainly not want to be picked up by a cabdriver anywhere near the murder scene. But there was a way of turning that to his advantage. It was about forty minutes' brisk walk along Bankside to Waterloo Station. He would travel that way (disposing of the raincoat, and any stray blood, en route), and catch the last Northern line tube from Waterloo to Charing Cross Station.

His bags were already at Charing Cross. His tickets were purchased. Tomorrow he would be lunching in Paris; tomorrow's dinner would be in New York.

After computing and rejecting several plans for slowly filtering the money into multiple bank accounts under the nose of Her Majesty's Inland Revenue, he had finally hit on a plan that let him enjoy it all immediately. The *Telegraph* reported that yesterday's ninety-seven-point drop in the American Dow Jones Average was being blamed on brokerage houses using computer programs to determine buy and sell orders. The programs had all commanded Sell, and the market had been dragged along.

Yates estimated it would take him less than three weeks to set up a system that would anticipate the anticipative programs. There was no prophecy so profitable as a self-fulfilling one.

He had arrived on the south side of the Thames. There was a small stairway leading down from the bridge approach to narrow, winding Park Street some twenty feet below. Yates descended. The Bear Gardens was just a short block ahead. He had visited the Museum as part of this afternoon's research; it had nothing to do with bear-baiting, but was dedicated to Shakespeare's old Globe Theatre, which had apparently been built around here someplace. Shakespeare was long gone, though. The place was purely industrial now.

"Gazellus," said the woman's voice, familiar now, and he saw her. She was just a few steps ahead, wearing what looked like a military tunic with epaulets, a bag over her shoulder.

"Good evening, madam," Yates said. "You have the money?"

"Come this way."

"Now just a moment. Do you have the money or not?"

"It's this way. In my car. Besides, it's a nice cool night for walking. For you and anybody with you, that is."

"I see." She was a thinker. Yates liked that. At any rate, she was indicating that they should walk west along the riverbank, exactly as he had intended. "Then I'd be delighted . . . though of course there's no one with me."

They strolled around the Bankside Power Station, a huge, windowless brick mass with a floodlit, medieval-looking smokestack. "Strolled" was the operative word. Yates resisted the urge to look at his wristwatch, but he could feel his timetable slipping away, sense the departure of the last tube from Waterloo. "It isn't . . . much farther now, is it?"

"No. Just up at the bridge."

Blackfriars Bridge had Romanesque brick arches, rippling with light off the river water. Parts of older bridges were decaying near it, arches broken off in midair. To the left, the framework of a new office block sent shafts of bare concrete and metal upward. The whole was like something in a Surrealist painting.

"Your car's here?"

"Just up there." She pointed. He saw a line of parked cars. This was the place to do it, he thought; he could get the key from her body and search the car himself. Perhaps even drive it to Charing Cross, park it somewhere, confuse the police further.

"Here, take the case," Yates said.

"It's only a little farther."

"It's all right. I trust you. Take it."

She paused. "Okay." She stepped toward him. He tightened his grip as he held the portfolio toward her. His left hand slipped into his pocket, and tightened as well on steel. Her hand stretched toward his.

There was something in it, something like a mirror. A truck rolled by, very loud. The mirror flashed light twice. Yates felt bees sting his throat, his jaw. The world tipped over. His chest felt crushed.

He saw steel rails that ran into a hole like a tunnel and thought that the last train was pulling out without him but the connections were wrong the trick you see was to know when they were all going to buy or sell and buy or sell before they did and dragged everything with them into the concrete hole all black. . . .

WAGNER stepped back from the building foundation. There were two wheelbarrow loads of gravel covering Yates's body. Tomorrow morning there would be a truckload of concrete on top of him, and in fourteen months, according to the sign, he would be under "One of London's Smartest New Addresses."

She took off Yates's plastic raincoat, shaking gravel dust from it; it had been much better protection than the throwaway paper coverall in her bag. She picked up the portfolio and went across the street, into a telephone kiosk. She dialed a number.

"Yes."

"Tell Palatine: Knight to Knight's Two." She hung up at once.

She looked up and down the street, past the parked cars—none of which were hers—and started walking north, across the road bridge toward Blackfriars Station. If she hurried, she could just make the last tube home.

■ ■ ■

At eleven the following morning, Cherry the courier parked his motorcycle in front of a quietly expensive City of London address, offices important enough that they did not need names on the doors. Couriers were allowed to park there, as long as they went about their business quickly. Cherry was always careful to obey the parking ordinances; his bike was his livelihood. For the moment, anyway.

He signed in with the guard and took the lift up. Mr. Palatine let him into the office, as always. Cherry had never seen anyone else in the office, not so much as a steno.

"You're doing well, Mr. Cherry, I take it?" Mr. Palatine said pleasantly.

"Pretty good, sir."

"That's nice to hear. You're a good worker, Mr. Cherry. You earn your pay. That's rare these days."

"Thank you, sir."

Palatine took an envelope out of his desk. "Delivery by tonight on this one, is that all right, Mr. Cherry? The usual bonus is enclosed."

"You got it, Mr. Palatine." He grinned. "Don't much like working weekends anyway."

"Excellent. Good day to you then."

"'Day, guv."

Cherry went out, rode north to an alley just off the Barbican Centre courtyard, and stopped to open the envelope. The "usual bonus" meant seven thousand quid. The address was a Ministry of Defence building, that new war-games place. A hundred million to play games and they call blokes like me layabouts, Cherry thought. He looked at the photograph then, and scratched his chin. It was a bird, a real looker, in a long white coat. The picture seemed to have been taken in a hotel room. He wouldn't have minded getting her in a hotel room, not at all. What the hell did Mr. P. want her dead for?

Well, not his to reason why. He'd done a bird once, a high-priced dolly who'd been about to write her memoirs. The contractor told him all about it, with a few choice excerpts, "since yer won't have no chance ta be readin' about it."

He let the photo and address slip drop to the ground, struck a match and tossed it after. There was a poof of purple fire, and then only ashes for Cherry's boot to scatter.

Cherry liked working for Mr. Palatine, all things considered. There was never any fuss, for one thing. With the East End boys, he'd do the job clean as you please, then read in the papers a week later about SO AND SO DEAD IN GANG SLAYING. When the hoods did for a bloke they wanted the world to know about it, didn't think they'd gotten their money's worth otherwise. Palatine didn't. He kept things tidy from his end. A real City type.

Cherry suspected that Palatine was a bosses' boss, probably owned

half the yobs in loud suits. That pleased Cherry. Every time he got on
the cycle for Mr. Palatine, he felt like a henchman to kings.

■   ■   ■

At five o'clock Friday afternoon, WAGNER was sitting in the Games
Centre coffee lounge, putting the finishing touches on her personal
part of NIGHTMOVE: page after page of

```
procedure Azimuth_Acquire
    IMPULSE : Dyn_String := Type_Convert
(MOTOR,X,Y,Z)
    DELTA,N := string (ENCODE)
procedure Command_Line
function Decrypt (LOCUS_STRING,
SIGNAL_STRING,
        POSTAUTH_STRING : Dyn_String :
CODE_SELECT : integer := K3)
```

She was reading through a pile of computer listings when she
heard a voice say "Hey," at her elbow. She looked up. It was Suze Bell.

"Thought you'd finished all that, late shift and all," Bell said.

"I thought so too, but the computer disagreed."

"Want me to look at it?"

"No, it's running now." WAGNER thought she had been just a
little too bold: If anyone could tell at a glance what the Sadie code
was meant to do, it was Suze. "Besides, isn't tonight your big evening
with Mick?"

Bell made a face. "That's what I came down to ask about. Mick's
got some sort of late duty tonight, last minute, you're-the-only-chap-
Captain, you know the drill, and he can't make it to the theatre," Bell
said. "I'm meeting him for supper afterward, but there's still the play
ticket. Would you like to go?"

WAGNER thought for a moment. The programming was done
now. There wasn't anything urgent to do tonight, except puzzle over
Allan's list, and a change of scene might be more helpful with that
than staring at it all night. Besides, she had worked hard to leave the
impression that she was starting a carefree two weeks' holiday; this

would confirm that. "What are friends for?" she said. "Give me half an hour to pack this lot up."

"Great." Bell looked up; Gareth Rhys-Gordon had come into the lounge and was fumbling with the coffee things, assembling a cupful apparently by touch alone. Bell said, in a stage-whispered stage-German accent, "Meet me at ze gate, unt bring ze plans. Vear ein hat zo I'll know you."

"It's no use telling me," Rhys-Gordon said, "I'm off duty for the weekend. Please do your spying on our night service, and we'll contact you on Monday."

"Downstairs, half an hour," Bell said to WAGNER, and went out. Rhys-Gordon looked after her for a moment, then sat down carefully, stirring his coffee with a ballpoint pen.

"Where do you go on the weekends, Gareth?" WAGNER said.

"I go where I'm sent, mostly."

"The sun never sets, eh."

Rhys-Gordon drank. "The sun never rises. Not on me."

WAGNER felt a chill. Footstep on her grave. As Allan had said. She gathered her papers and stood up. "Good evening, Gareth. Take care of yourself."

"Have a nice holiday." She started to leave the lounge, then stopped in the doorway, and turned, feeling his eyes on her; but he was just sitting, a thin brown stick in the fat orange chair, looking into his oily coffee.

WAGNER went down to the Documents Room annex and dumped the program listing into the incinerator chute. She pressed the igniter button, heard the soft *whump* of the gas jets, imagined the paper curling to ash, to Orwellian dust of forgetfulness.

She got her jacket and checked out of the building, sat in the foyer reading until she heard Bell's voice say, "Well, I'm ready."

WAGNER looked up. Bell had changed in the ladies', into the white Lagerfeld trench coat, the best thing she owned. "How do I look?"

"With you on my arm, I'll be the envy of every girl there," WAGNER said, and they went out giggling.

■ ■ ■

Cherry was sitting astride his cycle, watching as the target came out of the Defence building. She was wearing the same white coat as in the photo Palatine had given him. It was almost too easy . . . except that there was another bird with her. That could be awkward.

The two women flagged down a cab. Cherry kicked the bike to life and took off in pursuit. Not much of a complication: He could follow a taxi in his sleep. They crossed Waterloo Bridge to the South Bank Centre, and the taxi let them off at the National Theatre.

Cherry swore. If it wasn't one thing, it was another. Well, at least he knew where the target was going to be for the next couple of hours. And that being the case . . .

He went off to park the bike, then strolled into the National Film Theatre building, right next to the NT, for a sandwich and a glass of milk. Cherry never drank on the job.

■ ■ ■

The target and her companion walked out of the theatre building at ten-fifteen. Cherry was watching. They turned south together, on the narrow street between the theatre and the car park.

They stopped, hugged. Cherry shook his head. Such a waste of birdflesh. Then the other woman kept walking, south toward Waterloo Station. Cherry moved away from the pillar, to keep the target in sight.

The target entered the parking lot. Cherry stepped back into shadow. The target looked around, then went to an open roadster, a Triumph Stag. Cherry memorized its license number, took a step. She wouldn't notice him, starting the car.

She opened the passenger door, got in and sat down.

Cherry froze. So she was meeting someone. That was annoying. That was a positive nuisance.

Then he had a sudden wonderful thought. He walked on toward the car, the target, softly, softly.

He was only a pace behind her when his foot crunched on the concrete. The target turned as Cherry's shadow fell across her. She didn't say anything: All she could have seen was a dark shape against the light.

Cherry clamped his left hand over her face, bent her head to the side. His right hand slashed down. Flesh gave, bone clicked. The target twitched, light flashing from her big earrings.

Cherry stepped back, breathed easily again. Then he reached

down and straightened the dead woman's head. She had a long scarf under the white coat; he pulled that up, wrapped it around her neck. It was still a little bit crooked, but close enough to pass in the dark.

He walked around the Triumph, running a gloved fingertip along the curve of its rear fender. He liked the Stag: It was a sound English car from the days when nobody laughed at the idea. Whoever owned this one clearly thought so too: This one was a '68 model and looked new.

Cherry thought he could do a good trade in roadsters, when he had his garage. *Cherry's English Motors—Roadsters a Speciality.* And if anybody came through the door with one of those plastic fakes, he'd cave in its fenders with a sledge.

Tonight he was seven thousand closer to it.

A man had come into the garage, hands shoved into the pockets of a long coat. He was whistling, and walking straight for the Triumph. Cherry turned away, pretended to fumble at the lock of the car two spaces away.

"And with one bound, the mad Mick was free!" the man said as he rounded the Stag's rear bumper. "So how was the show, darlin'?"

Cherry shot his fist into the Irishman's temple and he went down across the Triumph's flank. Cherry braced him, pulled the car door open, rolled him into the seat. It took some careful wedging to get his feet in; the car was anything but roomy. He was almost finished before he noticed the rank pips on the man's shoulders.

Cherry unbuttoned the man's coat, patted down the uniform. No gun. That would have been just too much to ask for, he supposed. He unzipped his own jacket and took out the Beretta, glad he'd brought it instead of the Walther; easier to replace, and the light caliber wasn't going to be a problem tonight.

He reached inside the man's uniform blouse again. Pencil stuck in the left side pocket, so he was a righty. Righty-ho. Cherry slipped the gun into the Irishman's right palm, pulled the muzzle up and pressed it against the skin behind his chin. Cherry knew that a pillow made a good impromptu silencer; he supposed all the soft stuff inside a skull would do it as well.

He decided that it did.

Checking to be sure he'd left no bloody handprints or other souvenirs, Cherry took a step back to examine his work, then vaulted over one of the low concrete walls, loped back to his cycle, and rode off.

■ ■ ■

WAGNER opened her apartment door. She stood in the doorway, suddenly unable to breathe. Every drawer in her dresser was open, her closet doors wide, the mattress tipped off the bed. The rugs were shoved against the baseboards.

She took a cautious step backward, wondering if they were in there, waiting for her. She listened. There was nothing. She leaned into the room again, hand circling the knob, ready to pull it shut in an instant. Still nothing.

She slipped her handbag down on its strap, set it on the stand by the door, opened it and reached in for Palatine's cigarette lighter. Armed and dangerous now, she charged in, pointing the gun into the closets (unoccupied, in chaos), the kitchen (unbelievable mess on the table, the floor), the bathroom (also empty, the clothes hamper upset, the lid off the w.c.).

WAGNER closed the apartment door, sat down on her single chair; stuffing puffed from a slit in the cushion.

She nearly screamed when the phone rang. She let it ring three times, trying seriously to think, then picked it up carefully, half expecting it to fall to bits or explode. "Hello?"

"This is Gareth Rhys-Gordon, from the Games Centre," the voice said. Oh, God, she thought, the Secret Service had her now, the whole game was up, they'd searched her room with their bloody special powers and now—

"—wish to hell there was some other way to break this, but you're on the register as having left the Centre together."

"What?"

"You and Suze Bell," Rhys-Gordon said patiently. "If you think you can manage it, could you come down to St. Thomas's? We need someone to identify the body. Bodies."

"I'm afraid I'm not making any sense of this," she said, desperately afraid that she was in fact doing so.

Rhys-Gordon explained it again.

"Yes, of course I'll come . . . no, I won't need a car sent"—she looked around at the wreckage of her rooms—"I'll take a cab, it'll be just as quick. Yes, I'm sure."

She put down the telephone. Now she understood why the burglars hadn't waited for her. They hadn't expected her to be coming home. She was supposed to be dead, except that they had made a mistake. They had made an extremely large mistake, one that was going to prove very costly to them. Was it war now in earnest? Very well, she would give them a war. She would give them the end of the bloody world.

PART FOUR

A BELL SHALL RING

The watchword being given, a bell shall ring,
Which when they hear, they shall begin to kill,
And never cease until that bell shall cease. . . .

—**The Masssacre at Paris**, *I, iv*

It was a sunny Saturday morning just outside Cambridge. Professor Edward Moreton Chetwynd, OBE, was four steps from the door when he heard the study telephone ring. "Get that, will you, Margy?" he said automatically; on the next ring he stopped and shook his head. His secretary wasn't in this morning; he'd told her not to bother. So, naturally—the phone rang again, and once more while Chetwynd debated answering it.

He put down his suitcase and went back to the study, taking the opportunity to check the lights and the fireplace grate and the ashtrays. All dark, all cold. The phone, on the corner of his Hepplewhite desk, persisted.

"Chetwynd here. Oh. Good morning, Charles. No, just on my way out, actually. What's this about?

"Hansard? What does this—Oh, that's his name, I see. No, I . . . oh, yes, I do know him, slightly. He's here with *what?* Wait, I recall now . . . I suspect I do know where he'll have gotten it. That's right. Cut off the hydra's head . . . I'm talking to myself, Charles, that's what I'm doing. Look, I'm off to Canada in . . . oh, God, three hours. Just use discretion, will you? And, Charles—I mean discretion in the generally accepted sense of the word, not some quaint thriller euphemism." Chetwynd paused, tapped his fingers on the desk blotter, looked at the right bottom drawer.

"Charles, are you still—of course. Now listen. I think we have to consider this a purely academic matter, no pun intended, not like the other business. I believe I know how to handle it. Yes. Yes, I will. *No, Charles, no action on our part will be necessary.*

"Because, young man, through the grace of God and friendly governments we are allowed a certain number of immoral acts, but we are obliged to avoid merely stupid ones.

"Yes. That's right. I'm sure I'll have a splendid time. Oh, damn it, Charles, the Sheraton, I think; Margy's written it down for me—in Toronto, I remember that much. I shan't at all, if the plane leaves without me. Good-bye, Charles."

Chetwynd sat down behind the desk. He closed his eyes and began to massage his temples, knuckles white with the pressure.

The mantel clock struck ten. Chetwynd picked up the telephone again and dialed a number, hoping that the favor he was about to ask was neither stupid nor immoral.

■　■　■

WAGNER finished packing her suitcases. She'd had to buy a new one: Palatine's burglars had slashed her best bag apart, looking for circuit boards. She took a last look around her deranged flat, put the cases in the hallway, snapped off the lights, and locked the door. She went downstairs and loaded the bags into her rented car, and drove off without any further glances back.

Timing was everything. There wasn't anything sudden about her departure; the landlady knew WAGNER had a holiday coming. She wouldn't snoop, but in a week or so she'd take a peek in, just on general principles, and discover the break-in, neatly establishing that it had happened days after WAGNER's departure. After all, who would have lived in the middle of such a violent mess without saying a word about it?

The Saturday evening traffic was light. It took her just under half an hour to drive to her temporary flat, rented under a name just a few letters different from her real one.

She paused before the door, key just at the lock. Suppose she opened it and found it turned over, just like the flat she'd left? Suppose the turners-over had decided to wait this time? She put her palm against the door, perhaps to steady herself, or as a silly, magical gesture to sense danger.

The wicked flee where no man pursueth, she thought, and opened the door. The place was ordinarily empty. Small living-and-bedroom with phone and telly, little kitchen, plasticky but bright, shower and sink. Inside the kitchen cupboard, the briefcase holding the COPE LIGHT board sat patiently. All the comforts.

She went out again, to bring back coffee and milk and a dinner of cod and chips, sat on the bed to eat and watch a Hammer horror film on Channel 4. Tomorrow was Sunday. She would stay in tomorrow, get used to the new place, read and make plans. Monday would begin a busy, busy week.

■ ■ ■

Hansard had made a research appointment at the British Museum Reading Room at ten Monday morning. He was prompt. This was, after all, the British Museum.

"Hello, Dr. Hansard," the librarian said as Hansard showed his White Group identification. "In the country for long this time?"

"A couple of weeks, thanks." He knew he'd heard the fellow's name, but couldn't recall it at all. He pushed a request slip across the desk. "I'll need these. I think they're all one case of documents."

"Very good, Dr. Hansard. Shouldn't be more than fifteen minutes."

It took ten. Hansard signed for the box, took it to a table, sat down—careful not to squeak his chair—and began reading. He began to sink into the minutiae of Elizabethan daily life, as into a hot bath, relaxing and slightly dizzying at once.

"Psst," said a woman's voice, quite close to his ear. "Would you happen to have Weaver's *Household Annals Analyzed* in there?"

Hansard looked up. Standing next to him was a woman in a tweed skirt and a pink cotton blouse, a khaki cardigan tied across her shoulders. A huge and shapeless leather bag was slung over her shoulder. Her hair was dark blonde, her eyes blue and alert, her nose a bit sharp . . .

"Uh, yeah. Here it is," Hansard said, and burrowed for the pamphlet.

"Great. Won't be a moment with this . . . unless I might . . ." She gestured at the other end of Hansard's table.

"Please do." They had both mastered the art of murmured library conversation.

"Thanks." She sat down, smoothing her skirt primly. Hansard watched her for a fairly long moment as she unloaded notebooks and paraphernalia from her bag. Then he went back to his books. Then he watched her again. There was a little of Anna Romano in her face, a little of Louise in her hips and her dress . . .

Finally he started to get up, then thought better of it: Feeling a grin pinch his lips, he wrote a note and slid it across the table to her.

She noticed it at once. Much too quickly, Hansard thought, for her full attention to have been on her own work. She read the note, scribbled on it, slipped it back. He read his message—

MY RESEARCH GRANT COVERS MEAL EXPENSES.
DO YOU LUNCH?

and below that, in small neat letters, her reply:

DIVINELY.

She pushed the pamphlet she'd been using back to him, held up ten fingers for ten minutes, and went out.

Hansard signed the box back in. He walked out of the Reading Room, past the glass-cased Shakespeare folios and bills of attainder, illuminated Kindermaerchen and Magna Carta, through the long halls full of paper history, almost humming.

The woman was sitting on the steps, surrounded by curious pigeons. They rose in a fluttering wave as she stood, brushed her skirt, and said, "How fancy do you feel?"

Whatever he'd been expecting her to say, that wasn't it. "The, uh, the Museum Tavern is okay."

"Oh, come now. The Tavern is full of boring researchers and even more boring tourists. Do you like crepes?"

"Sure."

"This way."

She led him northward into Bloomsbury. On the way he learned that her name was Ellen Maxwell, she'd read history at Cambridge, and she was helping research a book on Elizabethan household life— "Just exactly what the world needs to solve overpopulation and nuclear tension, I'm sure you'll agree."

"I'm Nicholas Hansard. I teach at Valentine College, which you've never heard of."

"*Hansard?* Do you mean, as in—"

"As in the Parliamentary Record, yup."

They arrived at a little creperie with cracked gilding on its mahogany-framed windows and no two tables or chairs the same. Maxwell ordered mushroom crepes, Hansard chicken, and they split a bottle of Evian water.

"So, Dr. Hansard," she said over the salad, "What are *you* doing to advance Western thought?"

"I'm working on the Skene Manuscript."

"Oh, really? I saw a copy of that. A friend from University had one."

"They're scarce. Who's your friend?"

"Oh, you wouldn't know her."

"I might."

Ellen laughed. "All right, tell truth and shame the devil. My friend wasn't supposed to have it. Gilly couldn't even read the script, but she thought it was just divine to have it, lost work of romantic old Kit Marlowe and all. She was general sec-and-maid-of-all-work to some professors, and when Dr. Chetwynd asked her to make a photocopy—"

"She made two."

"Isn't modern science wonderful?"

"Chetwynd, you said." The name was familiar. Hansard thought a moment. "I've read something of his, about the Spanish Armada."

"*Papists, Playwrights, and Pamphleteers: A Study of Popular Propaganda in the Wake of the Armada.* Too many Ps and a rather weak pun, but Gilly—that's my friend, who was a secretary for Sir Edward—tells me it's a good book."

The Armada, Hansard thought. *In narrow seas I watched a tragedy/ With Hell's own flames my only light to see.*

"Are you all right?"

He realized his forkful of chicken crepe was suspended in midair, gone quite cold. "I'm fine. I'm stupid. The Armada was broken up by an attack of fireships."

"Yes?"

"When Didrick—that's the Assassin in the play—is first asked where he comes from, he talks about being a sea-foundling, from a burning ship. The story's not true—I mean, we find out later that Didrick's not really an orphan—but I wonder if he meant that he was a refugee from the Armada."

"Didrick is Spanish?"

"The play is set in something called 'The Kingdom of the Germanies,' but it's England if it's anything. So Didrick—well. This is all pretty half-baked right at the moment. I'm trying to connect the play to real history, which may be a complete idiocy."

"It sounds like a splendid idiocy to me."

"Well. Thank you."

"I'm serious. This sounds considerably more interesting than the price of cotton thread in the Lisle letters. Not to mention that *my* grant doesn't cover expenses . . . How would you like a research associate, Dr. Hansard?"

He looked hard at her. She looked hard right back. Anna had been like that, when he'd first met her. And Louise . . . God, she looked like Louise just now. "Have you read the whole play?"

"Just once lightly."

He opened his briefcase, took out the typed transcript. "Now you can read it once heavily," he said. "Where shall you and I and my grant meet for dinner?"

■ ■ ■

WAGNER sat in her new flat, in a vaguely comfortable armchair, her copy of *The Assassin's Tragedy* in her lap. She no longer doubted that it contained clues to the rest of Allan's NIGHTMOVE network. And now there was the matter of Nicholas Hansard. . . .

It was just luck she had been told he was coming, and been able to get a look at him. So he was trying to authenticate *Assassin*. That was interesting. It might also be very useful. She would have to watch him very carefully, for anything he might discover.

Nicholas Hansard, dear heaven. Allan's protégé.

Watching him would be no problem, she thought. Maintaining a safe distance from him might be a problem indeed.

■ ■ ■

Hansard and Maxwell met in a Greek restaurant on Denmark Street, just a block from the bookstores on Tottenham Court Road. The whole dining room was no larger than the kitchen in Hansard's bungalow, and the owner was never more than a step away to make sure everything was perfect. Which it was.

"So what do you think? Hansard said.

"The feta is usually fresher."

"I think you know what I mean."

She poked at her Greek salad. "It's like a first draft of *Hamlet*, isn't it? With a little of *Oedipus* and *Un Ballo in Maschera* thrown in."

Hansard laughed, and as the restaurant owner cocked a curious glance, Hansard and Maxwell leaned over the typescript.

Act One, Scene One.

An Inn near the sea. Storms without. Polydorus and Argelian are seated near the fire.

The Assassin's Tragedy opens on a wild black night, with a piece of human flotsam washed up at an inn called The Humours. A man calling himself Didrick, of mysterious ancestry, comes in from the storm, finding the inn occupied by a company of players.

The Company is no ordinary band of actors, however. They are all men with secrets, and one, Doctor Argelian, seems to be a genuine sorcerer with a gift of prophecy. They accept Didrick as one of their number, with a curious ritual and an oath "to never ask the truth of men's condition."

Left alone, Didrick reveals to the audience that he is intent on the murder of the good King Fabianus: "I shall turn over stones, and show thee worms: I shall cut into hearts, from which shall flow a filthy suppuration of the blood."

From that moment the play is a series of plot reversals and sudden revelations, with no one's loyalty certain. Didrick falls in love with Violetta, the innkeeper's daughter (and clearly its resident whore). He also is attracted to Corwin, the golden-haired "player's boy"—the young man who took women's parts in companies of the time, since women were forbidden to appear on stage. Didrick agonizes over "this secret heat, this gorgeous dark obsession of the soul," afraid to admit it to the virginal Corwin for fear of losing both him and Violetta.

Experimenting with the summoning of spirits, Doctor Argelian raises the ghost of Didrick's mother, who urges him on to murder the King: "Do this for me, or say thou lov'd me not." When the ghost has departed, Didrick demands to know if Argelian saw and heard what took place: The wizard replies, "I know not what you saw, nor what was said. The message was for thee, and thee alone." Later, when Polydorus, the Master of the Company, asks Argelian what happened during the seance, Argelian refuses to speak of it. The audience never knows if the ghost is real, a product of Didrick's imagination, or some demon disguised to trap Didrick's soul.

Eventually, overburdened with secrets, Didrick tells Violetta the source of his grudge against the King: He is Fabianus's illegitimate son by a woman of the court, now dead. He has joined the Players' Company as a means of getting access to the court, and the King's person.

When the Company is finally invited to perform for Fabianus, Didrick campaigns for the part of Wittol the jester: Masked and costumed, with a dagger hidden in his stick, he will stab Fabianus to death in the full view of Court and Company.

Violetta goes to the palace to warn the King—whether from loyalty, or the hope of a reward, is not made clear. She is admitted to his chambers, only to discover that Didrick is only too right about the King's private habits. The text is sparse (as in Lightborn's murder of Edward II); perhaps Fabianus rapes her, perhaps he only tries. She is thrown out, with a handful of silver tossed after. She never delivers her warning.

Learning of this, Didrick murders Violetta, in a scene that begins with Didrick enraged—"Down, strumpet, and down bastard hid within—" and ends with him sorrowful and pleading.

"And now I know thou did'st for love of me,
So let me prove to thee I love thee too—"

Kills her.

Master Polydorus reveals Violetta's death to Corwin, who proves to be Violetta's half-brother, and eggs him on to revenge. As Didrick waits in a small tiring-room for his cue to appear, Corwin stabs him to death.

Polydorus then explains to Corwin that, while he has "no love for Fabianus, nor any King in either Earth or Heaven," he and all the members of the Company are murderers, demonolaters, or worse, and they would all have been exposed in the wake of the assassination. He then welcomes Corwin as a full member of the Company, "baptiz'd in blood, and one of us at last."

In an ironic epilogue set before the court, all plots against divinely anointed Kings are denounced, and Fabianus promises to reward Corwin "as if he were my princely son and heir."

"So what's your first impression? Do you think it's genuine?"

Maxwell took a sip of coffee, a tiny bite of baklava. "That's a silly question and you know it. If there were any serious oddities or anachronisms, they'd have been announced and there wouldn't be any interest."

"Maybe it's silly. Remember the new Shakespeare sonnet?"

"Touché, Doctor. All right, just because a work is lousy doesn't mean a genius didn't write it." She put down her cup and flipped pages. "Violetta's true to Marlowe, at any rate. His female characters are all terrible."

"I'd say absent more than terrible. They're background . . ."

"Props and possessions, you mean? Or backstabbing whores? He doesn't seem to have known the first thing about women."

"If not understanding women were a sin, Ellen, we'd all . . . oh, the hell with that. Or are you suggesting he was gay after all?"

"Gosh, I thought it was 'generally accepted,' she said, enough acid in her voice to get across what she thought of those who generally accepted it. "I mean, 'all who love not tobacco and boys are fools,' right?"

"Touché yourself, Ms. Maxwell."

"Think nothing of it, Nick."

"No. Not Nick. Nicholas, please."

She looked rather startled. "All right. . . . Look, do *you* think Marlowe was homosexual?"

"I think there's not a bit of useful proof one way or another. Whether it's *relevant* to the issue of the play is something else again." He tapped a finger on his coffee cup. Every historian had private techniques, not easily explained even to another historian. Hansard knew very well his own were among the oddest.

"This has certainly got the thread," she said. "Of course, so does *Edward the Second*. But this can't have been an easy thing to put on stage."

"Now, you see, there's a useful point. *Did* they ever put this thing on stage? There ought to be some records, in household rolls or the accounts of one of the players' companies. . . . Finished?"

She emptied her cup. "Just."

"Shall we take a walk?"

They went down Charing Cross Road, past bakeries and music stores, peering into bookshop windows. At Cambridge Circus—"Look," Ellen said, "there's George Smiley's office," which made Hansard just a touch queasy—they went into a pub for bitter and light to read by.

But the documents stayed in the bag, and they just sat through a pint and half of a second each, other people's conversation and the ringing of slot machines fading to a soft carpet of background sound, looking at one another.

"Are you married, Nicholas?" she said finally.

"I was. Louise died. Several years ago."

"I'm sorry. Was it—"

"It was pretty awful. But it's over now." In a corner of the pub, a jukebox started up. "*Wonderful* guitarist," Hansard said, not certain if he was deliberately changing the subject or not.

"You play an instrument?"

"No."

"Did your wife?"

Hansard looked at her. Her open, curious look darkened suddenly; she bit her lip, said, "Oh. I'm sorry. Researcher's habit."

"It's all right." He wanted her to know that it really was all right, and went on: "She played recorder. She'd started with flute, in high school, but . . . well, she said it wasn't as much fun. She could carry a little plastic recorder around in her bag, and take it out and play it anywhere; with a flute, it'd be too—too—" He pantomimed holding a flute to his lips, waggled his fingers on the keys, suddenly seeing Louise seated on grass, luminous and hazy as in a perfume commercial, and was wholly unable to find words for the thought.

"Too formal," Ellen said softly, "by the time she'd assembled her long silver flute, people would have expected something grand and ethereal, when she just wanted to make pretty music."

"Yeah," Hansard said. "I gave her a little wooden ocarina on a neck cord. . . . Do you play something?"

"Strings, mostly. Guitar and lute. I was in a band when I was in school, along with three other girls, all of us history students. We called it Palimpsest—supposed to be rock written on top of folk, you see?"

"Like Fairport Convention, or Steeleye Span."

"That's it. We used to play in cellars around town. Nothing ever came of it, naturally. I guess it rarely does. Like history, eh, Professor Hansard? Great fun but not much of a living."

"Here's to," he said, and finished his beer. "Do you want another?"

"A half."

"Fine." He brought the glasses back, sat down. She reached out and put her hand on top of his. "You are a dear to be doing this."

"And you're a help," he said, beginning to feel the alcohol stiffen his tongue. "Socratic dialogue, you know? Makes it—" He stopped. That was not a subject for now. He was acclimated to the loss of Louise. But not to Allan. Not yet. He patted her hand, felt something cold.

"You're wearing a wedding band," Hansard said, feeling hot in the least sexual of senses.

"And you aren't," she said. "Six of one, half dozen of the other."

"Wait a moment," he said, and then he understood. "*Oh.* And I was so self-righteous about—God, I'm sorry."

"So now we're sorry for each other. Could we move along to a later geological epoch now?"

"How long . . . ago, I mean?"

"Fourth of May, '82."

He nodded.

She said, "Does that date mean anything to you?"

"No. Should it?"

"My husband went down with HMS *Sheffield*," she said.

"*Oh,*" Hansard said, unsure if she meant to stop there. *Sheffield* had been sunk by an Exocet missile during the Falklands War (the South Atlantic War, as the experts in Allan's circle called it). The ship had gone down very fast. Ray Rayven said that Exocet sales had taken a major jump. Everybody loves a winner.

"It was all rather sudden," she said, and then sighed. "What am I saying? Couldn't have been much more sudden. Just a man at the door with 'Sorry, Mrs. Maxwell, but England expects that every man, you know.' And he did, too. What England expected. I'm drunk, you know."

"Hmm."

"And quite gen'lemanly of you to put it that way, sir." She smiled at him. It shone through the glare and haze of the pub; it *shone*. I ought to call Anna tonight, Hansard thought, and knew damn well he wouldn't.

"Well, Nicholas? Are you a gentleman?"

"In what way?"

"Yeah, you are, I think. I like that in a man. Not the only thing I like, of course."

"Maybe I should take you home."

"Maybe you should," she said, and he could hear the edge of a sob in her voice; a tear got away from one eye. "I'm sorry, really," she said. "I don't know what the trouble is. I don't usually make passes at gentlemen . . . nor anybody else, I mean. . . ."

"It's okay," Hansard said gently, recalling himself like this, horribly like this. "'As well be hanged for a gentleman as a clown.'"

"What?"

"Oh. . . ." He pulled out the playscript. Give us both something to focus on besides each other, he thought. "There's this key line that Didrick keeps repeating—'As well be hanged for a something as for a something else.' Each time he speaks it, he ups the stakes a little more: 'a beggar as a slave,' 'a coxcomb as a bawd,' and so on, until finally, just before the court masque . . . here, look. He's getting into a jester's outfit, and the poisoned bodkin he means to kill the King with is hidden inside his stick."

DIDRICK, being dressed in motley. He dances, and shakes his staff in mock sword-play.

DRESSER. Take care, my lord, this stitching's old, 't will tear.

DIDRICK. I am a clown; shall I not caper?

DRESSER. Sir,
    I have seen clowns aplenty in my time,
    And those that know their craft best, know its place;
    While dancing is most merry, in its time,
    And jesting maketh laughter, in its place,
    To use them at the unappointed time
    May call forth anger in good humour's place.
    To curry laughs and fail's the direst thing.

DIDRICK. What penalty doth bootless clowning bring?

DRESSER. God's truth, sir, I have seen men killed for it.

DIDRICK. A death for silent laughter! O grave wit!

Yet if I cannot bring the highest down,

As well be hanged for a killer as a clown.

Maxwell was making a soft sound; Hansard thought at first she was crying, but then realized it was laughter. "Killers and clowns," she said. "That's the human race, all right." She looked at him again, smiling again, with not quite the glow of before but a genuine humor. "Thank you, Doctor. I think I ought to go home now."

They went outside. The Circus was brilliantly lit, a wilder glow coming from the West End theatres just beyond the traffic circle.

"Shall I . . . *accompany* you?" Hansard said.

"No, that's all right. The air's cleared my head nicely." She did sound quite sober now. "Thank you for the offer, though."

"Will I see you at the Museum tomorrow?"

"No. I'm awfully busy tomorrow."

"Oh."

"What about lunch on Wednesday?" she said suddenly, and pulled a little notepad from her bag. "Here's my number. You pick the place. Not too early, all right?"

"Sure," he said.

"Good night now, Dr. Nicholas Hansard," she said, still too fast, squeezed his hand hard and went walking quickly away from him. She was lost almost at once in the West End, the crowds and the neon.

Hansard watched after her for a while, then turned and started the walk to his hotel, whistling without a tune.

■ ■ ■

WAGNER followed Hansard from a half block or so back, watched him go into his hotel. She waited a few minutes, until a light came on in a window, and she saw his silhouette, moving about, finally drawing the curtains.

He would have been an interesting man to have known, she thought, with more than a little bitterness. Allan had spoken of him so often, so warmly. But she had never been able to meet Allan's friends, except as her own arcs of movement intersected theirs.

It had been the most illicit of affairs, conducted at the convenience of men like Palatine and the inconvenience of men like Gareth Rhys-Gordon. They had forever agonized between isolated trysts, where they might be invisible or else remembered, and crowded rendezvous, where they might be lost or else recognized. No trips to the theatre, no dinners in public; instead they had read plays to one another over hotel-room trays.

It was what there was; it had been enough.

Now what she had was a suitcase full of electronic parts, a handful of code names, and a plan. It would have to be enough, it was what there was.

■ ■ ■

Hansard's wristwatch alarm woke him from uncomfortable dreams. He stood up, then sat back down again hard on the bed, feeling dizzy and ill, unsure if it was mild flu, mild hangover, or mild depression, but certain he didn't want to go anywhere just yet.

He phoned the Museum to cancel his research time today, then crawled back into bed and darkness and sleep.

He woke again a little before noon, feeling less misused. He dressed, packed up his notes, and went out to a pub a few blocks from the hotel. He sat down in a moderately well-lit corner with a pint of dry cider and a ham and tomato sandwich, and contemplated killers and clowns.

Suppose, Hansard thought, the play was about a real assassin?

It was a perfectly reasonable idea. Marlowe's other plays had all been dramatized history, except for *Doctor Faustus,* and it was based on the actions of real wizards such as John Dee. Elizabethan theatre generally drew its plots from at least legend, if not life: stories the audience would be expected to know.

More importantly, it made sense. There had been a whole series of plots against Elizabeth the First, and through the efforts of Francis Walsingham's private spy network, a whole series of exposures. And executions. It was what a free press would have called a hot issue.

The press wasn't free at all, of course. One of Marlowe's contemporaries had gone to jail for a play that fictionalized the now-cold, now-hot war with Spain.

If *The Assassin's Tragedy* had found its way into the wall of Skene House because it steered too close to the truth, there was a whole new angle on this issue of its authorship. Authenticating it meant discovering what that truth was.

It also explained why Raphael, who was anything but an academic, had hold of a copy of the play; it pointed in the direction of why Raphael wanted *Assassin* analyzed.

It seemed more than a little ridiculous that a murder plot four hundred years old could weigh on the present; but when Major Montrose had come out of the river, and Allan had died, Hansard had been forced to recalibrate his sense of the ridiculous.

He sipped the crackling strong cider, started on his second sandwich, and drifted through his notes into the time of Elizabeth.

> POLYDORUS. He has borne the weight of secrecy too long,
>   Sick-swollen with his thought, unable to
>   Release himself into another's heart;
>   Such celibacy maketh all men mad.

Somewhere in Paris, an English spy paced before his Spanish spymaster. The Spaniard, whose name was Mendoza, straightened the letters and papers on his desk for the hundredth time that day and said, "I understand that you are dissatisfied."

"I am glad that you understand *something*," the spy said. "How should I feel? What is there for me to do, here?"

"Your reports on the Protestants have been of use."

"I am glad to have been of use," the spy said, with exaggerated deference. "But I tire of being *of use*. I wish to act, to do."

Mendoza nodded. "Would you be willing to return to England?"

"Of course!" The spy's eyes narrowed. "To what purpose, then? More of the tedious counting of pikes?"

Mendoza said carefully, "His Majesty of Spain proposes that if Elizabeth of England will not consummate the alliance she has so often spoken of, he shall act for her."

The spy pounded a fist into a palm. "*Invasion,*" he said. "How soon?"

Mendoza spread his hands. "You will be in enemy country. There are ways of making men tell dangerous secrets."

"Aye, true enough. They've had your Inquisitors to learn from."

Mendoza frowned. The spy said, "Oh, let it pass. I'll make a way for

your soldiers. I'll need some money, and papers—but you're good at
papers, aren't you?"

■ ■ ■

"'Nother pint, mate?" the barman was asking. Hansard said, "Sure."

Mendoza had run Spain's spy network from Paris for years before
and after the Armada; he was, by the evidence, a prolific writer of
reports, a methodical files clerk—and an utter disaster as a spymaster,
incapable of the rawest analysis of the reports he received. He had as-
sured Philip that England's Catholics were just gnawing the bit to rise
up against their Queen, given only a little bit of a push from outside.

Mendoza had been wrong about a number of other things as well.

Hansard's second pint arrived. The barman flipped him for the
change and won, flashed Hansard a grin and went off whistling.

The spy watched from Dover as his dreams were set afire.

He turned away. The fleet had been the wrong method, he knew
now. It was no longer a world for mighty fleets and gallantry: Mighty
fleets were wrecked by pirates and blazing pitch. The serpent slew the
lion with a treacherous bite from hiding.

If that was the world's game, then he was a man of the world and
would play it. It was as the Bible said, the spy thought, more than a
little blasphemously; the serpent would wound the woman's heel.

■ ■ ■

WAGNER put down the Penguin collection of Marlowe's plays, exhausted and relieved. Only one small lamp was lit by her chair; the
evening had gone by without her really noticing. But she had found
FRIAR BACON.

She had spent the last several hours reading through the plays, looking for friars. There were plenty of those, a whole houseful in *The Jew
of Malta,* but no Friar Bacon. Then, in the fourth act of *The Jew,* she
spotted:

ITHAMORE. So, let him lean upon his staff. Excellent! He stands as if
    he were begging of bacon.
BARABAS. What time o'night is't now, sweet Ithamore?
ITHAMORE. Towards one.

She looked at the clock. Half past eleven. An hour and a half to wait.

She puzzled over the last name. ROCK STAR. The first two, FRIAR BACON, KING BYRON—all right, those were vaguely classical. But ROCK STAR? She could hear Allan laughing as he composed the joke. But she didn't get it.

At one A.M. she picked up the phone.

"Roger Skipworth," said a man's voice, sounding not at all sleepy.

"This call is for Ithamore," WAGNER said.

"'S'a moment," the voice said, and WAGNER tensed, wondering if she'd gotten the number wrong, or worse, the code name. Then the voice came back, saying, "Okay, we'll make this fast. Got a pencil?"

"I'm ready," WAGNER said.

"You take the A259 east from Rye . . ."

■ ■ ■

Roger Skipworth had come late to the pleasures of corruption. His father, a machinist with his own small shop, had rigidly instructed him that thieves went first to jail and second to hell. Sometimes the instruction was less rigid: a strap, rather than a stick. Roger rebelled at first, was frightened at first; but locked in closets without a light, he learned patience, and the end of fear.

When Roger was eight, a friend of his father's gave him a paperback book on physical culture, and he learned strength. His father didn't mind; it made Roger more useful around the shop, carrying leaf springs and harrow blades, motors and wheels and chilled-steel plowshares. Roger had always been big for his age, and soon he was hard for his age as well.

There would come a day, Roger knew, when he would break his father's arms and legs and neck and back and skull. And if the police asked any questions, Roger would tell them that the old man had been a thief (which was the truth; the shop was full of tools and parts that had appeared by night), and that would settle matters.

When Roger Skipworth was twelve his father disappeared. Roger was at a loss: He did not know where a man could go, except home. His mother, who had also been at lessons these past years, tried to beat him usefully, but though Roger always cooperated it was physically absurd. Almost as absurd as the woman's attempts to run the machinery shop without a mechanic. The place was paid for (at least, there were no outstanding debts against it), but it was padlocked, and gathered dust.

At fourteen Roger lied about his age and enlisted in the Royal Marines.

Roger Skipworth's first epiphany was that here was a place that would clothe and feed and house him, and pay him cash in the bargain, while requiring in return only manual labor, verbal and physical abuse in quantities so small he scarcely recognized them as such, and the constant readiness to go somewhere and kill strangers. Above all, there were no confusing value judgments about whether one was being a good boy or not. Obeying orders was good, and that was that.

Roger and the military got along very, very well.

Roger's second epiphany came a year and a half after his enlistment, one rainy day in barracks. Skipworth was working out with a set of weights that belonged to one Private Bourne. Bourne was something of a bug on fitness; he spent a fair amount of time discussing exercise with Private Skipworth, and granted Roger the free loan of his personal equipment.

A few of the other recruits looked sidelong on this relationship, and one private, an ex-punk from Liverpool named Jack Fish, out-and-out warned Skipworth in the coarsest possible terms. Skipworth, partly from patience and partly from ignorance, let the advice pass.

Then Private Bourne made *his* pass, and that was in fairly coarse terms as well.

Private Skipworth stared at Private Bourne, not fully comprehending. Private Bourne made the request much clearer. Skipworth punched Bourne in the mouth, cracking two of Bourne's teeth. He hit Bourne in the sternum and the ribs, doubling him over. Bourne fought back, of course. They were both strong, tough young men, with the kind of experience at this sort of thing that one only gets in a military barracks; but they both knew that this was different. This wasn't a brawl. This was a fight.

It went on until Bourne lay facedown, bleeding from mouth and nose and ears, Skipworth's knee on his spine.

Skipworth looked up. He was breathing hard, but not at all tired.

Then he saw Jack Fish leaning against a locker, watching him. Some of his other barracks mates were standing by the doors, alert.

Jack Fish said, "Don't mind us, Skipper. No'un's gonna bother you two."

It took Skipworth a moment to get the full meaning of Fish's statement, but then he thought of his mother, standing by as his father swung the strap, and he understood. He felt terribly grateful to his mates. In their honor, he gave Private Bourne a box on the ear.

It felt very good. In an instant he grasped the lesson his father had been trying to teach him: the wonderful pleasure of beating someone who cannot retaliate. Doubtless, Skipworth thought, that was why his father had run away: He had seen his son about to outgrow helplessness.

Truly grateful, truly happy, Roger Skipworth poured his pent-up heart into Private Bourne's muscle and bone. When he was quite spent, he and Jack Fish and two of the others loaded Bourne into a Rover and drove off through the rain. They dumped Bourne, in his underwear and without his boots, in a distant corner of the base, at the bottom of a gravel hill Bourne might theoretically have hurt himself tumbling down. They left him on his back, so he would not drown in the mud. Then the four pals drove to the enlisted men's canteen—Skipworth looked barely roughed up—and hoisted one, discussing how they would close ranks if need be.

It wasn't necessary. There was no inquiry. Private Bourne was transferred before half his bruises had faded. While no officer ever formally voiced approval of the wet day's work, there were smiles, and there were nods, and Roger Skipworth found himself a favored young man at the base.

Advancement for Roger was not long in coming. He was, after all, an ideal soldier by several views. He spent the average amount of time on report for minor infractions, but always stayed well clear of the glasshouse. It was his observation that most of the men who ended up with bad discharges or prison terms were either drunkards or thieves. Roger had never developed a taste for more than a few pints in good company, and whatever else he might be or become, he was no thief.

This scrupulousness was noted. Seven years after Roger Skipworth's enlistment, he became the base Supply Sergeant.

Supply sergeants occupy a special niche of power in the world's armies, which goes far beyond their ability to provide or deny the small comforts, like nonabrasive soap and correctly sized socks. A soldier's kit is not his own, but the property of his government (whether HM or US or CCCP), and a soldier who offends the Supply Officer may discover that some article of that government property entrusted to him has been marked down as Not Returned. If the article is a weapon or a supply of petrol, the offense can be genuinely serious. One may protest that the item was indeed returned; but if the Supply Sergeant says it cannot be found . . . it will not be found.

Skipworth was no tyrant. For his mates, Jack Fish foremost among them, many things were available. Cheap petrol, for instance. Loans at preferential rates. Food a cut above the norm. Within a year, a liaison was established with the Regimental Clerk's office, and documents for every purpose could be obtained. There was also a kind of rental library for military equipment; handguns, mostly, but also Rovers, lorries, once a helicopter. No expendables were involved. Skipworth bought ammunition from an outside source, an Israeli arms dealer who offered fair prices and perpetually asked to buy some piece of major equipment.

But Roger Skipworth did not steal.

Ten years after he left home—his mother had died sometime back, he had forgotten just when—Sgt. Skipworth was running one of the most efficient entrepreneurships in Britain, built on the classical capitalist principles of using someone else's money and goods, and paying no taxes whatsoever.

Four months later, the roof fell in.

Jack Fish and three other men were surprised while burgling a warehouse. Shots were fired. Fish, trying to escape along a shed roof, slipped and fell, breaking both legs and an arm, but surviving to confess a considerable amount.

Sgt. Skipworth was nonplussed. Why on earth had Fish grassed? Skipworth could have made life very comfortable for Fish in the glasshouse. He was confused, and deeply hurt, that his mate hadn't closed ranks.

The regiment did, however. There was an official inquiry into Sergeant Roger Skipworth's record, but no court-martial. Skipworth was asked to voluntarily resign, for the good of the regiment and all concerned.

"I never stole a brass farthing," Skipworth told his military lawyer.

"Sergeant," said the lawyer, "we're doing our best not to look very hard at what you *have* done. I assure you, when we say that this is for the best, we haven't neglected your interest. You're coming out of it pretty damn well, I daresay."

But of course Sgt. Skipworth did feel neglected. As for the coming-out, he had told the truth about brass farthings. After continuous reinvestments in bigger bribes, prettier whores, powder and shot, broadening his operation like any good capitalist, there were no liquid assets for the young sergeant to take home. Roger Skipworth had become the Clive Sinclair of military graft.

There was only one thing for it, Skipworth thought. He had been absolutely virtuous in his single virtue, and it had brought him nothing but false friends and disgrace. He was not about to accept poverty on top of it.

One evening about two weeks after Jack Fish's misadventure, the end of his last full day of military service, Skipworth allowed his lawyer to buy him a drink and see him back to his quarters. Skipworth asked the time before they parted company: It was 9:13 P.M. He wanted to be certain the lawyer remembered. Skipworth went into his room, undressed, and sat reading until eleven-thirty. Then he dressed in civilian clothes, gathered a few things, locked the door, and left by the window.

He slipped off-base through a carefully concealed gap in the perimeter fence and went to a small shed. It contained an automobile, garaged here for just this sort of late-night excursion. God bless the peacetime army, Skipworth thought.

He drove to a hospital a few miles from the base. Getting in would have been ridiculously easy even without his Commando training. Skipworth entered a large, dark ward. Four men were sleeping there, all some distance apart. He went to each bed in turn, making a small adjustment to the patients' intravenous fluid bottles with the gear he'd brought along.

The fourth man was half-cased in plaster. Skipworth had been half expecting there to be guards, but what was the point? This fellow wasn't going anywhere. Skipworth touched him gently on the fore-head. The man's eyes opened.

"Hello, Jack," Skipworth said.

"Who's there?" Jack Fish said.

"Oh, you know me, Jack." Skipworth let Fish hear the knife snap open, see light along the blade. Then he put it under Fish's chin. "You've cost me a bit, Jack. There's somethin' I want from you."

"Christ," Fish said, a long hiss. "I've cost *you?* I'm goin' to the glass-house for twenty years, an' I've—" The edge of the knife shut him up. Fish's eyes flicked around, at the other patients; none of them stirred.

"That contract job you did for the Yid last month, Jack. I want the stuff from that."

"For God's sake, Skip—" It was not a shout. Fish's voice was pitched low. This was a foxhole conversation.

"You think I'm goin' to steal it? You know me, Jack. No such thing. Can I put this away now?" He raised the knife, closed it. "You're in no position to finish the deal, are you? And wouldn't a little money comin' in make life a lot easier?" Skipworth grinned. "We could even put it to work for you, Jack. In a building society. Compound interest, you'd be pretty well off when you got out."

Jack Fish relaxed. "You had me goin' there for a minute, Skipper. But you're a right bloke. I told 'em that, you know. I told 'em you were right."

Fish told Skipworth about the deal to steal missiles from the Navy, arranged by the Israeli for some secret third party. He told Skipworth where the stuff was hidden. He talked and he talked. Skipworth thought that he could have saved a lot by questioning the whores he'd gotten Fish; being horizontal did so much for his tongue.

As Fish talked on, Skipworth slipped off the clamp he'd put on Fish's IV tube, letting the liquid flow again. After a few moments, Fish's voice got thick. Then he stopped talking, and his eyes closed.

Skipworth checked the other patients. None of them seemed to be breathing. There had been twenty-four morphine Syrettes in the case he'd brought—stolen, there was no nicer word for it—five each for the others, nine for Fish, since only Fish really counted. The others were only for show. A diversion, that had a military ring. Skipworth's knowledge of medicine was limited, but he supposed nine shots direct down the old pipes would do the job.

Skipworth left the hospital, quietly as he'd come. He went back to the base that he had never formally left. The next day he turned in his kit—everything accounted for, naturally—and drove home to Kent, making a stop to collect a crate from a South London warehouse.

The next day Skipworth got in touch with the Israeli. The Israeli put him in contact with the American who wanted the goods. The American gave Skipworth a pair of code words—one meaning Go, the other Go to ground—and told him to wait for a phone call at a certain hour. He didn't name the day.

That was all right. Skipworth was a patient man.

■ ■ ■

WAGNER turned off the A road at a blue barn, as per instructions. There weren't any signs. She drove up a track for half a mile, then saw a Nissen hut, all to itself; she pulled to a stop in front of it. There was rust on the galvanized metal curve of the building, electric lights hanging askew, a faded sign that said MACHINE SHOP—FARM TOOLS. There was a large rolling door, and a smaller one, in the end. The small door opened, and a man in a gray camouflage parka, baggy pants, and Wellingtons came out. He had sandy hair, and a large hand held in front of his face.

WAGNER got out of the car. "Ithamore?"

"Whoever the hell he is," the man said. "You know who FRIAR BACON is?"

"If I called you that, you were to disappear instead."

"This little piggy don't run. But c'min, then," Roger Skipworth said, and held the door open for her. She looked around as he slammed it shut again.

Long fluorescent fixtures lit the hut's interior coolly, flatly. The building was full of metal: generators, tools, bits of machines, rows of steel shelves with cans of paint and still more parts. Everything that wasn't metal seemed to be concrete, or else grease.

"Do you have the goods?" WAGNER said.

"Be pretty silly bringin' you out here if I didn't." He walked around her, toward a bench covered with an extraordinarily filthy tarpaulin.

Skipworth moved with his head forward and what seemed an utter lack of caution, as if he expected the world to get out of his way. He was actually rather handsome, WAGNER thought, except for a fixed screw-you-mate expression.

He pulled back the tarp. Underneath were three long blocks of foam plastic, a little more than a yard long and a foot square on the ends. Skipworth lifted off the top of one of the blocks. Nested inside was a gray box, quite like a little coffin, stenciled with do-this-heres and don't-do-thats.

"They're called Sea Wasps," Skipworth said. He tapped the metal box. "The canister's storage and launcher both. You've got to give 'em twenty-four volts, like a car battery, in here." He pointed to a plastic-sealed socket.

"What about the arming unit?"

Skipworth looked sidelong at WAGNER. "True, they'd be little use without that." He went to one of the metal shelves, opened a battered toolbox, and removed another foam case. Inside it was a metal box with a row of lights and weatherproof switches. Skipworth reached into his breast pocket and took out a small yellow envelope, dropped it on top of the arming unit. "Arming key. Don't lose that."

WAGNER nodded, put the key in her bag.

Skipworth said, "Any questions?"

"Sea Wasp is infrared-optical fire-and-forget," WAGNER said, trying to sound as bored as possible . . . just like Suze Bell would have. Before somebody killed her. "Once launched toward a thermal trace, it pursues until impact. It's a short-range missile, under three thousand meters, reasonably resistant to false traces. Since it's meant for sea surface-to-surface, most of the air-combat countermeasures aren't—"

"All right," Skipworth said, with a bit of a grin. "You're a clever girl. Want some tea?"

"No, thank you."

"Well, I do." He went to a small, relatively clean table that had a vacuum bottle sitting on it. He poured a cup, gulped down half of it at once. "Ahh. Nothing like a cuppa on a cold day. You bring the money?"

WAGNER took the bundles of bills from her purse, put them down on the table. Skipworth picked them up, began counting. WAGNER dipped her fingers into her bag, for the gun.

One of the bundles struck her in the face. She took a step backward, off balance, and Skipworth shoved her in the chest, knocking her down. Skipworth stood over her, put his foot on her left wrist.

"Somethin' else in your bag for me, ma'am?" He bent down; she started to move and he showed her the knife in his hand. He cut the purse straps, then pressed the blade to her throat as he picked up the bag and dumped it on the floor. She moved her eyes to watch as he stirred through the items. The blade was warm against her neck, warm from his pocket.

Nothing in the pile seemed to catch Skipworth's notice. WAGNER said, "I haven't got any more money."

"No, I see that. Too bad. But I know who does."

"What are you talking about?"

"You're much too honest to be in this trade, lady. You think my little birds are worth ten thousand quid: There's others who'll pay more. Fifty thousand, maybe a hundred."

How had Allan ever come in contact with this man? How had they done business? "How much more do you want?"

"You're not a stupid woman," Skipworth said. "Not much more at all I want from you." He pressed his boot down on her wrist, puckered his lips and blew her a kiss.

She clenched her right fist and swung at his leg, hitting the shin just below the kneecap. He grunted, more surprised than hurt, and shifted his weight. She grabbed his trouser leg and pulled, rolling her weight behind it; pain lanced through her trapped wrist, and then the foot lifted. She pulled again and he fell forward, toward her. She rolled. He flung the arm with the knife out involuntarily; it scraped on the concrete floor as he landed. She tried to find the cigarette-case gun among the spilled contents of her purse, but he snatched at her ankle and she ran for the door, her low heels loud on the floor, praying that one didn't snag.

She nearly collided with the door, grabbed the handle and pulled.

It rattled but wouldn't open. Skipworth had locked it when she'd first come in. He'd never intended to let her leave.

She turned. Skipworth was walking toward her, holding his knife low. He was about fifteen yards away. WAGNER looked left and right: He could turn and catch her just as easily no matter which way she ran.

She braced her hands against the door. She watched him grin. She pushed off and ran straight for him.

He stopped. She sidestepped and passed him, close as she dared, and sprinted for the far end of the building, toward the clutter of tools and equipment. She heard his steps behind her, pounding almost as loud as her heart.

There were shelves at the back, more shop tables. She went behind one of the loaded shelf units, crouched down, not at all sure if she was out of sight. She looked around. There didn't seem to be any backdoor; in the far corner was an area boxed off with plywood sheets, a door in one of the panels, probably an office. She started to move, then held still: If there wasn't another way out through there, it was nothing but a mousetrap.

Not that hiding would save her. Skipworth had all the time in the world.

She looked up, at the lights hung from the ceiling. Conduits ran down the back wall of the hut, to three junction boxes fixed to the wall.

"I wasn't goin' to kill you, luv," Skipworth called out. "Wasn't goin' to do you any harm at all." He was terribly close.

She felt cold metal against her back and nearly screamed: It was just the edge of a shelf. She tried to ease away from it, without rattling the steel, but her heel scraped on the floor. She heard Skipworth stop and turn. "There you are," he said. "Just coming, luv."

She stood up, put both hands on the shelf unit and pushed. It creaked and rattled, but it was too heavily loaded: It wouldn't go over. She looked through the shelves and saw Skipworth eye to eye, not two feet away. His eyes were bright. His hand swept forward. The knife cut WAGNER's jacket. She turned and ran to the switch boxes, pulled the first handle. Nothing. The second, nothing. The third, and the lights went out. She was blind a moment, then the thin shafts of light through high shallow windows showed everything gray on gray. Skipworth was a black shape, sliding through the darkness.

She could see a pipe spanner on a shelf nearby, a metal club as long as her forearm. It might do to smash the hasp on the door, if she could get to the door, get past Skipworth. She picked it up. It was heavy. She took a light step, another.

There was a movement in the dark. Something clattered behind her, and she gasped. "There you are," Skipworth's voice said, and he closed in on her.

She raised the spanner in both hands, brought it down. It hit Skipworth's right shoulder, glancing off, but he dropped the knife. She swung at his chest, connected: He puffed out breath.

He grabbed the spanner, pulled it out of her hands.

She let it go. She turned and ran for the plywood office door, pulled it open, slammed it shut behind herself. There was a hook-and-eye latch; she fastened it, for what it was worth.

There was some light through a filthy window. A worktable, covered with papers and parts. Shelves with cans and jars. No door.

She went to the window. It was tiny. No way out.

There was a grating sound from outside the plywood box, footsteps, a faint rush of wind.

The door shook. The blade of an axe bit through the wood, a bright beak poking in. It pulled free, chopped again. The bastard wasn't even trying to cut out the latch, she thought: He knew she was trapped, he wanted this to last a while.

She looked around the office, touched a steel square, a block plane, nothing useful. She scanned the shelves, reading the labels on the cans. She took one down, tried its cap. Stuck.

The whole head of the axe came through the door, caught for a moment, pulled free. She could hear Skipworth panting. Her sweaty hands slipped on the can. She wrapped the hem of her jacket around the cap, twisted hard. Her wrist ached where Skipworth had stepped on it.

The door split. Skipworth kicked it open. The metal cap came free in WAGNER's hand. Skipworth came through the door.

She flung the paint thinner into his face, his eyes. He shrieked, dropped the axe, covered his face. She splashed him again. He groped for her, cursing, then sank to his knees and began to whimper. Back pressed to the flimsy wall, WAGNER edged past him, his clawing hands, stepped carefully over the axe.

He was still screaming when she reached the middle of the hut, picked up the cyanide gun. She went back, found him struggling to get to his feet. His flailing hand caught her arm. His face was a horror. She shoved the gun muzzle against his temple and fired. His hand spasmed. She pulled free and Skipworth crumpled to the floor.

Her own legs went weak. She walked a few steps, then leaned against a stack of shelves. She shuddered, felt herself starting to cry, held it back. Not for him, she thought. No tears for him.

She covered up the missile again, gathered the things from her purse, then realized that Skipworth had the key to the door. She went back, kicked his body for certainty's sake, then went through his pockets. The key was there. She tossed a dropcloth over the body, then stood looking at it, wondering what to do with it. It would be much safer to leave it here than try to move it; no one else should be in until the missiles were picked up, and in ten days it would make no difference who found Skipworth.

She wondered what he had planned to do with her.

Then she saw the paper sacks of powdered lime against the back wall, and guessed the answer. Well. They would do very nicely.

■ ■ ■

Palatine was in his City office, burning documents. The treated paper exploded with purple fire, and a small fan sucked the smoke through charcoal filters.

There was a knock at the door. Palatine switched on the TV monitor. He shook his head and opened the door.

"Hello, Mr. Palatine," Cherry said. "There's been kind of a noise about the other night."

"I'd think that puts it quite mildly," Palatine said.

"It's no problem, sir. Leavin' em out like that, guess it couldn't be helped."

"What are you here for?"

"The fella," Cherry said. "The soldier. Though I guess they were both soldiers. I wasn't paid for him, you know, sir. And nobody works free in this business, sir. Not in this business."

Exasperated, Palatine said, "You weren't paid for *either* of them, Mr. Cherry. That's the problem. You were given a photograph of the target. Did you look closely at it?"

"I—uh—oh. You mean . . ." Cherry grimaced. "It must've been

the other one. Sure, that was it. Birds swap clothes all the time . . . I'm sorry about that, Mr. P."

"You're an idiot," Palatine said. "You've caused more trouble than a regiment of coppers. I should . . . never mind what I should do to you. Just be certain that I never see you again."

"You really a Russian spy, then?"

Palatine stared at Cherry, unable to decide if the little bastard was trying to talk his way through fear or was really all brass and a yard wide. "I said I didn't want to see you anymore, Mr. Cherry. That begins immediately."

"Aw, I'll kill her for you," Cherry said, without any fear or desperation that Palatine could detect, certainly not whining. "I'm a man does a job right, 'n'e does it. . . . What's one bint more or less, eh?"

"Mr. Cherry," Palatine said coldly, "you no doubt think that you are safe, because I will not turn you over to the police. I assure you that I have no fear of the police, and that you have no such safety."

Cherry's insolent little smile finally wavered. "Sure, guv," he said, and zipped up his jacket and went out.

A moment later Palatine noticed that both his hands were balled tightly into fists.

Palatine opened the locked drawer in his desk. He took out the last copy of the NIGHTMOVE file, put it in his briefcase. Enough was enough. He would have to transmit a full report to Dzerzhinsky Street. They had approved the plan: They would have to figure out what to do now that it was out of control.

They would not be happy with him, of course. But there were limits to their power. It had become too awkward to kidnap people, too difficult to defame them (*o tempora! o mores!*). They could kill him; he knew only too well that they could always kill him. But if they did, what was that? He would be over, no more.

Allan Berenson had made the right preparation for the journey, Palatine thought. Berenson had never mentioned the remarkable WAGNER to him while he lived; Palatine wondered if Allan had known just what a protégé he had created. Something Allan had said came back to him, distorted and vague, something from the Italian Renaissance, about the object of birthing children being to have avengers.

As he turned out the lights, he had a hideous vision, of the darkness as a live thing drowning the room, but he blinked and it passed.

Palatine locked his office, arming the Chubb security system. The T Directorate had reluctantly authorized twenty thousand pounds to install it; it protected nothing—the machinery inside did that—but an office without the best modern alarms would attract attention. That was the whole of the game, ever since the Trojan war: looking right.

He walked down two flights to the building lobby, tipped his bowler to the building guard, and went out into Cheapside, one more City businessman on his way home.

He walked south to Cannon Street Station, turned and went a block under the railway viaduct, a massive bridge of black stone with crenellations along its top: Against the gray curdled sky, rain slicking its surface, it looked more Gothic than the real Gothic church just up Thames Street.

Palatine turned again, down a narrow lane that ran beside the viaduct to the river's edge. Halfway along was the entrance to his parking garage. He paused; there was a small pub at the very end of the lane, a good place for a pint when the traffic was bad. The traffic was. He looked at the sky. More rain was likely; better to get a start now. He walked into the garage, looking down automatically as he descended the ramp.

"Mind your 'ead, guv," Cherry said, and swung his arm, easily from the shoulder, the spanner in his hand striking Palatine's face just at the bridge of the nose. It hit with a crunch, driving splinters of bone into Palatine's brain. Palatine's whole body jerked and collapsed. Cherry let go of the spanner as Palatine fell: It was stuck in the dead man's skull. Palatine thudded full length at Cherry's feet.

Cherry checked his leathers for telltale bits, but there hadn't been much splash, except on his glove. He wiped it on Palatine's coat for now; he'd burn it later. He knelt and started to go through Palatine's clothes, taking his wallet and keys. There was nearly two hundred quid in the wallet; that'd pay for a new glove.

Cherry turned the key ring over in his hand. He recognized the car key at once, looked around and spotted the car: a Lotus, a raven-black Turbo Esprit. That was too good, he thought, just too good. Besides, he was doing this as a robbery precisely because robbery wasn't his usual scheme; do a robbery and you might as well do it right. Sort of severance pay.

He picked up Palatine's briefcase, opened the Lotus, tossed the case onto the leather seat. He took off his gloves and leather jacket, got in and drove out of the garage, snaking into the rush-hour traffic. He plodded along the river; it began raining, which was fine too, fewer people out looking, less attention paid in the rain.

He circled round the East End and turned onto M1 northbound. The Lotus was beautifully kept, drove like a dream in the rain, especially once Cherry was on the motorway and could give the turbocharger its head. In moments the car was doing 180 kph and feeling no pain, the water practically boiling off its sleek black body. Cherry supposed that he ought to have a Lotus, once his garage was going: something to impress the customers, not to mention the birds.

For a moment he thought about driving round to a particular girl's flat, just to take her for a spin. Spin-and-tumble, that is. But it was just a passing thought. Dreaming was one thing, stupid stunts quite another.

He turned off the motorway at Watford, got supper from a chip shop and made a phone call, munching the fried cod in the booth. "Get me the Duke. Tell 'im it's Cherry. Didn't ask you for help, did I, mate? Just tell the Duke. . . . Duke? Yeah. Got something I think'll interest you. . . . Ri-ight, mate. Tonight, I thought. Hour and a half or so. . . . Fair enough."

Cherry walked around until he found a big steel trash container. He chucked Palatine's briefcase in, then went back to the car and drove on to Birmingham. It only took an hour with the Turbo whistling. He pulled into a garage west of the city center.

The Duke came out of the office, wearing oily coveralls held together by racing patches. Duke was no desk jockey when it came to his business. "Oh, now," he said, as Cherry got out of the Lotus, "you said you 'ad somethin' *in*-ter-esting."

"And this isn't?"

"My pal Cherry calls, says 'a's got an interestin' car, I figure, mus' be a four-liter Bentley at least, maybe 'itler's Mercedes. But no, 'a brings me this ploughman's lunch."

Cherry grinned. "The ploughmen are puttin' out thirty thousand for these lunches."

"Oh, that's just it, innit. Anyone can get one of these for thirty thousand. Where's the fun in 'at?" Duke went to the Lotus, examined the interior, the finish. "But I'll tell you, you're my friend, an' despite that you want to be my competitor . . . fifteen hundred."

"I'd thought closer to five thousand."

"Had you."

"You'll get twenty."

"I'll get ten, on the best of days, if I can sell her whole. If she goes for parts. . . ." The Duke shook his head.

"Three thousand."

"Twenty-five hundred."

"Sold."

"All right, come on back." They went into the office, which was hung with photographs, old racing numbers, a few trophies. The Duke took out a bottle of Jameson's whiskey and two grimy glasses. "Help yourself, won't be a moment," he said, and went out. Cherry poured a shot, drank it, poured another and sipped. From somewhere in the shop, Cherry heard metal scrape. A moment later, Duke came back with the money, several packets of well-used fives and tens. Cherry riffled them for politeness's sake.

"It's a pretty car," Duke said, now that it cost nothing to say it. "She 'andle nice?"

"Smooth enough," Cherry said, and poured a whiskey for the Duke. "You really only get ten for her?"

"When you're ready to go into the business, come see me. We'll have some things to discuss." He drank. "Anything *particular* I ought to know about 'er?"

"The owner has no further interest."

"An' the owner's friends?"

"The owner has no friends."

"Ah, now. No man should be without friends."

Cherry retrieved his jacket, slipped the money into pockets in its lining. "I should be getting back. Call me a cab?"

Duke took a key from a peg on the office wall. "Here. The blue

Cortina out back. Park it in the station lot, key under the seat, we'll get it tomorrow."

"Thanks, Duke."

"Just be sure you lock it. So many thieves about, you know."

■ ■ ■

Gareth Rhys-Gordon got the call from Section C a little after eight P.M. telling him who was dead and what to do about it. He shoved the tinfoil tray with his half-eaten dinner into the refrigerator, looked out the window at the rain, still coming down hard and cold. He shrugged into a dingy tan mackintosh and cap. The night welcomed him as one of its own. He stood in a half-full car on the tube (where all was warm and bright, as the old posters had it), looking around at the other passengers, all wet and weary, wondering who among them had killed whom today, or wanted to. It was all the same thing, he'd been told in Sunday school. That had been years ago. When he went to Sunday school. Before he had a job.

Rhys-Gordon got off at Cannon Street Station, ducked under the railway bridge, and went into the garage, shaking off the rain. A camera flash was firing up ahead. He saw McAdam of the Murder Squad, and Cohan from Special Branch; then he came round a pillar and saw the mess on the floor that had been Their Man in London.

"Evening, Gareth," Cohan said. "Figure this one, will you?"

"You tell me."

Cohan said, "He was a City businessman. Import, export. All strictly legal, so far as we know, but some of his friends were on some of your lists." Cohan added carefully, "Anything you'd care to share?"

"No," Rhys-Gordon said. "Any chance it was a straight robbery?"

"A chance," McAdam said. He was standing above the body, swinging his arm experimentally, trying to reconstruct where the killer had been standing. "I'd bet against it, though. Too professional. One blow, from the front no less, through the pockets and away he goes."

Rhys-Gordon said, "Do you think it was someone he knew?"

"Because of the front blow? Not necessarily. It would have been from the side, like this—" McAdam demonstrated on Cohan, swinging his empty hand hard enough to make the Special Branch man flinch. "Victim probably never saw a thing." He pointed at the body. "Want to look him over?"

"No. You'll tell me if anything clever turns up on autopsy, of course."

"Of course," McAdam said, and turned to the ambulance crew. "Let's move him."

As the body was removed, the Special Branch man said, "You've got a couple of people dead, haven't you? In a garage?"

"You shouldn't read the Murdoch papers, Cohan. Give you ideas."

"So why is it you're here for this, eh?"

"I was ordered, just like you."

"Ah, but I'm the police and you're the government."

"I'm not having it, Cohan," Rhys-Gordon said, and Cohan shut up. The SB man was right, as far as it went: Rhys-Gordon had been sent here on the chance that something connected this death with Bell's and Doheny's. But there didn't seem to be any link. Other than garages, of course.

"All right," Rhys-Gordon said. "Why was he in this garage?"

"He parked his car here," Cohan said.

"Which one?"

"Isn't here. Looks like chappy took it, or someone with him. Attendant saw it go out, but not who was driving. Space was paid for by the month, so he just waved it past."

"Remind me not to leave my car here," Rhys-Gordon said. "Did he recall what make?"

"Lotus Turbo, raven black."

"That should be a bit easier to find than your standard white Cortina."

"Should be indeed," Cohan said. "Stupid of him to take it."

Rhys-Gordon was thinking about two other bodies in another garage. Pretty Suze Bell and Mick Doheny. In another year or so they'd have either broken up or gotten married, and either way Rhys-Gordon could have stopped snooping after their sex life. Another few months, but some bastard had killed them, and now he had to dig for all the dirt, with the computer's help and guidance. The computer was dull and picayune and plodding. It had a cop's best instincts. "If the lags weren't stupid we wouldn't stand a chance," he said. "Let's go ask after a car."

■ ■ ■

Sladen looked around the ruinously empty office of his predecessor. If there was any position on earth more precarious than being a new KGB chief *rezident* in a city such as London, it was being pushed into that position in the vacuum left by a man like Palatine.

Palatine had been one of those cursed British junior aristocrats, far more interested in the creation of interesting schemes for the triumph of socialism than in the article itself. Sladen was certain that England could have been made into something much like a workers' paradise a generation ago, if not for its utopians.

Palatine had been raised in the country, public school and Oxbridge. Sladen had grown up at Tyuratam, child of a rocket scientist and a propellant chemist. Well, actually, of the chemist and a truck driver. KGB cared very little and Sladen cared not at all.

Palatine had become caught between his upbringing and his work, Sladen thought. Sladen knew what he was: a peasant bastard with the ability to keep other men in line without excessive violence. He had no illusions that this made him better than his fellows, only somewhat more useful to the system, as his aptitude for English was useful, as his skill with interrogation hardware was useful. In this Sladen was the truest of socialists.

What had Palatine's skills been? Obviously, to hold too many things in his mind. Records were missing all over the place. Sladen had issued apparently calm requests to Dzerzhinsky Street for "verification copies" of Palatine's action files. KGB Headquarters had sent apparently polite requests for elaboration on why the copies were needed.

There was no doubt in his mind that Palatine had been very foolish, that he was better dead. The task at hand was to identify the damage, and limit it.

Glazdunov came in. He was a legal, an Amtorg economist with a nighttime allegiance to KGB Planning Directorate. Glazdunov was only just loyal enough to be trusted with a foreign posting, but he seemed to do his work well. And he had access to files, notes, a little of what had been in Palatine's crumpled skull.

"Well?" Sladen said.

Glazdunov opened a folder, spread its contents on Sladen's desk. There were painfully few papers there. "This is what we have been able to reconstruct of the Line ZN operation, plan NIGHTMOVE. In addition to the line head, Dr. Berenson, there are four agents. We know that Palatine contacted one, coded WAGNER. WAGNER is, we believe, a woman."

"You believe?"

"WAGNER could have been working through an intermediary. Or possibly be a transvestite. These things happen."

Sladen nodded impatiently. "Yes. Go on."

"WAGNER was issued with money and a concealable weapon—the old cigarette-case pistol, 1950s vintage, easily deniable. This all indicates that Palatine was continuing the NIGHTMOVE operation until WAGNER obtained the COPE LIGHT communications unit; this was done with the consultation and approval of S Directorate. Presumably the COPE LIGHT unit was obtained, because Palatine then paid one of the usual free-lance assassins, a man called Cherry, and dispatched a removal team."

"But Cherry killed the wrong woman?"

"It would appear so. The removal team found nothing, and the person at that address has dropped out of sight."

Sladen spat on the carpet. Clever stupid Palatine. "And therefore we have tipped our hand, for absolutely no return."

"Perhaps not completely without return," Glazdunov said, almost twitching with excitement. Sladen wondered idly if the man was homosexual. It was a common disorder with the planning types. They were all highly strung. Some of the best were half-mad.

"Go ahead," Sladen said.

"We have every reason to assume that WAGNER is continuing with NIGHTMOVE after the principal's death, without us. And assuming *that*—"

"We may yet collect the prize," Sladen said, interested again.

"Yes. Yes. But it is important that WAGNER not be interfered with—by the British services or any independent party."

Sladen nodded. "We have a file on this Cherry?"

"Yes."

"Bring it to me."

Glazdunov went out. His usefulness was limited, Sladen thought. A man of action would have already procured Cherry's file.

Sladen unlocked the vault drawer in his desk, took out a small leather datebook. He picked up the telephone and made a call.

■ ■ ■

Cohan parked the car in front of the Birmingham garage. The sky was heavily overcast, and a few drops of rain had already splotched the windscreen. Rhys-Gordon turned up his collar and got out of the car.

They went inside. A bell jangled above the door. There was a Jaguar parked on the oily floor. No one was in sight. Rhys-Gordon looked around at the racing stuff on the walls, nodded slightly. Cohan peeked into the Jag's windows, wrote down its license number.

A man in coveralls came in from the back. "Afternoon, gents."

"George Duquesne?"

"Nobody much calls me 'George.'"

Cohan flipped out his identification. "Special Branch, Mr. Duquesne. And this man's from the government. We'd like to ask you a few things."

"Well, you can call me George, then."

"I saw you at Brands Hatch a few times," Rhys-Gordon said. "You were pretty good."

"Yeah, I guess I was. Nobody stays good at it forever, though. Have to find honest work. What's this about, then?"

"We're looking for a Lotus Turbo saloon. Black. Leather seats, telephone, all mod. cons."

"Ah. Well, you can see I'm not a dealership—"

The Special Branch man said, "We've got a pretty fair idea of just what you are, Mr. Duquesne."

The Duke nodded, turned to Rhys-Gordon. "He's the bad copper, eh. That'd make you the good copper."

Rhys-Gordon smiled. "We want the car, but more we want any papers that might have been in it, and I don't mean the title. Almost as much we want the fella that had it for sale. Now I'd like to tell you it'd be in your interest to help us out, but what I have to say is that *not* helping us would not be in your interest at all. What we lose on the swings we make up on the roundabouts, isn't that right, Duke?"

"So you thought I was good at Brands."

"Stirling Moss was better. That's why he always beat you."

"An honest copper," the Duke said. "Pardon me, gents, but I just felt Hell freezin' over . . . come into the office and we'll talk a bit."

■ ■ ■

Cherry sat in his flat, flipping through a copy of *Fast Lane*. It was the same old stuff, Italian cars, Japanese cars, now even Yugoslavian cars, for Christ's sake. He threw the magazine on the floor and sat back, thinking about what he would do to replace the income from Mr. Palatine. Maybe raise the rate with the East End boys. That was tricky, might even be dangerous; but then again, they liked to be big spenders, liked everyone to know that their suits cost a thousand quid. Maybe he could get a reputation as a premium man, ten thousand a hit.

The phone rang. Cherry picked it up. "Yeah."

The voice on the other end was stiff, pretend-Oxbridge. "Mr. Cherry, I represent a firm you have done business with in the past."

"Get to it," Cherry said.

"Fifteen thousand pounds," the voice said, "but time is very short. The object would have to be completed tonight."

"If it's that important, it's worth twenty thousand."

"Yes. It is. Do you accept?"

Cherry couldn't help grinning. Doing for Mr. P had proven to be a sharp career move. "I'm your man."

■ ■ ■

"Right," Cohan said to the car radio. He turned to Rhys-Gordon, who was standing beside the car, smoking. "We've got the order. We can go in now."

"You've checked the address," Rhys-Gordon said.

"Yes, we're *quite* sure this is Mr. Cherry's flat."

Rhys-Gordon nodded and took a walkie-talkie from the car seat. He was tired. Rhys-Gordon found fifteen minutes with Cohan tiresome, and they'd just done the drive to Birmingham and back, all with just each other's company. He pressed the Talk key. "Rhys-Gordon to Support. We're about to flush the bird. You all on station?"

"Team One, roger."

"Team Two, on station."

"Team Three, roger."

"Let's go, then," Rhys-Gordon said, stuffing the radio into his raincoat pocket. He and Cohan moved to the door of the flat. Rhys-Gordon drew his pistol, held it muzzle-upward, and put his hand on the door handle just as it was opened from inside.

Cherry looked at him, at his gun. He punched Rhys-Gordon in the chest, hard. Rhys-Gordon staggered back, colliding with Cohan. Cherry shoved past them both and sprinted for the street, for the parked motorcycle.

Rhys-Gordon dropped into a firing crouch and shot twice. The front tire of the cycle exploded. Cherry looked back and snapped off a wild shot of his own, then put his head down and ran like hell.

Rhys-Gordon pulled out the radio. "All support teams, subject is fleeing on foot, southward. He is armed, I say again, armed." They followed, not quite running, a block south to Leicester Square, which was full of cinemagoers and tourists and half a million panhandlers and drunks. Rhys-Gordon quickly got his gun out of sight; he breathed hard, making his sternum ache, and looked at all the people and felt a proper bloody fool.

"We've tagged him," one of the teams said over the radio. "Headed for Piccadilly Circus."

Rhys-Gordon said, "For God's sake, keep him out of the tube station."

"We'll—" There was a sound of traffic, a squeal of brakes and tires. "Too late. Sorry."

Rhys-Gordon swore without any heat and started walking fast, west on Coventry Street toward the neon glow of Piccadilly. "All right, lads," he said into his radio, "down we go, all units." He passed a bank, a bum, a Burger King, and the tube stairs beckoned. Down he went.

The station was circular, a ring of corridor with ticket windows and cigarette kiosks, a double whirl of people walking round it in both directions. They spun off to the street through half a dozen exits; they funneled through the automatic gates and down the escalators at the center to the Bakerloo and Piccadilly tube lines. Ways out enough, Rhys-Gordon thought. If the bugger got really clever, the Piccadilly line would take him direct to Heathrow Airport.

"Hey!" he heard Cohan say, and looked up in time to see Cherry shove through an entry gate, and they were in business again. Cohan had his Special Branch card out, held up like a flag, and was using it to bull his way past a ticket-taker's booth, against the flow of passengers. Rhys-Gordon reached into his own coat for ID, and somebody who'd seen too many gangster movies screamed, and people fell away from him. Rhys-Gordon just used the space to get by, hoped they could get by with no more shooting.

Then Cherry stopped at the head of the Piccadilly line escalator, stuck a hand in his jacket and came out with a pistol, pointed at Cohan's middle from no more than ten steps away. Cohan tried to stop short, stumbled.

A Metropolitan copper nobody had noticed before stepped out and grabbed Cherry's gun hand, twisted his arm down hard onto the escalator railing. Cherry grunted, let go the gun, and then swung his left hand hard at the side of the policeman's head. The copper fell. Cherry rolled free, pulled himself onto the handrail and began sliding down it.

Cohan bent to check on the policeman. Rhys-Gordon dodged around him and started down the escalator. People were sprawled on the steps below him, knocked aside by Cherry. He hopped onto the railing and slid the rest of the way, vaulting off into the middle of a knot of gaping bystanders. Rhys-Gordon shouted, "Stop, Police," though he could no longer see the man he wanted, and started running. People either flattened against the walls or stood dead still; he dodged them, he ran on.

At the bottom of the moving stairs was a short, high-ceilinged room, opening onto the train platforms. There were a dozen-plus people coming from and going to their trains, none of them Cherry. There was a busker with a mouth organ on a wire brace, hastily stuffing his guitar back into its case. "Police," Rhys-Gordon said, and the man dropped the guitar, spilling coins. "Which way did he go?"

The busker pointed to a westbound arch. West went to Heathrow. "Thanks," Rhys-Gordon said. As he turned, he could see some of the flying units, and more bobbies, finally getting here. "This way," he shouted at them, and ducked through the short tunnel.

He spotted Cherry at once, running along the crowded platform, nearly to its far end. He crouched on the edge of the platform, jumped the few feet down to the tracks. People turned to look, pointed. Rhys-Gordon pushed them aside. He felt a faint draft in his face, looked up at the electric announcement board. Train in one minute.

There was a flicker of light in the tunnel, silhouetting Cherry crossing the tracks. Headlights appeared, white dragon eyes in the darkness. Cherry flattened himself against the far wall.

Then he jumped, away from the wall, into the path of the train. He took a staggering step toward the platform, fell against it, its edge against his chest, his arms reaching across the paving, as if he were trying to pull himself out. All around him on the platform, people backed away.

The train struck Cherry with a hollow bang of metal and a crunch of bones. Brakes screamed. Passengers stared. Cherry was dragged for twenty yards, caught between the train and the platform edge, his hands scraping bloody streaks down the floor as passengers leaped and stumbled clear, some fleeing entirely. The train slowed, stopped halfway into the station, and its sudden silence was like the letting out of a sigh.

"Is he dead?" someone was asking, a child or a hysterical adult, and Rhys-Gordon went to look. Cherry was nearly gone below the waist, twisted off like a bottlecap. All Rhys-Gordon wanted was two minutes from the man, a few words, one name, and then he could go to any Hell that would have him. Rhys-Gordon knelt, thought he saw a glimmer of movement—but no, Mr. Cherry wouldn't be talking.

"What in the name of sweet bleeding Jesus did he jump for?" Cohan said. "He was clean away."

"God knows—" Rhys-Gordon started to say, and then he saw the reason. "Wait. He didn't jump. Look." He pushed at Cherry's shoulder, pointed at one of the messy rips in the leather jacket.

"Oh," Cohan said. The Special Branch man had seen enough bullet wounds to recognize one more.

"We had a little help tonight," Rhys-Gordon said. "Now the question is, from inside or outside?" He drew his pistol. "Mine's been fired exactly twice. You'll check your lads', of course."

"'Course. Don't think we'll find anything, though."

"Naturally we won't." He turned, started to walk off the platform.

"Where are you going?" Cohan said.

"Won't be a moment. Just going to give a few bob to a busker."

■ ■ ■

Hansard took Maxwell to a small Italian restaurant in a Bloomsbury alley, a place loud enough that his enthusiasm would not turn the other diners' heads.

And he was enthusiastic. He led Ellen to a table. He pulled out his notes. "The Players' Company," he said. "They're the Scholars of Night, what else?"

Sir Walter Raleigh hosted a conversational circle of the best minds in England, who gathered late o'nights to push back the limits of knowledge. If the group called itself by any particular name, it has not survived; but Shakespeare called them the Scholars of Night, as fair a title as any. They included Hariot the astronomer-mathematician (and Earl of Northumberland), Doctor Dee the natural philosopher—yes, and sorcerer too, but at the time there was barely a hair's difference—Raleigh himself, poet and explorer and patron. They questioned science, they questioned philosophy, they questioned faith at the literal risk of their lives.

Wonderful, romantic Elizabethan England, Hansard thought with a sudden rising of bile in his throat. Lace ruffs and courtly manners, and the death penalty for homosexuality, for atheism, for anything the state decided was sedition. The same majesty of law longed for by certain prominent hatemongers in his own country and time.

Thinking of the Scholars made him think of Allan, of course, alive in his circle of working minds, and Hansard was suddenly unable to stomach the present any longer. He looked at Ellen—she was eager, the student who wanted to learn, the fellow scholar anxious to join the adventure—anchored his eyes on hers for warmth and light, and pushed off into the dark still waters of the past.

■ ■ ■

Raleigh had provided a roast bird for his guests, knowing that the life of the mind sickens when the belly is empty. Now the platter was cleared away, the good wine and the tobacco set out, and the doors locked against intrusions.

The new member of the group, who gave his name as Adam Dover, looked a bit surprised as the key was turned in the lock. "You do not trust your servants, Sir Walter?"

"They are people of discretion and trust, but not scholarship or understanding," Raleigh said, in an ordinary tone, no secrecy in it. "Our discussions are not their discussions."

"Now, if those qualities were only confined to servants . . ." another man said, and several of those present laughed.

"You come to us sudden, and a little curiously, Master Dover," Hariot said. "What's your heritage, what are your interests?"

"As Sir Walter saw from my letters," Dover said, "I was a student at Paris for some time. My parents having died, I returned to England to claim what little inheritance they left me. As for my interests, I like to think them broad . . . I am fascinated by the measurements of things."

"Small enough to span about comfortably, near enough to find in a bed in the dark," someone said, and the group laughed; Dover looked surprised, then joined in. "I had thought you . . . perhaps more serious than this," he said.

"Serious enough," Hariot said, "but still men for a'that. It distincts us from the Greeks. Tell me, Master Dover, when you were in Paris, did you hear of this new notion, that by laying lines upon an orrery, dividing its motions, that the physical seat of Heaven might be located?"

Dover hesitated. "Is this a test?"

"It's a question," Hariot said.

"No, I had not been introduced to that idea."

Doctor John Dee, a plumpish, white-bearded man who had been sitting quietly at the end of the room, said, "It is unlikely to succeed in its present form."

Dover said, "Surely Heaven is not so easily located."

"Indeed," Doctor Dee said. "The proponents of this astrometry adhere to the doctrine of the crystalline firmaments, which distorts their lines."

"You say that as though it were a mere matter of corrections."

"I suspect that it is," Dee said.

"And God, therefore, will allow himself to be discovered?"

"The discovery of God," Christopher Marlowe said, lighting his white clay pipe, "is a thing much taken for granted."

"It is one thing to doubt the nature of sunlight, or matter," Dover said—though he did not say it nervously—"and another to doubt the nature of God."

"God is vast," Raleigh said. "Can he not bear a little doubt? Look hard, friend, at any group of men you consider righteous. Some of them will have stolen, some killed, most all of them blasphemed and coveted, and a staggering fraction lain with other men's wives—yet they are forgiven by Christ's blood; yet a man who only asks after the true nature of God is liable to special damnation? Damnation, man, that's unjust! And I will not worship an unjust God."

"I begin to see your line of argument," Dover said quietly. "Yet God is God—"

"As the Mohammedans say," someone said, sloshing oporto.

"—and surely one does not make the God one wants, will-He, nill-He."

"Nicely phrased," Raleigh said approvingly.

"Yet that is what we do," Christopher Marlowe said. Marlowe sat in a corner, puffing on a pipe, his light eyes fixed on the new Scholar of Night, the one called Adam Dover. "We make God in our image, and set him high on a stage, with ingenious machineries to move the players and the sceneries of the world. But who is the playwright, after all, Master Dover?"

"You are a playwright," Dover said. "Do you put yourself with God then? Or above God?"

"Gently, Kit," Raleigh said.

Malowe waved his pipe. "It is like being a god," he said. "You move your hand, and there are storms and catastrophes, love and madness and murder; didn't I compass all the conquests of Tamburlaine with my pen and a stage? We here"—he waved the stem of his pipe around the room, like a wand—"we are in rehearsal to play at being gods. And why not? Why not our hands, if God will not show his?"

Adam Dover said, "You dare much, sir."

Raleigh said calmly, "That is what men do, sir. They walk about the earth and dare it."

Maxwell looked bemused. Hansard found the look delightful. Not to mention erotic. Ellen said, "Crystalline spheres?"

"'But is there not *coelum igneum et cristallinum?*'"

"From *Faustus*," Ellen said, and laughed. "Faust quizzing Mephistopheles about the structure of the cosmos."

"And Marlowe showing off a fair knowledge of the current astronomical theory. But as he has Faust say, 'These slender trifles Wagner can decide.'"

Maxwell said, "If the Players' Company is supposed to be the Scholars of Night, it's certainly an unflattering view of them."

"Black-humored, at least. But I don't think it's necessarily meant to be them particularly—just a group of thinkers, taking off from Marlowe's experience of the Scholars. Polydorus isn't Raleigh by any reasonable measure. Doctor Argelian could be Dr. Dee, but that's like saying that Faustus could be Dee. . . ."

Ellen was looking past him, into space. Hansard almost turned to follow her stare, then said quietly, "What is it?"

"Hmm? Oh—I was just thinking of an engraving I saw once. Dee raising a ghost, inside a protective circle, with the help of his man—what was his name?"

"Kelley. I remember the drawing. It was even a woman's ghost, now that you mention it."

"So they did do that sort of thing."

"I'd take anything Dee was supposed to have done with Kelley with the largest available grain of salt. Kelley seems to have been a professional swindler who conned Dee six ways from Sunday. He wore a cap all the time, because his ears had been cut off for some offense or another."

"Some things don't change much."

"Now, look at this." He flipped through the *Assassin* text, to the confrontation of Argelian with Polydorus just after the ghost-raising scene.

ARGELIAN. Their father is the father of all lies,
    Their guises legion . . . Do you know,
    How men in deserts, near to death of thirst,
    May see a lake of water on the sand,
    And, taken with th'illusion, plunge them in,
    And quench their tongues with burning
    draughts of earth?

Just so the shapes of devils in the eye.
POLYDORUS. Fah! All these sights are merest sophistry.
Go swim your eyes upon iniquity,
And make your tears to puddle on the stone.

"Dee had a 'shew stone.' I don't remember now what it was supposed to have been made of, rock crystal, I think."

"The skill of specular stone," Maxwell said.

"That must be a reference, but I . . ."

"John Donne. I should have thought you'd know that."

Hansard scratched his head. "Well, gosh, I'm sorry," he said lightly, "there are only so many hours in a day, and—"

"And?"

"'And we will all the pleasures prove,'" he said, and she laughed and let it pass, as he hoped she would. He had been about to say that no one had ever given him something of Donne's to authenticate. But that brought Raphael into things, brought the whole night world in. There was no room for Raphael at this table.

They left the restaurant. "I can get a bus a couple of blocks from here," Maxwell said. "Would you walk me, Nicholas?"

"I'd be delighted," he said, which was true enough, though the delight perched on a high heap of disappointment.

They reached the bus stop, stood there in silence for a minute, for two. Then Maxwell said, "Nicholas . . ."

"Yes?"

"You *are* a gentleman. I don't think I would have believed it." And she wrapped her arms around him and kissed him squarely on the lips. She pushed him away, said, "Here's my ride. Sleep well, Nicholas," and before he could quite do anything the big red London Transport bus swept her away from him.

But as he went back to his hotel, there was warmth within him, and a sweetness in his mouth that lingered.

WAGNER looked into the bottom of her teacup, seeing truth in the clutter of leaves, finally seeing the joke. ROCK STAR. Of course.

The wizard character in *Assassin* did not scry by stone or crystal;

he used cards and a fire. It didn't matter. The connection was there. WAGNER heard Allan's laughter as she dialed the coded number.

Then she stopped, put the receiver down. Allan was still having his joke. There was another connection she was supposed to make. She was certain of it.

She looked through the short dossier. *Works with a silent partner,* it said. Of course.

"H'lo?" said the sleepy voice on the other end of the telephone line.

"Kelley?" WAGNER said.

"Oh. Yeah. *Yes.*"

"Listen carefully. Thursday morning, eleven A.M. . . ."

■ ■ ■

Yes, Celia Everidge thought as she put down the phone, *yes yes I said yes,* and she laughed silently to herself.

A few weeks back, Everidge had read Allan Berenson's obituary in *The Economist.* Heart attack, the magazine said. She supposed it was possible; he hadn't been young.

She closed the shop early that day—she thought about putting a Death In Family sign up, but someone might have asked after it— and went home, to a cottage on the edge of town. She went around to the back, where the silver caravan was parked. It was all done, done and perfect and ready.

Berenson had given her instructions in case he could not finish the project himself: the code words, the telephone call. She wondered how long she might have to wait.

Everidge didn't care. She would wait ten years if she had to.

She went into the house, upstairs to her radio shack, fired up the transmitter. She looked at the clock, sat down at the key, and began sending CQ to anyone who was listening.

"Will you build this?" the man calling himself Bascomb had asked her, sitting in Everidge's radio-repair shop with the door locked and the shades down and the diagrams laid out on the table between the teacups. "You *must* understand what's involved. Nothing that you yourself do, or build, will be illegal, but something desperately illegal will be done with it; and if everything falls apart and you're caught, there won't be any distinctions drawn, of that you may be very sure."

"Then why tell me that?" Everidge said. "Sounds like we're all better off with me not knowing."

"Two reasons," Bascomb said. "First, because I don't want you having doubts later. There *are* things you'll never know about the project, for safety's sake; the names of the other people involved, for instance. But I'm going to be as honest about what I'm *not* telling you as what I am. Second reason, I don't like lying to people, or using them under false pretenses. Either you're in this consciously, knowing that you want to be part of it, or you're not in."

"What's the third reason?"

He looked her squarely in the eyes, as few men who wanted anything professional from Everidge ever had. "I don't like ignorance. I hold there is no sin but ignorance."

"I'll do it," she said.

"Knowing—"

"I said, yes."

"Yes," the man said, and immediately told her that his real name was Allan Berenson, and gave her five thousand pounds in cash to begin construction.

Everidge met Bascomb at a weekend trading meet for radio hams. There was a case of partly built satellite decoders in the auction; really just parts, but she could finish them in a week or two of soldering and scrounging, and sell them for at least twenty percent under commercial retail . . . especially since nobody was likely to bid against her.

But somebody did, a heavyset, graying American in an expensive dark suit. He seemed absolutely determined to top any bid she made, so she ran him up to about twice what the stuff was worth and left him there.

Later in the day, the American introduced himself as Robert T. Bascomb. "You know what these things are for?" he said.

"Sure I do," Everidge said. "I also know what they're worth."

"Then would you mind accepting them as a gift?"

"What?"

Bascomb shrugged. "Not a gift. I want to buy a little of your time."

Everidge dropped her hand on top of the crate of parts. "Sold. Shall we put it in my van?"

They moved the box into the back of Everidge's battered vehicle, which had CELTRON—Electronics Repairs Sales Service handpainted on the side. Bascomb bought two foam cups of tea from a tent vendor, and they sat down in the front of the van.

"Your time," Everidge said. "Start talking."

"I understand you used to work for Vectarray."

She looked hard at him, at his suit, at his black bag. "I did. So what does that make you? Government? Defense Department?"

"Independent contractor," Bascomb said, and opened his briefcase. "I have a project in mind that you're particularly qualified for."

He had some magazines: *Jane's Military Review, Aviation Week, Military Technology.* He had some of Vectarray UK's published papers, with her name circled. Everything referred to the Command Persistence system.

"I don't know anything about COPE," she said, supposing that he was a spy, or else a spy-catcher setting his snare. "I left before anything got out of the theoretical stage."

"You left before there were any working prototypes," Bascomb said, "but you worked on the first breadboards. And as for knowing nothing . . . if I read these correctly, you had quite a bit to do with the design."

"You work for Vectarray, right? I'm not going back. Sorry."

"I don't work for anyone," Bascomb said patiently. "Let me tell you what I *do* want, and why. Then I'll give you some time to think about it."

He told her what he wanted built. That was interesting.

Then he told her what he wanted it for. That was fascinating.

For a while as he talked, Everidge wondered when the trap would spring, the Special Branch or CIA or whoever came slithering from the woodwork. But then she saw in his eyes, in his voice, the thing that she had seen, clear as the light of uncontrolled fusion.

■ ■ ■

Everidge had never been political. CND member once, sure, wasn't everybody? But that had all been a lot of well-intentioned marching and singing, a mutual admiration society dedicated to the proposition that nuclear bombs were a bad idea. Well, hell, her University roommate had married a Captain of Royal Artillery, and *he* thought they were a bad idea: He'd actually admitted (drunk, at their house one Christmas Eve) that he knew they were the death of his wife and his kid and himself, knew they were the death of everything, good, bad, and indifferent. But it had been decided on levels he could not reach that the things were important to the National Purpose. . . .

Everidge watched the Captain, leaning against his mantel, his voice wound half an octave too high, sipping brandy eggnog to keep from snapping, trying to reconcile faith and loyalty with megaton yields. Celia wanted to say something helpful, something to ease his pain and confusion, but there wasn't anything to say, because there was no reconciliation. There was no way to reconcile the end of the world to anything.

At the age of eighteen Celia Everidge went to the University of Edinburgh, on a government scholarship meant to further the role of women in the sciences. She took with her a hundred-watt ham radio rig, two suitcases of clothing, a box of personal goods. She said good-bye to her family with real meaning. She would never again enter her parents' house.

Everidge did well at University, making some good friends (though she was terrible about keeping in touch), making some contacts. She was graduated with a Master's in Electrical Engineering, with honors. It was a good year to go into the market: The "Silicon Glen" near Edinburgh was just establishing itself, and there were jobs and money and optimistic feelings. She hired on with Vectarray, an American electronics firm whose new British branch wanted to prove that it was just as hot and brilliant as anything in the USA or (especially) Japan.

Vectarray UK started out with a commitment to consumer goods, but as the jobs, money, and optimism started to get scarce, they followed the hints from the American parent to Defence work. It did pay well. In fact, it paid ludicrously well, even for ludicrous ideas.

Then Everidge, along with one of the communications people and a software writer, brainstormed something called Project Tarncap, and they found the pot of gold at the end of the satellite downlink. NATO wanted the Tarncap system so badly, it was determined to force it into existence by sheer force of spending. More importantly, they were quite willing to take the project elsewhere if Vectarray UK couldn't deliver.

There were breadboards. There were computer simulations. There were a lot of progress papers. There was a great deal of pressure for a live test. Everidge pointed out, in the presence of a NATO liaison officer, that they were perhaps two years away from a live test.

Four days later Lester Borden, who was not even the head of Security but just a bloke who did the dirty work, informed Employee Everidge, C. that she had failed a special vetting related to Project Tarncap, and was no longer cleared to work on said project. She could accept a transfer to Consumer Products Research, or she could quit.

She quit. Her severance pay was surprisingly generous, enough to set her up in Lincolnshire with an electronics shop of her own.

Not long afterward, in 1982, she realized why they had been so generous. They had gone ahead with the live test. It had failed, as she had told them it would.

In '83 Celia's mother died of a stroke. Celia went to the funeral; no one spoke to her, and she did not press the issue. A few weeks later her father showed up at the shop. He had a brown paper parcel under his arm. He had partly shaved, and he smelled of whiskey.

"Well?" Celia said. It had been many years. Many things had happened. But not nearly enough years or things.

"I . . . wan'ed you t'have this," Mr. Everidge said, and put the package down on the counter with a loud clunk. "'Cause of the times, you see. You might need it, you see." He looked around the shop, the shelves full of refurbished televisions and radios, the satellite dish hung from the ceiling. "You're doing well here, Celia?"

"I'm doing all right. I can send you a few quid, if that's—"

"I don't want any money," Mr. Everidge said, and stood up nearly straight. "I don't *need* any money. I jus' . . . want you to do well, that's all, daughter. I want you to be safe."

She thought it was the worst thing in the world he could have said to her, but she didn't say anything. She didn't love him. She hated him. But hate was one thing, and cruelty was another.

"Good-bye, Celia," Mr. Everidge said, and as he walked, quite upright, out of the shop, she realized that he meant it seriously.

When he had gone, she opened the package. It was his World War Two service pistol, a Colt .45, loaded, illegal as sin. She looked after him, walking down the path to the coach stop, her lips moving, trying to say something but not succeeding. Charles had been his brother, she thought. Why had it taken her so long to remember that? She walked deliberately to the door, opened it, making the electric-eye signal chime. But Mr. Everidge had turned the corner. He was gone.

She never saw him again. He died less than a year afterward. She was not invited to the funeral. Instead she spent the night at her code key, DXing to islands, and got QSL confirmations from Bali and Tierra del Fuego.

When Celia Everidge was fifteen she was given an inappropriate Christmas present. It came from her Uncle Charles, a construction engineer. Charles Everidge was one of those magical uncles, like Old Drosselmeyer in *The Nutcracker,* whose gifts have a life of their own: things that a kid would never even know she wanted until the paper was off and the box open, and the model trains or the chemistry lab or the conjuring set revealed, and something awoke in the recipient's mind.

Charles gave Celia a Build Them Yourself Electronics Kit, with parts for a crystal radio and a solar-cell motor and a Morse-code practice key, along with Eleven Other Exciting Projects. On Christmas afternoon, while everyone else was playing with toys or arguing about whether American football was any damn use or just sleeping off dinner, Charles Everidge was teaching his niece how to use a soldering iron.

Charles insisted that they build the wireless code key first. Celia obeyed, but she couldn't see the value of it: It wasn't a real wireless set, it just went beep when you pushed the key down.

When it was finished, Charles took hold of the knob—with his whole hand, not just his index finger—and fired off a burst of signals. "Do you know what that was?"

"Of course not."

"That was MERRY CHRISTMAS YL CELIA OM CHARLES 73."

"And what does that mean?"

"YL is Young Lady. That's you. OM is Old Man. That's me. 73 means all best wishes."

Then Uncle Charles explained to her about amateur radio licenses, about the Morse-code test that one had to pass. "Now listen carefully, because I'm going to make you a promise. If you pass your exams, and get your ham license by next Christmas . . . I'll see you get a rig of your own."

From that hour—it was seven o'clock—Celia Everidge was obsessed by wireless transmission. She began reading the ham radio magazines, sent away for the license-exam textbooks. She learned the arcana of the upper frequencies, the iconography of the Armstrong oscillator, the unvarnished truth about superheterodyning.

The first bad moment came when Celia's mother impounded the manuals. The only reason given was that they were cluttering up the house, which given the dense litter of racing forms and film-star magazines was utterly beyond comprehension. Celia tried to make sense of it: Her school marks were fine, her housework got done, what was the problem? Her mother wouldn't say. After two weeks she hesitantly began to give Celia a lecture on The Changes in a Young Woman's Body . . . and it came out that Mrs. Everidge had confused "hysteresis" with "hysterectomy" and supposed that a hysteresis loop was some sort of contraceptive device. After a delay, the books were replaced; the originals (it emerged at length) had been burned.

The second bad moment came in the shadow of a brilliant one, on the Saturday after Celia's sixteenth birthday. Uncle Charles appeared at the house to drive Celia into London, to the Science Museum in South Kensington.

On the museum's second floor there was an operating amateur radio station, and the hams on duty greeted Charles by name, and opened the railing that usually kept them at arm's length from the visitors.

Celia was given a guided tour of the entire room-sized rig, the radiophones and the CW gear, the teleprinters and the Morse-to-text decoding computer. She smiled for a slow-scan television camera, and her still picture was bounced to someone in Calgary, Alberta, Canada. She examined the station's huge collection of QSL cards, postcards that radio hams mailed one another to confirm a wireless contact.

She couldn't send without a license, but was given headphones and a pad and worked at translating dit-dahs into English, comparing her work against the computer decoding screen.

No one said, "You're only sixteen!"

No one said, "You're not doing that right."

No one said, "But you're a girl!"

It got late very quickly. Charles thanked the operators and drove

Celia home. As he let her off in front of the house, he said, with a casualness that drove her mad, "License by Christmas, do you think?

"I know it."

"Right then. Promise made, promise delivered. Happy birthday, Celia."

"73, OM."

She walked into the house half-dazed, thinking of beat-frequency oscillators and moonbounce relay, and didn't hear the first words her mother said.

". . . said, what did you *do*?"

"We went to the Science Museum."

"You spent the whole blessed day at a *museum*? What did you do, I said."

"That's between us," Celia said, not really thinking; it *was*, that was all. She started up the stairs to her room.

"Young lady," her mother said, in a purely awful tone, and the air went chilly. It wasn't like YL at all: She said *lady* because she meant *child*.

Celia stopped, waiting.

After an empty moment her mother said, "I'll have a talk with you later, young lady."

But they didn't.

On the first of November Celia rode the train into London to take the Amateur Radio License Examination. One of the other applicants was a middle-aged blind woman, who left the code-proficiency examiner shaking his head in disbelief at her transcription speed. As they went off for the exam proper (the woman would have her test given orally) she made Celia promise to QSL her as soon as their licenses came through.

"I'm supposed to get my rig for Christmas," Celia said. "And besides, I still have to pass."

"How many women are here?" the woman asked.

"Just you."

"Counting girls, dear."

"You and I," Celia said, puzzled.

"And how many applicants all together?"

"Twenty, maybe twenty-five."

"You'll pass, Celia," the blind lady said. "You'll do just fine."

After the written test, Celia was certain she'd failed. She couldn't remember frequency numbers. The schematic for a Wheatstone bridge had vanished from her memory. Antenna shapes and transmitter wattages and harmonics rattled around loose in her head.

Then there were two intolerable weeks until the official envelope arrived. She was now a Licensed Radio Amateur.

She ran to call Charles. "Congratulations, YL," he said. "I never doubted it for a minute. 88, now."

"88 to you, too, Uncle Charles."

"What does 88 mean?" Celia's mother said.

Celia giggled. Nothing was wrong today. Nothing could ever be wrong ever again. "It means 'love and kisses,'" she said, and floated up to her room.

On Christmas morning there was a package, enormous and heavy, wrapped in white paper, with a card that was written in dits and dahs. She read it without the least difficulty. *Promise made,* it said, *promise delivered.* Opening it was easy—she knew what was inside: a 100-watt transmitter, BFO, receiver, phones and key, coil of antenna wire. The hard part was waiting for Uncle Charles.

By dinner he still hadn't arrived. She didn't have any appetite. That finally attracted some attention, since everyone else was gorging.

"Oh," Celia's father said slowly, "Charles called to say he couldn't come today. He's sorry."

Celia felt as if she had been struck hard in the chest. Couldn't come? Was *sorry?*

She got up from the table, went into the kitchen. Her eldest cousin was there, drinking scotch from a water glass. "Problems, dear?" he said indifferently.

"No," she said, felt herself starting to cry and fought it back.

"If you're lookin' for your dad's brother, he's not here. Not likely to be, either, after what your mum said to him." He took a long swallow, looked at her with his head tilted, and said almost kindly, "If you're looking for particular comfort, luv, you're in the wrong place. I'm a drunk and a bastard, but I'm not an adult—I mean, not an adulterous drunk bastard."

"What are you talking about?" Celia said, confusion bringing the tears again.

"Pretend you don't know? Pout your lip a little more, Our Lady Lolita-of-the-Wireless."

Celia gaped at him. Then she ran upstairs and tried to ring Uncle Charles's number, but the phone just buzzed without an answer.

At seven on Christmas night, a year to the hour from Celia's introduction to the etheric mysteries, the police paid a visit. An inspector with sad-spaniel eyes and an exhausted manner explained that shortly before six o'clock that morning, Charles Everidge had purchased a ticket from Birmingham New Street Station single to London Euston, gone onto platform 11, and then without any warning jumped in front of the arriving London express. A dozen witnesses agreed that the jump had been quite deliberate.

Celia carried the radio gear up to her room. Somehow or another she got it all connected, and a dipole antenna strung from her window. No one said anything to her at all. They all seemed afraid to.

A little before midnight she was on the air, key in her fist, headphones shutting out the world, sending to whoever was listening: sending MERRY CHRISTMAS, PEACE ON EARTH, GOOD WILL TO ALL, 73 EVERYBODY. As she sent, the frequency came alive with responses, 73s from the Continent, from Scandinavia, from the Americas, a chorus of voices streaming in from the air, comforting her though they did not know her grief.

■ ■ ■

WAGNER walked around the aluminum caravan. It was thirty feet long on two axles, with an umbrellalike satellite dish unfolded on its roof, cupped toward the sky.

"It's all self-contained," said Celia Everidge, otherwise known as ROCK STAR. "If you don't do any driving, the petrol tank will run the generators for a couple of days."

"That's fine," WAGNER said. She was wearing dark glasses and a scarf over her hair, and carried both a shoulder bag and a large briefcase.

Everidge tapped the side of the van. "She handles pretty well on the road. You ever drive one of these?"

"I'll manage it."

"Sure." Everidge was a short, stocky woman, plain though by no means unattractive, with short black hair and half-framed glasses.

She wore an Amateur Radio Association sweatshirt, jeans, and no makeup whatsoever. "Come on inside."

Everidge stepped up to the caravan's rear door and unlocked it. They went in. The interior was lined with electronic equipment, dials and switches and monitors. There was a cork-topped desk running along one side, with a swivel chair. Everidge pointed out the refrigerator, hot plate, and coffee maker.

"Can you get into the front from here?"

"Through here." Everidge crouched and slid aside a small panel, no more than twenty inches square. Through it, the front driver's compartment was visible. "It's a wriggle, I'm afraid." She shut the panel. "Let's get started. Want some tea?"

"That would be fine."

Everidge filled a kettle from a bottle of spring water, put it on the hot plate. She sat down in the swivel chair, tugged off her sneakers, and tossed them in a corner. WAGNER put the briefcase on the cork desk, opened it, and lifted out the COPE LIGHT circuit board.

"So that's the thing," Everidge said, and ran a hand over the gold-etched surface, without actually touching it. She opened a metal panel, slid out an open rack with a long multipin socket along its bottom. WAGNER tried not to think of Susan Bell.

Everidge lowered the board into the rack, rocking it gently into the socket. She fastened some jumper wires to it, adjusted some tiny switches with the point of a ballpoint pen. "Okay, smoke test," she said, and threw a switch on the main console, turned a dial slowly to the right.

Lights came on. An oscilloscope screen flickered with a loop of green light.

Everidge breathed out. "Works so far," she said. "There's a folding chair against that wall. Have a seat while I finish checking things out. Then I'll show you how she works."

Everidge spent the next hour probing and testing, then three more showing WAGNER how to operate the satellite receiving station. "The only thing you really have to remember is how to turn her on," she said, with a small giggle. "Once you're locked onto the Rhombic satellite, she'll track and record all by herself. You don't have to do anything except pack up the tapes when it's all over." She tapped a small monitor. "This one gets commercial TV if you get bored." Everidge turned the chair, rubbed her bare toes on the carpet. "Well," she said slowly, "that's all of it." She stood up.

WAGNER stood, facing Everidge, pushing her chair aside. "Thank you," she said, and picked up her shoulder bag.

"You're going to kill me, aren't you," Everidge said. Her hands were flat on the cork-topped desk. Ripples flashed light from her teacup. "Look, just let me go away. I don't even want the money . . . I mean, if you'd give me just a couple of hundred to get away on, everything I've got is in here. . . ." She stopped, swallowed hard, turned—just her head—to look at WAGNER. "I can't hurt you. What could I do? Please don't kill me."

WAGNER thought that Everidge didn't look a bit vulnerable, standing there tight as a spring. And her voice was—

WAGNER's hand was in her bag, already closed around the cyanide gun. Three seconds and this phase would be over.

This phase was a woman looking back at her as she must have looked at Roger Skipworth. WAGNER felt desperately sick, as if something green and dripping were crawling up her throat from deep within.

She brought her hand out of the bag. She put a stack of bills on the desk, then two more. "There's ten thousand," WAGNER said. "That right?"

Celia Everidge sat down hard, the swivel chair's springs shrieking. "Yeah," she said, with a hint of a giggle, "that's right enough."

"I won't be hearing from you anymore," WAGNER said crisply.

"No, you surely won't."

Everidge was holding a gun, a huge black Colt pistol. The bore looked cavernous. WAGNER held quite still.

She set it on the desktop, drew her hand away slowly. The pistol lay there like a dead animal. "My dad gave it to me, for burglars, you know," she said. "Hasn't been fired since 1945. . . . I made a clip for it, under the desk." She smiled nervously. "Saw that in a movie once."

"The Big Sleep," WAGNER said.

"Humphrey Bogart was in it, I remember that." Everidge picked up the money. "The fellow who asked me to do . . . this . . . did you know him?" She looked up. "Well, I mean?"

"Yes."

"He was quite a man. I mean—I never—I mean, I never would have done something like this without him. Never would have thought that I could. Do you know what I mean?"

"I know."

"I'm sorry he's dead," Everidge said, and she picked up her shoes and went out of the caravan.

WAGNER sat down in the swivel chair. She examined the Colt, found the spring clip beneath the desk, and slipped the gun back into place.

Everidge was envious. That was funny. Everyone else had accepted that Allan was dead; only WAGNER was doing anything to keep him alive, for these last few days and a bare few more.

And when those were gone? she wondered.

What would she do then?

PART FIVE

WHERE WE ARE LOOSE

Why, that was in a net, where we are loose;
And yet I am not free—

—Dido, Queen of Carthage, *III, iv*

Ellen appeared at Hansard's hotel precisely at ten on Friday morning. They walked two blocks to the car-hire agency, picked up a small red Fiat Uno, and threaded their way out of London toward Cambridge. The traffic was light, and the drive took barely an hour. They parked some distance north of the center of town, and walked down St. John's Street toward the colleges.

The banks of the Cam were still green, though the trees were turning; the sky was clear and the air was chill. Students sat on benches and the riverbank, lunching on fried fish and pasties. There were a few small bands of punks in dusty black leather and spiky hair, wandering aimlessly among the elegant architecture.

"Keep clear of them," Ellen said, after a pair with tattooed cheeks and extraordinarily hostile glares had gone by. "Cambridge hardcores make London skinheads look like children."

"They're *all* children," Hansard said, looking after the two punks, then turning back quickly as one glanced over his shoulder. "They couldn't have been more than seventeen."

"I'm afraid you're right," Ellen said, sounding slightly surprised.

Hansard presented his White Group card at the Library. There was a delay while someone telephoned someone, and a pinched-looking librarian appeared to look sidelong at Hansard. "Yes, sir. What was your specific research request?"

"The Skene documents," Hansard said.

The librarian shook his head, but said, "I see. Very well, sir, we've been instructed to cooperate with you. Just a moment." He disappeared through a door.

Hansard said to Ellen, "Something's very odd. I don't think they want to let me have the papers. That's never happened before."

"Did you tell them you had a copy of the play?"

"No."

"Don't," she said, very quietly. "I heard some of this from Gilly, my friend who worked for Sir Edward. The Skene papers are supposed to stay a British project."

"Oh. Great," Hansard said.

The librarian came back. "If you'll come this way, sir, madam."

They were led to a small wood-paneled room with several chairs and a conference table bearing a set of document cases. "These are the Skene papers, Dr. Hansard. You do understand that they're not to be removed from this room?"

"Of course," Hansard said, as patiently as he could. "What about photocopying?"

"I'm afraid not, sir. The documents are very fragile, and our conservator advises against it." He looked at his watch. "Will three hours be sufficient?"

"I doubt it," Hansard said, out of patience. "Look, I've been handling old documents since I was seventeen, and I daresay I know my way around them. If there's something wrong with my credentials, would you kindly tell me what it is, instead of giving me this uppity undergrad routine?"

"I'm sorry, sir," the librarian said, in a most unsorry voice. "I'll be back to look in on you in three hours."

When he had gone, Ellen said, "Seventeen?"

"What?" Hansard cooled off at once. "I was . . . kind of precocious." He looked at the boxes of papers. "Well, we've got three hours and no photocopier. What do we do?"

"What they did before photocopying," Ellen said. "We take copious notes." She flipped open her shoulder bag to reveal a stack of spiral-bound notebooks and a dozen yellow pencils.

"Where have you been all my life?" Hansard said, and they set to work.

■ ■ ■

In London, Gareth Rhys-Gordon sat in a carrel of the MI6 Main Files room, paging through surveillance photographs taken during the last days of Palatine's life. The pictures were grainy, black-and-white enlargements in plastic binder pages, low-priority and thus low-budgeted stuff. Satellites a thousand miles up took better pictures than these.

There was a clerk sitting opposite Rhys-Gordon, clearly unhappy to be working through his lunch hour. "Well?" he said.

"Seen better in the Sunpapers," Rhys-Gordon said, and flipped another picture. His fingers froze still in midair: the plastic slipped through and landed with a slap.

The hair was wrong, the face mostly hidden—but the white coat, the jewelry . . .

"Something?" the clerk said, as Rhys-Gordon riffled through the photo logbook.

> CONTACT 29 August
> LOCATION Hotel H2/Standard Contact Point
> IDENTITY Unknown
> SUBJECT OF CONTACT Unknown
> CASE REFERENCE None

"So do you recognize that one?" the clerk said, finally interested but trying not to show it. He tapped his fingers on a pad of yellow forms.

"Give me that," Rhys-Gordon said, and pulled the pad away. He tore off the top blank, put down *Bell, Susan Swensen* in the name block, filled her rank and assignment into the right spaces, put DECEASED in the reserved space. Under Case Reference he put PENDING, and then printed and signed his name at the bottom. He slipped the form into the photo holder.

"You'll want a copy of this?"

"No," he said, and snapped the binder shut. "Don't shelve that yet." He got out of his chair and walked to the house phone. A sign on the booth door said NO FILES TO BE BROUGHT INSIDE. Rhys-Gordon went in and dialed Department C, the case desk.

A few minutes later he went back to the carrel, took the photo binder back from the clerk. He slipped the yellow paper out, crossed out the PENDING case reference.

"You can't do that."

"What?"

"You can't alter a processing form." The clerk tore another yellow sheet from the pad. He took the first one from under Rhys-Gordon's fingers, picked up a rubber stamp, and hit both sheets with the date and a red number. The old one went into a lockbox, and he turned the new one to face Rhys-Gordon, squaring it with deliberate fussiness. "Now you're ready."

Rhys-Gordon, very calmly, filled in the new form. The case name he'd been given was ENGRAVER, and he wrote that down. The names didn't mean anything: A computer loaded with most of the dictionary picked them at random, so that anyone happening across the name couldn't draw any conclusions about the case. One of these days, Rhys-Gordon thought, the machine was going to draw the word PENDING, and the clerks would all go crackers. There wasn't any humor in the thought, just a sense of grim inevitability and the glimmer of a wish.

He went out of the files room, out of the building, up the street to a pub. So he had a case now.

Maybe he had a case. There were still too many variables, too much that couldn't be summed yet.

Eventually it would all total, he knew. Eventually it always did. And when that happened—

The barman put a pint of bitter and a shepherd's pie in front of him. "Hello, Gareth."

"Hello, Charlie."

"Long morning?"

"The longest. Death in the family."

"Sorry." Charlie's other job was as a policeman. He knew what Rhys-Gordon meant. "The wife still wants you over to dinner some night, Gareth."

"Some night I will," Rhys-Gordon said, neither meaning it nor lying, and Charlie left him to his lunch.

Sweet bleeding Jesus, Suze, Rhys-Gordon thought, tension making his scarred cheeks ache, What were you into, and who were you in it with?

■ ■ ■

"Now this is an odd lot," Hansard said, a half hour into the Skene examination. "The document list counts the playscript, some letters, and get this, the Skene household rolls."

"You're sure they weren't just added to the discovered documents?"

"It specifically lists them as being part of the discovery." He tapped the box of parchments. "What in hell were the household accounts doing sealed up in a wall with this other stuff?" He looked at his watch, sighed. "Read 'em and find out, I suppose."

Twenty minutes later he said, "Oh, now this is interesting."

"That sounds better than peculiar."

"Take a look." He pointed. "Item: 'The Costumes for Her Majesties Maske at Christmas, 20 shillings fourpence.' A fair amount of money."

"Three months' ordinary wages," she said. "But that's not your point, is it?" She tapped her pencil on the pad. "Christmas masques weren't that common in Elizabeth's era—not until James's court. And Marlowe was a long time dead by then."

"They were popular then, yes. But it's certainly not beyond reason to imagine one for Elizabeth; she seems to have liked the drama as much as anyone. And if something had gone wrong, it might explain why they *didn't* become popular. . . ."

"Why do you say something went wrong?"

He only partly heard her. He was starting to drift, to see the scene of confusion, costumes, and sudden violence . . . He pulled back to the present. "Because these records went into a wall, never to be seen again." He looked intently at her. "They deep-sixed the evidence, you see?"

"Maybe," she said slowly.

"Look at this," Hansard said, showing her the document list. "Item B: 'Letter from Thomas Walsingham to Christopher Marlowe.'"

"'Not yet authenticated,'" she added.

"But it all goes together. Now, we know Thomas inherited some of his brother's spy system . . . and we know he housed Marlowe for the last few years of his life. Now, where's the letter?"

"It isn't here, I already looked." She handed him a small white form. "Removal slip. Remember we were talking about Professor Chetwynd? He's got it."

"So these materials do circulate," Hansard said dryly.

They packed up just fifteen minutes short of the three-hour limit, purely to see the look on the librarian's face when he entered to find them ready to leave. It was mildly gratifying.

Lunch was at a small tavern a few blocks from the University. It was terrible, plastic ploughman's lunch and pasties that could have been used as paving stones. "No wonder Marlowe was always getting into fights over the bill," Ellen said, and Hansard laughed, and it made up for quite a bit.

They took a long way round going back to the car, turning more or less at random, the better to see hidden bits of architecture, court-yards off the main thoroughfares.

"This one, however, seems to be a blind end," Ellen said at the end of a rather dull brick alley, and they turned.

There were three punks, two boys and a girl, standing halfway up the alley, leaning against the walls, nearly blocking the path. They all wore black leather and boots with pointed toes. The boys had their hair in spikes, one orange, one blue. The girl's hair was jet black, pulled down viciously on one side of her head and clipped with a surgical he-mostat. Her belt was buckled with police handcuffs, and another pair dangled and clinked.

"Just go on," Ellen said. "They may not be anything to do with us."

But as they approached, one of the boys stepped directly into Han-sard's way, and held out a hand; it wasn't quite a punch, but caught him rather hard on the shoulder.

"You're in no hurry, areya, man? That's the trouble with the world, everybody's in too much hurry." The hand dropped onto Hansard's shoulder again. Hansard pushed it off.

"Didja see that, Bill? The fella wants to fight. You saw him start it."

Hansard looked around. The kids' eyes were wide and dark and hungry.

Suddenly Ellen tugged his sleeve. She was smiling, weirdly like the punks themselves. "Come on, George," she said, clearly to Hansard. "Tear 'em up."

The punk in Hansard's path hesitated. "Yeah, George," the other one said, "tear 'em up," but there was just the trace of a tremor in it.

Hansard swallowed and concentrated. He reached out and hooked a finger through one of the handcuffs on the girl's belt. "So you can wear those, huh," he said, hearing his voice rasp, hoping it sounded mean and not frightened. Or else frightened enough to be dangerous.

The boys were slipping out of their casual poses, tightening up.

Hansard tugged at the handcuff, looked the girl straight in the eyes and said, "You got what it takes to *really* wear 'em, love?"

Hansard felt himself smiling. It really wasn't intentional. It really wasn't forced, either. He felt sick.

Ellen was leaning against his shoulder. She wrapped her hands around his forearm, scratched with her nails. "Ooh, George," she said from deep in her throat, "you think she'll play? I'll bet she plays for *them*. I'll bet she's on those sweet little knees a *lot* for them."

The punks didn't exactly back off. Hansard and Maxwell didn't quite push their way through. There was just some confused motion, and Hansard was at the end of the alley, walking rather fast toward the car, realizing that he had his hand around Ellen's wrist.

He let her go quickly. They got into the car. Hansard didn't look back at the alley. He caught a glimpse of black in the rearview mirror, a flash that might have been something thrown after the car, but that was all.

"I'm sorry I got you into that," he said, when they were on the open road again.

"It wasn't so close as that," Ellen said. "They weren't hardcore. Barely even punks." She turned her head, and Hansard glanced at her face: It was set, and her eyes were terribly hard, so that he looked back at the road at once.

Ellen said, from a way off, "It was a question of whose stomach turned first. You can't upset real punks, not if you vomit on them . . . though that was the next thing to try. But they weren't the real thing. Just some kids out playing fancy dress. D'you know the song? 'He looks working class but it's all baloney, he's really middle class and he's just a phony. . . . '"

"I'm not . . . streetwise, I guess."

"You did all right." She said lightly, "If you ever have to try that again, look at the cuffs."

"Huh?"

"If the cuffs look rusty, never bluff."

"*Look* rusty—Oh, Christ."

"Indeed, when you see the wounds, you must believe." Ellen laughed, impossibly gay.

"*Stop*," Hansard said, pain in his chest, and she did.

A mile or two later, she said, "I'll sing, if you'd like. We did some good stuff in Palimpsest."

"In—"

"My band, remember?"

"Yeah. Yeah, that would be nice."

She leaned back in the car seat.

> *"There's a cold white moon reflected*
> *In a dead man's open eyes*
> *There's a raw dark wound where his throat had been*
> *And his blood is scarcely dry . . ."*

Well, I asked for it, Hansard thought.

> *"He was racing for the highway*
> *At the moment he was killed*
> *He ran like death was on his heels*
> *But death ran faster still . . .*

"I really need more voices on the chorus, but here goes," she said.

> *"So sister light your lanterns up*
> *And brother load your gun*
> *Awaken every able soul*
> *There's red work to be done*
> *Now meet me by the crossing roads*
> *And set the wolf-hounds on*
> *For full moon night the cry goes up*
> *The beast must die by dawn!"*

"Very cheerful," Hansard said, but the worst of his tension had in fact faded. Something about the grisliness of the lyrics, perhaps, a dramatic catharsis.

"You should hear the later verses . . . we did one called 'Song of the Plague Year,' too."

"I'm sorry. You've got a very good voice." No, it wasn't the words.

It was the sound of her voice, of a woman singing to him because she loved to sing.

"We seem to spend a lot of time apologizing to each other."

"True. What's the alternative?"

"I wish I knew," she said, from somewhere far away, and then said, "What's the plan now?"

"I want to know what's in that letter from Walsingham."

"Do you know Edward Chetwynd?"

"Not really. You?"

"Only well enough to know that you've got a job ahead of you." She looked over her shoulder. "If he was responsible for that warm reception we got at the Library . . . well."

"Hmm," Hansard said, then banged his fist on the steering wheel. "I know who'll have seen it. Claude Buck."

Maxwell's mouth dropped open. "Do you mean Claude *Conyngham's Rapier* Buck?"

"Claude *Conyngham's* fifteen weeks on the bestseller list, soon to be a major motion picture, *Rapier* Buck, please," Hansard said, and laughed, rather too loudly but glad to be laughing. "He was an academic before he hit the big time as an author. I knew him at school." And not through Allan, he thought, grateful that some parts of his life weren't bound up with death.

They stopped at a pub a few miles outside London. After a cup of coffee and a Cornish pasty, they crowded together into the telephone kiosk outside: Maxwell put a green telephone charge card in the slot, Hansard got the number from Information and dialed.

"Hello."

"Claude? Nicholas Hansard."

"Well! You're some time returning an invitation. Are you in London?"

"Doing some research," Hansard said. "That's actually the reason for the call; I need a favor. Have you seen the Skene papers?"

"Oh, you're involved in that?" Buck said. "Curious stuff. Yes, I've been through the papers. In fact, I thought I was the only token American to get a look."

"I'd like to talk them over with you."

"Well, all right, but it's going to have to be a social visit too, you know that, don't you?"

"Sure, Claude. Glad to."

"Fine. Unfortunately, this is one of those ghastly weeks . . . tonight's impossible, and tomorrow I'm supposed to give a platform lecture at the National Theatre on Josiah Shanks."

"Who?"

"Aha, Nicholas—caught the prodigy out at last! Tell you what, why don't you come to this lecture, give me a little moral support from the audience. You might even learn something, who knows . . . Afterward we can talk about Skene over dinner."

"That sounds wonderful, Claude. I've got a friend with me; may I bring her?"

"Dinner for three."

"What time is the lecture?"

"Seven, in the Lyttleton—you know the NT, don't you? No, that's silly, of course you do. Come by the stage door beforehand . . . let's say six . . . and ask for me."

"Sounds good."

"Well, I *hope* so," Buck said.

Hansard hung up. Ellen said, "Tomorrow in London, then?"

"Tomorrow in London, at the NT. He's speaking, on somebody I've never heard of."

"Well, it can't be anyone important, then."

Hansard was abruptly aware of Ellen's closeness, her warmth. "Shall I take you home?" he said, not at all certain what he wanted her to say in response.

"I think that's a very gentlemanly thing of you to say," she said.

Whatever he'd wanted, that wasn't it.

They drove back into the city without speaking. Ellen asked to be let off in front of a little grocery. Hansard felt just slightly nervous: Had he upset her? Offended her?

Damn it, was he lonely?

He drove around Piccadilly Circus and down Haymarket, to the American Express office. He went downstairs to the mailroom and showed his card. There was a thick letter. From Anna. He stroked his fingers along it, tucked it inside his coat as if someone were going to snatch it from him.

He drove back to his hotel, ordered a pot of tea from room service, waited for it to arrive before opening the envelope. A letter, and another envelope, with Hansard's name and College office address but no stamp, were inside.

Anna's handwriting sprawled on the page. Hansard read:

You will be pleased to know that I've been clearing tons of circulars and subscription offers out of your mailbox. If this doesn't please you, note that I'm piling them all in the fireplace scuttle, and I feel just the same about nice roaring fires (and what to do in front of them) as I did last winter. So there.

The enclosed is from Paul Ogden (Rich's friend). Thought you'd want to see it right away, and no I did not either steam it open. It's a damn good thing for him that I'm a sharing sort of person.

The dishes you left in the sink are washed and put away. Your bed is unmade because I slept in it last night. Nobody missed me in mine. Hoping you are the same,

A.

Hansard carefully refolded the letter and put it in the pocket of his suitcase. Then he opened the second envelope. The letter inside had been neatly printed by a Macintosh computer.

Dear Dr. Hansard:

I don't know if you remember me or not, but I was in the game of Kingmaker with you and Rich and Ms. Romano a few weeks ago. I'm a student at Valentine now. I like it here a lot. Frankly I think four years in the lower circles of Hell would be better than high school, but I honestly do like the College.

Anyway, I wanted to ask you again about being my faculty adviser. Mr. Marischal at the office said (I'd better quote this exactly) "If you can convince Nicholas to take you on, I'd be stark staring crazy to object to it."

The truth is, I don't really know that well what college advisers do. My adviser in high school spent most of his time telling me that I ought to be doing stuff like running for Student Council, all that school spirit crap. I told him that school spirit was what got us into the war

*with Russia in 1918. He didn't know we'd had a war with Russia in
1918. I guess you get the idea.*

*I know that you do research and are away from the College a lot,
and of course I'll understand if you say no. Either way, I'm looking
forward to seeing you when you get back from England, and to
playing more Kingmaker. I've already enlisted Rich and a couple
more people from the dorm in my fantasy campaign, and I'd be
very happy to have you join us.*

Yours awfully,
Paul Ogden
aspiring protégé

Hansard shook his head. He knew Paul Ogden; hell, he'd *been*
Paul Ogden eighteen years ago. Leaving high school for college had
been like climbing out of a lake of molten sulfur into fresh clean air.
Eventually you discovered that the air wasn't all that fresh or clean,
but the shock was wonderful while it lasted.

And since there wouldn't be any more research trips for Raphael,
maybe it was time he did advise a student. Settle down a bit.

Hansard and Anna and Paul. Instant nuclear family. Or add in
Rich, and Shen and Bob and some of his other regulars: Were they
Scholars of Night?

That last thought soured the feeling. He put Paul's letter with Anna's
and went to bed, sleeping neither well nor badly.

■ ■ ■

Sladen walked into the private upstairs room of a dingy Hampstead
pub. The bar was shut down, the room lit by one table lamp. Behind
the lamp sat a little man with unkempt hair and an ugly grin, cracking the knuckles of his enormous hands.

"You asked to speak to me?" Sladen said.

"Pleased you accepted," Gareth Rhys-Gordon said. "Sit down,
won't you."

Sladen sat. "Is this your usual channel for official statements?"

"I'm not making any kind of official statement at all, Mr. Sladen.
I'm just speaking as a British citizen. A couple of close acquaintances
of mine were murdered the other night, and that makes me angry,

and now one of your rankers is dead, and that makes me angry too. I can't even begin to tell you how angry I am that someone feels he can plug . . . *interested parties* that I've put some effort into chasing."

"Many things seem to make you angry," Sladen said.

"Oh, yes, that's me, charter member British Society for the Easily Pissed Off."

"That is too bad, Mr. Gordon."

"Rhys-Gordon, Mr. Sladen. People getting my name wrong also causes me tension. Now, come let us reason together like a couple of good old cold warriors. You've had your fingers in the jam jar, deep, and now you're trying to get them clean. That's fine with me, I like your sort to have clean hands, it makes my day much pleasanter. But you don't seem to be able to wash up without mucking up the whole damn lavatory, and that, Mr. Sladen, is going to stop, and I mean stop *right now.*"

"I'm not certain I understand," Sladen said. "What is it, precisely, that I'm being accused of? What am I supposed to stop?"

Rhys-Gordon smiled, the scars twisting his face into a mask. "I'm willing to have you tell me, Mr. Sladen. I'm even willing to help you with it, speaking as a private British citizen who believes in charity, that is." He stood up, took a dirty raincoat from a hook, tossed it over his shoulders.

"Is that all you have to say?"

"One more thing. I know about the woman, and Palatine." With a sudden flare of heat he said, "You're lucky to be alive." He cooled instantly. "That's all. Your pitch." He stood there for a minute, watching Sladen. Sladen fought down the urge to spit. Then Rhys-Gordon said, "See you 'round the jam factory," and went out.

Sladen was annoyed that the stupid little Englishman suspected him of knowing more than he told, and ten times annoyed that there really was no such information. Only a handful of scribbled code names, and Glazdunov's plan to let an operation run completely blind.

And if Sladen *did* know about the woman, about WAGNER—

He went downstairs, took a taxicab back to the office.

■ ■ ■

Just after eleven P.M., WAGNER dialed one of the numbers she never wrote down.

"Good evening," a bored-sounding voice said.

"My name is WAGNER," she said, rapidly, crisply. "Sometime ago we placed an order with Mr. Palatine. We've been out of touch since then."

"I'm sorry, but Mr. Palatine is—"

"I know that. I'll talk to whoever's replaced him."

There was a pause. "If you'd like to make an appointment—"

"No, I would not. I'll wait exactly thirty seconds, no longer."

After twenty seconds a heavy male voice said, "Yes?"

"You're in authority?" WAGNER said.

"What exactly is this about?"

"Command Persistence."

There was a moment's silence, a faraway sound. "I don't have any—"

"My line isn't tapped. Is yours?"

"Go ahead," the man said.

"The operation will be completed as planned. But I need someone removed, and I can't do it. You're not very good at it either, but you're the only service in the phone book."

"I am afraid I do not understand."

"That's too bad. I'm going to call you from another telephone with particulars, PINE KEY interval. You should understand by then. And while you're learning, learn this: If you botch this—if you hurt anyone other than the target—I'm going to do as much damage to you as I can, and that's more than you think it is."

She rang off. Her chest hurt with tension. She looked at her watch: PINE KEY meant a callback in exactly twenty-seven minutes. She had to make sure she was at a functioning telephone then, while still keeping an eye on Nicholas Hansard.

She'd been much too angry with whoever was on the phone, she thought. Her nerves were beginning to scrape thin. That was very bad.

■　■　■

Sladen put down the telephone. So WAGNER had come back to them, wanting someone dead in exchange for the NIGHTMOVE plan. That was interesting.

Sladen thought about death as a carpenter thought about a crosscut saw: a tool, no more, not a general solution but indispensable in its place. One did not saw boards without reason, because maintaining the tool had a cost; but if a board had to be of a certain length, no amount of clever talking would shorten it.

Sometimes the board came out too short, that was true; but lumber was cheap. In twenty-two years of active service, Sladen had never seen a situation made worse by a killing. He had seen plenty of them destroyed by leaving someone alive.

He looked up PINE KEY. Twenty-seven minutes until the woman called again. They would not trace the call. She had the basic skills. Sladen could respect that. He pressed the intercom and called Glazdunov.

The planner came in, looking tired and raw-nerved. Sladen knew the condition; it came from knowing one was about to be returned to Moscow, or possibly somewhere farther along the railroad. They called it "Eastern eyes."

Sladen said, "The agent WAGNER has contacted us. She wishes a person eliminated. You will inform Department Eight, and they will do so. If the operative can identify WAGNER, she is to be eliminated as well."

Glazdunov looked nervous. Sladen took some pleasure from that. Glazdunov said, "Suppose she has made preparations—left documents—"

Sladen's hand struck the desk blotter. "I don't care *what* she leaves behind, as long as she is dead. We will find the device."

"We—"

"I have seen women like this," Sladen said. "In Hungary, in Poland. They have strong wills and they are ruthless. They achieve great things with small cells and scarce resources. But if you remove them, all that energy goes away, like nothing." He wondered if that meant anything to this twitching little faggot. "Shall I tell you what I did in Poland? We tried to kill the one there, but we could never get close enough to her. Her cell worshiped her, like a saint, like Saint Joan of Arc. But there is always a means of access. With this one, finally I found what it would be. I had the abortionist move his knife just half a centimeter. Better than burning Joan. It makes no martyrs."

"I will call Department Eight," Glazdunov said, looking a bit sick. "Do you expect that the woman will be there?"

Sladen smiled. "She demanded precision of us. As much as she wants this person dead, there will be someone nearby she wishes kept alive."

■ ■ ■

The stage-door entrance had a tiny lobby, papered with posters of NT productions. A pretty young woman in a startlingly stylish leather blouse sat behind a desk. A man in a topcoat sat by the windows, reading *City Lights*.

"Excuse me, I'm Nicholas Hansard. Dr. Buck is expecting me."

The receptionist ran her finger down a list. "Oh, yes, sir. Go on back, won't you? Dressing room twenty-four."

"Thanks."

It took less than five minutes for Hansard to get thoroughly lost. He had been backstage at the NT more than once, but it was a maze of stairways and little corridors, signs that changed as the productions changed. People bustled by now and again, but no one gave him a glance, and he was too embarrassed (not to say stubborn) to ask directions.

There was a story the tour guides always told, that an actress (usually Beryl Reid, but there were variations, like any good myth) on the way to her dressing room had taken a wrong turn and emerged on stage in the middle of an entirely different play.

He found a narrow corridor lined with doors painted a sickly green color, bearing actors' names in archeological layers. Finally he saw number twenty-four, and knocked. After a moment, the door opened. It wasn't Claude, but a man in a leather jacket, mostly a silhouette in the dim dressing room. He held a wallet out with an identity card. "Special Branch Scotland Yard, sir. Mind telling me your business here?"

"I'm here to see . . ." Hansard's eyes adjusted to the dark, and he saw the man on the floor, the color of his hair . . . "My God," Hansard said, thinking suddenly, uncontrollably, of the assassin Didrick dead in his dressing room. "What's happened? Is he dead?"

"Quite dead, sir. Would you close the door, please, sir? We don't want everyone seeing him."

Hansard shut the door behind himself. "How did this happen?"

"Just what we'd like to know, sir. Now, would you tell me who you are and what you're doing here?"

"My name's Hansard, Nicholas Hansard . . . I had an appointment to meet Dr. Buck, and discuss . . ."

"Yes, sir?" the Special Branch man said, and reached into his jacket, as for a notebook.

"A play," Hansard said, and then, suddenly angry, he turned sharply to face the policeman, shouting, "A god-damned silly *play*." His arm, flung out as he spun in the tiny room, bumped the Special Branch man in the chest, and Hansard saw something like two pieces of green pipe in the policeman's hand twitch and cough, and heard the bullet ring against the thin metal wall. The pipe buzzed and clicked. The policeman's teeth were showing whitely.

Hansard smashed his fist against the killer's shoulder, throwing his whole weight behind it, knocking the other man backward and nearly toppling himself after. The gun coughed again, shattering a jar on the makeup table. Hansard grabbed the pipe barrel with his left hand and pulled the gun away, pinned the killer against the wall with his right arm and hammered the gun butt against his forehead. The man grunted. Blood ran down his face. Hansard hit him again. He sagged. Hansard fumbled for the door, jerked it open, stepped out into the too-bright hallway. He looked up and down. People flashed by at the ends, intent on their errands.

He needed some time to think. He couldn't go back to the car; Ellen was expecting him in the auditorium. He couldn't be sure how badly the killer was hurt, or if he had company; if he just grabbed Ellen from the theatre and ran they might be waiting just outside . . . He needed a little time in a safe place.

The sign at the end of the hall read TO LYTTLETON STAGE. Hansard put the gun into the inside pocket of his jacket and stumbled that way.

He pushed through a door, and found himself backstage, surrounded by lights and bits of scenery, muslin and plywood backing up the brass and lacquer of the *Alchemist* set. There were strips of masking tape on the floor, and cables, and pieces of broken crockery from the laboratory explosion that climaxed the play. He stepped around all of it, following the auditorium lights, walked past a black view-blocking flat and was abruptly on stage. There was a small table, with a chair and a water carafe. There was an audience of fifty or sixty people.

They applauded.

Hansard froze. Then he took a step, and then another, moving automatically to the table. He touched it to steady himself, then sank slowly down into the chair. He wanted a glass of water, but didn't dare touch the pitcher; it might have exploded at his trembling.

He scanned the seats for Ellen. She was in the third row, left center aisle. She looked puzzled. And damn right too, Hansard thought.

"Well . . . good evening," he said. The audience applauded again.

Relax, he thought. They're here because they know less than Claude did. It's just like a lecture class at the top of the term.

Well, maybe they were a little more motivated than the average students. Besides, what were they going to do if they saw through Hansard—call the police?

"When I first started to study the work of Josiah Shanks, I was rather overwhelmed by the enormity of the project . . . perhaps less by what there was to know than what I couldn't possibly know."

People in the audience smiled, settled in. It always helped to admit you weren't any smarter than they were.

"Suppose," he said, "that we put old Josiah into his historical perspective." He scanned the audience. "You all know when he did most of his work?"

They sat there for an agonizing moment, a few nodding. Then, finally, someone held up a hand. Hansard pointed. "Yes?"

"Sixteen-eighty to seventeen hundred," the woman said, and Hansard relaxed. He could get twenty minutes' worth of "historical perspective" out of the Restoration without breathing hard.

Maybe Claude had been right, Hansard thought with the blackest possible humor. Maybe he would learn something.

He kept expecting a sudden challenge from the audience, a sudden appearance of armed men in the wings, alarums and excursions, noises off. But the audience was perfect. They sat, and they listened, and they approved. Hansard allowed five minutes for questions and answers, which were thankfully all on the order of "When will you write another book like *Conyingham's Rapier?*"—which he could have answered with absolute precision, but didn't.

Hansard's watch bleeped. Seven-forty-five. "I'm afraid we're out of time," he said, "or, as Shanks put it, 'Go tell the watchmakers, passer-by, that here, obedient to their chimes, we lie.'"

I must be mad, he thought, but the applause was terrific. Hansard looked at the wings. They were dark, frightening. He had no idea if anyone was waiting there, but simply could not bring himself to walk that way. It was only four feet down from the stage. He vaulted it easily. A few of the audience members glanced at him; he ignored them, went straight to Ellen, took her arm and tugged her toward the exit.

"Come on," Hansard said, and grinned at the people waving at him.

"Where's Dr. Buck?"

"Dead," he said, still smiling, feeling his armpits dampen. "Come on, now."

As they passed the bookstall, just a few steps from the door, a squat man in a trench coat stepped directly into their path. He reached into his pocket.

Hansard felt his stomach sink. He thought about the assassin's gun, still in his jacket. So what was he going to do, have a shootout here in the theatre lobby?

The short man held out a paperback book. It was Claude's *Lives Upon the Wicked Stage.* He said something, Hansard couldn't hear what through the hammer of blood in his ears. He took the book. Ellen handed him a pen. He scrawled *Best wishes, Claude Buck* on the flyleaf and pushed the book back. The man nodded and smiled and got out of the way.

Hansard walked on, his arm locked on Ellen's. The room seemed tilted, the doorway ahead skew, as in an old German movie about sleepwalkers and death.

Then suddenly they were through the door, and cool night air struck him, bringing back a little reason. He looked at Ellen. She seemed terribly beautiful and vulnerable, an easy target. She said, "Where to now?"

He didn't want her to die. He said, "To the car. Out of here."

They turned down the side street to the parking garage. Street lamps threw their shadows before them, black on gray; Hansard thought of cameras tracking them, of eyes behind the lenses, of gun muzzles below the eyes.

"I'll drive," Ellen said, and put him in the passenger seat. She started the car, paid the attendant, turned into the gray night streets. "Where do you want to go?" she said.

"Christ, I don't know."

"You were improvising pretty well a minute ago."

"You're joking."

"Well, yes, Nicholas," Ellen said gently, "I am."

He did laugh faintly then, from the release of tension; as he bent forward, the gun in his jacket jabbed him, stopped him cold. He pulled it out with two fingers, dropped it on the floor of the car. "I can't think just now," he said, closing his eyes, rubbing them with both hands. "Do you have any ideas?"

"Sure." He clearly heard the excitement in her voice.

They stopped in Leicester, a little more than an hour and a half north of London, and checked in at the biggest, most nondescript international chain hotel that presented itself. Settled in the cold, garish, synthetics-and-laminates room with a pot of instant coffee from room service, Hansard sat bent forward, letting Ellen massage his shoulders. "Talk," she said.

"About what?"

"About anything. Just talk. Tell me about your wife."

"Are you—"

"Yes, I mean it. Tell me about her. I want to know."

Such celibacy maketh all men mad, Hansard thought, and started to talk. "It might not have been Louise," he said. "The first woman I might have married—I mean, seriously cared about in the right way—I lost to my own confusion and uncertainty. And for years after that I thought, well, that was that, opportunity knocks once, and so on. I was so utterly damnably convinced of that, I nearly missed the woman I did marry. Because Louise loved me enough to let me walk past if I wasn't certain. . . . Sounds like Shakespearian comedy, doesn't it? Comedy of errors."

"Go on," Maxwell said.

"Louise had cancer in her pelvic bones and lower spine." He looked past Maxwell, at some distant point. "Sometimes, when she wasn't sick from the therapy . . . we could make love. If I was very, very careful. If I wasn't careful, I made her scream."

"You mean the cancer made her scream."

"Yeah. Sure, that's what I mean."

"There's nothing wrong with gentleness, you know. Last I heard, it was gaining popularity by leaps and bounds."

"I wasn't gentle. Just scared."

"Did you have a lover on the side?"

He looked hard at her. She was just sitting there placidly, her eyebrows lifted just a bit.

"No," Hansard said.

"I imagine you were gentle enough, then."

"Sometimes she screamed . . . without being touched. In the night."

"Why in God's name are you torturing yourself?"

"I just want you to know what it was like, that's all. Historian's curse. We want so badly to know what it was like, really like, in some long-gone time or another, what was it *like* for Bess of Hardwick to have Mary in the sewing room working on embroidery and plots, and after spending sweat and shoeleather and hours reading crabbed manuscripts and worse modern books, thinking you have a two-finger grip on the truth, here comes reality, cast lead and a yard wide, and you know why I'm running on at the mouth like this, don't you?"

"My best guess would be that you're sexually aroused, Doctor Hansard."

"Excellent guess, Doctor Maxwell. And yourself?"

"Within reason."

"Always within reason."

They looked at each other for a moment, and then Maxwell said, "So, you want to drown in me like I was a pint of best bitter. You want to quench the glowing sword in hot salt water." There was a casualness to her tone that struck Hansard as exceptionally vicious. "You want to spread me on you like cream on a tart. So, do you love me a bit?"

"I haven't got the faintest idea."

She nodded, then said slowly, "No. Neither do I yet. Do you want to anyway?"

"Sure," Hansard said, "but just for the hell of it, let's not. I'll flip you for the couch."

He won the toss, offered her the bed anyway, but she refused. The lights went out. There was a faint yellow-orange glow through the windows, from the mercury lights in the parking lot outside.

"Ellen," Hansard said into the half dark.

"Yes, Nicholas?"

"I've been suspecting that this damn play is more important than anyone told me. Now I'm sure of it."

"What on earth are you talking about?"

"I had a friend," he said slowly, "who was a Marlowe scholar. And he died."

"Yes."

"Well, after he died, I . . . it's kind of complicated."

"I'm listening."

He tried to explain it to her, without naming names, but of course Berenson's came out. "I've been lying to myself, see. I've been pretending that I'm doing this to forget about what happened to Allan. But I was really trying to . . . fit things together. Find a connection if there was one. Now I've got to finish it. . . . I don't expect you to understand."

"I think I do," Maxwell said. "I'd like to help."

"No."

"Just like that?"

"Ellen, people are *dead* over this thing. If anything happened to you, I'd . . . *no.*"

"Thank you, Nicholas. That's really very dear of you. But in the first place, I'm already involved. Safety in numbers, right? And in the second, I've got a couple of things you need."

He looked at her, awed and appalled by her sincerity, and then laughed. "All right, what's the second one?"

She laughed too. "Dirty-minded scholar. One, I've got a place to hide. Two, I know a way to get the Walsingham letter."

■ ■ ■

Raphael was watering the hanging ferns in his marble office. Just past the plants, the wall screens flickered from commercial television to surveillance cameras in the D.C. Metro to the C-SPAN Congressional cameras to weather satellite transmissions. The door slid open and Stringer came in, his trouser waistband slipped dangerously below his pot belly, his half-glasses precarious on the end of his nose, a stack of stiff report folders in his thick hands.

"We've lost track of Dr. Hansard," Stringer said, irritably. Stringer abhorred a data vacuum.

"Was he properly handled in Cambridge?" Raphael said without apparent concern.

Stringer snapped a folder open and flipped pages, making a clicking sound with his tongue. "According to the Library callback, he was shown the papers but denied any cooperation, as per request. They would like a clarification of why the request was made."

"I'm certain it wasn't so very difficult for them to do. No clarification."

"They also report that Dr. Hansard was accompanied by a woman, apparently a research assistant."

Raphael lowered the watering can, looked thoughtful. "Yes?"

"They don't identify her."

Raphael looked upward, at the softly whispering ventilator grille. "Well. He has disappeared in a woman's company. That should be interesting." He sprinkled another plant. "Identify the woman. Don't begin a search for them. And for contingency . . . whom do we have available, that Dr. Hansard knows?"

"Colbert in Geneva, Rulin in Munich. Pollard is in Athens, but not readily available."

"Rulin will have Donner with him. That's useful. Move them to London and ready status."

Stringer made a note. "Professor Edward Chetwynd is returning to the UK tomorrow. Shall I notify him?"

"Why not just call Moscow direct?" Raphael smiled slightly as Stringer raised his pen. "No action. Besides, Professor Chetwynd has already done the American services one great favor. He has yet to be properly repaid for arranging the termination of Allan Berenson."

■ ■ ■

It was just after eleven on Sunday morning. Hansard was driving, Maxwell navigating; they were a little less than a mile west of Cambridge, winding through a small town, a couple of pubs and a petrol station.

"Now we case the joint," Maxwell said, swallowing giggles, and pointed to a red telephone kiosk a short way ahead.

Hansard parked the car. He stood in the door of the phone box while Maxwell dialed. "Right," she said, and held the phone to Hansard's ear. He heard a woman's voice, under the scratch of tape, saying ". . . wynd's office. The Professor is not available at the moment. If you will leave a message—"

Maxwell hung up. "The answerphone, the modern burglar's best friend."

"It doesn't necessarily mean no one's home," Hansard said, thinking of the number of times he'd stayed in bed and let the machine front for him.

"Yes, it does. You noticed Margy's voice on the tape? The Professor hates the thing, won't have it on when he's at home. It's one of the few things he never, ever forgets. And even if for some earthshaking reason Margy should be in on Sunday, she'd never let the machine answer if she was there. *Quod erat demonstradum.* Let's go."

They drove a little more than a mile out of town, turning at an access road with brick pillars flanking it. "There's the house," Maxwell said.

The house was large; Hansard guessed fifteen to twenty rooms. It was of brick, two stories, with diamond-paned windows and monumental chimneys. The walls were thickly ivied, the rose trellises and the flagstone path trimmed with micrometric precision. Extending behind the house was a yard-high garden wall, topped by another three feet of dense, squarely cut hedge, running for sixty feet or so.

"Charles the First?" Hansard said.

"Very good! Now, was the owner Roundhead or Royalist?"

"That's a bit much to ask from one look . . . well, it's a small manor, so I'd guess Royalist."

"You're being romantic, but you're right. Park over there."

Hansard stopped the car by the garden wall. There was a gateway just ahead, near the far corner of the enclosure. Ellen got out of the car, went to the gate, and lifted the latch. "Well? Coming?"

"We're not even going to try the doorbell?"

"No. We aren't. This way."

The garden was square and rigidly formal, a pavane of roses and small conical firs, paths of herringbone brick framing and constraining it. It was fully enclosed by the wall and hedge and the back wall of the house, which showed several windows and a pair of white-painted French doors.

Hansard said, "I hadn't considered breaking and entering to be part of this project."

"We're not going to break, just enter." She went to the center of the garden, stood facing the rear of the house. "'Three rings for the Elven-kings, under the sky,'" she said, and took three steps forward, and turned right. "'Seven for the Dwarf-Lords, in their halls of stone . . .'" Seven steps, and a left turn. "'Nine for mortal men, doomed to die . . .'" After nine paces, she bent down and turned over one of the stones edging a flowerbed, dug into the soil beneath with her fingers. Her hand came up, shaking dirt from something. "'One for the Dark Lord, on his dark throne.'" She turned to face Hansard, holding out an oxidized brass key. "Or, as the office help used to say, 'Edward Che-twynd, OBE, never can recall his key.' This way."

The key opened the French doors, and they went into the house, into what had to be Professor Chetwynd's office.

"I don't suppose there's an alarm system," Hansard said.

"Tape on the windows, against housebreakers," Ellen said, "but he'd never remember to turn off one of those ultrasonic-radar gadgets. Have the police out four times a week. I've got an idea where the letter will be; just give me a moment."

She sat down behind the desk. Hansard examined the room. The office was all honey-colored wood and old brasses, with carpet of a billiard-cloth green. There were books, of course, hundreds of books on the walls, an Oxford English Dictionary with one volume open on a reading stand, and shelves built-in and brass-bracketed holding the thousand accumulated curiosities and keepsakes of the historian's packrat life. Hansard irresistibly found himself reading the artifacts, like an archeological dig: framed photographs and oddly shaped stones, a six-inch metal figure of a mounted knight in armor, and an old Military Cross in a velvet-lined box.

"Over here," Ellen said. She had a desk drawer open, and several file folders spread out on the blotter. She tapped one of them. "Thank goodness he didn't put it with the Secret stuff."

"*Secret?*" Hansard felt a sudden cold shock to his nerves.

Maxwell looked up, surprised. "The Professor's one of the old University Intelligence recruits, you know, George Smiley, old school tie, and good night, Kim Philby, wherever you are? . . . There's a vault around here somewhere, and that *does* have an alarm on it. And *that* drawer—" she pointed at an oak filing cabinet next to the desk—"has a scrambler telephone in it. Want to call Number Ten? Or the White House?" She frowned at him, playfully. "Oh, come *on*, Nicholas. I don't have a key for it. Besides, I hadn't figured you for such a law and order type."

"I'm not. It's just . . ." He looked around at the room, not so much different from his own house. ". . . this is someone's house, that's all. Personal property." There wasn't time just now to explain it to her, explain his fear, his revulsion. "Is there a copier around here somewhere?"

"There is, but it's got a copy counter. And while the Professor would never notice, Margy would spot it in a second. We'd better just borrow the folder, and hope nobody needs it for a few days. Do you want to leave a charge slip?"

"No!"

"All right, Nicholas, I'm sorry." She replaced the other folders in the drawer, closed it.

He put his hand on hers, tightened it harder than he really meant to. "You know too much," he said.

She looked up at him, eyes wide, pupils huge, genuinely scared. "I—I what? Nicholas, you're not—I mean, you're not with one of the security things—"

He let go at once, took a step back. "No. But you know too much about this place to have gotten it all from a friend. The key in the garden, the alarm, the copier counter." He paused, took a short breath, tried to sound less accusing. "Are you 'Gilly'?"

She nodded.

"Why?"

"I was afraid that you knew Sir Edward," Ellen said. "That you'd . . . mention me to him, and he'd know I was helping you with Skene. That's more than my job is worth. So I was somebody else. See the gillyflowers outside the window? Local habitation and a name."

"But you are helping me."

"I'm glad you noticed."

"Could I ask why?"

"Because I think Chetwynd and his friends have been perfect asses about the Skene Manuscript, that's why," she said explosively. "I don't like them carrying on as if it were some sort of national secret. So when I met you in the Reading Room, I, well, I . . . haven't you ever wanted to be a secret agent, Nicholas?" She seemed close to tears.

"It's all right," Hansard said, wishing she hadn't brought secret agents into it, but understanding all the same. "I should be apologizing to you. Or at least thanking you."

She rubbed her eyes. "I guess we're even-all so far. Still partners in crime?"

"Still partners."

They checked for disturbed objects, closed the French doors carefully. Ellen reburied the key. Hansard had a watched feeling, seriously expected to find police waiting by the car. But there wasn't anyone. They drove away with no audience but crows.

Hansard felt his gut untightening as they turned onto the main road. "Back to Cambridge now? Or London?"

"That way," she said, and pointed west. "To the A1, then north."

"What's north?"

"Home," Ellen said. "There's no place like home."

■ ■ ■

By four o'clock the A1 had taken them into the Cheviot Hills, along the North Sea coast. Inland, there were fewer cattle dotting the fields, and to the right a squall line was just visible across the water.

There was a gray building on a point of land, concrete boxes jumbled together, with spiderweb antennae whirling. Hansard pointed to it. Ellen said, "Lindisfarne Station. You don't want to know. Secret, you know?"

"Yeah."

A few minutes later, just after a sign indicating twenty miles to the Scottish border, they turned off the A road, stopping in a tiny townlet at a whitewashed house with a Bed and Breakfast sign.

"This is it?"

"Yes," Ellen said, in a peculiarly soft voice. "It is. Come along." She got out of the car, went to the door, and tapped a large iron knocker.

When Hansard stood up beside the car, there was a woman at the door, about Ellen's height, with curly dark hair frosted with gray. She was just a touch plump, not heavy, and she moved and smiled with that particular grace that makes plain women beautiful and beautiful women radiant.

Ellen hugged her, turned to Hansard and said, "Nicholas, this is Felicia Maxwell, Peter's mother."

"Hello," he said, and held out his hand, stiffly.

Mrs. Maxwell took it easily. "Pleasure to meet you, Nicholas," she said, in a Northumbrian accent that launched Hansard on thoughts of Harry Hotspur . . . *of guns, and drums, and wounds. God save the mark!* "Do call me Fel. Now, come in, the both of you. There's no guests today, so I'll have to put tea on, but I was just making cookies."

"Cookies," Hansard said vaguely, and then Ellen took his hand and pulled him inside, into the scent of cinnamon.

There was a strong black tea and oatmeal cookies that bid fair to derange the senses. "It's the malt whiskey," Fel confided. "The lady I had the recipe from, she said, 'Oh, use a blended scotch, it's only cookies, after all.' Can you imagine such a thing?"

After tea, Felicia went out on an errand more implied than described. "I hardly expect anyone this time of year, but if the phone rings, Ellen, you know how to give them directions. I should be back in plenty of time to make dinner, but if you just can't bear the strain, there's cold beef in the fridge. . . . Oh my, must run now. Back as soon as I can."

"Why do I get the feeling," Hansard said as the door closed behind her, "that your mother-in-law was doing her best to leave us alone together?"

"Maybe you're just more sensitive than most men."

He snorted. "Sensitive to what? . . . I'm sorry. But all I have a sense of right now is impending . . . I don't *know* what. Doom. Damnation." He got up, went over to poke the living-room fireplace. "'The devil will come, and Faustus must be damned.'"

It was no use. It made him think of Allan and death. Everything made him think of Allan and death.

"*Must* Faustus be damned?" Hansard said suddenly.

"You mean, before the actual end . . ."

"Yes."

Ellen frowned, thinking. "Obvious enough on the face of it. The good angel tells him that he can repent, while the bad angel says he can't; but the good angel can't be lying."

"Right so far," Hansard said.

"'So far,' eh? All right, Professor. You're asking if, after Faustus has been determined enough to ignore all the warnings and sign over his soul, he could find the strength to change his mind."

"Failure of will, I'd call it." Hansard sat back, nibbled at one of the cookies. "You know what the doctrine of continuous confirmation is?"

"Confirmation? It sounds terribly complicated, not to say Papist."

Hansard laughed. "It's nothing to do with Heaven, my dear. It says that an airplane on its way to deliver a nuclear bomb has to have a continuous line of communication with headquarters, and HQ has to keep sending go-ahead codes until the bomb goes off. Theoretically they can disarm the damned thing after it leaves the bomb bay."

"That's a comforting thought."

"Isn't it? Except that on a modern battlefield, there's all this stuff called electronic countermeasures, that's specifically intended to break those lines of communication. So there are counter-countermeasures, and counter-counter-counters, and so on down the hall of mirrors. If an atomic weapon goes off, things get fifty times worse, with electro-magnetic pulse and ionizing radiation. Now, if I know this, you can bet the generals do, right?"

"A fair assumption."

"So you tell me: Knowing that the whole world is out to interrupt their fail-safe signal, knowing that something surely *has to* interrupt it for at least a moment or two, do you really think they're going to give up and go home the first time the green Go light flickers a little? And that's not even considering the problem of the bomber crew suspecting that they may no longer have anyone to take orders from, or a home to fly back to."

"Up with that I won't put," Ellen said lightly, and then more seriously, "Yes, I see. Once committed to a course, it's very hard to abandon it. . . . Or were you thinking of the loss of communication? Faustus is damned because he's broken his link with his God? That's very Christian-mystical, you know. Almost Charles-Williamsy."

"I wouldn't know anything about that," Hansard said, too sharply, and they were both silent for a moment. Then Hansard said, "The friend I told you about . . . the one this was for . . ."

"Yes?"

"I think . . . he must have made Faust's bargain." Hansard felt his chest tighten, felt the tension of imminent tears. If he were wrong he would despise himself.

As if he didn't already.

Ellen said, "And you have to understand it?"

"Yeah."

"All right." Just like that.

They sat in the living room for twenty minutes or so, looking at one another but hardly moving. Hansard felt the tension increase— not honestly comprehensible arousal, but something completely shapeless, just tugging at his viscera. What did he want to say to her, what did he want to do? And whatever he said or did, what would he say or do to Anna, when this was all over and he was safe and warm at Valentine, and men on motorcycles no longer brought him photographs of corpses bearing secrets. . . . He thought he must explode, any moment now. Then there was a knock, and a voice, and Felicia was back. The spell broke, and they both stood; Ellen gave Hansard one short look, almost unbearably like a lost child, and then went into the kitchen to help with dinner.

Hansard walked around the living room, sipping cold tea to anchor himself to reason, reading the objects on the walls. On the mantel, so prominent that he wondered why he hadn't seen it before, was a framed photograph of a young man in naval uniform. Peter Maxwell's hair was short and straight; he had a neat mustache and an easy, broad smile. He supposed that the look alone meant nothing, that wife-beaters and serial killers looked just that way. But on Peter—Hansard could see the sort of fellow Peter had been, in his photograph and his widow and his mother's oatmeal cookies, and he felt diminished not to have known him . . . diminished and angry to have lost the chance for the sake of the stupid little Falklands War. "'Accurst be he who first invented war,'" he heard himself say, and then noticed a movement behind himself.

"That's a quote from Christopher Marlowe, am I right, Nicholas?" Fel Maxwell said brightly.

"Yes, that's right," Hansard said, embarrassed.

"Yes," she said, and there was a moment's silence. "I do read a lot, Nicholas. Is there anything of yours I might have read?"

"I doubt it . . . there's only one book, and it's kind of technical."

"About history?"

"Yes . . . historical methods, actually. It's kind of obscure."

"I must see if I can find it. As I say, I read, and there are the guests, but not so many of them anymore. Peter's friends used to visit, with their companions; it was so alive then . . . but they don't come any longer. I believe they think they're doing me a kindness." She shook her head. "Well. Dinner should be ready. Come along. . . . Oh, by the way, Nicholas . . ."

"Yes—Fel?"

"Do you play gin rummy?"

They played gin for a couple of hours after dinner, Hansard losing extravagantly to Felicia. Then Fel hugged Ellen, told them both good night, and disappeared into the back of the downstairs house.

"I—uh, good night, Ellen," Hansard said, and went upstairs, leaving her sitting before the fire, watching him with yellow light reflected in her eyes. He went into his room, closing the door slowly, slowly, so that neither hinges nor lock made any sound at all.

The room was an utter improbability, something from an old novel or a *New York Times* Sunday magazine piece. There was a handsewn quilt on the double feather bed, a needlepoint hunting scene on the wall, oil lamps near the electric ones. A wood and wicker rocker stood by the small coal fire, and next to it a table with an electric teakettle and a plate of cookies. His suitcase was open, and his robe and pajamas and slippers were spread out on the bed.

He switched on the kettle and changed clothes. As he started to settle down with the Walsingham letter, a whimsy seized him, and he lit the hurricane lamp—the matches were already set out—and switched off the electric light. Turned up properly, the light was quite sufficient, and very friendly. Hansard poured water over a teabag, sat down in the rocker, took a bite from a cookie.

You have asked a great Why, the letter began. . . .

The door opened, with just a whisper of sound. Ellen came in. She was wearing a flannel nightgown and fuzzy white slippers.

"Oh," Hansard said, both genuinely surprised and feeling a bit silly for being so.

"Oh," she said, very seriously, and shut the door behind her. "Is there another teacup?"

Hansard looked. There was. And the pot had been filled for two cups. He fumbled with it, spilling a little of the steaming water.

She took the tea, leaned against a bedpost, crossing her ankles. She laughed, and Hansard realized he was staring.

Ellen said, "'O my good lord, why are you thus alone?'"

He nearly spilled his own tea, then said, "Lady Percy?"

"I knew you'd know that. I brought another friend here, once, and all he could do for an hour after meeting Fel was quote *Henry IV*."

"A male friend."

"Yes, Nicholas, this is my mother-in-law's place. She's also the best friend I have in the world. And she's been a widow longer than I have . . . longer than you *or* I have." She paused then, suddenly, and said, "But I haven't asked you . . . you've got someone?"

"It's open," he said, and put down his teacup. "I suppose that sounds very casual, but it's the truth. I love her, but it's . . . open." He thought of Anna's letter: *Damn good thing I'm a sharing sort of person.* He wished now that she had sent him a nice, polite, businesslike letter, one he could have shown to Ellen. This letter wouldn't do. This letter was honest.

In the pause, Ellen relaxed a bit, and Hansard felt the effects directly. She said, "Yes, I'd thought that might be it. . . . So, do you want to work tonight?"

He chuckled, and she began to laugh, a beautiful noise. He set the letter aside. He stood up.

Ellen pulled the ties on her flannel gown, slipped it off. Underneath she was wearing a pale blue satin camisole, shining in the lamplight. It hurt Hansard's eyes to watch her move. She pulled back the bedspread, kicked off her slippers, and entered the featherbed like a swimmer.

Hansard dropped his robe into the chair, turned down the lamp. He stood by the bed.

"It won't work," he said.

"No?"

"I'm scared," he said, "just like after Louise died."

She sat up, drew her knees up and pulled the covers around them. "I won't die if you make love to me, Nicholas, and I won't die if you don't."

"I know that."

"Then act like you know it. If you want to punish yourself for something you didn't cause and couldn't prevent, that's just fine, but count me out. It isn't my kink to be on either end of the whip, d'you understand?"

"Yeah."

More gently, she said, "Your lover back home. Is she pretty?"

"Are you asking me to be objective?"

"Not especially."

Hansard looked away from Ellen. "She's very slim. Like you. Shorter. Her face . . . is like Loren's, a little."

"Oh, well then."

"I only meant—"

"I know what you meant. I asked the question, remember? Thought maybe if I got you thinking about the living instead of the dead . . ."

"Don't—twist—the knife, Ellen," Hansard said, suddenly tired. "Do I want you? Yes, I want you. But there's so much else going on right now, so many other people I *can't* get out of my mind—room's just a little crowded now, do you see, Ellen?"

"I see, Nicholas. Do you want me to go?"

"No," he said, without any hesitation at all.

"So what can I do?"

"Just let me hold you."

She held out her arms. She started to say something, then didn't. He didn't want to know what it would have been. Probably a question; under the circumstances he would have had a bunch of questions. But he appreciated her not asking any of them. He slipped into bed, put his arms around her, stroked the small of her back. She sighed, touched the back of his neck.

Very softly, her lips almost against his ear, she said, "If you want to—"

"Sssh."

"—it's perfectly all right."

"Thank you. Sssh."

He fell asleep holding her.

■ ■ ■

Hansard woke up alone. He dressed, tucked the folder with the Walsingham letter under his arm, and went downstairs to juice and tea, eggs on toast, and Ellen at the table. Fel Maxwell set out Hansard's breakfast, smiled at him—there was nothing of conspiracy in it—and said, "You'll excuse me now, I take breakfast over to Mrs. Lansing across the way every morning," and she was gone.

Hansard sat down. "Does she really?"

"Yes. She really does."

"About last night . . ."

"Isn't something supposed to happen before we get to the 'about last night' business?"

"I used you like a teddy bear. That was selfish. I'm sorry."

"You're bewildering."

Hansard laughed dryly. "Yeah. I suppose I am."

"What is this, guilt without sex? You didn't hurt me. You didn't use me. You didn't, now that I've had a chance to think about it, even disappoint me."

"Really," he said, rather more flatly than he had meant to, looking into his tea.

"What sort of fancies have you been making up? It isn't always two-way. You don't always give as good as you get, or vice versa. You just do what you can, give what you can, try to be fair about it. You think you owe me one? Very well, you owe me one."

Hansard nodded slowly. Ellen said, "Now, shall we get back to work?" and cleared his plate away, set the document folder neatly in front of him.

Hansard opened it, began to read the letter from Walsingham to Marlowe.

You have asked a great Why, concerning the man called Adam Dover, lately deceased: and as we are greatly in your debt over this matter I shall attempt to answer it.

That man's ancestry is somewhat as you suspect, yet at once not so. Though he indeed once professed to be of a Certain origin, this was a falsehood of the most calumnious sort. . . .

"Very modern sort of letter," Hansard said tiredly. "It says a lot, absolutely none of it definite."

Maxwell said, "Not all that modern. Remember 'By my order and for the good of the state, the bearer has done what has been done'?"

"Touché," Hansard said. "But we knew who Milady de Winter wanted dead. What about Walsingham?"

"Hmm. Well, can you think of any original calumnious falsehoods?"

Hansard thought about the times. Calumny was cheap. As for origins . . . Finally he said, "Arthur Dudley."

"You mean Robert . . . No, you mean Arthur, don't you."

"You've heard of him?"

"Every schoolgirl in England knows about Great Elizabeth and Sir Robert Dudley. Nooky in high places, you know."

"You think that they actually had an affair? That 'Arthur' might actually have been their son?"

"I'm not so romantic as *that*, Nicholas. It *is* an awfully good story, though—and it's a fact that Elizabeth spent hours in private with Sir Robert, while Dudley's stick of a wife sat at home alone, rotting with cancer—Oh, bloody hell, Nicholas, I'm *sorry*—"

"It's all right. It's all right." Hansard concentrated. "Now. Philip of Spain entertained someone calling himself Arthur Dudley, self-proclaimed royal bastard, at court for a while, even allowing people to gossip that Dudley might be used to press a claim for the English crown. Which is absurd, since Philip himself had a Habsburg dynastic claim that was at least as sound—"

"Which is to say, no more worthless."

"You've got it. 'Arthur,' whoever he is, goes on being a royal pet until a few months before the Armada sails. Then poof, he vanishes from view, never to be heard from again. That's convenient, but big deal, it's an age of convenience in death."

"You're assuming a lot."

"Of *course* I'm assuming a lot! I've got fragments, I've got a play that I'm making a wild guess was based on a real event there are barely even fragments recording—I'm a history professor, I'm not God."

"But it's like being a god," Ellen said gently, quoting Hansard back to himself, breaking his tension, making him laugh.

"Okay. Okay," he said. "I can't let it go now."

She put her hands on his shoulders. "So what's the next act, Doctor?"

"Change of scene," Hansard said.

"Noises off?"

"Skene House."

■ ■ ■

The last cog clicked into place in WAGNER's mind, and she knew who the last agent, CROWN PRINCE, had to be.

A year and a half ago, Allan had chartered a boat, to take them around the Hebrides. He'd asked the captain all sorts of technical questions about the vessel. That had meant nothing to her, of course: Allan was always interested in the details.

It hadn't been that much of a boat, just a little cabin cruiser, skipper and crew of two. But it was big enough to launch the Sea Wasps.

What was the name, now? Something-or-other Charters of Stornoway. It was the captain's name. Light. No, Licht. Captain Owen Licht. Licht Charters.

She called Information for the number. Then she dialed CROWN PRINCE—or as she would call him when he answered, Didrick.

■ ■ ■

It was Tuesday morning on the Kentish coast, less than an hour after sunrise. The sky was overcast, like a pink mattress. The odd light made the Nissen hut that said MACHINE TOOLS seem even more alien, like one of Wells's Martian cylinders half-buried in the soil.

A blue Land Rover parked in front of the Nissen hut, and the man inside got out. He went around to the side of the metal building as he'd been instructed, looked at the ground where dirt met corrugated tin. There was a tiny flash of yellow. The man bent down, picked at the yellow spot, pulled it; the tag came out of the soil, a key dangling from it. The man brushed dirt from the key, fingered the yellow plastic tag. Then he opened the door, and squinted at the dusky dark within.

Owen Licht was fairly tall, solidly built. He wore a faded blue parka and a black peaked cap; his beard was reddish and full. He looked like a sea-captain, or rather, a Victorian engraving of a sea-captain. Licht hated the beard, it itched and needed constant tending, but the customers expected it on him, like the coat, like the cap.

Not just the anoraked tourists, either, out for a glimpse of the Orkneys, looking for Sir Gawain's mum. The mercenaries, themselves decked out in epaulets and oversize sidearms and badges from un-fought battles, the smuggling magnates in their expensive suits and dark glasses, all wanted their boatman to dress the part too.

Licht found the missiles easily enough. He opened one of the foam cases and examined the unit inside. Licht had mounted missiles on the boat once, the idea (and demand) of a crazy Levantine gold smuggler. Licht had agreed to it before he saw them: gas-pipe bombs, home-brew imitations of a German design from Hitler's war. The smuggler spent the voyage sitting on the deck, trigger in his lap, hoping for a coast boat to shoot at. It was just as well they hadn't seen one; Licht had snipped the ignition wires half an hour out.

But these, now, these were something entirely different, neat and impressively compact. So this little coffin could kill a ship? That was damned unromantic.

Licht smelled something, above the oil and metal; it was like meat gone off. He put down the missile and strolled to the back of the hut. He examined the hacked-apart door, then the heap of lime powder on the floor, the lump beneath the heap. Then he went back to the missiles.

Licht had never been a romantic man. It ran in the family.

Owen Licht's father had sold food and fresh water to German sub-mariners. His grandfather had run guns to Ireland; Owen had built that trade up a bit, branched it out.

Grandfather Licht had also invented the family tradition: gorgeous lies of an ancient line of smugglers and blockade-runners, who had carried every sort of contraband and every variety of refugee: French aristos, Covenanters, Armada sailors, Normans, Romans. It was part of the Licht myth that no Licht sailed to war except for money, and that war money, hard cash paid under cover of fear, was the true Licht fortune. There would, Grandfather said, always be wars, and Lichts would always take their share.

A few weeks after Owen's father had died, Owen found an old paper in a frame, a blank bill of lading from *Queen Morgause of Orkney*. Written on its back was:

> *Dunkirk—Dover, 1940*
> *To Captain Sean Licht—*
>   *Thanks for the lift. Going back soon to petition Herr*
> *Hitler for your fare.*

Thirty names were signed below. Owen took down the logbooks. The trip was entered, and therefore real. Sean Licht might have drawn up a fake souvenir to impress the tourists, but he would not have falsified a log: There were kinds and kinds of lies.

It had turned Owen's world inside out. His father had been a hero after all; Licht amorality was as false as Licht history. Then Owen began to learn about nuclear war, the great light and the great darkness, and realized that not even that part of the great fraud was left to him. There would be no perilous charters or sealed cargoes for him in the event: There would be only poison ashes on an empty sea.

Owen had no wife, no son, no more crew than he needed. He had dead-reckoned his life for twenty years, until the American had shown him a light to steer for. He had come to realize at last that Licht men all made their own myths. His grandfather had claimed to have a heritage. His father had claimed to be a cynic. Owen would scatter ashes on the sea.

He adjusted the tarp covering the missiles in the back of the Land Rover, shut the rear hatch, went round to the side door. He paused to look at the sky. He could smell rain coming.

Licht got into the Rover and started driving north.

■　■　■

Skene House was larger than Hansard had expected, four or five times the size of Sir Edward Chetwynd's manor. Scaffolding caged two sides of it, where workmen were restoring the half-timbered walls, and chimneys were shored up with steel angles.

The door was opened by a slender young man in a green silk Italian suit and tennis shoes. He had curly blond hair and rimless, round-lensed glasses. "Yes?" he said pleasantly.

Hansard held out his White Group identification. "My name is Nicholas Hansard, and I'm a historian—"

"*Ellen?*" the young man said, looking past Hansard.

"Hello, Hugh," Maxwell said quietly.

Hansard stepped aside as the man in the green suit walked past him. "I . . . uh . . ."

Maxwell said, "Nicholas, this is Hugh Keane, the twentieth Baronet of Skene."

"Twenty-second, but who's counting?" Keane said, and held out his hand. As Hansard shook it, Ellen said, "Hugh, Nicholas would like a look around the house . . . if it's all right?"

"Well, *certainly* it's all right, Ellen. Come in, come on in, both of you. Good God, Ellen, you haven't been here since before Dad the Twenty-first died. And may I say, Mr. . . . ."

"Hansard. Nicholas Hansard."

". . . Mr. Hansard Nicholas Hansard, it's a pleasure to invite such a lucky bloody bastard into my humble house. Ellen, love, give a bereaved man a final hug, will you?"

"Oh, really, Hugh," Ellen said, and hugged him. Hansard watched, slightly surprised but not (he supposed) bewildered. Or maybe, he thought, he was bewildered but not surprised. At any rate, the hug went on for a good long while, and then the Baronet of Skene said, "All right, ladies and gentlemen, this way please, watcher boots inna museyroom," and they went inside.

Keane showed them the priest's room where the Skene documents had been hidden, until one of the masons had unsealed it for the first time in four centuries. "We were hoping there might be a skeleton or somesuch in there," the Baronet said, "a little bit of color, a decent ghost story at least. But no such luck." Hansard tried to imagine the person who had put the papers in, and bricked up the doorway, but there was no image, just a closet full of cobwebs and dust.

Keane said, "I'm really not much on papers, that's Ellen's department. And yours too, I guess, Nicholas? But this is the bit I like." On a table near the opening was a glass case, looking brand-new. Inside it, on clean red velvet, was a blackened metal object . . . a metal tube, with a sort of crank at one end. Two leather straps, badly disintegrated, ran around it.

"Wheel lock pistol?" Hansard said.

"That's it," Keane said. "But you notice, it has no stock. The straps must have been used to fasten it to something, maybe a polearm—"

"An arm," Hansard said, thinking. One strap at the wrist, one below the elbow, the lock in the crook of the elbow, the trigger—

". . . and the barrel's awfully short," Keane said. "With the powder they had at the time, the muzzle velocity would have been ridiculously low. You couldn't have used it from more than a few steps away."

"That's right," Hansard said. "That's absolutely right."

"Eh?"

"I was just thinking, that's all," Hansard said. "What's next?"

The Great Hall was some sixty feet long and twenty-five floor to ceiling. There was an overhead gallery, wood-paneled with narrow windowslits, reached by little enclosed stairways at each end. The floor was tiled checkerboard, black and white. "Were you here the Christmas we played out the game from *Alice,* Ellen?" Keane said.

"I was Queen's Pawn," she said, rather distantly.

"That's right, you were. And I was King's Knight's Pawn, and . . ."

Hansard's mind drifted as he examined the room. At the bottom of one of the gallery stairs was a small antechamber, just right for dressing for an entrance.

DIDRICK. I would be Wittol. There's a clever role.

POLYDORUS. A foolish one, you mean. Why, would you not
  Prefer the Sage, or Archer, or the Duke?
  These all have cleverness, with dignity.

DIDRICK. Nay, I would be the jester. *Aside.* For 'tis he,
  And he alone, who may approach the King.

"Write me a part," Dover said. "Make me . . . make me Genius, that I may touch the Queen."

Marlowe thought a moment. "You'll play Athena, then? She'd fancy that, I think. She likes for people to think she burst from Great Harry's head. Yes. We shall have Athena appear for Elizabeth's sake, and . . . Diana for Dudley's." Marlowe grinned. "Oh, they shall be charmed and quite furious, but 'tis Christmas and all's merry."

"It *was* here," Hansard said softly.

"We should go, Nicholas," Ellen said. "It's still a long drive back to London, and it's starting to rain."

Hansard looked up at the windows opposite the gallery. There was a flash of lightning through the stained glass, and long seconds later a low roll of thunder.

Keane said, "Why drive to London through the storm? You're welcome to stay here. Nineteen bedrooms, no crowding. Just like college weekends, eh, Ellen? And you can even have the two with the secret passage between—"

"Hugh, stop it," Ellen said, sounding not amused.

"Ellen, I'm happy for you, *really*," Keane said, in a hurt voice. "I just . . . well, bloody hell, I hadn't expected it to be somebody your father would have approved of—"

Maxwell slapped him hard enough to send his glasses flying. "We're going now," she said, and took Hansard by the arm.

"Just a moment," Hansard said, and pulled free of her. He retrieved Keane's glasses, handed them to him. "I have absolutely no idea what's going on between the two of you," he said, "and I don't really think I want to know. But thanks for the look around."

"My pleasure," Keane said, without any apparent sarcasm. "And don't mind this . . . you *are* the world's luckiest bastard, you know. You and Peter . . . well. Good-bye, Nicholas. Do visit again."

"Thank you, Hugh."

Ellen's face was set, expressionless. She went out of the house with Hansard without saying a word.

Hansard turned the car out of the drive. The last he saw of Skene House was the Baronet standing in the doorway, one hand raised. Raindrops plashed on the windshield. Hansard said, "If you don't want to tell me . . ."

"I think you know I don't."

The rain came harder. There was a forked bolt of lightning to the west. Hansard switched on the wipers, which squeaked hideously. "Okay, then I'll tell you. Your father is Sir Edward Chetwynd, isn't he?"

"Did you guess?" she said, in a tiny voice. "Or did you know . . ."

"I didn't know until now," Hansard said. "Since I sure as hell don't have any money or City manners, it's the only sensible explanation for Hugh's comment about your father approving of me. And once I'd thought of that—well, 'Gilly the secretary' might have known her way around the office, but you were just *at home* at Chetwynd's house. You lied to me—"

"I *was* a secretary there, Nicholas."

"All right, you only half lied." He paused. She didn't say anything. He said, "I'm not angry, I'm just confused. Why didn't you tell me?"

"Because he set me on you," Ellen said, sounding almost frightened. "He sent me to spy on you, make sure you didn't find out anything about the play without his knowing."

"So you've been—"

"No! *No!* I haven't told him anything, not one word! He's been out of the country, damn it—and even if he'd been here, I wouldn't have . . . but I don't suppose you believe that." She sounded close to tears.

Hansard tried to decide if he did believe her, decided he did, and said so. "But you should have told me."

"I'm sorry," she said, and Hansard supposed he had to believe that too. "I was . . . having fun, you know? Being a spy, having a secret identity." She swallowed hard. "I thought you'd figure it out when Hugh mentioned my father. He blew my cover, do you see? That's why I got so angry with him. I'll apologize . . . Hugh's really a gent, too. Oh, he talks fresh, he did all through college, but he'd never . . ."

"Never?"

"Well, hardly ever," Ellen said. "Nicholas, do you have a place to stay in London tonight? I mean, arranged already?"

"No."

"Yes," Ellen said.

■ ■ ■

By the time they reached London it was full dark and the rain was coming down hard. They had half a block's soaking walk to Maxwell's flat. Once the door was closed, she hung her coat and peeled off her dress. "Go thou and do likewise," she said, and he shrugged and did.

Maxwell made hot milk with nutmeg and whiskey. It did wonders. Dressed in nightclothes, they sat drinking it slowly.

"Time to take stock," Ellen said. "What's your opinion of Skene now?"

"I think it must fictionalize some real event. A real assassination, by someone Marlowe knew. Suppose—"

The fat man sat in the corner of the Cheapside stew, where he always sat, half-visible through the dense air. Marlowe thought he looked like a turd left by some not very fastidious mongrel, and told him so.

"And greetings to you as well, Master Playwright," the fat man said pleasantly.

"I want to know about a man named Dover," Marlowe said. "Adam Dover. He says he's from there. A small gentleman."

"You're no longer part of our company of players, Master. Some things are secret from the world."

"Death's no secret. Blood's sticky stuff. Blood and shit both."

"Now really, Master Marlowe, you are off your familiar stage—"

"No, I can't see it," Hansard said.

"Go on. You're doing fine."

"No, I'm not. The characters aren't coming from anywhere but me." It didn't do any good to make the private spy fat and greasy instead of slender and immaculate: He was still Raphael, still cool, superior, calm in the face of whatever was thrown at him—"I'm just angry."

"Can't you get angry? Let it out?"

"*Of course,*" Hansard said, and then more softly, "of course. But I won't, not as long as I can help it."

"Noble," she said. "And useless."

"Reason isn't useless."

"Yes, Professor. . . . This friend of yours, the one you keep talking about—did he teach you that? Never to get angry?"

"He only got mad at me once. I mean, we had some knock-down-drag-out arguments, but he only got really angry once."

"Tell me about it."

"It was very late. We were already having an argument, about . . .
I don't remember what about now. I think it was Germany, modern Germany and the Thirty Years' War. That was one of Allan's
favorite—"

"He didn't get angry over the Thirty Years' War."

"No. I was trying to be very wise. That was dangerous in front
of Allan; he could tell wisdom from pomposity at fifty yards blind-
folded. I said something about a historian's job not being to make
policy but to guide it. To provide continuity. I know I used that word,
continuity.

"Allan's face got red. I'd never seen that before. I thought—" Maybe
he did have a heart attack, Hansard thought. Sure. And maybe Major
T. C. Montrose was playing a practical joke on the High Command.
"—anyway, he blew up.

"He said, 'Damn it, Hansard, the past isn't a refuge, it isn't some
scholarly retreat: It's the corridor that leads to where we stand now.
All the side doors are closed. The only branches are in front of you.
If you want to do something about the world, you can't do it in the
past and you can't reach the future. Now is all you have.' That part's
verbatim. I can still hear him, see him saying it. 'Now is all you have.'
And he's dead and I don't know why." Hansard's whole body was a
clenched fist. His eyes hurt, his throat, and he leaned forward and
began to sob.

"What *did* you do?" He looked up. Her voice had burned.

"It's an odd story," he said.

"Go on."

Hansard said, "There was an assistant professor at Valentine, po-
litically pretty far out, but Valentine likes to consider itself open . . .
at least, we rarely make issues of things. Anyway, this guy was caught
with a high-school girl. Not quite statutory, but . . . well.

"Of course there were demands he be thrown out. And there were
rumors that he hadn't done the seducing. And his politics came into
it, naturally. The arguments got really very vicious. It got to be quite
confusing: Whether you wanted him kept on or not, you couldn't
ever quite decide *why* you did."

"Which did you want?"

"I never said anything. I never did anything. When he finally did resign, I drank two beers at the farewell party, and went home, and slept with one of my graduate students."

"That isn't all the story," Ellen said. Of course it wasn't.

Allan had raged at Hansard to *do* something.

Raphael, all golden calm and sweet reason, had given him something to do.

People were dying.

What *was* the rest of the story? Hansard was a historian. He found connections. He had never been afraid of history before.

"No, that's never all of it," Hansard said. He looked at Ellen, so very close, so very *available* to him. She had been lying to him about who she was, how they had happened to meet. So had he. They both knew it. So what was next?

"You still have now," Maxwell said, resting her hand on his shoulder. "You can still get angry. Angry enough to do something."

He was about to ask what, when suddenly her fingertips were inside his collar, and her other hand was working at the buttons of his pajama shirt.

He looked up at her. She kissed him on the forehead. Her damp hair fell across his face.

What did I do? Hansard thought. Ellen's nails scratched his chest and he felt slightly dizzy. "Is this . . . the one I owe you?"

"Yes."

"All right," he said, though she hadn't asked him at all if it was all right, and he stood up while his legs would still allow it. He tugged gently at the sash of her robe.

"It's a small bed, love," she said. "You'll have to hold me close."

They began tenderly. They finished quite sweetly. In between there was a long and confused phase of awkward struggling, weight in the wrong places, roughness that could not be excused as inexperience or playfulness.

What they were doing, Hansard thought, was consummating the relationship, in all directions: all the fear and the mistrust between them, as well as the attraction. The trouble with being afraid was that you needed to frighten someone else in turn; the trouble with lying was that you needed someone to believe you. The trouble with attraction was that it gave you someone.

And this was so much easier than telling the truth.

Hansard could no longer think for breathing hard. In the dark, up close, Ellen looked like Anna. In the dark, Anna had looked like Louise. In the dark, Louise had tried not to scream.

Ellen cried out and Hansard fell upon her neck. In the dark none of it made any difference.

THE
DAY
OF THE
FIRESHIP

PART SIX

MEN UPON THE BRIDGE

Go place some men upon the bridge,
With bows and darts, to shoot at them they see,
And sink them in the river as they swim.

—The Massacre at Paris, *I, vii*

Hansard dreamed of graveyards, silent under snow. He wandered in the cold, looking away from the worn stones so that he would not read the names carved on them, shuffling through the drifts until whiteness blinded him completely.

He woke up, flat on his back in Ellen's bed, sunlight flooding his eyes, one arm and one leg dangling, the sheet a sort of toga across him. Roman jokes floated across his mind, but he just got up and walked into the little kitchen.

It was empty. So was the bathroom. He pulled on his undershorts and shirt and leaned in the doorframe between rooms for a moment, finally spotting the note on the kitchen table. In her small neat researcher's handwriting, it said:

*NO MILK. I REFUSE TO DRINK BLACK COFFEE THIS
MORNING. BACK IN A TICK.*
                LOVE, ELIZABETH THE FIRST.

Hansard sat on the bed to pull his trousers on, and then noticed the corner of paper sticking under the front door. He pulled it in, unfolded it. The message was not neat at all, awkward block letters drawn in thick black pencil.

DR. HANSARD, it said, WE ARE HOLDING THE GIRL.

Hansard felt his fingers ache, as if the paper were burning them.

DO NOTHING FOR 48 HRS & SHE WILL BE FINE. YOU
KNOW THE ALTERNATIVE.

He sat quite still. The alternative. Allan. Claude Buck. The alternative. He knew. He looked at the clock. It was 9:43 A.M. How long had she been gone? *Do nothing for 48 hrs.* As opposed to what? What in God's name was someone afraid he would do? Whether in an inn at Deptford or old and gray somewhere else, Christopher Marlowe was centuries dead.

He looked at the windows, at the windows beyond them. Were there eyes behind one of those panes, watching him, wired to a gun or a knife against—

Hansard stood up and yanked the drapes closed across all the windows. He sat back down on the unmade bed, making the springs scream, feeling the sound like a knife in his heart. He knew what the alternative was.

Do nothing? What constituted nothing? He went into the kitchen, made a cup of coffee, drank it black. There was some sausage and cheese in the small refrigerator, a loaf of bread, some butter. He began cataloguing: in the cupboard, two cans of soup, a box of Ryvita and a jar of Tiptree orange marmalade, both unopened. There wasn't much else in there, only a couple of plates and pieces of flatware. It would do. He could stay in for two days. He wasn't very hungry anyway.

He went back to the bed, lay down on it, closed his eyes. Nothing happened. Just as well, he thought, getting up, going to the kitchen again. Dreaming just now was inviting horror.

He opened the marmalade, spread some on bread. It tasted bitter, not much else. The coffee had gone foul somehow. He walked out of the kitchen into the bathroom, opened the medicine cabinet, looking for at least an aspirin, maybe something stronger.

There was nothing in the cabinet. Nothing at all.

He began to walk around the small flat, opening every cabinet and drawer as he passed. There were some clothes, some absolute-basic housewares. But there was no redundancy: Hansard didn't know of anyone who had only one bottle opener, one set of salt and pepper shakers. All the silverware matched exactly; there wasn't one odd spoon. Even the glasses were all from the same lot, no empty jam jars or replacements that didn't quite match.

And there was no junk at all. No bric-a-brac, no keepsakes. For God's sake, Hansard thought, *college dorm rooms* had personal clutter.

She had been a folksinger, and there was no guitar here. Nothing to make music with at all.

He analyzed. It was what he did best in the world. And the analysis was idiotically simple. Nobody lived here. Oh, presumably it was Ellen's flat—these were her clothes, she'd had the key—but she didn't *live* here.

Hansard sat down on the bed, confused and frightened and angry. Yes, he thought, very angry.

Angry enough to do something about it?

Hansard opened his wallet, slid out his telephone credit card. He picked up the phone and began dialing. It was now 5:11 A.M. in Georgetown. That didn't matter to Hansard. Raphael didn't sleep. Only human beings had the need for sleep.

■ ■ ■

In the Games Centre Situation Room, digital clocks showed 10:28 A.M. London and 5:28 Washington time. The Main Display had a map of the North Atlantic, ships marked in green. They were real ships this time; the BLUE CRYSTAL naval exercise was beginning its first full day.

At the four tiers of consoles facing the Display, signals and monitor officers were at work, pecking at their keyboards like battery hens. In the Machine Room to one side of the big screens, programmer Pruett (who had replaced the late LCdr Susan Bell on the COPE systems pilot operation) supervised the loading of thoughts into Freon-cooled mechanical brains. Three floors above, a specially cleared team of reporters and technical writers sat with coffee and doughnuts and notepads and lap computers, ready to pound out the play-by-play on the NATO navies' most expensive pretend-war to date.

And just below the reporters, the navies' top brass were settling into their own chairs, having just finished a briefing brunch. Centre Director Lambert, wired for sound, stood in front of them, feeling quite schoolmasterly.

He held onto the feeling for almost twenty minutes, directing the gentlemen's attention here and answering questions there and calling downstairs for elaboration over *there*. He had forgotten, Lambert thought with more than a touch of rue, just how grindingly dull this sort of thing could be. He wondered how Bell had stayed sane—and then he stopped thinking about that at once and deliberately.

At 11:04 London/6:04 EDT, prompted by the UNICOM 1 phone in his ear, Lambert said, "The next stage of the exercise is a navigational drill, in which—"

The three-note warning chime for attack cut Lambert off. A red nuclear-burst symbol, a semicircle atop a triangle, like an ice-cream cone, appeared on the main board; then there was a second, a third, a fourth.

The data screens went black. The scrolling LED data line printed: THIS IS NOT A DRILL THIS IS and then died too.

"Oh," one of the American admirals said, "oh, my . . ."

"Shut down the links to the press room," the Director said over the SPECCOM channel. "Shut them *all* down. No, don't drop the curtains yet . . . they're not going to get any more off the Board than we are, dammit. And get me the Machine Room on Uni 2 . . . Pruett? This is Lambert. What's going on? No, I'll be right down."

Lambert said to the observers, "We've had a programs glitch, I'm afraid. If you gentlemen will excuse me, I'll see what's being done. We should be on line and running again very shortly."

"Mr. Lambert," a British admiral said quietly, "those are not computer simulations, out on the water . . . they're actual ships, with sailors on them. Do get this straightened out quickly."

Lambert nodded. As he went to the lift, he said softly to the Duty Officer, "Don't let them call out."

In the Machine Room downstairs, a half dozen of the equipments staff were standing around a table covered with manuals, diagrams, printouts; another half dozen programs people worked furiously at video terminals.

Pruett looked up as Director Lambert came in. "It's gone full automatic," he said.

"What's that supposed to mean?"

"We've got green lights. It's not a malfunction. Or if it *is* a malfunction, the hardware's hiding it."

"What in hell are you talking about?" the Director said.

"What am I talking about?" Pruett exploded. "What am I *talking* about? The goddamn mainframe is running a goddamn exercise all by its goddamn self, that's what I'm goddamn talking about," Pruett said. Lambert took a step backward, turning a vivid red. Pruett held up a crumpled pile of printouts. "It's running just like it's supposed to, only *we didn't program this.*"

"Who had access?" Rhys-Gordon said, seeming to suddenly appear from the wall.

"Look, we don't even know if it's hardware or software—"

"Who had access?" Rhys-Gordon said again.

"The programming staff, the equipments and maintenance staff, the installers," Pruett said, in desperation.

Rhys-Gordon said, "There are days when I'm so proud to be part of my country's security, I could just vomit." His pager whistled. He slapped it to his ear. "Yes. There's—he's here on *whose* authority? All right." He turned to Pruett. "Try to narrow it down to the population of the Home Counties, will you?"

Rhys-Gordon met Nicholas Hansard at the main security gate.

"You're the Security Officer?" Hansard said. Rhys-Gordon thought he looked in a proper sweat.

"For a while yet, yeah," Rhys-Gordon said. "We're rather busy now, Doctor. What's this about?"

"A friend of mine is missing. I think it might be important: I've only just found out she works here, you see, and—"

"Who?"

"Ellen Maxwell."

"Jesus holy Christ." Hansard gaped. The gate staff did too. Rhys-Gordon grabbed a telephone. "Machine Room. Now."

Hansard was hastily issued a pass and dragged through the Games Centre corridors to the second-level observation room, which had been converted into an emergency operations room by plugging in terminals and bringing in a select few Intelligence and command personnel. What Hansard saw was a rats' nest of cables, and a cluster of people knee-deep in coils of printout looking at him with a sort of horrified awe.

"Anything come through?" Rhys-Gordon said.

"Not a bit," someone told him.

Hansard said, "I got a message saying they'd kill her . . ." He let it pass.

A man in a dark suit looked Hansard up and down. He spoke with an American accent. "Just how much have you learned about the Berenson network, Dr. Hansard?"

"The Berenson *what?*"

The man stopped talking. Rhys-Gordon said to the dark-suited man—CIA? NSA? Who cared?—"Yes, I don't suppose you'd care to enlighten the rest of us?"

The American looked nervous. "It was reasonably common knowledge that—"

Hansard said, "What do you fucking mean, *common knowledge?*"

"Now, look, some of you aren't cleared for this."

"What are you cleared for, you son of a bitch?" Hansard snapped. "Raphael's right after all. 'You're all in bed with each other, you all snoop on each other. . . .'"

"Raphael?" the man said. "I'm sorry, sir, I didn't know you were—"

"I'm not," Hansard said, "so don't tell me anything, okay?"

Rhys-Gordon said, "I doubt there is a network any longer. The boys from Moscow tried seriously to kill Mrs. Maxwell a few days back, did kill a couple of people we know of. They're not going to have missed them all." He turned to Hansard. "What we need to know now is what this little surprise"—he pointed at the huge computer screen outside, which was blank but for nuclear symbols—"is supposed to accomplish. We're confused, right enough, but that's not an end in itself."

"Well, actually . . ." said Pruett, the computer man, "we're really just isolated, not disrupted. The exercise is still proceeding under computer control. The data is even being stored. We just can't *read* any of it yet."

Director Lambert said, "But we will be able to?"

"We don't dare shut down the system now, while communications are out—it might restore the links, but it might not. But after the exercise has run, we can access everything that happened."

Lambert went to the window, to stare at the board. "Then I don't understand at all. What's it *for*? How can they even tell—"

The voices all stopped, leaving only the whir and rattle of the machines. "Oh, my god," someone said, "COPE is running."

"So what does that mean?" an admiral said.

Pruett sat down at one of the video terminals, stared into the noise on its screen. "It means the channels aren't out at all. COPE CHANTER is making sure the data is still collected, PHAGE is making sure there's a transmission channel, and LIGHT is receiving. But not *our* LIGHT. We can't read it, but somebody is." The technician threw up his hands. "We can't even *stop* it."

Rhys-Gordon said, "COPE LIGHT." His voice sounded gritty.

"It's logical," Pruett said.

"I can see the *logic*. Where did they get . . . oh, Christ." He turned away from them all.

Lambert said, "Gareth—"

"I'm thinking. . . . It's not enough," Rhys-Gordon said. "They could get maneuver data with a man in here. And they *had* a man in here," he said, with a long look at Hansard.

Someone said, "They're after the codes."

"Not enough," Rhys-Gordon said. "They could sit tight in Archangelsk and pull the codes off the satellite. But Mrs. Maxwell was in London until last night."

". . . something provocative," one of the men in dark suits was saying. "It would be logical to do something to stimulate communications— the more traffic, the better the traffic analysis."

Hansard thought about a Korean jetliner and kept his mouth shut.

"A submarine," one of the admirals' attachés said.

"Christ, yes," said an admiral. "The water'll be full of Russian pigboats, they're always there during exercises, we've run 'em down twice. Suppose one of them lets go a fish or two, and a couple of ships go down, who's going to pin the blame?"

Freedonia's going to war, Hansard thought, beginning to understand what was going on on the board, in this room. It was a game, all a grown men's game with live pieces, expensive delicate ships. He said, "No, wait . . . Ellen wouldn't do that . . . I mean, her husband was on *Sheffield,* for God's sake . . ."

No one seemed to be listening to him. There were calls going out for RAF Buccaneer aircraft with antisubmarine gear to be scrambled, sweep the sea under manual direction. Outside this room's window, on the floor of the big theatrelike chamber, a table showed a slide-projected map of the North Atlantic, and young officers were spreading plastic markers out on top of it.

Hansard said one last time, "Ellen wouldn't sink a ship," and Gareth Rhys-Gordon took his arm and led him away, saying, "That's the thing about this business, Dr. Hansard. You never know just what anyone will do until they do it." There was nothing gentle or comforting about Rhys-Gordon's voice; it was hard as bare bone.

Hansard said, "Do you think . . . Allan Berenson set this up?"

Rhys-Gordon said, "I've never heard of Allan Berenson 'til this morning, Doctor. Your countrymen seem to know a good bit about him, though. Why don't you ask one of them?"

"Countrymen . . ."

"My country, right or wrong, that is an American saying, isn't it?"

Hansard only half heard him. "And Ellen's father . . . he's something in British Intelligence, isn't he?"

Rhys-Gordon rubbed his chin, ran a finger along the deepest of the scars on his face. "Yes, sir, that is true, he is most certainly *something* in that area."

"'O stately, measured dance of venery!'"

"Excuse me?"

"That's a quote from a play . . . it's about a man who wants to destroy his father, bring down his father's court. I know what it's for, now." Hansard laughed. "Something worthy of him."

"Well?"

"To make you all look like fools," Hansard said, grimly delighted by the beauty of the idea.

"Right," Rhys-Gordon said, with combined wonder and distaste. "Anything further to add, Doctor?"

Hansard struggled to think. "You say that Ellen's tapping the ships' communications somehow."

"That's a fair guess. If she'd turned the gear over to the other side, there wouldn't have been any need for her to disappear. Of course, she might have done it today . . . in which case I think you can count her no longer among the living." He started to walk away.

"What if we found her?"

Rhys-Gordon stopped, turned. His eyes were hooded. "What time did she leave you this morning?"

"I don't know."

"What's the earliest she *could* have left?"

"I didn't check my watch."

"Pity. I thought you historians were good about such things."

Hansard said nothing.

"All right. Where do you propose we begin looking, Dr. Hansard? This isn't such a vast country, but it's big enough to hide quite a lot." Bitterness fairly dripped from Rhys-Gordon's voice.

Hansard started to speak, then paused. Rhys-Gordon was watching him carefully, measuring Hansard with his eyes.

Hansard said, "I want something in return."

"Doesn't everyone?" Rhys-Gordon's voice was calm and cold. "I can't promise to give her immunity. I can't even call it possible or not. I'm not even entitled to call it a damn shame we stopped hanging traitors in this country—at least, not in my official—"

"I want to go with you."

Rhys-Gordon said, without sarcasm, "You know where she is, then."

"Yes."

"And if I won't take you? Will you hold your breath"—he pointed at the blank boards outside the room—"till some particular number of people've died?"

"I—"

Rhys-Gordon turned to the American Intelligence man in the dark suit. "I'm borrowing this national of yours to identify our target. He's waived his constitutional rights to be kept alive."

"Fine by me," the man said, with a look of utter indifference at Hansard.

"Come on, Professor, roll up for the mystery tour," Rhys-Gordon said. "Where is it we're going?"

"Dover," Hansard said. "She's in Dover . . . watching the Armada burn."

"Fair enough," Rhys-Gordon said. "On the way you must tell me all about it."

■ ■ ■

Marlowe ran through the gallery, flung himself down the little staircase. He half fell against the tiring-room door, and it swung wide.

Adam Dover, or whatever his name was, was fully dressed for his part, just tying on his mask. He looked up, eyes like sparks behind the silver mask's holes.

"Stand away, Friend Playwright," Dover said, "or I shall miss my entrance, and the court will blame your play."

Marlowe kicked Dover in the crotch. Dover groaned, and his costume tore, and the dagger in his hand fell to the floor. He staggered back against a table.

"Lord of killers, are you?" Marlowe said. "You wouldn't last two breaths in a Cambridge stew," and then his own gentlemanly knife was out.

Dover muttered something he lacked the wind to say clearly, and pushed himself forward, groping with his right hand at his left sleeve. He shuffled. His eyes shifted. Marlowe followed the look—the feint—but was not distracted; he stepped and thrust, through the costly beads and satin into the slot between the ribs.

Dover's hands closed on Marlowe's wrist. They were cold, and had no strength. Marlowe pulled his knife out, and there was blood enough to drown in.

Dover wobbled. He reached up, touched the mask loose around his neck. He pulled it away. His lips were bloody and his face dripped hate. He fell down, scattering beads.

Someone was pounding at the door. Marlowe opened it. The Master of the Revels was there, saying, "Master—oh, Master Marlowe, Dover's part is—" and then he saw the blood, and reached to his belt.

Curious how hands seek out knives, Marlowe thought.

"What has happened?" the Revel-Master said. More players were crowding up behind him. Someone gasped.

Marlowe reached down to the sleeve of Dover's costume, the one Dover had tried to pull open. He ripped it apart, and light shone dully from the pistol barrel against the undersleeve.

"The foe is fallen, celebrate the day," Marlowe said, "now call for men to bear the dead away."

He stood there for a moment, staring at the dead, twisted face. *No more answers here,* he thought. Then he snatched up the mask and pushed his way out of the room, to fill a little part in Hell.

■ ■ ■

"Or as the play says, after Didrick dies in a small tiring-room, 'Now take my knife, thou murd'rer, spill thy blood/And decorate a chamber down in Hell.' There's a similar line in Shakespeare's *Richard II*."

"Very colorful," Rhys-Gordon said. He upshifted, and the black Lotus Turbo left London in its wake. "Any evidence for it?"

"Some," Hansard said, too tired to be insulted. "The Skene rolls account for the costumes, and the Queen's visit. But there's no record of the masque itself . . . which is itself evidence. Or at least," he said dryly, "I choose to call it evidence."

"That's fair."

Hansard said, "The man I saw at the theatre wasn't really police, was he? He did kill Claude."

"I'd suppose he was the killer. As for the other bit, I wouldn't venture a guess. Policemen *have* been known to do jobs on the side. Barman in my favorite local's a Metropolitan." Rhys-Gordon tapped his fingers on the wheel, looked slightly at Hansard. "All kinds of people do all kinds of odd work." The Lotus passed a pair of Cortinas. "How long have you been in the trade?"

"I'm not in . . . the trade."

"Oh, that's right. You're one of Raphael's brain trust."

"I suppose I am, at that . . . but my main interest is the truth. I guess I've fallen in with the wrong crowd."

Rhys-Gordon laughed once, and Hansard knew he had to stay out of battles of sarcasm with this man. Rhys-Gordon had unlimited ammunition.

"I was at CIA headquarters once," Rhys-Gordon said. "There's a sign just inside their door. Do you know what that sign says, Dr. Hansard?"

Hansard did. "'Ye shall know the truth, and the truth shall make you free.'" Yes, no way at all to beat the Intelligence man at double meanings.

Rhys-Gordon said, "Of course we lie. And it's no good to ignore the lies, or minimize them, because the lies are very honestly the point of it. It's a liar's trade. First the liars prosper most, then the lies are needed just to break even—then just to stay in business, stay alive. Truth kills."

■ ■ ■

Sladen was looking out the office window when Glazdunov came in, his arms full of notes and maps. He dropped the papers onto Sladen's desk.

"What is this mess?" Sladen said. "The English are already on their way to apprehend WAGNER."

"Only one vehicle was dispatched," Glazdunov said, with a distinct sound of excitement.

Sladen went to the desk, looked at the papers. "And?"

"There is a chance to reclaim the entire NIGHTMOVE operation," Glazdunov said. "If WAGNER can be given a small amount of time . . . she is not far from the shore, and the pickup boat is on station."

Sladen looked at the clock. "How much time?"

Glazdunov looked at his map of the Dover coast, measured a distance with his fingers. "Two hours."

Sladen folded his hands. He had no illusions of suddenly, heroically salvaging the situation. Only planners like Glazdunov, like Palatine, could reduce things to such a schematic level. The consequences of a disaster were real, there was no point in ignoring them. Glazdunov's "delaying action" meant killing the British agent and the man with him. And then if they did get the woman WAGNER and the tapes onto the boat, they would have to kill her, certainly at sea, incommunicado. And she would know this, she had proven thoroughly that she was no fool, no amateur! So—

Sladen thought about Rhys-Gordon, the unpleasant little man, on the road in Palatine's car.

"Very well," he said, and Glazdunov nodded furiously.

■ ■ ■

"There's a helicopter just above us," Rhys-Gordon said. "I don't believe I like that."

"Could it be support for us? Maybe it's—"

"You don't send people 'support' without telling them about it.

That leads to serious misunderstandings." There was a sound like a brick hitting the roof of the Lotus, then another. Rhys-Gordon's hands clenched on the wheel and he slewed the car into the right lane, then back again as an oncoming car blew its horn and screeched its brakes. The helicopter fluttered up slightly, then down again. Another brick hit the roof.

"They're shooting at us," Hansard said.

"That's right. But that's not a misunderstanding, I'm afraid."

The car slid around tight two-lane curves edged by pubs and stone retaining walls. Hansard could see the helicopter cut across the tightest bends, to be there when the Lotus arrived. "Why don't you stop?"

"Because that's—what they want," Rhys-Gordon said, and downshifted to take another S-curve. "Doubt they really want to kill us. Then again, if I figure Mr. Sladen right . . . sorry. Private grudge, that."

Hansard stared at Rhys-Gordon. The world truly belonged to the madmen now. "I don't suppose the car's bulletproof," he said, as the window a foot behind his head starred. "Or has rocket launchers, or turns into an airplane, or . . ."

"*Do* hush, Dr. Hansard."

Hansard shut his eyes. He was thrown against the door, then back again.

Rhys-Gordon said, "I do have a gun, if you'd care to shoot back."

"Will that do any good?"

"How good a shot are you?"

"I've never fired a pistol in my life."

"That's too bad."

They passed another car, dodging back again as a van bore toward them. "What I need is some open space," Rhys-Gordon said. "This thing will do 220. They can't." Another shot went *spat* against the sheet metal. "But we have to go all round Robin Hood's barn . . . Ah. Stupid me. Pick up the phone. Call—"

The telephone rang. "Bloody hell." Rhys-Gordon grabbed it. "Yes? Do tell." He held it out. "It's for you."

Hansard said, "Hello?"

"Nicholas, this is Vince Rulin."

"*Vince?*—I . . . Vince, what did you give me for Christmas last year?"

There was a chuckle. "Very good, Nicholas. I gave you a tomb seal. Now, tell Rhys-Gordon to just keep the pedal down, and we'll be along in a moment . . . I can see you now. We're in a red Porsche about five hundred yards behind you. See us?"

Hansard looked back. It was hard to see much of anything through the narrow slot of the Lotus's rear window, but finally he spotted a streak of fire-engine red, dipping and sliding along the curves of the road. "Yes, I see you." He turned to Rhys-Gordon. "The cavalry's coming."

"Really. When this is over, I'll be interested to know who called them."

The helicopter lifted away from the Lotus. "What—" Rhys-Gordon said as they rounded a left-hand bend. A truck was stopped in the lane dead ahead, big as a house. Rhys-Gordon shoved the car right to dodge it, putting them head-on with another van. Its horn blasted. He inhaled sharply and threw the Lotus back into the left lane, slipping by as the two trucks scissored past.

"Handles well, she does," Rhys-Gordon said thickly.

Hansard heard horns blow behind them. The Lotus went over a bump, nearly getting airborne, and the black trucks disappeared. The helicopter pulled low again, and there were thumps on the car roof, and a sudden star on the windshield.

Hansard turned again. The red Porsche bounced over the rise. "They're here," he said to Rhys-Gordon.

"Right." Rhys-Gordon downshifted and braked. The helicopter shot ahead of them, the Porsche closed in, pulled alongside. The helicopter closed in. Hansard couldn't see the gun in the red car, or who was shooting, but he heard *punt, punt, punt,* and then the helicopter was climbing like a mad black angel.

"Remember the Alamo," Rhys-Gordon said, double-clutched the Lotus and floored it.

■ ■ ■

Owen Licht had put out from Stornoway before dawn, alone with the Sea Wasp missiles. The fog had been heavy then, and had barely broken at all; he was navigating by dead reckoning. The boat had radar, but the woman on the phone had warned him not to use it. It was a simple enough job of sailing, as he understood it: head out into the open water, find a warship, fire the missiles. Supposedly some sort of device would keep the warships from spotting him, as long as he didn't use the radar. That was fine, but not so very necessary; Licht had been in the water with the big ships before, and they tended not to notice little boats, or just to ignore them. Tankers were the worst—they knew they couldn't turn worth a damn, and would crush you anyhow—but the navy ships weren't much better.

Damn them all, he thought, and plowed on through the fog.

■ ■ ■

"I think that's what we're looking for," Rhys-Gordon said, and pointed to a silver van on the green Dover clifftops, pointing a mesh-work dish at the cloudy sky. He slowed down. "Nice coverage of the approaches," he said. "The way I see it, we have two options: fast and close or long and slow." He glanced at Hansard. "I vote fast and close. And I'm the only one voting."

The car picked up speed as it left the roadway, bouncing over the greensward, directly for the caravan.

"You're going"—Hansard said, holding on tight—"just to go in shooting?"

"Not unless I have to. But if"—they bumped and bottomed, kept going—"I have to, the gun won't do me much good stuck in my trousers, will it, Dr. Hansard?"

The Lotus braked to a stop a few feet from the caravan door, throwing sod and gravel. Rhys-Gordon released his seat belt and drew his pistol. "Now *look*. I'm going to go in there and stop the lady doing what she's doing before ships get sunk, and there's a good chance I'll have to hurt her very badly in the process. If you're not on for that, then just sit."

Hansard unfastened his belt. "I'm coming."

"Suit yourself." Rhys-Gordon was out of the car in an instant. There was a hollow bang of metal, a crash of glass. By the time Hansard was fully out of the Lotus, he saw Rhys-Gordon standing in the caravan doorway, gun leveled. Rhys-Gordon went inside. Hansard followed him.

The inside of the caravan looked like a TV studio, much compressed. Screens were flickering, reels of tape turning, lights flashing. There was a long, narrow, cork-topped desk along the consoles on one side. Ellen was sitting in a swivel chair, a book of *Telegraph* crosswords in one hand and a pencil in the other, looking at Rhys-Gordon and Rhys-Gordon's gun, and then at Hansard.

"It seems like we're always apologizing to each other, Nicholas," she said.

"It's all . . . real, then," Hansard said.

"It's been a lot of very hard work," Ellen said. "Yes, it's real."

■ ■ ■

Owen Licht looked up. There was a pair of search planes coming, fat old Buccaneers by the look of them, black spots in the fog scraping the bottoms of the clouds.

Maybe they weren't looking for him, he thought. Fat chance, he thought. He lifted the lid on the missile arming box, took the key from the pocket of his parka. All he needed was a little time, all he needed was a ship. The papers said there were at least forty of them out there, playing their war game. He couldn't sail by them all.

The planes flew over, whipping spray across Licht's boat. They began to circle back.

All he needed was one goddamned ship, and they wouldn't need to report him. The world would already have heard.

■ ■ ■

Rhys-Gordon said, "Are you ready to shut it down now?" He was standing at one end of the caravan, Ellen sitting in the swivel chair at the other. Hansard stood next to the Intelligence man, just staring from one of them to the other.

Ellen said, "I don't know how to shut it down. I just watch the lights."

"Now you don't expect me to believe that. Suze Bell could teach old admirals new tricks. She could surely teach you."

"Leave Bell out of this! . . . Leave her out."

Rhys-Gordon shook his head. Still holding the gun dead level, he picked up Ellen's handbag from the desktop, turned it over. Makeup and a wallet fell out, coins, keys, a silver cigarette case. Rhys-Gordon picked up the cigarette case. "Oh, now, I haven't seen one of these since I was a Boy Scout. Palatine give you this?"

Ellen put her hands in her lap.

"Palatine's dead too, you know. Or did you have a hand in that?"

Ellen said, "Nicholas . . ."

Hansard took a step forward. "They said in London . . . that someone was going to attack a ship."

"Did they?" Ellen said.

"You might as well tell us," Rhys-Gordon said. "It's all over now but the shooting, and there doesn't have to be any of that."

"A ship, Ellen?" Hansard said, trying to make some sense of her. "'Sorry, ma'am, but England expects that every man, you know . . .'"

Ellen's hands came up from below the desk. There was a monstrous black pistol in her grip.

Rhys-Gordon had a gun, and now suddenly Ellen had a gun, and Hansard had a wild wish to grab them both and shake them until their teeth rattled, wake them up from the dream of guns and killing.

But he knew, and was sick for knowing, that they weren't dreaming, that he was, and he was terrified that any moment now he would wake up to find a gun in his own hand. *How much more like a god might one man be,* Marlowe had written, if it was Marlowe at all who wrote the damned play, *to strike another dead, and yet be free.*

"Nicholas," Ellen said, "do you understand what this is for?"

"I don't understand any of it." He looked at the gun, pointed as much at him as at the Intelligence man, and thought of the sudden slap at Skene House, of Hugh Keane's glasses against the wall. The Baronet had blown her cover, she'd said.

"She's going to start World War Three," Rhys-Gordon said, sounding amused. "No hard feelings, you understand. It's just to prove a philosophical point."

"That's just it, I'm *not.* Nicholas. This is Allan's plan. Do you think he'd have done any such thing? We're going to prove a point, yes— we're going to prove that the command system doesn't work. You told me yourself about the command doctrines; you know how insane the whole thing is. We're going to show the idiots in command what we already know."

"Codswallop," Rhys-Gordon said.

"We," Hansard said.

Maxwell said, "Yes, we. Allan and I. And you, if you'll help me. Do you remember, last night, how angry you were? Be angry, Nicholas. But *use* the rage for something."

Rhys-Gordon said, "Can't have you angry, Doctor, there isn't room in here." He had his gun in both hands, leveled.

"Oh, Gareth, damn it," Ellen said, and put the gun down on the desk. Rhys-Gordon lowered his own pistol. Ellen brushed by Hansard. Her hand moved very quickly.

Rhys-Gordon made a small, sharp sound. Blood flew. Rhys-Gordon staggered back, a hand to his face, and hit the wall. Hansard saw what seemed to be a rigid red streak of blood spouting from Ellen's hand, then realized it was some kind of transparent knifeblade.

She pushed Hansard aside, knocking him off balance, and dove for the floor. She pushed open a little panel, started to crawl through into the front of the vehicle.

Hansard tried to bend down, and half fell onto Maxwell's legs. He wrapped his arms around her calves. *"Nicholas,"* she said, but he held on, squeezing his eyes shut. "Nicholas, please, let me go—"

"No," he said. He opened his eyes and looked up. She was holding the pipe-fitting gun that had killed Claude Buck. Or maybe it was another one. Guns were a dime a dozen now.

Hansard heard movement behind himself, felt a hand on his shoulder, a hard steady pressure against the back of his head. "We'll do it on three, Mrs. Maxwell," Rhys-Gordon said, "and when you're sitting in your cell for the next fifty years, you can have that little bit of doubt about which bullet killed the fellow. One."

"Oh, stop it, Gareth," Ellen said.

"The hell I will. Two."

She tossed the gun aside. "You're a good team," she said, without much inflection at all. "A regular Burke and Hare, for digging up old bodies. For smothering people."

■ ■ ■

Licht turned the arming key, and the three lamps lit green, haloed in the fog. He pressed the first button. With a bang and a furious hiss the first Sea Wasp exploded from its launcher. There was almost no smoke, just a pulse of yellow light, rising toward the search planes.

A black shape blossomed red, metal peeling apart, light mirrored off the sea and the fog. Then the sound arrived.

But it wasn't good enough. He needed a ship, and there wasn't one, and the second plane was already turning, to destroy him.

Then he saw it: a lovely fat cruiser, like a cliff in the fog, showing its broadside to him. He could have thrown the missiles with his bare hands and hit it.

Owen Licht stabbed the buttons, and the two Sea Wasps burst their coffins and flew.

He had done something real, he thought, and something unique: In any war, there can be only one first shot.

■ ■ ■

Maxwell stood up slowly. Rhys-Gordon pulled Hansard away from her with one hand, holding his pistol level with the other.

"You've won, Gareth. You don't need a hostage."

"Just do the work, dearie." His voice was neither angry nor sarcastic; it was like a machine, a tape recording.

Maxwell reached to the control boards, flipped a switch, another, another, turned a knob a full twist over. Lights went out, tape reels stopped turning, a jittering green line on a monitor went flat as the trace of a dead man's brain.

"Now I've done it," she said, looking at the flat line. "I've betrayed absolutely everybody."

■ ■ ■

Owen Licht saw volcanic eruptions of fire from the ship, a red hail of steel like no weapon he had ever seen before. The Sea Wasps collided with a solid wall of bullets and exploded in midair. Owen just had time to feel the heat before the Phalanx rounds reached him, and tore him and his boat to splinters.

■ ■ ■

"I didn't kill Suze and Mick," Maxwell said. "Not even indirectly."

"Like hell not indirectly." Blood was still oozing from the gash in Rhys-Gordon's cheek. If it hurt him—and it had to—he was showing no sign of it.

"I didn't."

"Oh, I believe you," Rhys-Gordon said. "You can't think it forgives anything, though."

"No. Of course not."

"Right enough. Shall we take a drive, then?"

Hansard looked back and forth between the two of them, trying to get a little of whatever their mutual understanding was. He had been denying that this was his world, but it was in fact. It was the world he lived in, though he knew nothing of it at all.

Ellen went out of the van, Rhys-Gordon and his gun right after. Hansard was left alone with the silent electronics, the spilled purse, the abandoned pistol. No one seemed to be interested in him at all.

■ ■ ■

It had required a special phone call before Hansard was admitted to the RAF base; then his clothing was searched and his person swept with a metal detector. He was asked to leave his keys and wallet and ballpoint pen outside.

At the end of a long blank corridor, Gareth Rhys-Gordon was leaning against a wall. It made him look folded-in on himself, crumpled.

Hansard said, "I just wanted to see her . . ."

Rhys-Gordon said, "I supposed so. You can. For a while, I suspect you can get anything you want. You may not realize it yet, but you're the bloke of the hour. Saved the whole stinking world, with seconds to spare. James Bond could do no more."

Hansard banged a hand against the wall. It hurt. "What in *hell* is your problem?"

"No problem at all." Rhys-Gordon smiled, wrinkling the plaster stuck down the side of his face, and there was all the bitterness in the world in it. "I was just welcoming you to the little fellowship of heroes, Dr. Hansard. Welcome to the depths of the shithole."

Hansard went through the door. Beyond was a little room, absolutely bare but for a small table and a chair. An RAF base policeman stood by the door; Ellen stood against the far wall, in a shapeless gray shift and cloth slippers.

"Go away," Hansard told the guard, and he went away, closing the door.

Hansard said, "Ellen—"

"We're not private, you know," she said. "We're on audio and video. They're afraid I'll kill you with my teeth and hang myself with your shoelaces."

He tried to smile, but it wasn't a joke. There wasn't any humor to take away from the situation. There didn't seem to be anything at all to take away.

After a silence he said, "I did love you."

"Allan loved me. And he loved you. Do you know how much Allan loved you, Nicholas Hansard? He'd tell me, 'There's this young man, he's my best hope, I wish you could meet him.' But I couldn't meet you, because Allan and I couldn't ever be connected, because of peeping Toms like that little Welsh gargoyle out there, listening at the door right now . . . he kept us apart, and my father the knight had Allan killed, and whose side are *you* on?" She held out a hand, pointed it at him. "You had the note—just stay silent for two days, to save my life—and you went straight to the coppers. What should I make of that?"

"Tell me what side you're on," Hansard said, "and I'll try to figure out where I stand."

"You're everything good that Allan was," she said, not sadly but spitting the words as if revolted by them. "You're kind and decent and intelligent as men are made . . ." Hansard thought that the world was full of revolting things this morning, but he could not think about them too much, dared not make it all make sense.

"If I'd met you before," Ellen said, "had you even to talk to, after he died . . . maybe I could have let it drop. But I didn't. You had all of Allan's friends. I didn't have anything." Without any particular feeling, she said, "Where were you when I needed you, you bastard? Do you see how you've hurt me?"

She was perfect, Hansard thought, she was whatever person the situation required. He said, "I could have . . ."

"No," Ellen said. "Too much history between us."

She began to laugh, a light, throaty, hideous noise. He couldn't hate her, couldn't begin to do that, but the bright awful laughter did allow him to turn away, and as he did he recognized it for a kindness, perhaps the only unalloyed kindness she had done him.

He went out of the room, past the guard, past Rhys-Gordon without sparing him a glance, down the empty corridor, alone with his echoes.

LAST ACT

PART SEVEN

SINCE WE HAVE THEE

Thus he determin'd to have handled thee,
But I have rather chose to save thy life. . . .
. . . for, since we have thee here,
We will not let thee part so suddenly.

—The Jew of Malta, *V, v*

Hansard had not known what to expect of Edward Moreton Chetwynd. The man he found was surpassingly ordinary; a dumpy, balding fellow in a gray tweed suit and a club tie, sitting behind his desk, next to his fire, amid all the bric-a-brac that Hansard had found fascinating when Ellen had brought him here before, but now only reminded him of the visit, and Ellen, and lies.

"Ellen said that I should ask you who killed Allan Berenson," Hansard said.

"A very complicated question, Dr. Hansard," Chetwynd said evenly. "One which you yourself know part of the answer to, I believe; was it not you who analyzed the Montrose papers?"

"Yes."

"Dr. Berenson would have known in a matter of days, if he didn't already know, that the Montrose documents compromised him. His exposure would have been . . . embarrassing. His defection would have been a disaster."

"Embarrassing and disastrous for *whom*? He wasn't in Secret work!"

"Allan was in *everything*, Dr. Hansard. You know that just as well as I."

"So you decided to kill him."

Chetwynd shook his head slowly. "Sevenage did. In actual fact."

"Who's Sevenage?"

"Sevenage is a computer."

Hansard stared.

Chetwynd said, "It belongs to the National Security Agency, in Virginia. They have so many . . . this one analyzes the importance of certain people, and purports to predict their actions. Do you catch the significance of its name, Dr. Hansard?"

"'All the world's a stage, and all the men and women merely players.'"

"Yes . . . Sevenage insisted that the only way to prosecute the Berenson case—this is technical, trade terminology I'm using, Dr. Hansard, and my personal feelings have nothing to do with it—was to terminate him."

"But you did it."

"I had given Allan a copy of the Skene playscript. I wanted it back. As a document of . . . questionable provenance, it was likely to be seized by the American police, if not the Intelligence services. So an arrangement was made."

"You killed him in exchange for your *manuscript* back? For a *copy of a play?*"

"You aren't listening," Chetwynd said. "Allan was going to die. He was tried and condemned by a helium-cooled supercomputer. All that I did was rent out the assassins. The Skene Manuscript wasn't the *reason* for anything. It was my *price.*"

"No reason," Hansard said, feeling numb. "No reason for anything."

"I don't see why it's necessary to remind you of NIGHTMOVE, Dr. Hansard. It was not one of Allan's games. People were killed for it, and it was part of the plan that even more people be killed. Or do you agree with Ellen? Do you think that those deaths would have been in a good cause? That the end—" Was that pain in Chetwynd's voice, or something else? "—justified the means?"

Hansard said nothing. Chetwynd was right, that far at least.

Chetwynd said, "Allan might have been my second son-in-law. And it would not have made any difference. He would still be dead . . . and it would still be a shameful thing. So very shameful. I'm ashamed, Dr. Hansard. You can't ask me to be anything more than that."

Chetwynd picked a typescript from his desk. "This is the last of the Skene documents. It is not catalogued with the others. I suggest that you read it."

It was a letter from Thomas Walsingham to Robert Poley, the shadowy spy who had done nameless things for Walsingham's brother, and been present in a never-explained capacity at the death of Christopher Marlowe.

Hansard looked up from the letter. "This says that . . . 'Adam Dover,' Arthur Dudley, whatever his name was, was one of Francis Walsingham's agents in Spain."

"Very clever piece of work, eh?" Chetwynd said. "One might have expected an English double agent to denounce Elizabeth as a heretic devil, but to claim to be evidence of fornication . . . well."

"He tried to *kill* Elizabeth."

"That," said Professor Chetwynd, "is the fault with double agents . . . Red Pool, whatever you want to call them. One trains them in the enemy's thoughts and beliefs . . . and success is measured by how like the enemy they think. Should we be surprised that sometimes they also come to believe? I made Ellen what she is, you see; and well, much too well."

"She didn't meet me by accident . . ."

"Of course not. I set her on you . . . I put her exactly where she needed to be."

Hansard looked at the letter again. *As Marlowe hath no understanding of where to cease his work, I regret we must Cease it for him. . . .* "So this is it. Marlowe's death warrant."

"The Playwright's Tragedy," Chetwynd said.

This work raises too many questions that no man wishes answered . . . . "Poley was supposed to destroy the manuscript," Hansard said, "but he didn't. He hid it—hid *all* the papers—in Skene House."

"A long-standing habit of Intelligence employees," Chetwynd said, "salting away an incriminating paper or two against a rainy day."

"Poley died rich. Do you suppose he actually blackmailed Walsingham?"

"I'm no longer interested in suppositions," Chetwynd said, sounding tired, tired.

"All right," Hansard said gently. He picked up the typescript. "Where's the original of this letter?"

"Do you mean, the unmodernized original? The one that provides the proof?"

Hansard started to speak, but didn't.

Chetwynd said, "It could all yet be one grand hoax, of course . . . the play to prove the letters real, the letters to prove the play. Who knows what it is we are supposed to be convinced of?"

"You're a historian—"

"She was my *daughter,* don't you understand? We're going to be crucified, Ellen and I, in the press, in the books that bright young men like you will write. I won't have it done in the literary journals as well. No, Dr. Hansard, I believe that Walsingham had the right idea. He only chose the wrong vehicle for it." He looked at the fireplace, shook his head.

Hansard turned. In the hearth, old dry paper was burning, pages curling away to silky ashes, crumbling into flakes of yellow fire.

"You do know why she hates you," Hansard said suddenly.

Chetwynd looked up sharply.

"Arnold Rayven of Vectarray Technologies is a friend of mine," Hansard said. "He was part of Allan's circle."

"Yes."

"Ray told me that COPE LIGHT was prototyped several years ago, as the Tarncap Project."

"Dr. Hansard," Chetwynd said coolly, "you're speaking of old matters. Closed matters."

"Was there a Tarncap prototype aboard HMS *Sheffield* when she was sunk?"

Chetwynd said, "Very well, Dr. Hansard. You are, I suppose, entitled to hurt me. Congratulations. You'll be leaving now, of course."

"Yes, I'll be leaving now."

"I doubt I shall see you again."

"Not unless it's professionally, Sir Edward."

"Professionally, Dr. Hansard . . . professionally I could destroy you utterly. But I haven't, and I hope I won't have to. Do remember that, young man."

■ ■ ■

When Hansard got off the plane at Kennedy, a small plane was waiting for him. He watched out the window as the coastline streamed by. At Washington National, there was a blue Mercedes for the trip into Georgetown. Everyone on the trip was very helpful and considerate, including the young man in the White Group foyer. Hansard did not even have to wait in the lounge; the elevator door was open. Raphael was waiting, behind his glimmering desk in his white stone office, dressed in a suit of dove-gray silk, hands folded before him. His cufflinks were of knotted silver cord.

"I'm very pleased to see you, Dr. Hansard," Raphael said smoothly.

Hansard thought he would be polite, play it cool. But there wasn't any point in that. He couldn't beat anyone at their games; not Rhys-Gordon at sarcasm, not Ellen at hiding feelings, certainly not Raphael at cool. "I don't think I'm pleased to see you," he said.

"Yes. I believe I can understand that."

"And do you understand why I'm angry?" Hansard said, letting his voice rise, not caring if he screamed. "Do you understand how I'm beginning to think I should have let the plan go through?"

"I do. Except that you are certainly not 'beginning' to consider that. It has been on your mind for quite some time."

"Yes. That's right. Did you get that from the computer? From Sevenage?"

"You are not in the Sevenage database, Dr. Hansard. Though it is somewhat erratically chosen. I did not know at the time of the Montrose analysis that Dr. Berenson was in the base . . . frankly, I have little use for it. Sevenage is a misuse of computers, not least because the present state of the art is inadequate to its concept. But it was inevitable that someone should build the system . . . and, in a way, it is a positive evolution: The more that humans rely upon computers to make decisions, the more accurate a Sevenage analysis will become. But Dr. Berenson's plan came from the wonderful complexities of his mind. We used other complex minds against it."

"You used me, you mean."

"Yes, of course, Dr. Hansard. And I was right to do so."

Everyone's right, Hansard thought. Everyone who's still alive is right. "And if I'd gotten killed?"

"You were of too much use to be killed. WAGNER herself was your best protection . . . Surely you don't think it was your innocence protecting you? This was a salvation by works, not faith."

"No," Hansard said, "not a bit of faith involved, is there."

"That's a matter of individual choice."

"Did you know . . . *did you know* that WAGNER was Ellen Maxwell?"

"No, Dr. Hansard. I did not know that."

Hansard leaned with his fists on Raphael's desktop. "Did you *guess?*"

Raphael's smile showed sparkling, even teeth. "You are the best mind we have, Dr. Hansard. We have never rewarded you appropriately."

"I told you I was quitting."

Raphael reached beneath the desktop and produced the white envelope with Hansard's resignation. "I told you you were free to do so." He held out the envelope, smiling. "I have certain faults, Dr. Hansard, but I never lie."

"'Accurst be he who first invented war,'" Hansard said, to the walls, to the air, to anything but Raphael. "That's from *Tamburlaine.*"

"'Is it not a pleasant thing,'" Raphael said calmly, still holding the envelope, "'to be a king, and ride in triumph through Persepolis?'"

Hansard stared at Raphael, at the golden hair, the pale eyes, the face smooth as Dorian Gray's. If Raphael did know all things, did that make him a scholar? He supposed it did. They were all scholars together, scholars of forbidden things and unspeakable, Scholars of Night, Scholars of Darkness.

"All right," Hansard said, "I'll stay with the devil I know."

Raphael dropped the envelope into a slot on the desk. There was a faint whir of machinery as the paper was eaten and digested. "We have come into possession of a map of Bavaria, supposedly dating from the Thirty Years' War. If you'd care to have a look . . ."

"I'd be delighted," Hansard said. "But there's something I want."

"If it's something I can arrange, I shall do my best, Dr. Hansard."

"Oh, I hope so. After Santa and the Tooth Fairy, there's so little left a man can believe in."

■ ■ ■

Through the windows in Hansard's living room, the sun was just setting. Hansard poured himself a glass of seltzer, took a sip, set it on the bar; he adjusted the position of a chair, checking that the path to the front door was clear. He heard a car pull around the drive, then another. He took another swallow of water and went to the door.

Two long black limousines were parked at the end of the walk, drivers standing at attention as the passengers debarked, three from the rearward car, a man and a woman from the other. The man was unfolding a wheelchair.

From the road came the sound of tires screeching, and a ghost-silver Mustang tore around the corner, whipping inside the curve of the limos to double-park neatly against their front and rear fenders. Anna Romano got out, waved to Hansard. She opened the passenger door of the Mustang, and Paul Ogden, the history undergrad, emerged. Paul and Anna came around the black cars to shake hands with Arnold Rayven and Augustina Polonyi.

Hansard looked back inside the house. Seven chairs and a space for Dr. Polonyi were set around the glass-topped *Diplomacy* board. He had adjusted Allan's Doctors-only rule to include a student observer.

It was necessary to show someone young the games the grownups played, so that the students could learn in time not to play them. To kick the board over before it was too damned late. The children were growing up angry, without any help at all. If he could teach Paul Ogden to think through his anger—

If anyone could teach that to anyone, then there was hope.

He went back to the bookshelves, took down the mug labeled HEMLOCK, poured the glass of seltzer into it. He stood in the doorway again, holding the cup aloft as the players came up the walk.

A toast, he thought.

To love, to war, to heresy.

And rage.

ALSO BY JOHN M. FORD

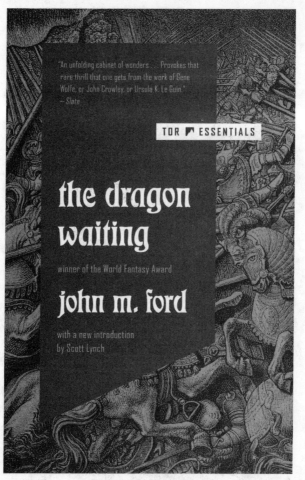

ISBN 978-1-250-26901-0
US $15.99 / CAN $21.99

"An unfolding cabinet of wonders . . . *The Dragon Waiting* provokes that rare thrill that one gets from the work of Gene Wolfe, or John Crowley, or Ursula Le Guin. A dazzling intellect ensorcells the reader, entertaining with one hand, opening new doors with another."

—*Slate*